A
Heart
Most
Worthy

Books by

Siri Mitchell

A Heart Most Worthy

She Walks in Beauty

Love's Pursuit

A Constant Heart

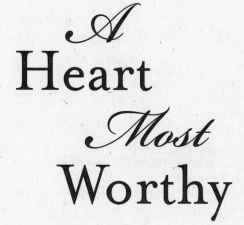

A Heart Most Worthy

SIRI MITCHELL

BETHANY HOUSE PUBLISHERS

Minneapolis, Minnesota

A Heart Most Worthy
Copyright © 2011
Siri L. Mitchell

Cover design by Jennifer Parker
Cover photography by Kevin White Photography, Minneapolis

Scripture quotations are from the King James Version of the Bible.

Published by Bethany House Publishers
11400 Hampshire Avenue South
Bloomington, Minnesota 55438

Bethany House Publishers is a division of
Baker Publishing Group, Grand Rapids, Michigan.

Printed in the United States of America

Library of Congress Cataloging-in-Publication Data

Mitchell, Siri L., 1969–
    A heart most worthy / Siri Mitchell.
        p.   cm.
    ISBN 978-0-7642-0795-2 (pbk.)
    1. Italians—United States—Fiction. 2. Upper class—Fiction. 3. Family secrets—Fiction. 4. Boston (Mass.)—Social life and customs—Fiction. I. Title.
    PS3613.I866H43   2011
    813'.6—dc22

                                                                    2010041268

To the immigrant in all of us.

SIRI MITCHELL is the author of nearly a dozen novels, among them the critically acclaimed Christy Award finalists *Chateau of Echoes* and *The Cubicle Next Door*. A graduate of the University of Washington with a degree in business, she has worked in many different levels of government. As a military spouse, she has lived in places as varied as Tokyo and Paris. Siri currently lives in the D.C.-metro area.

LIST OF CHARACTERS

Some readers have a habit, when confronted by a long list of characters, either to become discouraged or to assume the story to follow is much too complicated either to like or to read. I know you're not one of those kinds of readers, but just in case you are, I promise that you'll come to like the people on the list below. Most of them, in any case. But I don't want to get ahead of myself. I'll present you with the list; you'll make up your own mind. And if you're not completely discouraged by their foreign-sounding names or their great number, then I hope that you'll allow me to tell you their story. Being the intelligent and discriminating reader that you are, I'm quite certain you really wouldn't want to miss it.

Madame Fortier—Genovese; a gown shop owner who employs Luciana, Julietta, and Annamaria

Luciana Conti—Roman; a beader at Madame Fortier's gown shop

The contessa—Luciana's grandmother

Julietta Giordano—Avellinesi; an embroiderer at Madame Fortier's gown shop

Little Matteo Giordano—Julietta's youngest brother

Mauro Vitali—a doctor, and Julietta's oldest brother's friend

Angelo Moretti—recently arrived immigrant from Roma; Julietta's love interest

Annamaria Rossi—Avellinesi; a smocker at Madame Fortier's gown shop

Theresa Rossi—Annamaria's younger sister

Rafaello Zanfini—Sicilian; Annamaria's love interest

Mrs. Quinn—Boston blueblood; Madame Fortier's first and most annoying client

Billy Quinn—Mrs. Quinn's son

Patrick Quinn—a second generation Irishman and national congressman

Boston
1918

1

On May 2, 1918, a short article appeared in the *Boston Globe*. It was only three sentences long; not an article really. Just a mention. It appeared on page twenty-four on the outside column, where most people hold on to a newspaper. I'm sure you wouldn't be very surprised to know that few people noticed it as they read the paper that morning and several people smeared jam on it as they turned the page. Only a very few read it.

COUNT BLOWN UP
Heiress Disappears

On the night of April 12, the Count of Roma was assassinated by an anarchist's bomb at his house in that eternal city. His mother, the contessa, and his daughter were not harmed in the blast, but were later found to have disappeared. The new count suggests sinister persons may be involved.

Rare was the person who consulted the *Globe* those days for any news other than the war. There were no tears in America to spare for luckless Italian counts and their vanished daughters; there were still too many left to shed for lost sons and wounded fathers. For the scores—the hundreds, the thousands—being killed on the battlefields of Europe every day. So it could be expected that a small article about an insignificant foreign incident, buried in the depths of the newspaper, garnered little attention.

Except that actions committed on one side of the world have a way of impacting the other. And people previously unknown to one another happen to meet all the time. In the Italian-speaking North End that day, copies of the *Globe* were used to wrap fish and line cupboards, while up on Beacon Hill, the newspaper was read from page to page, top to bottom. And in one particular house, the lady of that mansion sniffed as she sipped her tea and thought how it was just like an Italian to be blown up by one of his own kind.

Two of the people mentioned in the article had access to the paper that day, but the hapless heiress couldn't read English, and the sinister persons were too busy hatching evil plans to bother with a propaganda tool of the capitalists' machinations. And so the fact that there had been an assassination registered to no one in particular. And life went on just the way it usually does.

But fate has a way of laughing at human ignorance and God spins mysterious plans, and by August that Italian count's death would start to matter very much to quite a few people who had never known him at all.

———

Stealthy and silent as the cats she so admired, Julietta Giordano slipped past her papa and mama, her elder sister, and her three brothers as they ate breakfast at the table.

Or she tried to anyway.

"You forgot your *salame!*" Mama leaned toward the sideboard, grabbed a sack, and passed it to Dominic, who tossed it to Julietta.

"I told you, Mama. Madame doesn't want any salame. Not in the shop. It stinks."

"Of course it stinks. It stinks like a good salame."

"It stinks like garlic. And it makes my hands greasy."

There was hardly a break in the rhythm of the family's eating. They all had work to do and somewhere to be. It was the nature of an immigrant family. Which made it all the easier for Julietta to lower the salame to the floor behind her legs and leave it leaning against the wall as she slid toward the door.

Little Matteo looked up at her as she turned the knob.

She winked at him.

He hid an answering smile in the palm of his hand.

"Tie your scarf tighter beneath your chin!"

Julietta jumped at her older sister's order and dutifully tightened her scarf, although her knot left something to be desired. . . . A stiff wind, perhaps, to carry the hated thing away and deposit it into a gutter.

While she was busy with her scarf, Julietta's oldest brother, Salvatore, leaned his chair back on two legs, scooped up the salame with a sweep of his hand, and pitched it up to her. She'd have given anything to have hit him with it, but if she didn't leave then, she knew she would be late. She did, however, glare at him.

He answered by flashing her two fingers held up in imitation of horns. He thought she'd given him the evil eye? She'd show him! She knocked him on the head with the salame and then slid out the door before Mama could yell at her.

Don't forget your salame?

She wished she could. Along with scarves and garlic. More than wishing she could forget them, she wished she could throw them all into the street. Or give them to old Lorenzo, the ragpicker, to sell to someone else. All the *salami*, all the scarves, all the garlic in the world. He could have them. And good riddance!

Once outside and down the block, she turned onto Prince Street, made the sign of the cross as she walked through the shadow of St. Leonard's Church, and then ducked down North Street. Had you known where she worked, you might have wondered at her circuitous route, but Julietta was a firm believer in the sanctity of women's rights. She believed that a woman like herself had the right—nay, the obligation!—to give every man in the North End a chance to admire her singular beauty. As she walked in and out of the slices of light that probed the breaks between buildings, a curious change came over the girl. Her chin lifted, her shoulders rolled back. The scarf that had so lately been secured beneath her chin had, in one deft move, been drawn from her head, twisted, and then secured around her neck in a fashion that befitted only the very smartest of debutantes up on Beacon Hill.

Her fingers pushed in and out of her waistband until, in very gradual increments, her skirt had been shortened by at least two inches. Any decent person—me, perhaps, and you for certain—would have wanted to grab the girl by her shoulders and shake some sense back into her, but by then she had become almost unrecognizable. By some sleight of hand or dark magic, her dusky complexion seemed to have lightened and, with her shoulders rolled back, she seemed to have grown several inches. She had shed the very essence of her self. She had ceased to be Italian.

In fact, that was her greatest desire and most secret plan. More than anything, she wanted to be not Italian—not some person bound by family ties and the traditions of the old country—but American. There was a whole city—a whole world!—that warm summer day, just waiting to be discovered. And she wanted to explore every single part of it!

———

Two blocks up the street and three minutes later, Annamaria Rossi left her own family's apartment. The leaving was less strenuous than Julietta's, even though her youngest brother, Stefano, wrapped his arms about her waist and refused to release her; even though her mama handed her a string-bound pile of newly hemmed trousers to be dropped off at old Giuseppe's; and even though her sister, Theresa, whispered into her ear to tell that handsome Giovanni Sardo that she would meet him down in the alley after dinner.

Surrogate mother, servant, maid. Deliverer of secret messages. The day was no different than any other. Her leaving that morning was less strenuous than Julietta's only because she knew her return would be more so. The bulk of her work that day would be done not at Madame Fortier's Gown Shop, where she was the expert in smocking, but that evening at home where she was also her mother's eldest daughter.

Two girls there were among a family of three boys. And as the eldest of them all, Annamaria was destined to be indentured in service to her family for most of the rest of her life. That night, she knew she would have to coax Stefano to do his English lessons and try to persuade Theresa to help her pull in the wash. And in the meantime she would help Mama prepare for putting up some plums on the weekend.

As Annamaria stepped out into the bright summer's morning, she clamped the stack of trousers under her arm as she unknotted the scarf beneath her chin and then, grasping the two ends, cinched it tighter. She retied the knot, pulled the scarf further forward on her head, and started down the sidewalk.

Ducking into Giuseppe's tailor shop on the way down North Street, she nodded at his gap-toothed greeting. But this time, for the first time, she dodged the old man when he tried to pinch her bottom. And she deliberately, *on purpose*, walked right by the Sardos' shop without passing on Theresa's message. She spent the next three blocks rejoicing in the feeling of triumph that buoyed her spirit. And the three blocks after that feeling exceedingly guilty for having been so jubilant. So contrary. But she hadn't known before just how satisfying it could be to say *no*.

Take your own trousers.

Deliver your own message.

In truth, it wouldn't have done for her to say either of those things to her family. Not at all. Not for Annamaria Rossi. Wasn't hers the life that had been fated as the eldest of the daughters? Indeed, the life that had been demanded of eldest daughters for generation after generation in her family's small village in Italy? And hadn't her Aunt Rosina, her mother's own sister, warned her against the bitterness of resentment? She pulled her aunt's medal, the medal of Saint Zita, from her blouse.

Saint Zita, that pious woman who had known the blessings of neither husband nor children. Nothing but a life of toil as a servant. Annamaria kissed the medal and then let it fall back to her chest, where it slid between breasts that would never know the caress of a lover's touch, nor the pull and suck of a newborn babe.

It might seem strange that a person so young would deny herself those things that most of the rest of the world took for granted: a husband, a child, a family of her own. But Old World customs were strange, and stranger still were the traditions that had been formed in the small villages that nestled in the rolling hills of Avellino. To those not used to having choices, it's very difficult to even imagine their existence. So we must not think less of Annamaria or be impatient with her to shed her family's odd strictures. The poor girl only wanted to do what was expected of her. We cannot blame her for that.

She stayed in the North End, hugging the shabby buildings, not straying from the filthy sidewalks, inhaling the mingled scents of garlic and coffee just as long as she could. When finally she was confronted by Cross Street, she did what she had to do.

She crossed it.

And then walked west, eventually consigning her person to

that bane of modern existence, the close, cramped quarters of an electric car. But still, as she squeezed herself onto the bench, a smile curled the very tips of her lips. How easy, how delightful it had been to be disagreeable.

———

You might have thought that Julietta, having left several minutes earlier and intent upon arriving at the same place, would have reached Madame's gown shop in advance of Annamaria. But you would have been wrong. Other people, other more experienced, more knowledgeable people than you, had also been known to be wrong about Julietta. She was a sly and evasive one. Though kindhearted and loyal, she was just a bit . . . well, more than a bit, stubborn. On this point and at this moment you'll find yourself having to trust me, but I think that I'll be proved right before long. Suffice to say that in this case, on this morning, she stopped along her way to work.

She hadn't stopped to talk. Not necessarily. Although she would have been quite willing had the opportunity presented itself. No. She stopped mostly to see. And to be seen. Which are the two main objectives in the lives of most eighteen-year-old girls, be they from America or Italy or from any other place in between.

She was really quite extraordinary, and she knew it. You might have taken offense at such extreme vanity except that she made such a picture that morning, standing in a patch of early morning sunlight, across from Zanfini's *frutta e verdura*. At least that's what Rafaello Zanfini thought. He paused in his labors when he saw her, breathed in a sigh, and immediately dropped a crate of cucumbers onto his foot.

Which caused his father, Mr. Zanfini, to swear, and his mother, Mrs. Zanfini, to berate his father, and the deliveryman, Angelo Moretti, to look up at Julietta over the flatbed of his truck. She only stayed a moment more, but that one moment was long enough for Rafaello to forget his pain and Angelo to lose sight, for just one second, of all his mad schemes.

But perhaps, in fact, it was one moment too long. Before she continued on her way, Julietta saw a flash in Angelo's eyes that made her wonder, for just an instant, if he was what she wanted after all. She pondered that thought as she walked along, finally deciding that of course he was what she wanted. Why wouldn't he be what she wanted? He was entirely and absolutely what she wanted by virtue of her wanting him.

And so they went to work, those two girls from the North End, separated by several blocks and the inseparable gulf of two differing perspectives. The one planning to escape her family just as soon as she could, and the other resigned to stay.

2

Later that afternoon, as Julietta and Annamaria were working on the third floor of Madame Fortier's Gown Shop, Luciana Conti ventured from the shadowed entrance of a North Bennet Street tenement building. Looking first up the street and then down, she took a cautious step off the stoop.

To her left, three women had blocked the sidewalk with their chairs. Gesticulating wildly, revealing large gaps between their teeth as they grinned at each other, they spoke in a dialect that Luciana didn't even try to decipher. To her right, a group of young girls was playing hopscotch. But it wasn't old women and children that worried her.

Luciana lifted her chin, eyes traveling the length of the rows of windows in the tenements across the street. If it weren't for the laundry hanging slack in the still summer air, she might have been able to see who sat in the windows behind them. She knew they were there, those faceless people whose laughter and banter bounced between the buildings and echoed down the street.

They had to be women, didn't they? At this time in the afternoon?

She put a hand to her scarf, reassuring herself that no one

would recognize her. She didn't look at all like the heiress she'd been three short months before. That's when her father had been blown up by an anarchist's bomb . . . and all her prospects of a brilliant future with him. What is an heiress without money but a girl in search of means? And what is a girl with no means but destitute? Destitute is doubtless what she was, the family estate having been entailed to a man—a cousin—she'd never met. A cousin who hadn't even bothered to come to Roma after her father was murdered. Abandoned and penniless, a stranger in a strange land, she had no doubt she was being hunted by the man who had killed her father. She'd seen him. Once. Right there on that North End street.

She pulled her scarf down over her eyes with a trembling hand and started away from the steps. As long as she didn't go out to the corner, she wouldn't encounter any men. She shouldn't. None but the shopkeepers. And those she could not avoid.

Not if she wanted to eat.

She took hesitant, measured steps, pausing to look up and down the street between each one. Two storefronts down, she paused in front of a window. A *macelleria*, it dangled a few rabbits from its ceiling, skinned but for their round, fuzzy tails. An enticing chain of salami hung beside them, caught up in a snare of twine. There were roasts displayed on a shelf behind the window, encased in white marbled fat. But the glass also reflected back a pair of men, sauntering down the street.

Luciana bolted toward the door. Opened it and fled inside.

The man behind the counter smiled as she entered. "*Buon giorno, Signorina*. What do I get for you?"

At least that's what she thought he must have said. She wasn't certain. She couldn't make sense of his accent.

He raised his brows, opened his hands behind the glass of the case. "What do I get for you?"

She shook her head.

"*Inglese?*"

English? Is that what he was asking her? She scarcely knew a word.

He shrugged. Decided to help the girl settle on what it was that she wanted. *"Insaccati?"*

Ah. Now there was a word she understood. But no. No preserved meats for her. The contessa wouldn't know a salame from a *cotechino*. She'd think for certain someone was trying to poison her.

Luciana took a step farther into the shop so that she could peer out the window. Those men were still there. They'd stopped in the middle of the street. The reason they'd stopped, of course, is that they'd seen one of their friends. But Luciana didn't know that. And when she saw the dawn of recognition light their faces, she feared the worst.

"Prosciutto?"

She jumped.

The butcher was holding up a hunk of aged ham.

Luciana shook her head. She was getting hungry now. She took another step farther in, toward the case, to hide herself in the relative recesses of the room.

"Agnello?"

Her mouth began to water. She hadn't had lamb in . . . far too long. If only they had some *casoeula*. That would be worth the money. Tender meat stewed with sausage and bacon. Served with white cabbage and polenta. What she wouldn't give for a taste of that once more. But it was so very difficult for Luciana to know what to ask for when she had never cooked before.

"Coniglio? Polpette?" Rabbit. Meatballs.

The contessa had grown tired of watered wine and cheese and bread. Luciana had too. *"Bistecca?"*

"Bistecca?" The man raised a brow.

Beefsteak. That sounded like what she had asked for, didn't it? Enough like it that she nodded. And then hoped. And prayed.

Maybe if the contessa had a real meal, she would sleep through the night. And then Luciana could too.

"*Una?*"

She nodded, knowing she only had enough money for a single steak.

"Una bistecca." She watched as the butcher picked up a large thick steak, wrapped it in paper, and tied it up with a string. "Something else?"

Something else. Did he have a *Carabiniere* or an arrest warrant hidden behind his counter? Could he buy her passage back to Italy or breathe her father back to life? A beefsteak would have to do. She counted out the precious coins as if they were her last. Laid them on the counter, fingers lingering atop their warm, shiny surfaces.

The butcher wiped his hands on his apron and then swept the coins into his palm with a deft hand. "*Arrivederci.*"

Luciana paused at the window. Looked past the salami in their string cages to the street outside. The men were no longer there.

She drew open the door.

The women were still on the sidewalk, sitting in their chairs, sighing over a shared memory. Looking beyond the crumbling sidewalks, gazing past the tenements, back through the years into the golden age of their youth. To the days when Tommasina still had all of her hair and Generosa had all of her teeth. Hadn't the boys come sniffing around? And hadn't they been the talk of the village back then?

Luciana didn't care about old women. Her thoughts were on things more basic. More immediate. She cared about life. Or if not about life, then she cared about death. And she didn't want to bring it to her door. Not again.

Sì. The men had gone from the street.

She slipped away from the butcher's door and out into the day. Bolted for her tenement building. She couldn't do it without skirting those old *nonne* and stepping into the street, but she did it quickly and then she was back up the stoop and into the building.

She was safe.

As safe as she could be in a falling-down tenement, filled with the poorest of immigrant classes. She was, perhaps, as safe as she would ever be again.

Slender and light as she was on her feet, she ran straight up the stairs. All four flights of them. As she twisted up their heights, the air grew hotter. Closer. More stale. At the top, she felt more than saw her way down the gloomy tunnel of a hall. Passing a cluster of giggling girls and a rack of *maccheroni* set in front of an open doorway to dry, she reached the door of her apartment.

She closed and locked the door behind her—testing it—before she placed her package of meat on a narrow shelf. Then she unknotted her scarf as she walked toward the window and the straight-backed old woman who sat before it, hands folded within each other on her lap.

At least they had a window.

Others on the floor, a dozen in the building, had no such luxury. And though the glass itself could have used a good cleaning, it was open this afternoon. No rays of light came through it just now, but across the street, windows glowed where the sun still touched them. And sometimes when light itself cannot be had, then a glimpse of it will suffice.

"Contessa?"

The woman raised her head, turned just an inch, as if to summon Luciana closer.

The girl obliged. And when she entered the old woman's peripheral vision, the contessa offered up a hand. Luciana took it, curtsied, and then kissed it.

"Si?"

"I have come to prepare your dinner."

"*Grazie, ragazza.*" The old woman withdrew her hand before Luciana could think to hold on to it.

Ragazza. Girl.

Luciana would have given her own heart to have heard the words *mia bambina* fall from the old woman's lips. My little girl. For when a child of any age has been orphaned, all she longs for is to find a safe place, a firm lap to climb into, and be comforted. But the contessa would comfort no one. She simply sat in front of the window all day long, back straight as a rod, never touching the slats of the chair, speaking to no one, requiring nothing, treating Luciana like a servant girl.

While Luciana spent her days in the shadows, pacing the length of their sad set of rooms, using the window at periodic intervals to scout the neighborhood, the contessa sat and gazed out, impervious to shadow or light. Sometimes the strained notes of a song came out in a feeble hum. Once or twice, Luciana thought she had heard the woman speak, and several times when she looked into the contessa's eyes, she thought she'd seen her *nonna* looking back. But most of the time the old woman was silent.

Luciana had given up hope. It was no use calling her "nonna" any longer. That engaging, warm, vital woman was lost in the far reaches of a grief-stricken mind. Gone was the proud mother, the doting grandmother, the competent administrator of the estates of the conte di Roma. The woman all Roma had once referred to as *Contessa Formidabile* had disappeared.

Luciana would have kissed the top of her head had the woman displayed any sign at all of her former person. But she did not, and so the girl went to the shelf, took the steak from the wrapper, and prepared it as best as she could. Which I must say, if truth be important, was not so very good at all. After wasting three matches trying to light the stove, she cooked the steak at too high a temperature. So when the contessa sat down to her dinner, the beefsteak was burnt on the outside and raw on the inside. But the butcher was an honest man if he was a clean one, and neither Luciana nor her grandmother got sick that night.

The contessa slept without waking, but Luciana could not sleep at all. Aside from a trip down the hall to the communal toilet, she did not leave their rooms. But she knew the next morning that she would have to. It was unavoidable. The beefsteak had taken the last of their money. The next day she would have to find a job.

3

Madame Fortier was going to need another seamstress. More than a seamstress, perhaps. She was going to need an artist. She knew it as sure as she knew the latest modes from Paris.

Taking up the sample book the postman had just delivered, she walked from the floor of her oriental-carpeted, chandeliered shop back behind a glass case filled with gloves, tasseled bags, handkerchiefs, and belts. Placing the sample book on top of it, she opened the front cover. Pen and watercolor-print illustrations bordered with squares of fabric filled the pages.

She flipped through the book quickly, giving the designs a cursory look. And she approved. Of most of them. After she was done, she had proof to bolster her suspicions. She would have to hire another girl.

Julietta was a genius with all kinds of embroidery, though Madame frequently wished the girl would alter her attitude. Annamaria, though she rarely spoke, smocked like no one Madame had ever seen. The girl's interior work, the back side of her designs, was impeccable. But the styles for spring were going to be more ornate. And beadwork was just as tedious as embroidery or smocking.

It required someone with a steady hand and abundant patience. And more than that, it required someone who knew what happened when beads were joined to fabric. Someone who could anticipate how their weight would pull and stretch the material. It was true handiwork. A lady's work. And where was Madame going to find a lady who was willing to work?

For what Madame Fortier could afford to pay her?

She frowned before she could remember not to. Madame Fortier never frowned. Rarely frowned. Why was it so difficult, after all those long years, for her to remember the role she had laid out for herself to play? She went back through the book. Stopped for a moment to consider an illustration. Simple and sleek. But such dark colors. Black. Navy blue. Only one or two of the styles she'd examined were offered in green.

Dark green.

It wasn't easy to remember the gowns women had bought before the war. But how could anyone in 1918 think of wearing Copenhagen blue or Nell rose? Lavender or terra cotta? What she wouldn't do to be able to order a bolt of silk crepe in a reseda or a Russian green! But how could anyone think of looking cheerful when a war was being fought? When thousands of boys were dying in Europe's trenches?

Madame crossed herself, some habits being nearly impossible to break.

She sighed as she turned another page. When would it all end? When could she stop making black gowns and selling veils to match? When could she stop converting fanciful patterns meant for shimmering beads into sober lines intended for black jet? And when—oh when!—would she be able to order charmeuse again? Or chiffon? Her fingers itched to touch a whimsical voile.

It's not that she missed those fabrics exactly.

She missed their innocence. Their charm.

Julietta brought her own kind of exuberance to the shop, but she was a restless, impatient sort of girl. Which was too bad.

Julietta had style and taste to go with it. She needed a girl like Julietta; Madame Fortier could not be Madame Fortier forever. It was too exhausting. The strain showed in places she didn't know to look. It showed in the depths of her brown eyes and the slant of her shoulders. It showed in her walk and in the measured way that she talked.

None of her clients noticed it. Why would they? They only saw what they wanted to see. Madame Fortier, recognizing this, had long ago given up her fear of being discovered for who she really was. It had been absurdly easy for her to cease being Cosimo the Tailor's daughter and become the celebrated Boston *modiste*. Indeed, the city was filled with modistes, all of them Madames who had never set foot on France's fabled shores. It didn't matter. As long as Madame Fortier did nothing to break the illusion she had created, her clients were simply grateful to figure themselves on her small and exclusive list.

Madame Fortier was a gown maker. That's what the sign on her shop said. *Madame Fortier, Gown Maker*. She didn't make dresses and she never had.

Making a notation in the margin of the sample book, she fingered the square of navy silk that accompanied the illustration. It would look so much better in an organdy. In bright pink. But Madame knew Mrs. Rutherford, with her charitable work on behalf of the war, would want it just the way it was presented. Even more perhaps if the waist were raised just a tiny bit and the hem lengthened by an inch. Not everyone looked their best in the new short styles. Length had its virtues.

She sighed as she shut the book, wishing for something she didn't have the words to define. For something . . . different. Something *else*. Something other than what was. But she could not afford to investigate her feelings more deeply. She had chosen, you see, to leave her old life—her Italian life—far behind and now there was no going back. Not even when, quite often, she desperately wished to.

———

It had taken some time for Luciana to work up the nerve to leave the building. The hardest part had been getting dressed. She'd shed the rags of her peasant's disguise but had yet to put on the clothes of her old life.

They lay there—the beribboned satin pumps, the silk stockings, the beaded satin gown—across the bed that she and the contessa shared. The satin wasn't right at all for that July morning. It was too heavy and the color much too bright, but it was the only thing she had to wear. The shoes were utterly ridiculous, if you will excuse my saying so. And they were still marked by ashes. Luciana took up the hem of her discarded skirt and rubbed at the stains, but only succeeded in widening the smudges.

If she went out, she might be recognized.

If she stayed, they would most certainly starve to death.

She had to go. She had no other choice. She would just have to do it.

Luciana picked up a comb and pulled it through her hair. It delayed her getting dressed by a few minutes. Gathering her long dark locks, twisting them into a bun and then fastening the bun with pins took a few minutes more.

And then she could delay no longer. She took up the stockings, unrolled them and pulled them up over her knees, and then she fastened them to her corset. She pulled on her drawers and a chemise; a petticoat. And finally, closing her eyes so that she could not be goaded into remembering the last night that she had worn it, she took the gown from the bed.

She would not remember.

She refused to remember.

She stepped into it, pulling it up over her hips. She had to open her eyes in order to fasten it in front, but after sliding her feet into the shoes, she did not look down at the gown at all. But still, fear made her heart drop to the bottom of her stomach.

Even if her father's murderer didn't recognize her, others would surely know her. Know of her. Enough to decide that she did not belong in the North End, not in a gown like the one she was wearing. And if he did find her, what would he do to her then? She needed a disguise. Though she couldn't do anything about the shoes, perhaps she could cover the gown.

With her scarf, maybe?

She grabbed it from the pile of clothes on the floor and unfurled it across her shoulders. But no matter which direction she turned it, regardless of which end pointed down and whether it was placed in the back or the front, it did no good at all. The confection of beads that was sprinkled across the long, flowing collar of the gown still caught the morning's light, winking at her as if they meant no harm at all.

She could think of nothing else to use save the blanket.

It was a ratty, holey old blanket of indeterminate color that had been left in the rooms by the previous tenant. The fact that it had been left, and what's more, not stolen, might have told Luciana all she needed to know about its provenance and condition. But refugees are grateful for whatever they can come by and just then, during the stifling nights of July, it hid the stains on the mattress and succeeded somewhat in helping to level the lumps at night.

She decided to try it, draping the blanket across her shoulders and drawing it to a close beneath her chin. It made her look . . . well, I hate to say how it made her look. Even fearful young women on the run from sinister persons would like to think, I'm sure, that they have at least something to do with modern fashion. That something, hidden underneath the clumsy folds and holes of a moth-eaten blanket, could signal the beauty hidden within. She knew it couldn't look at all stylish, but she told herself it didn't matter. Just a few short months before she'd been known as one of the most fashionable women in Roma. But that was when she'd wanted to be noticed—when she'd craved all the attention society had to offer.

Once she ventured out—with the blanket—into the light of day, she made it from North Bennet Street to Cross Street without suffering any untoward glances. Indeed, without incurring a second glance at all. At that intersection of Boston proper and old-world Italy, once she crossed the street and the air shed the scents of sewage and rotting garbage, she dropped the blanket into a gutter, gathered her old airs around her and, lifting her chin, started off down North Street. But then she stopped. And very nearly caused a man walking behind her to trip. But there was no help for it; she had hit upon a snag.

She had to find a job, that was certain. There was only one thing she knew how to do, it was true. But where, in that vast and crowded city, was she to find such a place of employment? She only knew where it wasn't: It couldn't be within the district of tenements and slums she now called home.

But where, in fact, might it be?

She needed to find the most fashionable and stylish place in the city. And for a girl who spoke no English, this was a daunting task indeed. But by and by, after having hit upon the means of following the most fashionable people down North Street and then down Washington Street, she happened upon just such a place. Happened in fact upon *the* place.

Temple Place.

Now, Temple Place was the one location to which two kinds of women in Boston aspired: those who made gowns and those who wore them. It was that type of legendary, mythical, magical place that whispered the words that every woman wanted to hear: *You have arrived.*

As so she had.

Luciana glanced down, took a moment to straighten the sash at her waist, and then opened the door of the first dress shop she came to.

And was ushered right out just twenty seconds later.

She went into the next dress shop and lasted only a bit longer. Went on to the next one and lasted only slightly less. Her gown, it seemed, was acceptable. It was only when the modistes' gazes had fallen to her shoes that they lost some degree of respect. And when they swept up to her face, well, by then there was no warmth, no welcome left at all. They had spoken just one word she was able to understand before they showed her the door. And they spoke it with disgust.

Italian.

Sì. She was Italian. From the house and lineage of the conti di Roma. Italian born and bred. Was it her fault she couldn't speak English? She spoke Hungarian, German, and Italian.

Proper Italian.

From a distance, she looked like any other of the hundreds of young women who entered such establishments every day. In the right season. Of course, July was not the right season and the women who wore gowns such as Madame Fortier's were out at Newport or in the Berkshires. And the girls who hoped one day to wear such fashions were either hard at work in the city's sweatshops or gazing off into the distance over the pages of their novels.

There was just one shop left on her side of the street. Did she hesitate, just an instant, before taking hold of the door? Did her resolve waver for even a moment? If it did, I would have no way of knowing.

———

It was with much surprise that Madame Fortier saw Luciana walk into her shop. She looked like a client. But no stranger had ever entered Madame's shop. Her business was conducted by appointment only; her shop was immune to the hustle and bustle that was endemic to Temple Place. And besides, all of her clients were away on holiday at the shore or in the mountains.

She fixed her shopkeeper's smile onto her face before she realized that the girl was not of the class of her normal clients. No. The girl was something else, something different altogether. It is said sometimes that soul speaks to soul and need cries out to need. As Madame approached the stranger, the desperation in the girl's eyes kindled an unexpected response. It had something to do with the way the girl held herself. And something to do with the quality of the beading on her gown.

Instead of turning her out, Madame Fortier took a step closer. "Where did you get this?" The words came out in Italian, northern Italian, though Madame Fortier had not intended for them to.

"I—" Just what was she to admit to? How truthful did she have to be? "It is mine."

"Si. Granted. But the beading? It is extraordinary."

"I did it myself." She had. Because in all of Roma there had been none to rival her artistry, her skill at the craft.

"Can you do it again?" The woman was looking at her as if she wanted nothing so much as to reach out and stroke the design on her collar.

"Si." She could do it whenever she wanted, had done it whenever she wanted, but that was when she'd had access to beads. And jewels. That was before. When her every wish had been anticipated. And granted so quickly that she'd hardly had to wish at all. "Si."

"Can you do it . . . now?"

"Now?"

"You need a job, don't you? Can you start today?"

It was all just a bit much for a girl who had been raised never to work. For a girl who now rose each morning and went to bed each evening in fear of her very life. Luciana's eyelashes fluttered, her cheeks went rosy. She opened her mouth, intending to speak, but then she burst into tears instead.

"*Madonna mia!*" Madame was uncomfortable with emotions. She'd had so very little use for them in her life. But her hand went out to the girl as her glance went out toward the street. No one was passing by. She turned her attention back to the girl. Pulled her over to the fitting area where she could be hidden behind the screen. "Sit."

Luciana sat in an ornate overstuffed chair. For the first time in months.

"Are you pregnant?" It would be just Madame's luck. Some of her best seamstresses had been taken from her by way of motherhood. Matrimony did not matter quite so much. With a husband, one could still work. With a baby? *Impossibile*.

But Madame Fortier's blunt question had a completely unforeseen result.

Luciana, having recovered control of her emotions, leaped to her feet. Offense colored the tops of her cheeks. "Pregnant? Positively not! And I'll thank you, *Signora*, for your time." She had already spun on her satin-clad heel, pushed beyond the screen, and begun walking toward the door.

4

Luciana was not the granddaughter of the contessa di Roma for nothing. Though, in truth, she felt no little regret at having to leave. And you probably would have too. The shop was undeniably elegant from the carpeted floors to the chandeliered ceilings and papered walls. It had an air of discreet good taste that, in Luciana's experience, only the best shops in Paris and Vienna shared. And even in that short time, it had provided a refuge, not only for her person but also for her soul.

"Wait!"

Luciana stopped.

"I need you." Oh, how it cost Madame Fortier to say those words!

Luciana let go of the door and turned. Reconsidered as she looked once more at Madame's tidy and elegant shop. She nodded. "I can start. Today."

And with that, the odd reversal of roles righted itself and Madame Fortier became, once more, the formidable owner of the gown shop, and Luciana, an anonymous immigrant girl begging for work.

Madame led the way up the back stairs, past the second story workshop to the third floor of the building. "This is where you will work."

Luciana peered around Madame's shoulder and saw two girls sitting at a long table, looking back at her. One of them was staring, eyes lit with challenge. She raked Luciana with a gaze before returning to her work. The other glanced up and then immediately returned her attentions to her work. "Julietta. And Annamaria."

"Buon giorno."

Neither of the girls replied, though Annamaria smiled, for just an instant.

Madame Fortier continued the introductions. "This is—" Madame paused in her speech, rather surprised that she hadn't even thought to ask the new girl's name.

"Luciana."

"This is Luciana. She's to take over the beading."

"*Grazie a Dio!*" Thank God! Julietta had been afraid she'd have to do it herself. Which was why she'd been progressing on her embroidery with such uncharacteristic slowness. "You have to have the patience of a saint for that."

Annamaria smiled once more, though her meticulous stitches were the only witness. She was normally the sole audience for Julietta's many and varied opinions. She usually only half-listened to the chatter, but still, it would be nice to share that burden with someone else.

Madame Fortier led Luciana around the worktable. "We are working on the gowns for an autumn wedding." She wished she could start the girl on the wedding gown itself, but that would have been too risky. What if she had lied? What if she couldn't perform the magic she had promised? Madame would know soon. She would be able to tell from the lay of the beads and the pull of the fabric. "You'll start with the collar of one of the attendant's gowns. I've based it on this illustration." She pushed a page from a sample book over to Luciana. The girl took it up.

It was a simple gown. And the beading on the collar was equally as plain. "In bugle beads?"

"Seed beads. Of alabaster."

"And the fabric? Is it georgette?"

"Messaline."

Luciana frowned. Georgette would have taken the beads better. Messaline was slippery and not as easy to work with.

Madame Fortier had said that very thing, in fact, to her client. But the bride's mother had settled upon messaline and messaline it would have to be. No amount of coaxing had moved her from that decision. Mrs. Henry Haywood's daughter had been married the previous year with bridesmaids in messaline and it seemed that nothing else would do.

"What is to be used for the lining?"

"Sarcenet."

Sarcenet. That was correct. Luciana shot a glance up at Madame. "It will have to be several thicknesses then."

Julietta raised a brow at the girl's words. And her boldness! Even Julietta had never presumed to advise Madame on anything having to do with the gowns.

But Madame only smiled. "Sì." Exactly. The new girl understood exactly.

Luciana nodded. "Do you have the collar? I'll start it now." And then she could have the whole afternoon to figure out how to ask for an advance on her pay.

———

Sometime around noon, Julietta and Annamaria put down their work. They cleared the table of scissors and thread, pincushions and yarn. And then they retrieved their lunches from a cupboard. Julietta's had bread, a not-too-pungent hunk of smoky *provola* cheese, and a juicy tomato to go with it. Annamaria had brought a slice of ham to go with her own bread. But she eyed Julietta's tomato with something very near envy.

"Mama hasn't been able to find any good tomatoes."

"In July? In the city? Where's she looking?" No good tomatoes? Annamaria's mama had to be blind!

Annamaria shrugged. "Maglione's frutta e verdura. On North Street."

"Then she should come over to Hull."

Julietta and Annamaria were both Avellino by birth, but they came from two different villages. Those from Julietta's village had settled at the northernmost tip of the North End. Those from Annamaria's village along the eastern edge of the peninsula. It was expected that, as they had in the old country, villagers would do business only with fellow villagers. So Annamaria shrugged and tried not to think about tomatoes while Julietta began assembling herself a sandwich.

They had just crossed themselves in blessing when they realized Luciana had not joined them.

"Aren't you going to stop? To eat?" Though Annamaria was known for her industry, she still looked forward to the break at lunch. If for no other reason than to rest her eyes and seek relief from the headache that often pressed against her temples.

Luciana didn't even look up from her beads. "No."

Annamaria reached over and laid a hand on Luciana's arm. "But it doesn't have to be finished today. Madame's clients have all left for the summer. No one will be back until August."

"And even then, they won't come into the shop until September." Which suited Julietta just fine. She never worked harder than she had to. "So where are you from?"

Luciana took so long to answer that Annamaria and Julietta exchanged a curious look.

"The south."

"Where in the south? We're from Avellino. She's from Taurasi. I'm from Chiusano San Domenico. Maybe we know your people."

Luciana dismissed Julietta's friendly interest with a shake of her head. "You don't know my people."

"Then you're Abruzzi? Or . . . Calabrese?" For she surely wasn't Sicilian. Her clothes, though fancy, were clean. She didn't stink. She wasn't even very swarthy. And if she were from Abruzzo or Calabria, then it would account for her strange accent.

But Luciana was neither. And she couldn't tell them she was Roman. They didn't know her people, but they might know others. They might know the person who had killed her father. Though . . . what were the chances? She considered telling them the truth. But, no. No. It wasn't worth the risk.

"You don't sound like you're from the south." Julietta might not have liked work, but she had nothing against riddles. And this new girl had presented a good one. Her gown said she came from a good family, but her shoes said she'd fallen on hard times . . . though not quite hard enough to overcome the lift of her chin and the accent of her words. "You're from the north." That was the only possible explanation.

Annamaria looked up at Julietta's accusation.

Luciana looked up from her beadwork. "North Bennet Street." And she was. Now.

North Bennet Street. That was unexpected. "Then you're . . . Genovese?"

Abruzzi, Calabrese, Genovese. What did it matter? Just as long as they stopped asking questions. She nodded.

"Would you like some of my bread?" Annamaria couldn't bear conflict in any shape or form. Neither could she bear anyone looking so haunted, so hungry as Luciana. She had three brothers, after all. She knew what hunger looked like.

"No. Grazie." How could she eat when she knew the contessa had nothing? But then, that's what the old lady had been eating since they'd come to America. Next to nothing. Nothing more than a bird. She ate nothing, she said nothing, she did nothing. Just sat and stared out the window.

"Really. I have more than I want."

Julietta didn't. She'd finished every last crumb of her bread. And now she was pouring wine for the three of them.

Luciana waved her off. "No. I shouldn't."

"I don't see why not. Madame provides it. As part of our wages." When Julietta saw that Luciana was unconvinced, she enlisted Annamaria. "Doesn't she?"

"She does. Always. Every day."

Luciana leveled a look at each of them. And then she nodded. Accepted the glass that Julietta pushed in her direction. Better something than nothing.

But Luciana was very much regretting her decision an hour later. She couldn't seem to focus her eyes, and her head felt as if it were going to float right off her body. Soon it did that very thing. But heads being so heavy, hers crashed right down onto the table as her eyes rolled back into her head.

5

"*Che rumore!*" Julietta jumped at the thump Luciana's head made as it hit the table.

Annamaria slid out of her chair and knelt beside the unconscious girl. "Forget the noise. Help me!"

Julietta came around the worktable, curious but not wanting to get involved if things became very messy. "Do you think she's . . . sick?"

Annamaria slid a hand beneath Luciana's shoulder and pushed the girl back against the chair. They could both see her face now; her cheeks had gone pale. "No. She's just hungry. Here—take an arm. Help me lower her to the floor."

As the two girls moved her from the table, a necklace slipped from the collar of Luciana's gown. Its lavaliere glinted rubies and diamonds before it slid around its chain and disappeared behind Luciana's neck as they lowered her to the floor.

"Go down to the second floor and ask one of the girls for a cushion."

Julietta's nose wrinkled at the thought of associating with the second-floor girls. "You go."

"Sometimes when people faint like this, they vomit when they wake."

Julietta disappeared faster than a plate of cookies at a festa. She returned, several minutes later, bearing a small pillow in her arms. She handed it down to Annamaria, who tucked it under Luciana's head. "Why don't you wet your scarf? We can lay it across her forehead."

Julietta's hand went up to the scarf that encased her neck. "Why can't we use yours?"

"Because I put it away in the cupboard, but if it's easier for you to find it . . . !"

Julietta wasn't used to being talked to in that sort of tone by Annamaria. And you mightn't have liked it much either. Madame, of course, used that tone all the time. But Madame was formidable with her dark-colored gowns and dignified ways. Annamaria was not. At least not normally, though just now she looked as if she might like to strangle Julietta with the very scarf she was wearing. Quickly, Julietta stripped it from her neck and dipped it into the wash basin in the corner, wringing it out before offering it to Annamaria.

It was several minutes before Luciana began to stir. "Papa? Papa!"

Annamaria handed the scarf back to Julietta. "Wring it out again and bring it back."

"No! *Assassino! Fermati assassino!*" Though she hadn't yet opened her eyes, her voice had become louder.

Julietta brought the scarf back to Annamaria, who placed it once more on the girl's forehead. "What do you think she's talking about?"

Annamaria shrugged. "Her papa?"

Luciana's eyes opened, her gaze traveling about the ceiling before coming to rest upon the two girls. Her eyes grew wide, her hand went to her head, and she tried to sit.

Annamaria wouldn't let her. "Lie there a moment. Take a rest. Will you eat something?"

Luciana started to shake her head, but stopped with a wince.

"Just to take the edge off the ache in your head? Sometimes it helps."

Luciana considered this for a moment. Maybe it would help. And she could accept a bit of bread if it helped. She wouldn't accept it for hunger, wouldn't accept that the house of the counts of Roma had been brought to the brink of poverty, but she would accept anything that would help her keep her job.

Under Annamaria's watchful eye, she ate the bread that was offered. And when color had begun to seep back into her cheeks, Luciana took the hand that Annamaria offered and was helped back to the table.

"Is your father all right?" The girl had seemed so distraught that Julietta couldn't keep herself from asking.

The color that had just come back into Luciana's face drained out, and Annamaria scowled at Julietta, afraid the girl would faint again. "Why do you ask?"

"You mentioned him. While you were on the floor."

"What did I say?" Her eyes burned with an unearthly intensity in her pallid face.

"You cried out for him. Said something about assassins."

She should never have accepted the wine!

"Is he all right?"

"Fine."

Julietta might have asked more questions, but the look on the girl's face precluded any more inquiries. They worked in near silence for the rest of the afternoon, Julietta fearing that Annamaria's promised illness might come at any time; Annamaria fearing that Luciana might faint once again; and Luciana fearing both that she had revealed too much and that Madame might deny her request for immediate pay.

At six o'clock, Julietta and Annamaria put away their work, cleaned up their areas, and prepared to leave.

"Are you coming?" Annamaria searched the girl's eyes for any sign of hunger or illness. She saw only a strange sort of resignation. And . . . panic.

"No."

"We'll see you tomorrow?" The question was posed with the quiet optimism of hope. Annamaria had liked the girl, even though she hadn't said very much and even though what she'd said were mostly lies. She'd heard several Genovese speaking once, and they hadn't had the accent the new girl did.

Luciana heard the pair walk down the stairs. Heard the exit of those other faceless, nameless girls on the second floor. And just when she figured that no one was left, she heard the sound of a person coming up the stairs. She felt a sudden pounding in her chest, and a draining of warmth from her face. She knew there was no reason for the terror that clutched at her. Knew there was no one more sinister than Madame Fortier in the shop. She tried to still her trembling hands by laying aside her work and tidying her space.

Madame soon appeared in the doorway. "May I see what you've accomplished?"

Luciana held out the collar.

Madame took it into her hands. Ran a finger over the beads. Hardly a gap could be felt between them. And there was nary a pull in the material beneath. She turned the collar over, praying as she did so, that she wouldn't be disappointed. She wasn't. The stitching was as neat and precise as if she'd done it herself. She nodded. "Nicely done."

Luciana swallowed. Took in a breath for courage. "I need money, Signora."

"And you'll have it. Work like this will be well paid."

"I need money now."

Madame raised a brow even as Luciana's collapsed in upon

themselves. It wasn't going right. She'd meant to ask, not demand, but the problem was that she wasn't used to doing either. The contessa's granddaughter was used to having her needs met, even anticipated. And at first, in America, she'd had money to speak for her needs. But she had abandoned her title in this new country and now her money was gone.

"Who are you? Exactly." Madame put the collar down on the table and looked at her newest hire.

"An immigrant."

"As are all my girls."

"I am Luciana Conti."

"Who is not from Abruzzo. Or Calabria. Or Sicily. Where *are* you from?"

Luciana didn't answer. "I'm an immigrant and just one among so many. Why should it matter who I am or where I'm from?"

Everything matters. But because the girl was trying, so desperately, not to let it, Madame Fortier decided not to pursue the matter. "I will pay you for two days' work, and I'm trusting that you'll return to the shop tomorrow."

Two days' work. It wouldn't be much money, but it would be something. And at that point, something was everything.

———

Luciana did return the next day, a Friday. And on Monday and Tuesday. By that time, her oddly elegant gown had lost its allure for both Julietta and Annamaria. And her satin pumps were showing holes in their soles. Meant for the gleaming floors of a Roman ballroom, they were entirely out of their element on the cobblestoned streets of Boston.

That afternoon, Madame Fortier came up to the workshop, carrying a pile of gowns in her hands. She deposited them on the worktable in front of Luciana. "Some of these are mine, but most are discards from seasons past. They aren't really of the mode at the moment, but I suppose they'll do well enough for you."

Julietta looked over at Luciana, envy sparking her eyes. Gowns—a whole pile of them—all for the new girl! When she herself was used to wearing nothing grander than blouses and skirts. She frowned. Snuck another peek at them. Not of the mode? Nothing an adjustment here and a tuck there couldn't fix. She could think of a dozen ways in which the gown Mrs. Leavenworth had deemed unsuitable and the gown Mrs. Morgan had refused to pay for could be redeemed.

"Of course, you would have to make them suitable for day wear. But the colors are dark and the lines simple. It shouldn't be too difficult."

Luciana put a hand atop the stack to claim them. "Grazie." It cost her a piece of her pride to say it, to admit that the daughter of the Count of Roma had been relegated to accepting discards from a dressmaker. But she realized that airs and attitudes would not clothe her. And that there was nothing so important as remaining in Madame's good graces.

Madame turned to leave. But then she paused in her step. "Please take what you need—needles, thread, shears—to alter them."

Luciana nodded, knowing that needles and shears could not inform the hands of a girl who could not use them. She had never made a gown, never altered anything in her life, never stitched two pieces of material together. Why should she have had to? She had ordered everything she'd wanted from a couturier in Paris. What she *had* done, the beading she had learned, had simply been a parlor trick. A society-sanctioned way to pass her hours when she had tired of books or music or painting. The donation of gowns was very nice, but she had no way to put them to use. She pressed her lips together in apprehension as she wondered how long she had until Madame would expect to see her wearing them.

6

Annamaria had left work in a hurry that evening, riding the electric car back to North Station and then walking to St. Leonard's Church. She was going to confession so she could be absolved of all her sins.

But what had she ever done? Besides dodge old Giuseppe and walk on by the Sardos' store? She wished she could do something that really needed confessing.

Annamaria clapped a hand over her mouth as soon as she deciphered the thought. Had she just—had she really . . . ? Where had that come from? She made the sign of the cross, and then clutched at the medal that dangled from her neck.

But as she stood in line at the church behind signora Tubello and signora Rimaldi, feet shuffling against the stone of the floor, she pondered the thought. Most people did things that needed confessing. Her sister Theresa did, nearly every time she opened her mouth or set foot outside the apartment. Mama did. So did Papa. So why shouldn't she? Why shouldn't she be allowed the same right to sin as everyone else?

Because it was wicked, that's why.

But still. Why was so much expected of her when nothing was expected of anyone else?

Did that mean she wanted to be . . . bad? She didn't think so. At least that wasn't what she meant to think. But what did it mean? Where had those thoughts come from? And how could she get rid of them?

When her turn came, she stepped into the closet-like space, closing the door behind her. Inside, it was dark, the air close, smelling faintly of the rosemary that tainted signora Tubello's breath and quite strongly of the peculiar odor of signora Rimaldi's sweat. I might have fanned my hand in front of my nose, you might have pinched yours shut entirely, but Annamaria found the scents rather comforting.

Annamaria searched for the comforting sight of Father Antonio's shadow on the other side of the screen that separated them. Having seen it, she closed her eyes. Clasped her hands. "Bless me, Father, for I have sinned. It has been seven days since my last confession." She paused. Normally, she would have immediately started confessing sins, but the things she'd done the week before, the thoughts she'd had that evening, refused to be categorized. They had seemed sinful . . . but were they really? What gave old Giuseppe the right to pinch her? And why should she do something for Theresa that Theresa was perfectly capable of doing for herself?

Those weren't sins.

But . . . maybe her feelings were. Though she'd been exhilarated by her actions at first, they'd left her feeling peevish and foul-tempered. And hadn't she just thought about doing something wrong? More than that she'd tried to justify the doing of wrong, hadn't she? And worse, she'd *desired* it.

"I've had thoughts, Father."

"Of what, my child?"

"Of doing . . . wrong."

Annamaria Rossi? Doing wrong? On his side of the screen,

Father Antonio leaned forward. What on earth could the girl be planning? "Have you done something wrong, then?"

"No. I've just thought about it."

"About what?"

"About . . . being bad."

"Why? In what way?"

Here, then, is where it began to get tricky. Annamaria's thoughts were subversive in the most dangerous sort of way. They were thoughts meant to entice. Thoughts that could, very possibly, seduce one into sin. But Annamaria hardly had the words to explain it, and Father Antonio could not conceive of it, at least not in conjunction with Annamaria Rossi, and so he remained dismissive and rather bemused when he should have been quite concerned.

"It's just—I'm not—it's not fair, Father! It's not fair that I should be kept from the things that I want. Not when everybody else is allowed to have them." She despised herself for the tone in which she had spoken the words. Father Antonio must surely think her nothing but a whiny child. She wished she'd said nothing at all. But that was the point of confession, wasn't it? To say things?

"And what is it that you find yourself wanting?"

"I want . . ." to be free. "I want a family, Father. I'd like to get married. I want to have children. What's wrong with that?"

"Nothing. There's nothing wrong with that. But your life must be given over to service. You know that this must be."

"But . . . why? How do I know that this is what God demands?"

"He made you, didn't He?"

He had.

"And He placed you in your family, didn't He?"

He had.

"And what is the commandment that He gave to sons and daughters?"

"Honor your father and mother . . . "

"That your days may be long in the land which the Lord your God gives you." How Father Antonio liked Annamaria Rossi! She was one of the only ones who still remembered her catechism.

That my days may be long? Dear God, please, don't curse me like that! How lonely all those days would be. "It just doesn't seem fair that those are the things everyone would want for Theresa while they're all denied to me."

"Nothing in this life is fair. And remember, our Lord Jesus came to serve, not to be served."

To serve. Suddenly the weight of the medal that hung around her neck seemed so heavy.

"You know, my child . . . you can't confess to a sin that you have not committed. I must ask if you have any others."

Annamaria's cheeks flushed with shame. Of course she couldn't. She hurried through the confession of her true sins and finally, she prayed. "O my God, I am heartily sorry for having offended thee. I detest all my sins because of thy just punishments, but most of all because they have offended thee, my God, who art all good and deserving of all my love. I firmly resolve, with the help of thy grace, to confess my sins, to do penance, and to avoid the near occasion of sin. Amen."

And so Father Antonio granted her absolution when he ought to have warned her to take great care. He prayed for her and assigned her ten Hail Mary's and three rosaries as penance. "Give thanks to the Lord for He is good."

"For His mercy endures forever."

Annamaria stepped out of the booth, and Father Antonio remained, hoping for a parishioner just a little more . . . interesting. For someone who really needed his help.

As Annamaria walked down Prince Street, she couldn't keep herself from wondering if, in fact, she could do something that needed confessing. Something so . . . rebellious, so . . . wicked, that it had to be wrong. Wouldn't that be something? But doing something, and being *able* to do something, were two very different things. Unfortunately, meek, kind, gentlehearted Annamaria had cultivated the two most lamentable, most damning traits known to womanhood: She was nice. And worse, she was good.

———

Julietta, on the other hand, could have confessed to any number of sins. But she didn't. At least not on a weekly basis. She had developed a more efficient method of confession that fit in rather nicely with her personal philosophy of work. Why go to St. Leonard's for confession every week and admit to sins by ones and twos, when making a confession once a year, at Easter, was so much more convenient? It made her feel more devout in the same way that it made her feel more contrite. She could repent and be sorry in a much more satisfactory way if she had the benefit of having all her sins lined up together in a nice long row.

And that evening, she added one more sin to the pile.

The Settlement House lady visited the Giordanos again. Julietta loved it when she came. The girl could examine her clothing—and her hats!—and then, later, try to imitate the American accent. But to Mama Giordano, the Settlement House lady was the devil incarnate, always telling her the things she shouldn't do and handing her an ever-growing list of things that she should. She couldn't understand Americans! Mama had offered the woman a bowl of her spaghetti with tomato gravy and the woman had turned it down. And not just that. She had done it with a sniff.

And a grimace!

Mama took the bowl from the woman and put it down in front of Little Matteo. He knew what was good for him. Then she looked over at Julietta. "What did she say?"

Julietta understood English much better than she could speak it. "She says we need to eat more meat. Every starch needs a meat." That's what the lady always said, and Julietta

51

was inclined to agree with her. That's what all Americans ate. They ate meat. Mounds and mounds of meat.

"More meat? She going to give us some?"

The Settlement House lady was a bit worried. It was always tense in the Giordano apartment and now the mother of the brood was frowning. She turned toward Julietta. "What is your mother saying? She doesn't look happy."

"She fine. She fine." She wasn't, of course, and that's where the sinning came in. Julietta had lied.

"She going to give us some? That's what I want to know." Mama stepped toward the Settlement House lady, arms lifted as if in supplication to heaven. "When are you going to give us this meat?"

"Ma."

The Settlement House lady was looking back and forth between Julietta and her mother. "Maybe . . . I know meat is expensive. But so many vegetables—it's just not healthy for you! I know you people eat noodles . . . maybe you could just eat them with meat. With . . . meatballs!" That would work, wouldn't it? Meatballs couldn't be as expensive as a roast or a chicken. And hadn't she seen Italians making meatballs? Somewhere in that filthy and derelict old building?

"What did she say?"

"She says maybe we can eat our maccheroni with meatballs."

"What? Like this spaghetti? With meatballs? Who ever heard of such a thing!"

"Ma."

"She's crazy. Loony." She swept her gaze from Julietta to the Settlement House lady. "Get out of my house." Turned back to Julietta. "Tell her to get out of my house. Got no time for crazy people. Got enough people here as it is." She shuffled back to the stove, muttering to herself.

"What did your mother say?"

"She say . . . that's good idea, but . . . she got to think about it."

"Think about it?"

"She got to think about . . . about . . . what we have for dinner now we can't have vegetables."

"It's not that you can't have vegetables. It's just that you shouldn't have so many of them."

"*Pazza!*" Mama had brandished her wooden spoon along with her words.

"She say, Thank you for coming."

"Italian's a very strange language, isn't it? It uses so many less words."

"Crazy! *E' proprio fuori!*" Mama poked herself above the temple with a finger.

"Please . . . she say, Don't trip over the door."

The lady turned and flashed a smile toward Mama Giordano. "Thank you."

Mama placed her hand beneath her chin, palm down, and then flicked it away from her face toward the woman.

Julietta blanched at the gesture. Turned to push the lady out the door. "That mean God bless you."

That was a gesture the Settlement House lady hadn't seen before. The southern Italians were such a strange race of people. Always using their hands whenever they talked. She sighed and then lifted her shoulders, endeavoring to be as pleasant as she could with these destitute illiterates. She put her own hand beneath her chin, repeating the gesture. "And God bless you too."

Julietta waited until the door had shut before she turned on her mother. "What are you thinking?"

Mama looked up from her pot. "What was *she* thinking, that's what I want to know."

"You can't treat them that way! I had to tell her you had blessed her."

"Blessed her?"

"That's what I told her. That you'd said God bless you."

"God bless you? To that woman? 'God curse you,' more like. God curse these people who think they can come into my house, my own kitchen, and tell me what to do! Did you see her? Did you see that hat she wore? In Chiusano San Domenico only two kinds of women wear hats—"

"Ma!"

"You should be thanking me I got rid of her."

"She's only trying to teach us how to be American."

"Why do I have to be American? What's wrong with being Avellinesi?"

"Everything!" Julietta said the word before she could think not to. But once she'd said it, she was glad. "If Avellino was so good, then why did we leave? And if America is so bad, then why do we stay?"

Mama Giordano put her spoon down and turned to face her girl. "Why do we stay? Why did we leave? We left *la miseria* because it offered only one thing: misery. That's why we came here."

"But you brought the misery with you!"

"What is this? What's wrong, *cara mia*?"

"You! You're what's—" This time Julietta had the grace to put a hand over her mouth, but not before she saw hurt color her mother's eyes. "Look around. Is this why we came? Is this all there is? Two crowded rooms and a pair of raggedy old curtains? Is that all we get for living in a pig's pen and working like slaves, turning our paychecks over to Papa every week? That might be fine for you, but not for me. I want more. The only thing wrong with this country is people like you!"

7

As Luciana walked up Salem Street that evening, a piece of pink paper, buoyed by a sly and lazy wind, twirled up toward her hand. When she brushed it away, the wind abandoned it and the paper fell to her feet. She began to step over it when a symbol on it caught her eye. She bent over and grabbed it with one hand. Then she spread it flat on her thigh and tried to read it.

She couldn't understand the words, but she did comprehend the color of the paper. Pink. And though she couldn't translate the sentences into her language, she did grasp the message of those blaring black phrases. Her hands shook as she stared at them.

Anarchists? Here? A shiver crept up Luciana's spine.

She'd known that her father's murderer had followed her to America's shores, but she'd assumed that here there would be no anarchist political party or organization. And she had hoped— hoped still!—that in this country, she could become one of many. One of a very many immigrants come to America in order to leave the past behind. To begin life anew.

He hadn't found her yet. She knew that if he had, she would already be dead. And it had been so many weeks since she'd seen him, she had started to hope that he had given up his hunt.

She tore her gaze from the paper, searching the street for anyone looking suspicious. She examined those foreign words too, hoping to discern something that looked familiar. There was no mention of *assassinare*.

But what did it say? She wanted to know what it said! What it said was:

> There will be bloodshed; we will not dodge; there will have to be murder; we will kill, because it is necessary; there will have to be destruction; never hope that your cops, and your hounds will ever succeed in ridding the country of the anarchistic germ that pulses in our veins. . . . Long live social revolution! Down with tyranny!

THE ANARCHIST FIGHTERS

But she had no way of deciphering it. And in any case, she had already divined the general idea. Letting the sheet drop from her hand, she began to run. She flew by the crowds on the North End sidewalks, heedless of protecting her identity. She almost shouted at the greengrocer to hurry when she stopped long enough to buy some fruit.

Finally, she reached the door to their rooms, overwrought and out of breath. Trembling with trepidation. What if . . . what if her father's murderer had discovered where she lived? What if he'd already been to the apartment? What if he'd taken . . . ? She unlocked the door and pushed it open, then almost melted with relief. The contessa was sitting there, just as she always was, oblivious to person or to place.

Luciana set the fruit on the sideboard and unknotted her scarf with fingers gone stiff from fear. In the bedroom, she slipped out of her gown and then pulled on her worn peasant's skirt and blouse. Sat on the mattress as she tried to calm her nerves.

This wouldn't do. This wouldn't do at all. She had to have information. If there were other anarchists in this country, then he was sure to have found them. She had to know what they were planning to do. She was worse than an illiterate in this country. She was deaf and mute too!

Papa. Papa! She pulled the pillow to her face so that her grief could not be heard. She pressed it to her face with her knees as she beat upon the ends of it with her fists.

Why had this happened? Why had she been left all alone?

Why are you doing this to me, God? Sì. You, God! Keeper of widows and orphans. You who don't see and don't care and won't answer. Why have you done this to me?

Of course God had done no such thing, though you can probably see why she might think so. But it's no good preaching to a grief-stricken soul. And it can actually cause much harm. God is long-suffering in His patience, however, and infinite in His kindness, so we shall leave it to Him to draw Luciana to himself in His own time.

She fell over onto the bed and rolled onto her stomach, letting the pillow absorb both her sobs and her tears. After a while, once her tears had stopped, once perspiration had dampened the hair at the edges of her face, she sat up and wiped the remnants of grief away. And then she stood. Took a deep, stuttering breath.

Grief was too much a luxury to allow herself to indulge in for long. If God wasn't going to look after them, and clearly He had decided not to, then she had to do it herself. She left the room and went to the old woman's side. Kneeling beside the contessa, she kissed her hand. "Dinner is ready." Such as it was.

"Grazie, ragazza."

"Dinner isn't ready." Mama Rossi spoke the words as Papa pulled his chair from the table and moved to sit down.

"What do you mean dinner isn't ready?" Annamaria's family held its collective breath as Papa Rossi scowled at his wife.

"It isn't ready. Maglione the greengrocer gave us bad tomatoes.

I can't make salad with them, so I have to make a gravy instead. It isn't ready." What she really wanted to do was to remind him that seventy years ago, back in the old country when Maglione's was run by the present Maglione's great-grandfather, that man had overcharged her great-grandmother for a zucchini. And since then, hadn't the Magliones always given her family the worst of the produce? Hadn't the Magliones always taken great care to ensure that they received only the most rotten of fruit? And hadn't they been a curse to her family ever since? They'd been eating terrible food for the past seventy years. And she didn't see why it had to continue now that they were in America. Enough was enough! But of course, that wasn't really worth mentioning.

Papa opened his mouth as if he was going to say something, but then he gave up and shrugged instead.

The family sighed in relief.

"This is the third time this month that Maglione's given me bad tomatoes." Mama spoke over her shoulder as she stirred her gravy.

Papa looked up from his wine to see if Mama was exaggerating.

She wasn't. "Third time."

Papa shrugged. "So what do you want me to do about it?"

"I want to go to Zanfini's."

"Zanfini's? Who's Zanfini?" Papa could be forgiven such a question. He worked as a pick and shovel man downtown on a public works project. That meant that he rose when it was still dark and came home late. He trudged, head down to his labors, and then he trudged, head down, all the way home. And who would have blamed him? But the rest of the family knew Zanfini's. And they all turned to look at Mama as if she had suddenly gone mad.

"Zanfini's. Across the street."

"Across the street . . ." Papa's eyes screwed up as if he couldn't exactly picture where that might be. "Across the street?"

Mama nodded.

"Across the street. As in the other side of the street?"

Mama nodded once more.

"Where the Sicilians live?!"

Everyone cringed when they heard the *S* word. Sicilians weren't fit to speak to, let alone buy tomatoes from. Avellinesis bought tomatoes from Maglione, and Sicilians bought tomatoes from Zanfini. *Only* Sicilians bought tomatoes from Zanfini.

"I want to buy tomatoes from Zanfini."

"Zanfini the Sicilian?" Papa Rossi tugged on an earlobe as if he weren't quite sure he was hearing right. And then he shook his head. "No one in my house buys tomatoes from Sicilians." And that was the end of that.

But Mama Rossi was not to be swayed so easily from her course. She was sick to death of mushy tomatoes, and Zanfini's produce always looked pretty good. At least what he displayed outside on his cart did. And those Sicilians seemed happy enough with it. She wanted nice, firm tomatoes, and she was going to have them. It would just take a bit more time. And a bit more convincing.

But for now, Papa had spoken and there was a semblance of peace. Everyone was glad to be done talking of treason and tomatoes and Sicilians. And besides, when Papa said no, everyone knew what it meant. It meant that he meant no until Mama made him realize that what he really meant was yes.

And so, Mama Rossi finished her gravy, and Papa Rossi ate his dinner in blissful ignorance, happy that for once his wife had listened to good reason. And all the while, his children sent sly glances down the table in their mama's direction, wondering exactly how, this time, she would manage to get her way.

The next morning, Julietta wondered the very same thing: How would she manage to get her way? That she would, eventually, get her way and wrangle one of Madame's old gowns away from Luciana was not in question. And she quite intended to be upfront in the doing of it. She could have just as easily filched the thing, that pink and white silk embroidered net over messaline gown. Had she taken it, she was almost, very nearly, certain that no one would have missed it. But it wouldn't do to have her character placed into question. Not when she was hoping to be taken into Madame's confidence.

As Madame had said, it was outmoded. Done up in the fussiest of styles. All high-collared propriety, dripping with lace and wrapped up with a ridiculously large-bowed satin sash. It might have turned some heads a few years ago, drawn a few admiring glances. Oh, there was grace and elegance at the core of it, for wasn't it one of Madame's own designs? But its lines were stifled. They needed to be liberated.

Just like the Marne needed to be liberated from the Germans.

She'd rip that cage of lace from the neck, narrow the collar, slice the sash by half. Pull out the tucks in the tunic, lift the hem by five inches. No one would ever recognize it.

As she embroidered, she cast a longing glance in the gown's direction. It was buried beneath gowns made in heavy navy moiré and aubergine wool crepe. All those lovely gowns and the new girl had left them right where Madame had placed them! What was wrong with her? Didn't she know how it looked to wear the same tired, faded gown, day after day, to the city's best gown shop? Didn't she know how it must look to Madame? To see no sign of—no appreciation for—such a generous gift?

Luciana was eyeing that very same pile of gowns, wishing she knew what to do with them. She wasn't sure, exactly, if she should take them home. If that was what Madame had intended. She could, of course—and with gratitude—but what would she do with them once she got them there? She had no tools and no ability to turn their dated lines into something more pleasing.

Oh, she could see their potential. The pink and white messaline gown with its silk embroidered net, for example. She would feel so much cooler walking through the city in a gown like that. She could picture herself fairly floating. It needed something, of course. It needed to be different. To be simplified. It was too . . . much. At the moment. But how was she supposed to make it something less?

Maybe . . . should she ask? For help? Surely the other girls would know what to do.

Annamaria did gorgeous smocking, but she didn't seem to see the need for anything fashionable of her own. Julietta was quite the opposite; Julietta was the person she should ask. And she would, if only she didn't feel such disdain, such judgment, every time the girl looked at her.

Perhaps that evening, after work, she would spend a few moments looking through the pile. She knew how to bead, didn't she? Sewing couldn't be that much more difficult, could it?

As Julietta and Annamaria ran down the stairs after work, Luciana lingered in the room, caught between the desire to turn to her advantage Madame's generous gift, and the knowledge that she was inadequate for the task. Which was better? To take and wear one of the gowns as it was and look like she didn't know frippery from fashion, or to keep wearing the one gown she owned and look exactly like who she was: a girl, pathetic and pitiable, who had fallen upon hard times.

She passed a hand over those luxurious silks and wools, pausing to admire a dated, though finely worked, lace fichu. Perhaps . . . perhaps tomorrow. Perhaps tomorrow she would ask for help.

———

Mama Rossi had determined that tonight be *the* night. It was the night that she was going to advance her cause. Little by little. Step by step. Papa still had to be persuaded, but Mama had to have her tomatoes.

She set a plate of food before her husband and then took her seat.

He narrowed his eyes. Lowered his head to sniff at it. "What is it?"

"Parmigiana di melanzane."

"Parmigiana di melanzane?" He took up a knife and used it to lift the heavy layer of cheese that was draped over his slice of eggplant. "Where's the gravy?"

Mama pushed from her chair, collected a handful of chopped garlic and oregano from the sideboard, and sprinkled it on top of Papa's cheese.

"I want the gravy. Parmigiana di melanzane has a gravy."

Mama shrugged. "I don't have any tomatoes."

"And how do you make it without tomatoes?"

"I make it with the garlic and the oregano." She gestured to the plate.

Papa frowned at her.

"What? I'm not buying tomatoes from Maglione anymore. He's cheated me for the last time."

Papa shook his head, put a fork to his plate. What was it to him if his wife didn't buy tomatoes? He took up a piece of the eggplant. Tasted it. Disaster! That's what it was. "You can't make parmigiana di melanzane without tomatoes. There's got to be someplace that sells good tomatoes. You could go . . . you could go up to Hull."

Mama Rossi sniffed. Took up her own forkful of parmigiana di melanzane without tomato gravy. "I'm not going to a Hull frutta e verdura when there's a perfectly good greengrocer across the street."

"No wife of mine is going to cross the street for tomatoes."

She looked over at her husband, reproach molding her brow. "I wasn't going to. I would never do that. You know I would never do that."

Papa looked up from his plate, suspicion sharpening his gaze. She wouldn't? And when had she ever done as he had asked?

She smiled at him.

Well. Maybe things had changed. Maybe this time she was actually going to listen to him. "*Bene*. Fine then. There will be no more talk of tomatoes."

Mama nodded. "I was going to have Annamaria do it."

8

Annamaria nearly choked on her food. Mama was going to have her do it? But—

"It wouldn't do to have Emilio Rossi's wife buy tomatoes from a Sicilian, but if his daughter did it . . . you know how these young girls are since they've been living in America. They've gotten bold. They've forgotten the old ways."

Papa was staring at his wife in horror. "You want . . . ?"

"Annamaria can do it."

Mama was going to make *her* do it? She was going to make her own daughter cross the street and deal with Sicilians? Annamaria had always done everything and anything that her mother had ever asked, but buying tomatoes from Sicilians? Surely not even Saint Zita, with all her pious ways, would ever have allowed herself to be used so poorly. It was one thing to know that your life was destined for servitude, but quite another to be told to grovel in the doing of it. "I don't—"

Mama quelled Annamaria's protest with one black look.

Papa's fist hit the table. "No one is going to buy tomatoes from that Sicilian. And I *will* have tomatoes in my parmigiana di melanzane! Am I clear?"

Perfectly. And, surprisingly, Mama didn't seem too upset by his decree.

———

Julietta, on the other hand, was extremely put out by what she was observing. She walked into the third floor workroom the next morning, only to see Luciana pulling the pink and white messaline gown from Madame's pile.

Her messaline gown!

The girl held it up to her shoulders and then stood on her toes, trying to get a look at herself in the mirror.

"It doesn't suit you."

Luciana started and spun around, clutching the gown to her waist.

"You're too pale."

In fact, Luciana was pale. Paler than Julietta, in any case. She held the gown out away from her and sighed. "I know. I just . . . it seemed . . . I don't know what to do."

Julietta raised a brow. "You don't know what to do? With what?"

"With those." Luciana swept her hand toward Madame's pile. "With any of them."

"You're to wear them. That's what Madame said." Julietta wanted to add, *The sooner the better*, but she didn't. What was it to her if the new girl got in bad with Madame?

"But first, don't you think . . . I'd have to remake them."

Julietta nodded. Of course she'd have to remake them. Or risk being laughed at as she walked up and down Temple Place.

Luciana raised her chin against Julietta's impudent gaze. "I don't know how." She was not in the habit of asking for help and didn't quite know how to go about doing it.

"You don't know how." What was the girl trying to say? It was difficult enough to understand her uppity northern accent, but the words she was saying had no sense to them. She didn't know how to do . . . what?

"I don't know how to sew."

"You don't—but—?" What did the girl do every day but sit at the end of the table, beading?

"I know how to bead. I don't know how to sew."

"Like . . . like this . . ." Julietta made a motion with her hand as if she were doing just that.

Luciana, poor girl, stretched to the limits of humiliation, decided that Julietta was exactly the wrong person to ask for help. She bundled the pink and white messaline up into a ball and determined to take it home with her that night. She'd figure something out.

Julietta, seeing her dreams about to be whisked away, threw out a hand toward the girl. "I'll help you!" She tore the gown from Luciana's hands.

"You'll . . . what?"

"Help. I'll help you." Julietta set the gown down on the table and went to Madame's pile. Digging through the gowns, she pulled out a navy moiré, an ivory messaline, an aubergine wool challis, a dark green crepe de Chine, and a wine-colored crepe poplin. "You could fix these."

"Don't you think the moiré is a bit heavy?"

"It's nearly autumn."

"And this ivory messaline . . . ?" Luciana looked over at the table where the pink and white messaline lay, discarded. "It doesn't seem quite so . . ."

It wasn't. It wasn't nearly as elegant as Madame's design. The ivory messaline had been ordered readymade from a dressmaker in New York City for a client. "The color is better, though. For you."

Luciana sighed. She supposed that it was. "But what would I do with it?"

Do with it? Why, Julietta could imagine a dozen things! "You'll want to clip the collar away from that rosette at the bustline and let it hang down a bit at the corners. And lower the inset at the neckline."

Sì. Of course. Luciana could begin to see it. Much better.

"And then shorten the hem of the tunic. And cut away the bottom of the skirt."

Luciana nodded.

"And you could use those pieces to lengthen the sleeves. See?"

"You don't think the pink and white messaline would be better?"

"For you? No." Julietta shook her head with all the confidence she had acquired in her eighteen years.

"I see what can be done, but . . . I still lack the skills."

"I could do it. I could do them all for you."

"You would?"

"I *could* . . . for the right price."

The right price. That's what Mama Rossi had had to calculate. What was the right price? What would make Papa change his mind, yet spare him complete humiliation? A man had a reputation to uphold, after all. As she set his dinner before him that night, she prayed that she'd made the right choice. That she'd done the right underhanded thing.

He smiled. "That looks like parmigiana di melanzane."

"It is."

"Made with tomatoes."

"Indeed."

Papa sniffed at it with all of the delicacy of a connoisseur. This now—this!—was what a parmigiana di melanzane was supposed to look like. And smell like. He wasted no time in tucking into the eggplant, scooping some tomato gravy onto it, and putting it into his mouth. But just as promptly, he spit it out. "What kind of garbage is this?!"

"The kind made with rotten tomatoes from Maglione's frutta e verdura."

He picked up his glass of wine and poured the remainder down his throat. "No more tomatoes from Maglione's. Do you hear?"

Mama folded her hands beneath her apron. Nodded as demurely as she was able to. "I could get them from Zanfini's. Annamaria could get them for me." She slid a look at her daughter as she said the words. She knew that she was asking the girl to sacrifice her virtue for the family. But hadn't her family been sacrificing their reputation to the Magliones for generations? They'd been played for fools long enough. Wasn't the sacrifice of a daughter a small price to pay for shaming the man? For letting all the neighborhood know that the greengrocer was so detestable that the Rossis preferred to buy their tomatoes from a Sicilian instead? It was the Magliones' turn to be shamed.

Had she been less stubborn, had she not already committed to her course, she might have realized that the disturbance she felt in her stomach was not indigestion but rather the pricking of her conscience. But Mama had long treated her conscience the same way she treated Papa. And over time they had both decided it was much easier to simply acquiesce than to try and argue with her. Besides, it was the family's honor at stake, and sometimes honor had the habit of masquerading as righteous indignation.

Papa sighed. "If the Sicilians are the only ones who sell good tomatoes, then buy your tomatoes from the Sicilians." A man couldn't eat his pride, after all. And it made him want to weep, thinking of all that good parmigiana di melanzane gone to waste.

Julietta fairly wept herself the next morning. She was late. If she didn't reach Zanfini's frutta e verdura in time, she wouldn't be able to see the man. And if she didn't see him today, then she wouldn't see him again until Monday.

Dio ce ne scampi! God forbid!

In her haste she stepped right out of her shoe. Shoving it back on to her foot, she started up once more. She rounded the corner onto North Street and then stopped. He wasn't there. He'd already gone. A wave of disappointment and regret swirled through her stomach.

He was gone.

"Buon giorno."

She nearly jumped right out of her flimsy shoes. The voice was male, so she fixed a smile to her face before she turned.

It was *him*!

In all his handsome glory. Dark, curling hair. Thick, dramatic brows. He was perfect. Bold and daring. She knew he had to be. He wore colored shirts, didn't he? Instead of the boring white ones propriety always demanded? And what he didn't wear was a hat. Or a tie. She flipped a look toward him that was both bold in its directness and demure in its brevity. "Where's your truck?" A strange question to ask, perhaps, but Julietta had always been one for going directly after what she wanted, and the truck was part of the man's great appeal. She'd never been in a truck before. Or a car, for that matter. And she wanted to go for a ride.

He smiled. "I gave it to my friend."

She couldn't know it, but her face had fallen.

"For the day. I gave it to him for the day." He shrugged. "And night." And now that he was finally standing here, talking to this girl that he'd been watching, he began to wish that he'd kept it. There were such wonderful discoveries to be made at the end of dark alleys, in the cab of a truck.

"Oh. Well . . ." She looked up at him once more. Smiled. "Arrivederci."

Good-bye? "But—" He was already talking to her back. "Wait!" Wait? Did he have to sound so desperate?

She turned on her heel. Stood there, hand on her hip. "Do you have a name?"

"It's Angelo. Angelo Moretti. But—"

"Then good-bye, Angelo Moretti."

"But I don't—hey!—what's *your* name?"

He was speaking to a phantom. She had already turned the corner. She was gone.

Laughter erupted behind him as a second man emerged from the alley. "But, but, but—" He snorted. "You sounded just like your backfiring truck."

Angelo shoved a fist into the man's chest and a sheaf of pink papers into his hand. "Shut up, Armando. And go distribute these."

"Sure. Anything you say."

"And be on the lookout."

They always were. They may have kidded around while they went about their business of distributing produce, but they were dead serious about their true calling. And as they made their way through the North End distributing leaflets, they left a pink blizzard of terror in their wake.

———

That Sunday, Luciana tried to coax the contessa to church. They hadn't been since they'd come to America, and she didn't want to give God any more reasons to punish them. Besides, church was the one place she was absolutely certain her father's murderer wouldn't be.

"No, ragazza."

"But you used to in Rom—I mean . . . it's Sunday."

"You must learn to speak more clearly, girl."

Luciana took up the old woman's hand and knelt in front of her. "It's Sunday."

"Sunday." The contessa said the word as if it were foreign.

As if there were no responsibility, no obligation inherent in its meaning.

"Sunday. On Sunday we—*you*—go to mass."

"Mass."

"We'll be late."

The old woman looked up from Luciana's hand and into her eyes.

What Luciana saw in that gaze chilled her to the core. There was nothing—no one—there. She might have said the woman was absent her soul. And so, she did the only thing she could do. She pushed to her feet. "I'll be back when it's over."

"When it's over . . ." The old woman had already turned her face toward the window, her profile dismantled by the interplay of shadow and of light.

Luciana locked the door behind her. She took one step into the hall and then stopped. She wasn't sure she should leave the contessa by herself. She'd done it every day for work, of course, but that didn't make her worry any less about the old woman. Luciana had actually found her standing a time or two, in the middle of the room, when she'd come home from work lately. She didn't have to work very hard to imagine the contessa going to the door, turning the knob, and walking right out of the apartment.

And what would happen then?

Her throat constricted, and she felt her nostrils flare in compensation. She closed her eyes as she struggled to breathe. It had begun to happen quite often, this problem with breathing. But now she recognized the signs. The fluttering of panic in her stomach, the grip of fear in her bowels, the stranglehold of dread around her throat.

What would happen then?

How could she, a destitute heiress, alone and friendless, manage to make a life in this strange country? For both her grandmother and herself?

She didn't know.

As she stood there wheezing, as her vision began to tilt, she pressed her fingernails into her palm, desperate to feel something besides the cold clutch of fear. Sometime, someday, she would have to figure out what to do. Soon. But today was Sunday and Sunday was for mass. If nothing else, she wanted the satisfaction of confronting God in His own house.

Once at church, Luciana pushed herself into the corner of the back pew. Looking at the crowd of people crammed together in the pews in front of her, she knew it wouldn't do them any good. It wouldn't do them any good at all to try to sit so close to the altar.

God didn't care.

He didn't care whether you went to confession every week of your life, or if you only went to mass on Easter. It didn't matter.

It hadn't mattered that in Roma, Luciana slid into the very front row every Sunday that she could remember. It hadn't mattered that she held parties for the ladies' parish organization, or that she had given a donation every month to the orphans and widows fund. That she had wrapped bandages for countless soldiers or that she had kissed the ring of the Holy Father himself. On several occasions.

Why hadn't it mattered!

It was supposed to matter. God was supposed to care.

But He'd allowed her father to be murdered and then, when she'd found herself turned out of her own estate, He hadn't even bothered to help her. He'd abandoned her. She'd always been there for God, just like she was supposed to be. Why wasn't He there for her? Where was He?

Where are you?

She stood when she had to and kneeled when she was supposed to. She even prayed along with the priest. But she couldn't bring herself to partake in Communion. And so she sat in the back pew like a heathen, watching the parishioners stream to the front of the church. She ought to have left, but there was only hopelessness waiting for her at the tenement. Had she been able to be completely honest with herself, she might have admitted that the fact that her grandmother depended upon her so completely frightened her. But you know as well as I how fear can make even the eloquent inarticulate.

So that's where Father Antonio found Luciana after church. In the back pew, still pressed into her corner, after the rest of his parishioners had melted away.

"You are new?" He spoke in the synthesis of dialects that the immigrants, of all regions, relied upon to make themselves understood.

Luciana glanced up at him and then inclined her head, unwilling to lie to a priest, but unwilling also to reveal any particular knowledge of herself.

"Are you well, my child?"

Well? No. She was hardly well, but she was healthy. She was not hungry. She was alive. And she recognized that in spite of all her previous assumptions to the contrary, those things were not assured to any person in this new county. She nodded.

"May the Lord lift up his countenance upon thee, and give thee peace."

Peace. Sì. Peace would be a start. "Grazie, Father."

"You are from the north?"

Once more, she inclined her head.

"What is your name, child?"

"Luciana."

Light. Child of light. Then why did her eyes seem so shadowed by darkness? She should be singing. Or dancing. Laughing.

"How can I help you?" For it was quite clear to the father that she was in great need. Of something.

Help? Her? "No one can help me, Father."

"Perhaps it seems that way to you, but God can do the impossible."

She wanted to laugh. Oh, how she wanted to laugh! God had

already done the impossible. He'd killed the one person she'd loved the most and taken her away from everything she'd ever known. But she didn't laugh. She smiled. A very bleak, very sad smile. "My problems are too difficult, even for Him."

Father Antonio was used to speaking to the wounded of the faith, but he'd never before encountered one so set on God's impotence. Usually people were longing to be reminded of His great power and great love. But the words he'd meant for cheer seemed only to deepen the girl's despair. He reached out a hand to touch her, to bless her, but she slipped away from him and was gone.

9

Twenty minutes earlier and fifteen pews up, Julietta had been nursing a smile that had nothing to do with the rites of mass or the sacrament of the Eucharist.

Angelo.

Angelo Moretti.

Such a nice name was Angelo. For such a nice handsome face. For such nice thick hair that curled so delectably over his ears. And such nice brown eyes that had glowed as he'd looked at her. And his lips . . .

Julietta bit her own lip.

His lips were . . . divine. They were large and . . . and . . .

The word that she wanted was sensuous, but even she couldn't quite bring herself to think it while the father was conducting mass under the patronage of God's all-seeing, all-knowing eyes. There was something about his lips. Something about the way they curled up at one corner. In almost a kind of . . . It wasn't a sneer, really. Not quite. It was just that . . . he didn't seem quite . . . nice.

Julietta's lips suddenly curved into a full-blown smile. She'd figured it out.

He wasn't quite nice.

And that was exactly the reason she liked him so much. Who better to rescue her from the chains of propriety and the shackles of decency than a man who wasn't quite nice? She couldn't wait to see him again. And again.

And again.

———

Madame Fortier sat behind her desk on Monday, pulling her appointment book from some cards of buttons and a pile of trimmings. The twenty-ninth of July.

Mrs. Quinn.

A painful, insistent thumping began in Madame's head. And heart.

She had known this day was coming; she just wished it hadn't come so soon.

Mrs. Quinn.

What days and weeks and years had gone by that Madame hadn't wished for, hadn't hoped to hear, the glad tidings of that woman's death? But then, what days and weeks and years had gone by that she hadn't looked forward, with anticipation, to the client's next visit?

The woman was a witch. A *strega*.

A real, true witch, born at midnight on Christmas Eve, an occasion which an annual birthday ball had been conceived to commemorate. Who but a strega would think of celebrating something like that? Mrs. Quinn's Birthday Ball had been the event of the season before the war. It used to be that Madame Fortier had worked for months on Mrs. Quinn's gown for that gala occasion. These days, with the concussion of guns resounding from Europe and extravagant expenses abandoned for the cause of patriotism, the ball had been converted into a small dinner party with an influential guest list. And for it she would need a simpler, but no less brilliantly fashioned, gown.

Which in no way made up for Madame's loss of income from events like the Ace of Clubs Ball or the Junior League's Gala, which had been indefinitely postponed until the end of the war; until victory had been won and freedom wrested from the cruel, warmongering Boche.

Madame put a hand to her aching head and sighed.

A strega she was and a strega she would always be. Ever since Mrs. Quinn, née Howell, had chosen Madame Fortier to make her wedding gown, the woman had been a constant and abiding thorn in the gown maker's flesh.

Madame opened a drawer in her desk and pulled a flask from it. Reached further back to retrieve a glass. Poured herself two fingers' worth of clear, strong grappa.

Perhaps you might have been inclined, until that moment, to sympathize with Madame Fortier. To, at the very least, tolerate Madame Fortier. She was not an easy woman to like; she did not, in fact, even like herself very much. Though that last bit, of course, is a secret, and we must do her the courtesy not to mention it, not even to think of it too often before she can realize it for herself. But before you convict her for fortifying herself with liquor, consider for one moment that you have not yet met the woman she was fortifying herself against. And consider for a second moment that if you had to work for Mrs. Quinn, if you had to satisfy that voracious and unslakeable thirst for the highest, most distinctive of fashions, if you had to hear her speak of her husband, the congressman, over and over and over again, you also might feel a great and sudden thirst for grappa.

Or something very much like it.

You see, it's all very well and good to judge and moralize, but there are some whose morale has been broken. And for these, sometimes, we just have to let them survive, in hopes that one day they will decide to do more than survive. That they will decide, in fact, to live, in which case they can cast off their own crutches and endeavor for themselves to face their problems directly.

But Madame Fortier had not yet reached that point, and we must not run ahead of her to the place where we would like her to be. And so, we will let her drink her grappa in private, and brood on the appointments of the day.

———

It was some time later that she climbed the stairs to the third-floor workshop, supporting her steps by placing a heavy, discreetly jeweled hand to the wall. Once she'd reached the top of the stairs, she paused a moment, hand against her chest, to catch her breath and to buttress the last of the quickly waning courage that still resided there.

Once she had collected herself, she walked across the landing to the workshop. "Luciana."

The girls looked up from their work in surprise. It was not often that Madame paid them the favor of a visit. Least not midmornings.

"Si?" There was something in Madame's eyes, something in her demeanor that made Luciana reluctant to be singled out for that woman's attentions.

"I would like for you to assist me at this afternoon's fitting."

A fitting? What did she know about fittings? "But—"

"It will be at two o'clock."

"I don't—I can't—" She hadn't taken the job with Madame in order to work in the shop's window, visible to every passerby. She wanted to be hidden, not exposed.

Annoyance was beginning to creep into Madame's eyes.

"I can't—speak English." There. Now Madame wouldn't want her.

"Don't worry. Mrs. Quinn won't be conversing with you."

Luciana flushed from both the miscomprehension and the implication. "I don't think—"

"That's right. You don't! Because if you think that I'm giving you options instead of orders, then you can leave right now!"

Luciana flinched as if she had been slapped. She'd never been given orders as if she were a mere—an ordinary—working girl. She couldn't bring herself to even think the word *servant*. But leave? She couldn't—she wouldn't! She would do whatever it took to be allowed to stay. Even if it meant creeping out of her third-floor hiding place. "I'm sorry—I didn't mean—of course I'll—"

Madame was already regretting her words, though not her feelings of frustration. Mrs. Quinn was nearly on her doorstep. What she needed was an ally, not a recalcitrant employee. "Two o'clock."

As Julietta and Annamaria had observed the conversation, their eyebrows shot up toward their foreheads. They hardly waited until Madame had gone before speaking. "Mrs. Quinn!" Julietta was already crossing herself. She couldn't decide whether to bless her good luck or curse her misfortune. In the past, Madame had always asked her to assist with the clients. But there were clients and there was Mrs. Quinn.

Mrs. Quinn? Luciana already hated her. "Who is Mrs. Quinn?"

"A strega." On that point, both Julietta and Annamaria were agreed.

A witch? Surely not. But Luciana, looking over at the other two girls, could not ignore their reactions. They couldn't actually believe in witches, could they? Surely they were more educated, less ignorant, than that.

Mrs. Quinn herself would have been completely surprised and not a little hurt at that assessment of her person. She'd lived her life as an activist, after all. Those who knew her considered her to be remarkably and gratifyingly modern. A bastion of tolerance, a scourge against racism. She'd married an Irishman, hadn't she? She had been hard at work in the National Women's Party to advocate for women's suffrage. *And* she patronized Madame Fortier's shop.

It helped, of course, that the woman was the best gown maker in Boston. And it didn't hurt that she was truly European instead of second-generation Irish. Most of the other dressmakers had Gallicized their names and sprinkled their sentences with French phrases. Madame's accent, however, was authentic. And that counted for quite a bit in Mrs. Quinn's mind. She could not have said for certain from where exactly Madame had come, but she presumed it was some place respectable.

Mrs. Quinn was a Champion for the Downtrodden and a Defender of the Meek. The poor, the weak, the destitute could have no better friend than she. A witch, she was most definitely not.

She did, however, have a blind spot on the topic of Italians, as did most people in America with any kind of intelligence. Especially southern Italians, whom everyone knew to be inferior in every way to northern Italians. They were no more than over-grown children, really. Of limited intelligence and questionable virtue. Intractable and stubborn. They seemed to always think much more highly of themselves than they ought. And their homes! They swarmed to the North End like rats from a sinking ship. What sort of intelligent people would live like that? Why would *any* kind of person live like that?

Justice, liberty, tolerance.

Those were the topics that employed Mrs. Quinn's abundant energy and considerable intelligence.

If Mrs. Quinn had known the gown maker's thoughts, however, she would not have been pleased. And she wouldn't have used the word *strega*. She preferred to think of herself as clever. She had an uncanny nose for politics. She could sense a softening of resolve like a wolf sensed a change in the wind. She could ferret out a man's hidden interests with nothing but a well-phrased question. And she could plot betrayal as if she herself held the knife. Most of her husband's success in Boston and then in Washington was due to her instinctual mastery of the world of politics and her ability to call on just the right people, to do just the right thing, at just the right time.

———

At lunch, Julietta pulled a package from her sack, along with a length of bread and a wedge of cheese. "Here." She slid the package across the table in Luciana's direction.

Luciana opened it and held up the contents, exclaiming with something quite near delight. Her gowns! Several of them, in any case. New gowns had been in such generous supply at the estate in Roma, even in spite of the war, that their presence had never come close to eliciting that lift of delight in her spirit that these did.

She pushed aside her lunch and rose to her feet, holding one of the gowns up to her shoulders.

Julietta tried to look at it with an appraiser's objective eye. She'd worked harder than she'd meant to on it. On all of them. Dedicated more time on Saturday and Sunday nights than she had intended. But the results had been quite astonishing. Gone were the awkward, overwrought, over-decorated silhouettes. They'd been replaced by svelte, clean lines. No dowdiness, no stuffiness remained within their folds. The gown Luciana held in particular exuded charm, and grace. And the fresh, carefree *joie de vivre* of summers gone by.

Before the war.

And before the anarchists.

Annamaria smiled as she watched Luciana. "Try it on."

Oh, how she wanted to! But . . . "Now?"

"Sì. Now." Julietta had gone to help Luciana from her old gown. "Please! To spare us both another look at that old rag you've been wearing."

Rag? That was hardly fair to the handiwork of the preeminent

81

Parisian modiste Luciana had patronized before . . . everything . . . but she didn't quibble; she was too grateful. And she didn't even pause to consider what had happened to the pink and white messaline she'd given over to Julietta that past Friday. Or the lavaliere that had accompanied it. Though she hadn't minded the absence of the one, she truly missed the other. More than she thought she would. Its rubies and diamonds had been formed in the shape of her family's crest.

If Julietta noticed the fine weave of Luciana's corset cover or the quality of the detailing on its yoke, she didn't say so. She simply held up the gown as Luciana stepped inside it and then stood off to the side as the girl fastened it in the front. But her pride of workmanship was unmistakable, and she looked quite like Madame did whenever the shop owner had accomplished a particularly fine piece of work or an especially difficult draping. She quietly picked up Luciana's old gown from the floor and dropped it into the wastebasket.

Annamaria was watching the transformation with undisguised good cheer. She had never been the beneficiary of any of Madame's castoffs, had never expected to be, but that didn't keep her from sharing in the happiness of the girl she was starting to consider a friend. "*Che bella!*" How beautiful. How beautiful Luciana was.

There was a moment when Luciana wondered if she ought to thank Julietta. And another moment when Julietta wondered if she ought to be bothered by Luciana's failure to offer up gratitude. But Luciana couldn't settle on the correct words, so Julietta counted it against her as one more instance of arrogance. Exchanging wary glances, they sat down to lunch, not as friends but as prospective enemies.

———

Just before the hands of Julietta's clever little pendant watch pointed out two o'clock, Luciana descended the back stairs. She did it with trepidation and no little reluctance. She didn't want to assist Madame Fortier. She didn't want to meet the woman's customers. She only wanted to be left alone.

But Madame had been good to her. Mostly. She had offered Luciana a job. She had provided clothing and money during a time when such things had been difficult to come by. If Madame required her assistance, then assist she would do. She'd just pray that nothing bad would come of it.

Pray. As if God were listening!

As she came toward the shop floor, she saw Madame escort a woman to a seat behind the screen. The very seat in which Luciana herself had collapsed two weeks before.

The woman was tall. She carried herself with confidence, if rather a bit too much dignity. She ought to have been beautiful; she had every feature required for the task. Her hair glowed with soft highlights that might have reminded you of the best of summer's butter. The kind Luciana hadn't seen for months. And the curve of her lips brought to mind the bow of the moon; there lay upon her cheeks a healthy glow that had nothing to do with artifice.

Yes, she ought to have been beautiful, but she wasn't.

It is an old and tired motto that would have us believe true beauty lies beneath the skin. You might have suspected, as have I, that it is only the truly gorgeous who must think so. But as Luciana looked on Madame's client, she came to discover that no light, save that of intelligence, shone forth from that woman's soul. No warmth emanated from within. Those beautiful features with which God had chosen to bless her responded not to need nor to fellow man, but to principles and honor and duty.

At that moment, just as Luciana was appraising the strega, the woman looked over at her and did the same. Through narrowed eyes.

10

Luciana stepped back, for an instant, behind the protection of a doorframe and made the sign of the cross. She might have said a prayer for the woman, but she did not know, not at that point, what ailed her. And it was always a dangerous business to pray for a witch. But Luciana, from the depths of her own fear and unhappiness, had responded to a soul in pain in a way that Mrs. Quinn never had. Luciana had perceived; she had felt. She had sympathized.

It was only when she stepped into the shop once more that she realized the woman had been accompanied. By a man. A man who was handsome in much the same way as the woman, though he exuded a vivacity of spirit that the strega didn't seem to possess.

He sent a smile in Luciana's direction.

She cast her gaze to the floor and stepped toward the screen, placing herself at its side where Madame could see her.

Madame Fortier had asked the strega a question, and the woman was answering as she pulled off her gloves and folded them into her lap. "The same. The same as every other autumn. How many of these seasons have there been?"

"Twenty-one." And Madame could recount them all in painful detail. "And how is the congressman?"

The woman turned her head away from Madame as if she couldn't be bothered to answer. But then she sighed. Turned back. "Mr. Quinn? The same. The same as every other autumn. The same as every other year. He works all day." She lifted a slim shoulder. Let it fall back down. "We entertain at night. I scarcely have time to think of him, let alone speak to him."

"He is an important man. He is doing great things. You must be very proud to be married to him."

Mrs. Quinn considered that statement.

"I'm sure any woman would give her . . . how do you say it? Her right arm? . . . to be married to him."

At that, Mrs. Quinn scowled. She knew for a fact that was true. Knew for certain that there *had* been someone, some mysterious woman, that her husband had been in love with before they had married.

"It's not what they might expect. . . ." She said it in a tone so low that Madame could scarcely hear her.

It's not what Adeline Quinn, *née* Howell, had expected. He'd been so utterly charming, despite the melancholy she saw hiding behind his twinkling eyes and his quick smiles. And he'd been so ambitious. He'd spun visions of a new kind of city. A city where men and women could work together and immigrants could be encouraged to improve their plight.

The right sort of immigrant. The smart, hardworking, intelligent kind.

How they'd talked back then! Of anything. Of everything. As they'd shared their dreams for the future, she'd talked herself into believing that the difference in their backgrounds hadn't mattered. That her blueblood parents would accept her marriage to an Irishman. She'd thought of it as the first step in their plan. Their first advancement for the cause.

It was to be a marriage of minds and goals.

Encouraged by their shared passions, she had hoped for love and companionship. But she had tumbled from those glorious daydreams after the wedding, straight into the treacherous seas of matrimony where she'd found herself sailing alone.

Oh, she'd known of the other woman before she'd married. Patrick Quinn was nothing if not honorable. She knew she'd turned his head and captured his imagination, and she'd told herself that she could also heal his heart. But still, after twenty-one years, she hadn't been able to expunge the memory of that ghost. The toll that it had left on her, the weight that it had caused her to carry, had become debilitating. For how could she live up to a memory, an ideal, of some other woman when she didn't even know who that person was?

An immigrant.

That's all Patrick had ever told her. Knowing he had been raised in the North End, it wasn't difficult to guess what kind of immigrant, what sort of woman it had been. And at this point, with dreams of romance behind her, she could admit that the thought of it disgusted her. Patrick had fallen in love with an Italian.

Madame could read her client's face as easily as she could read the pull of a thread against the grain. The best cure for both was to smooth things out. "Nobody ever said marriage was easy. Perhaps a smile when he arrives home. A pleasant word or inquiry about his day?" Isn't that what any man would want?

"You think I don't do those things?" Adeline Quinn had taken to hovering near the door every evening until his return. Even when that hour kept creeping ever later. It was crass, undignified, and completely out of keeping with her class and station in life . . . and still, she could not seem to control herself. She just wanted . . . desperately craved . . . *something*. Some vitally important, nameless, missing thing.

Mrs. Quinn took the sample book that Madame Fortier offered. Began to flip through it. Black, brown, taupe. Wool jersey, wool tricotine, wool poplin. Buttons and beads and braids. Why should a new gown make her feel any more pleased, any more happy than the last one had? And if it did, how long would that satisfaction last? Until the season's first ball? Until Thanksgiving? Or Christmas? Until Patrick passed by her bedroom door again without stopping to say good-night? How sick to death she was of expectations! And hope! And the city and the war and people not knowing what they were meant to do or how they were to act!

She shut the book and shoved it back into Madame's hands. "If I wanted to order what everyone else has, then I would patronize Madame Connolly's. Please tell me you've something to offer other than what I've already seen half the other women in Boston wearing."

Madame had grown round-eyed at the diatribe, causing a swell of perverse pleasure in Mrs. Quinn's breast. It made her despise herself all the more. And it made Madame Fortier try all the harder. She knew from experience the strega would be contrary about her gowns until she had become satisfied, once more, with her life in general. "Perhaps . . . sometimes men seem to shrink from obligation. Men are contrary that way. They crave attention, but they don't want to think that they are your sole occupation."

"Do you think so?" Mrs. Quinn looked at her with an appraising eye. Madame's advice always sounded so sensible. So eminently reasonable. Mrs. Quinn had actually been tempted to think, once or twice, that the gown maker actually knew the man. With a nudge in this direction or a push in that one, Mrs. Quinn's marriage had been steered from perilous shores, on more than one occasion, by the skillful hands of Madame Fortier. And that thought, that knowledge, galled her to no end. "I suppose it's easy for an old maid like you to dispense advice about marriage. It doesn't cost you anything, does it? And you haven't the ability to experience the consequences of your advice."

Madame Fortier tried to smile. "No. It does not. But then, an old maid like me does not have the pleasure of sons, either."

Mrs. Quinn jerked toward the screen, behind which she supposed her son was waiting. Her son. If nothing else had come from her marriage, at least she had him. She took a breath. Looked up at Madame Fortier. "Have you another book?"

Madame passed the first one to Luciana and then handed a second one to the strega.

Luciana left the safety of the screen and placed the book on the counter, avoiding any contact with or any glimpse of the man.

Mrs. Quinn turned the pages, pausing halfway through. "I don't see why you didn't put me in a design like this last spring."

"Because we had decided that it did not properly highlight your stature."

The woman sent a sharp look at Madame through the mirror. "Yes . . . yes, I suppose I do recall you saying something like that." But it had ruffles and lace. And contrary to everything she had ever believed about herself and fashion, she had come to crave ruffles and lace. Less of what was and more of what was not. She wanted something different.

Madame coughed delicately into her handkerchief. "I should think you would want less of the distractions of ruffles and lace. So that the eye is drawn to your face and fine features."

The woman frowned and fiddled with her cuffs. Her face and fine features. It always came back to her face and fine features. But what had those things ever done for her? And why couldn't she trade them in for something different? Something new? "Bring me that first book again."

Madame bowed. Looked at Luciana. Inclined her head toward the shop floor.

Luciana ducked out from behind the screen and made for the counter where she'd left the book. But the man had already found it and was holding it out to her. Her gaze darted to the floor, but she accepted it from him and then turned and took it to Madame Fortier.

The strega seized it from Madame's hands. She was flipping through the pages toward the middle of the book when she suddenly stopped. "This one. This is the one I want."

Both Luciana and Madame tried to contain their dismay. They couldn't imagine, either of them, that anyone would want a gown like that one. There were more than a dozen horizontal tucks circling the skirt that made the design read like a cone, wider at the hips than it was at the bottom. Patch pockets were placed at such an angle on the hips that they might as well have been potholders. It was an avant-garde gown intended for someone living at the bohemian fringe of society. Someone who cared little about what others liked or thought or expected. Someone as far from Mrs. Quinn as a Hollywood starlet could be.

Madame considered it for a moment before replying. "Perhaps if we substituted georgette crepe for the wool jersey." That way it wouldn't flare out quite so much at the hips. If it lay flatter, then maybe . . . maybe. But Madame feared a gown like the one the strega wanted would be an unmitigated disaster. It would take on the look of a costume. And a gown maker didn't do herself any favors by letting her clients walk around in unbecoming gowns. Sooner or later, either the client would realize the mistake—and blame the gown maker—or the client's friends would see the catastrophe—and blame the gown maker. Either way, Madame's business had not become what it was by letting her clients walk around in whatever pleased them. There was an art to gown making that required far more than familiarity with needle and thread.

Mrs. Quinn pursed her lips as she considered the suggestion. The model in the illustration was the kind of person she wished she could be. Bold and bohemian. All dark, sleek hair, with a slash of red lips. Arresting and intriguing. Exotic. Exactly the kind of person Mrs. Quinn was not. "Maybe. Maybe if you do it up in georgette, then I can see if I want it."

Madame nodded. "And might I suggest that it be made in

this lovely color?" She flipped a few pages further and revealed a sample of gray-colored silk that had a supple hand.

"Is this a new shade for spring?"

It was. One of them. In a particular shade that would set off the woman's eyes.

"I'm still rather partial to taupe." She always had been, though she'd rarely ever ordered a gown in that color.

Taupe! It always came back to taupe with Mrs. Quinn. The strega might be partial to that color but, just between you and me, taupe was not at all partial to her. "Perhaps." It was as close to *no* as Madame would ever come. "Perhaps the pockets could be made of taupe. With wine-colored beading." That would be acceptable.

Mrs. Quinn squinted at the design, trying to imagine it in a different color and with a different material, but she had never been very good at imagining what she couldn't actually see. "I suppose. I suppose . . . yes."

"There's a new sleeve that's being shown for spring. Would you like me to incorporate it?"

"Does anyone else have it?"

"No." For no one else was as eager, as willing as Mrs. Quinn, to return from vacation three weeks early just to get her orders in first.

"I won't have what anyone else is having."

"Of course not. In fact, I'm sure you'll be happy to know that everyone else will have to content themselves with wearing what you're wearing."

The strega smiled at that thought.

"That is what I always tell them. 'Of course you know that Mrs. Quinn will be wearing the same.' "

"I did like all that beadwork. On the pockets. And I'd want the same on the collar. But I'll want mine done up in jewels." Mrs. Quinn had moved from her seat, past the screen and up to the counter. There, standing beside her son, she took from him a velvet pouch and spilled its contents onto the counter. "These were my father's."

If Luciana hadn't missed her guess, she thought she'd already spied one or two made of paste among the batch. Clearly the woman's father knew very little about fine gems.

Madame's heart had nearly stopped in her chest when she'd seen the tumbling, flashing jewels. Now she moved to sweep them back into their bag. "So many of them! The gown will gleam like a prize." There. She'd almost recaptured every one. "I've found a fabulous girl for beads. I'm sure you'll be very happy with her work." She gave Luciana a long look as she spoke, tying off the sack with its ribbon, and then handing it back to Mrs. Quinn.

But the woman handed it right back. "They're to stay here. For the gown."

Madame set the bag on the counter. "I don't have the ability to keep such fine jewels for such a prolonged period." Nor did she have the insurance.

"Surely you're not saying your shop is not safe."

"No. I am simply saying that I would feel more comfortable if you kept them."

"And I want them to stay here." She didn't say it, but she had lately begun to suspect that some of her maids were stealing from her. And though Madame was both a shopkeeper and a foreigner, she judged her jewels were more safely kept there instead of the Quinn mansion. "I must insist. As long as you don't . . ." Her gaze traveled to where Luciana stood, holding the sample book. "As long as you don't have any Italians working here."

11

Italians? Of course not." Madame Fortier had long since ceased to be Italian. She had given up her heritage to embrace proprietorship and had become all things to all people. She hardly noticed anymore when people disparaged her fellow countrymen. What's more, she was inclined to agree with them. So although the building was filled above the shop floor with Italians, she lied through her teeth and had no compunction about doing so.

Since Mrs. Quinn insisted on leaving her jewels and Madame could not imagine life without the dual blessing and curse of her patronage, the shopkeeper finally acquiesced.

Now, Billy Quinn had been leaning against the counter all that time, watching the goings-on. He wasn't opposed to stopping in at a dressmaker's the way some of his friends might have been. To his mind, dresses and girls went together. And why would he forgo the opportunity to haunt the former if it guaranteed the presence of the latter?

Madame Fortier's.

It had been a while since he'd been in the shop. He'd graduated from college, and then they'd gone away for the summer. He hadn't minded so much being dragged back to the city. He was tired of sun and sand and surf, though he wouldn't have wanted to admit it. Not to his set. They wouldn't have understood. But he'd run through all the girls in his crowd. They only knew how to giggle, dance, and flirt. It didn't seem quite right, in his opinion, to carry on that way, as if nothing in life were serious, when half the world was dying a mere continent away. He supposed that meant that he was growing up. And that a job at his father's bank and marriage couldn't be far behind.

A job and marriage. He stifled a yawn.

No, he hadn't been to Madame Fortier's in a while. A trip to the shop was usually just a prelude to distributing leaflets on behalf of the National Women's Party, or charming his mother's friends over tea. Sometimes even stopping by his father's office on the way home. The shop hadn't changed much, and neither had Madame herself. She was an interesting one. Not French. He'd spent enough time in the vicinity of the family's French chef to know that her accent was not from that country. If he had to guess, he would say Hungarian, or Romanian. She had that dark look about her.

His eye settled on the girl standing to the side, over by Madame Fortier. Not quite behind the counter, yet not quite on the shop floor. She didn't seem to belong to either realm. She wasn't a customer, of course. She'd been assisting Madame Fortier, hadn't she? But he wasn't yet convinced that she was a shop girl either. She seemed to hold herself apart, from all of them, through an act of choice rather than deference. She was, however—

Luciana looked up at him just then.

She was beautiful.

Her gaze sank from his again just as surely as it was weighted with a stone. And it told him, just as surely, that she wasn't American. American girls in Boston didn't mind meeting a man's look straight on. So this girl wasn't American. Her skin . . . it wasn't swarthy. Not like the Italians'. It had more of the golden tones of Madame Fortier's. Her hair was dark, it was true, but he'd have bet anything that it didn't tend toward coarse. And her eyes . . . he'd caught a glimpse of startling sadness in their sable-colored depths. But if she wasn't American—and she wasn't Italian—then what exactly was she?

He removed himself from his end of the counter and draped himself closer to hers.

Alarm fired the look that she gave him, and she moved back toward the screen.

He'd never have the chance to speak to her if she kept moving away like that!

"You'll have the gown finished by November?" The strega had put up a hand to adjust her hat.

Madame nodded. "But I'd like you to take a look at another design I just got in."

Mrs. Quinn had already turned from the counter toward the door. "I haven't the time."

"It's a lovely gown that mixes wool serge and silk satin."

"I haven't the time to be lounging around here all day, looking at books." Indeed, she didn't. There were so very many tedious things that had to be done oneself if one wished them to be accomplished properly. "Send them later. With your girl."

Billy lifted his hat toward Luciana before he put it on his head and sauntered out of the shop behind his mother, regretting that he hadn't been afforded the chance to speak with the girl.

———

Both Madame and Luciana let out a sigh of gigantic proportions as soon as Mrs. Quinn and her son had left the shop. Madame retreated behind her counter, pulled the sample book close, and turned to the design Mrs. Quinn had ordered. And then she turned to the page after it.

Luciana raised a hand to hide a smile. It seemed Madame Fortier had persuaded Mrs. Quinn from the gown her heart had been set on into another gown entirely. The one on the very next page.

Madame looked up and caught the glimmer of humor in the girl's eyes. "Sometimes it seems my clients don't know what they really want. In that case, it is my job to tell them."

Although, that wasn't quite the truth. Not in this case. During many other appointments over the years, with many other clients, Madame had done exactly that. But with Mrs. Quinn, things had always been different. Madame had a particular image and particular look she had in mind for Mrs. Quinn. She always had. Ever since the beginning. Ever since she had made the woman's wedding gown. And so it wasn't so much a case of Madame talking Mrs. Quinn into a particular style or color; it was more a matter of trying to talk Mrs. Quinn into the person Madame thought that she should be. And Mrs. Quinn had always been amenable. Until now.

Madame summoned Luciana once again, late that afternoon, placing several sample books into the girl's hands. "I need you to deliver these to Mrs. Quinn. She may look at them while you wait, but she is not to keep them."

Luciana nodded, though she couldn't imagine what she would do if the woman tried.

"She shouldn't keep them. If she tries to keep them, then I won't be able to order her new gowns."

Luciana nodded.

"You can remind her of that."

But of course she couldn't. Luciana didn't speak English. A fact that Madame had conveniently forgotten if she had ever known it at all.

The shop owner frowned. She wasn't sure about this. She'd never sent her books to any of her clients before. Without her books, Madame was worse than useless. She was impotent. She was nothing. Her customers made appointments to view them at the shop. That's how it was done. Before now. But what else could Madame do? Mrs. Quinn had changed the rules.

Madame glanced at the girl before her. A very frightened-looking girl. "I'd send Julietta, but the girl is sometimes too bold for her own good."

Sometimes?

"I've called a car for you. You'll present Mrs. Quinn with the books, and you'll wait to bring them back. You must bring them back."

———

Luciana was handed into the car by the chauffeur. She cowered on a seat in the back, not quite daring to look out the window for fear of being seen as she was driven from Temple Place around Boston Common and up Beacon Hill. Down not-quite-straight Mt. Vernon Street, lined with its bow-fronted faded brick townhouses. It was here that she started to relax. What could happen to her in a motorcar, after all? And wasn't it wonderful to be riding in one again?

At tree-lined, iron-fenced Louisburg Square, the plethora of cats that sunned themselves in the dappled shade and the general feeling of serenity reminded her of nothing so much as Europe before the war. Of languid and leisurely summer days spent in the tidy boroughs of Germany and the dignified neighborhoods of Vienna. They made her long for all that she had lost. So it was not with a sense of great awe or meek humility that Luciana descended the car; it was with a familiarity and ease, a sense of coming, if not home, then into her rightful domain.

Which is why, you see, she ought to be forgiven for walking right up to the front door.

The butler, upon understanding what her visit entailed, tried to shoo her around to the back, but Luciana didn't understand him. She didn't know what he was saying and her only acquaintance with a service entrance had been at Madame Fortier's. In front of that house in Louisburg Square, she had quite forgotten, for a moment, whom she had become.

Eventually, Mrs. Quinn, bothered by the commotion at the front door, came out of her sitting room and into the hallway. Upon seeing her, Luciana stepped forward and offered up the sample books as the doorman made his mistress aware of the girl's breach in etiquette. Soon both the man and the strega were berating her.

Luciana didn't understand the words, though she understood the intent. She was being scolded. And the daughter of the Count of Roma didn't take well to scolding. The more voluble Mrs. Quinn became, the more remote, the more patrician Luciana became. Until screeching at the girl became as satisfying as trying to engage her husband's attention.

Finally, she did something Luciana understood. She pointed toward the door at the far end of the hallway.

Luciana went toward it as she was bid, though she had no idea what to do or where to go once she had reached it. She stopped once, halfway down the hall, and turned back toward the front door, but Mrs. Quinn and the doorman had disappeared.

Narrow doorways set into dark corners of hallways were not within her usual realm of existence. Before having fled to the North End, that is. In her experience, such things had usually been meant for servants. She was rather enjoying the prospect of a brightly lit hallway that smelled of nothing but furniture wax and carbolic. It was a well-proportioned hallway at that. Not marble, like she had been used to, but the wood paneling on the walls and the floorboards at her feet gleamed with quiet dignity. So she decided to enjoy that place of quiet and relative peace. And as she stood there, she made a decision. She decided that she needed to learn English. If for no other reason than to be able to understand people like the strega when they yelled at her.

For then, she would be able to yell back.

In any case, that's where Billy came upon her. He'd long ago shed the suit he'd worn downtown. Clad now in his white duck outing pants and white canvas oxfords, he was on his way to The Tennis and Racquet Club.

Luciana was standing in front of a picture, head tilted, wondering if, in fact, it was the Canaletto it claimed to be. She had her doubts.

But he didn't. It was definitely the beautiful girl from Madame Fortier's shop who now stood in his hallway. "Delighted to see you again!"

12

Luciana jumped at his words.

He put out his hand in welcome. "I'm sorry! I didn't mean to startle you."

Forgetting who she was trying to be, she put her hand into his. She expected that Billy would raise it to his lips, so she let it lie in his palm.

Billy, having expected to be given a hand to shake, had no idea what to do with such a treasure. But he was not his father's son for nothing. Smiling in a way that displayed all of his innate Irish charm, he led her to the bench that sat in the hall. The invitation was unmistakable.

Luciana sat.

And he sat down beside her, elbows on his knees, spinning the racquet that was in his hand.

"I'm Billy, by the way. Quinn. Billy Quinn."

Luciana smiled.

"And you are . . . ?"

Luciana smiled once more.

" . . . going to make a game of this? Make me guess?" She was a coy one, wasn't she? "All right, then. I'm up for the sport." He stilled the racquet between his hands, turned to face her, head cocked to one side. "You're not a Florence, are you?" He narrowed his eyes. Florence? He hoped not. He hadn't much admiration for the Florences he'd met, though he had no doubt she could change that impression.

She said nothing.

"A Louise perhaps?"

Her brow rose.

"No? No." Definitely not a Louise. "Are you a Marie?"

She shrugged.

"Helen? Hélène?" He said it more to himself than to her. He studied her eyes, those beautiful, shining eyes.

She said nothing.

"Lucy?"

Ah—he was so very close! If only he had known it. But Luciana had an Italian-sounding *c* and she did not recognize her name in his. But she caught the question in his tone and shook her head ever so slightly.

"No?" He lowered his head, raised his brow.

She shook her head once more.

"No. Fine, good. Then are you . . . Carolina?"

Nothing.

"Suzanne?"

A door near the entry swept open and Mrs. Quinn stepped out into the hall. "Smith?" She called for her butler. He materialized quite suddenly from . . . it was difficult to tell exactly where. "Will you have that girl come—" She paused as she turned toward the back of the hall and saw her son. "Billy?"

He saluted her with his racquet.

"Is that Madame's girl there?"

"It is."

"What's she doing? I told her to go through and wait in the kitchen." She was used to servants rushing to do her bidding, and to her way of thinking, the shop girl was one of them. So it was irritating that the girl should stay seated when she was being spoken to. "You—girl. Come here. I'm done with you. I'll have to keep these books for another day. I don't have time to go through them now."

Billy stood, and when he did, Luciana did the same. She looked at him inquiringly. He shrugged. Gestured her forward. She walked to where Mrs. Quinn stood and held out her hands for the books.

But Mrs. Quinn would not relinquish them. "Come tomorrow. I'll be done with them then." She disappeared back into her sitting room and shut the door.

There was nothing to do about it. The strega had the books, and she wasn't letting them go. Luciana thought of trying to make an appeal to the butler, but that venerable personage had already vanished, and even if he had been there, she wouldn't have known the words to say.

Billy opened the door and gestured her through. They both went out into the summer's bright sun, supremely unsatisfied. Luciana was going back to Madame's without the books. And Billy still hadn't learned her name.

Julietta, however, was supremely satisfied with herself as she started home that evening. The embroidery she was working on at the shop was almost done. Though she'd enjoyed the novelty of working with the gold- and silver-wrapped threads, she was looking forward to the next project even more. She had the pleasures of a new pink and white messaline gown to revel in, and there were so very many good things in the coming weeks to look forward to. There was Saint Marciano's festa, there were Saturday evening dances at the Sons of Avellino Hall. And there was also Angelo Moretti.

"Buon giorno."

For a moment, as she turned a corner from the glare of Temple

Place into the shade of Washington Street, she thought she'd managed to summon the spirit of her beloved. She looked over in the direction of the greeting, expecting—oh. Her hopes died. It was only Mauro. She smiled. But it was purely reflexive.

"I was thinking I could walk home with you."

She looked him over from the top of his head to the tip of his toes. He was carrying his bag. But that didn't mean much. He always carried his bag. He was a doctor, after all. One of the few during the war who had been allowed to stay and work in the North End. Though that didn't explain what he was doing downtown. "You want to walk me home?"

He shrugged. Shifted his bag to his other hand. "If you want me to."

If she wanted him to. She didn't. Not really. And she refused to think of him as Dr. Vitali. To her he was, and always would be, Mauro. Mauro, her big brother Salvatore's friend. *Old* Mauro, she might have added. He had to have been at least thirty.

But she smiled. And inclined her head. It wasn't in her nature to turn down male companionship. "All the way to the North End?"

"Of course. It's just I was hoping . . . there's a war concert at Boston Common. If you want to go." He smiled at her as if he hoped, very much, that was exactly what she would want to do.

"You want to take me to a concert?" This was both better and worse than she had imagined. A concert! A real one. But with him?

Julietta had never been able to attend enough war rallies and parades for her liking. When she did, she would clap and cheer and wave her flag with all the zeal of a newly converted soul. At rallies and parades she felt American in a way she never did in the North End. In the middle of a crowd singing "Over There," she sang as loudly as the rest of them. Standing in line to buy liberty bonds, she knew that her money was as good as anyone else's.

"I don't know, Mauro. I'm sure Mama is expecting me."

"She is. I mean, rather . . . she's expecting you to be with me."

Julietta's eyes narrowed. "She is, is she?"

"I asked her just this morning where it was that you worked. And when you would be done."

"So she told you. And she said that you could ask me. To a concert."

Mauro nodded.

She was perfectly amenable to enjoying a concert when there was one to be enjoyed. Even if that meant she had to do it with Mauro. But when she got home? Was Mama going to hear about it! She linked her arm through Mauro's, and they started off down the street.

At Boston Common they dodged roving groups of children and women pushing baby carriages. An almost festive atmosphere prevailed. It was as if by hoping fervently enough, by singing loudly enough, by praying hard enough, Boston knew she could finish what those Huns in Germany had started.

Oh, if only it were true! If only the slaughter could be stopped!

Caught up in that swell of zealous, nearly reckless patriotism, Julietta almost wished she were wearing the new messaline. On further thought, however, she decided that pleasure would have been wasted on Mauro. But he always looked so distinguished that it might have been nice, in the midst of what seemed like the entire city of Boston, to have felt as if she matched him.

He steered her toward a vendor's cart and bought her an ice cream. Though it was already past six o'clock, the sun was still so blaringly hot that she ended up eating it rather more quickly than was ladylike. And at the end, after he threw away the cup for her, there was still a splotch of it left on her chin for him to blot up with his handkerchief.

"Grazie, Mauro."

He winked at her.

"Aren't you going to do that magic trick? The one where you pretend you've captured my nose? Like you always did when I was little?"

He slid a sidewise glance toward her. "You aren't so little anymore, Julietta."

Nice to know that he'd noticed! Even if he was just Mauro. Such a nice, funny sort of man. In his proper hat and his proper suit, carrying a proper doctor's case. Mauro was just too proper. He did have very nice teeth, though. Thick and straight and white. That couldn't be said about everyone's teeth. And he had a nice deep laugh. She'd always liked hearing it.

Their progress toward the bandstand gradually slowed as they joined the crowd surrounding it. Mauro wanted to stop at the outer edges, but Julietta grabbed his hand and pulled him right into the middle. By slipping around women and dispensing smiles at the men, she tugged him through the throngs, emerging, finally, right in front of the bandstand itself.

"But—"

"Don't you want to be able to see?"

He bent close so that he could speak into her ear. "It's a concert. I only have to be able to hear."

Nonsense. He didn't know what was good for him!

The orchestra began tuning their instruments, and soon the first soloist climbed the steps to begin the concert. Fluffy red, white, and blue bows nearly obscured her face, but when she opened her mouth, her voice soared far beyond those ribbons. That soloist was followed by another and another. Ten soloists performed that night. And after, a treat: an exhibition of ballroom dancing.

Julietta watched, enraptured. Oh, how she would have loved to have been whisked about on a dance floor by someone strong and lithe like Angelo! To be twirled and promenaded. Dipped and spun. All too soon the spectacle ended and the last notes of the orchestra drifted away into the evening's golden light.

She sighed.

Mauro offered her his arm. "Did you enjoy it?"

"So much!" She stood up on her toes and kissed him on the cheek. A cheek that smelled of soap and antiseptic and had more stubble than she remembered. She twirled, inspired by the music and intricate dance steps. "Wouldn't it be lovely to go to a ball?"

He considered her question with scientific detachment. "I've never been to a ball."

She stopped mid-twirl. "An important doctor like you? Never?"

He shook his head. "What do you think people do there?"

Had he gone mad? "They dance."

"I've been to dances."

She'd never seen him at any. Not at the Sons of Avellino Hall. Of course, she usually snuck out the back door with an escort. Early on.

"Do you like dances, Julietta?"

She shrugged. She liked dancing. And she certainly liked what went on in the alley out back.

"Would you go to a dance with me?"

"With you?"

He smiled.

"To a dance?"

"This Saturday at the Hall?" There it was again, that little boy smile. As if he hoped very much that what he wished for was finally about to come true.

She did a swift calculation, factoring in all the dances that she would miss because she'd have to save them all for him. Which wasn't really that many, considering she didn't usually stay at the dances for very long. But then she had to figure in all the extra time she would have to stay in the Sons of Avellino Hall because it wasn't as if Mauro was going to take her out back to the alley. And it wasn't as if she wanted him to.

She snuck a glance at his face . . . at his lips, if you want to put a fine point to it.

No. She didn't want him to, although it might be interesting if he did. Nothing very bad was bound to happen if she accepted Mauro's invitation, and intuition told her that something very good might come from it in the end. In the form of some of the boys not taking her as much for granted anymore.

It wouldn't be like going with Angelo Moretti, but she didn't even know where Angelo lived. And besides, he had never asked her to go anywhere, or do anything with him, at all.

"I'll go with you."

A smile lit his face, making it appear, for a moment, at least ten years younger. Poor Mauro. He had lost his heart to a girl too young and wild to appreciate that sacred trust.

13

Eventually, Mauro walked Julietta up to her apartment. And came in when it was made clear that Mama wouldn't let him leave. But that didn't bother Julietta any. The men and boys talked among themselves while the women tended to their own affairs, Mauro being one of them.

"Mama."

She turned from the stove where she was cooking a soup for the next day's supper.

"Mauro said you told him that he could walk out with me."

She smiled, nodding her head as if Julietta were thanking her for the favor. "He's a good man."

"He's an *old* man."

"Old!" Her older sister Josephine's eyes had snapped wide open. "You don't know old from a boot!"

Mama joined with her eldest daughter. "He's not too old to know how to be nice to a girl."

"Ma!"

"He comes from a very fine family."

"In Avellino. But we're in *America*."

Mama pointed her spoon at Julietta. "I want you to be nice to him."

"Why?"

"Be nice." After two shakes of the spoon, Mama put it back in the pot and used it to stir the soup.

"I'll be nice to him." She had to, didn't she? "But I'm not going to marry him."

"And why not?"

"You *want* me to marry him?!"

"I want you to marry a nice man from a good family. He's a doctor. He owns his house."

"I am sick to death of everybody telling me what I should do!" The men were looking over at them from their side of the room, so Julietta took a step nearer her mother so she could speak in relative privacy. "When I want to marry a man, it will be a man that I choose. That *I* want!"

"Oh, it will, will it?"

"Si!"

"Why can't you be a good Avellino girl like your sister, Josephine?'

"Because we're not in Avellino anymore, Ma. We're in America!" She didn't care at that moment who heard her. Why was it so difficult for everyone to understand? They were in America. And what was the use of being in America if you couldn't act like an American?

"You'll marry whom I tell you to marry. And you'll be glad for it!"

Julietta's reply was the slamming of the tenement door.

———

Annamaria only wished she could talk to her own mama the way Julietta spoke to hers. Today was the day. Mama was going to make her cross the street.

"You got the basket?" Mama asked the question for the third time.

"I have the basket." Annamaria's fingers were clenched tight around its handle.

"You got the money?"

"I have the money."

"Remember. You don't have to speak. You just have to get the tomatoes."

Just get the tomatoes. Annamaria took a deep breath, nodded, and then walked out of the apartment. Down the stairs. Out into the evening. She paused as she stepped down onto the sidewalk. She felt as if everyone were watching her. And she was right. Everyone was. All along the sidewalk. The nonne in their chairs, the children playing hopscotch. Above the street, the housewives pulling in their wash, and more nonne watching out their windows. All along North Street, everyone stopped what they were doing and watched Annamaria Rossi cross the street.

Some of them even hurriedly made the sign of the cross.

She ducked under the green awning that had been spread above the door. Slipped inside. She felt as if she were entering a foreign and hostile country, but quite soon, as her eyes took in the tidy bins of onions and stacks of eggplants, she loosed her grip on the basket and felt her shoulders relax. It was just like Maglione's. Cleaner perhaps. And brighter.

Zanfini's son was standing behind a display of tomatoes, wiping his hands on his apron. He was a slim lad with a square jaw and eyebrows that lifted from the bridge of his nose in a shallow diagonal. Had you been there with Annamaria, you might have been tempted to reach out and grab a few of those rosy tomatoes sitting in the pyramid before him. And you might have been surprised that Annamaria didn't. They were so impossibly red, so impossibly shiny. But those fat tomatoes, the pungent onions, and the plump eggplants might have been little bright-eyed, fat-cheeked children. Annamaria knew that the more those cheeks were pinched and pulled and poked, the more their spirits faded. And so she kept her hands to herself, though she admired the produce just the same.

Crossing her arms around the handle of the basket, she walked up to that pyramid of tomatoes and raised her eyes to meet those of Zanfini's son.

His words caught in his throat. He swallowed. He'd never seen her before or he would have remembered. She wasn't Sicilian . . . which meant that she'd probably want nothing to do with him, let alone speak to him. But he'd never seen such a beautiful face or such delicate features. That other girl, the one who slunk by on her way to work of a morning, she was striking, but this girl?

This girl was an angel.

For her part, Annamaria was simply and completely . . . amazed. There was an expansiveness in her breast. A new resonance to the beat of her heart. A sudden clarity in her mind. As if, finally, she understood what her purpose was. As if, in crossing the threshold of that Sicilian frutta e verdura, she had stepped into her life.

But how could that be?

They both asked themselves that very question. How could it be that such beauty existed? How could it be that the entire world had fallen away in an instant? And resolved itself into something new and fresh and vibrant? They searched for the answers, for one long moment, in each other's eyes.

And then Zanfini's son spoke. His words came out soft. And hoarse. "What do I get for you?" He would have given her anything, everything she wanted.

Annamaria opened her mouth to speak and then remembered that she couldn't. Shouldn't. She pointed to the tomatoes instead.

"Tomatoes?"

She nodded.

"How many?"

She inclined her head. She didn't know. She hadn't thought to ask.

Such loveliness, such grace in her gesture. And in it he read both the beginning and the end of every lover's poem, every romantic's dream, every fairy tale that had ever been written.

"You want two? Four?"

She lifted a single, frail shoulder. Shrugged.

He wanted to take her by it, enclose her in his embrace and hide her from the world forever, but he had no right to do any of those things, so he held up another tomato instead. "Five?"

She nodded.

"Six?"

She was just about to shake her head when she realized that doing so would end their conversation. It would only speed her home. So she nodded.

He held up another.

She nodded again.

By the time Annamaria left Zanfini's frutta e verdura, she was carrying twelve tomatoes in her basket. But more than that, she was carrying new thoughts and new vistas in her mind. She may have walked into the store the eldest daughter of the Rossi family, but when she walked out the door, she did so as a woman.

———

"Twelve tomatoes? You brought me twelve tomatoes? What am I going to do with twelve tomatoes?" Mama was putting them back into the basket one by one, recounting them just to make sure.

"Did you talk to him? You didn't speak to him, did you?" Papa Rossi had watched from the window the whole time, but still, he had no way of knowing what had taken place inside that shop.

Annamaria heard her parents speaking, saw her brothers and younger sister watching. Indeed, they all saw her listening and watching. They just couldn't make her speak. She was pondering all that she had heard and seen in Zanfini's shop. And she was feeling, with newfound wonder and tremulous delight, the stretching and growing of her heart.

"Annamaria!"

She blinked. "Sì, Mama?"

"Twelve tomatoes?"

"Sì, Mama."

"Just like a Sicilian. I suppose you asked for three and he forced twelve on you instead."

"No, Mama. He was very nice. But I didn't talk to him."

Papa walked up to her and clasped her by the arm. "You didn't speak to those people?"

"No, Papa." But she smiled as she said it.

"So . . . he didn't force them on you?" Mama was still trying to work out how it was that she'd ended up with twelve tomatoes.

"No."

"But he gave you twelve."

"Sì."

Clearly, something had happened. But since it didn't have anything to do with talking or tomatoes, Mama and Papa looked at each other and shrugged. What did it matter what happened, as long as she was safe, back home on the right side of the street?

14

The next morning at the shop, Madame's fingers closed around Mrs. Quinn's bag, pulling the jewels from the safe. *Grazie a Dio*, they were still there! She shook her head. Nearly made the sign of the cross. She'd never dealt with such a thing: a treasure chest's worth of priceless gems from a client. She refrained from peeking inside, not wanting to tempt fate. What was the woman thinking? That she was a jeweler now, as well as a gown maker? That she could advise on gemstones and marriages as well as patterns and fabrics?

At least they had already been drilled—they were meant to be strung or wired. At least she would not have to worry about that. But, really, she shouldn't have to worry about them at all. What had the woman been thinking, to commend such costly treasures to her care? Madame didn't like the responsibility such a trust brought with it. She cast a longing glance toward the drawer of her desk, but decided it would be foolish to waste such precious drops of liquor on the thought of that witch . . . when soon enough the woman would be appearing, once more, in person.

She muttered vague pronouncements and rather specific

curses under her breath as she climbed the back stairs to the third-floor workshop.

All three of the girls looked up at her appearance.

Madame walked to Luciana and then placed the pouch on the table before the girl. "These are the jewels that Mrs. Quinn left. We might as well see what she's given us so that I'll be able to place an order for what else will be needed."

Julietta gasped as Luciana shook them out onto the table. "*Bontà mia!*" She'd never before seen such a bounty of riches. "What are they?" Her fingers itched to touch the lovely, glittering stones.

Annamaria's eyes had gone wide at their sparkling brilliance.

Madame shrugged. Picked up several. "Besides the sapphires, these look like . . . garnets."

"Rubies." At least the two that Madame had chosen were. Luciana had corrected her without any thought or hesitation. Only a ruby could exhibit such a deep bloodred color. Garnets tended toward the brown.

Madame handed them to Luciana.

She took them and put them back among the others, proceeding to separate them out by stone and then by size. As she thought back to the gown the strega had ordered, a pattern began to take shape in her mind. A simple Florentine pattern of blossoms and scrollwork. Perhaps, if she placed the design on the vertical, like so . . . her hands worked to shape a line as if it were decorating one half of a collar. And then, another line on the other side. Soon, two lines had blossomed on the table in front of her.

Sì. Like that. Just like that.

Madame looked at Luciana's idea for a long moment. Measured off the length and width of the bodice in her mind. Imagined the collar. She reached down and shortened the line a bit by pushing the jewels closer together. "Sì. That will work."

Luciana nodded. "With some jet beads in addition."

Madame cocked her head as she looked at the pattern. Reached down to draw on the table with one long finger. "Here. Like this?" She traced a design through the bottoms of the blossoms.

"Si."

Madame nodded. "I'll place the order. The beads and fabric should come in next week. And I'll put these back into the safe until then." She swept the jewels into the bag and then proceeded toward the door, leaving Julietta and Annamaria to marvel at the magnificence they had just witnessed. And Luciana to remember, with regret, all the treasures she had left at the estate when she had fled. All the jewelry she'd had to sell once she came to America. She wished she'd kept some; she could use the money. But the lavaliere she'd given Julietta in exchange for altering the gowns was the last piece she'd had.

———

Madame hefted the bag as she descended, imagining what she might do with the small fortune the bag represented. She could expand the shop's offerings into . . . shoes. Or hats. She could buy out the shop next door. Or import some of the more notable designs from Paris herself. A small fortune. What a foolish woman the strega was! Perhaps she *should* increase her insurance. To protect the shop.

Which reminded her!

She halted her descent, turned around, and started back up the stairs.

"Julietta."

The three girls turned in unison at the sound of Madame's voice.

"I need to speak to you."

Annamaria and Julietta exchanged glances. When Madame made a point of coming up to the third floor, it had always been to speak to both of them about the detailing of some gown or the work that would soon be sent up from the second floor.

Julietta shrugged and set her embroidery down. Madame beckoned as she turned toward the stairs. Julietta followed her all the way down to her office and remained standing as Madame took a seat behind the desk.

"My business is growing, Julietta."

The girl nodded.

"Growth is good. But new clients create new work."

Julietta nodded once more.

"It is possible that at some point in the future, I will need to take on a partner."

"A partner?"

"Someone to share my business. Someone who can run the shop while I am out. Someone who knows gowns but who also knows people."

Julietta could hardly believe her ears. She had known Madame would need an assistant; she had envisioned herself many times in that role. But a partner? With a share in the business?

"I would consider you for such a venture if you prove that you are worthy of the work."

Work? How could it be work? Work was making ruffles and flounces and sewing them onto skirts. Work was embroidering endless vines and flowers onto a collar. A partner? In the shop? That meant being downstairs. That meant waiting for clients to come for their appointments. Flipping through the sample books. Choosing fabrics. Why, that was no work at all!

"It would mean spending extra hours with me at the end of the normal workday. And it would mean learning to speak English. Extremely well. Do you know English?"

Julietta inclined her head. She used to. Long ago, when she had gone to school at the Settlement House. But she hadn't really used it since she'd left. "Some."

"I would need you to speak English with only the faintest of accents."

"I could take a class. At the Settlement House. I could start tonight."

Madame permitted herself a smile. "If you are that eager in wishing to learn, and if you show me that you are worthy of my trust, then I will increase your pay commensurately."

Julietta's eyes widened. Papa would like that! Shame she wouldn't be able to keep any of it, for paychecks were always handed over to him on Fridays, still sealed within their envelopes. If she just had access to some of that money, think of all that she could do with it!

Julietta returned to the workshop, dreams of fortunes dancing in her head.

Annamaria wasn't going to ask what had transpired. Julietta would tell them sooner or later. Luciana, however, didn't want to wait to find out. In Roma she'd felt no shame in asking any of her maids to tell her exactly what she wanted to know. "What did she say?"

"She says she needs a partner in the shop. And she's chosen me."

Annamaria slid a glance at Julietta. A partner? Julietta was moving up, moving on, while she was stuck in the same position as always, doing the same things she always did. She jabbed her needle so forcefully into the material that it came out the other side, straight into her finger.

Mannaggia!

She stuck her finger into her mouth, but not before a drop of blood had stained the fabric. What was wrong with her? Why had good news for someone else become bad news for her? What had happened to the kind and meek Annamaria who had nothing but good words and a helping hand for everyone?

Poor Annamaria. Thoughts of the grocer's son had filled her head and haunted her dreams ever since she'd come back from Zanfini's with all those tomatoes in her basket. What she wanted more than anything was to go back and buy some more. But she couldn't. Not until Mama told her to. She couldn't do anything unless Mama told her to. She'd spent her entire life doing what Mama told her to. And Papa. And Theresa. And the boys.

Indignation colored her cheeks as she thought about just how many years she'd spent doing things that other people wanted her to do. She ought to be doing things that she wanted to do, shouldn't she? Just like everyone else? So, what did she want?

Here it must be said that Annamaria faltered. Oh, she wanted something grand! She wanted the thing that had made her heart beat faster standing there in Zanfini's store. She wanted to go back and see the grocer's son. But it wasn't her place to reach out for what she wanted. It was her duty to reach for what others wanted to give her. And so duty and desire warred within her breast.

What was wrong with thinking about a man?

He was a Sicilian, that's what was wrong with it.

What was wrong in wanting something for herself?

She was born to serve others.

But what was wrong in wanting something . . . more?

Because a person was supposed to be grateful for what she had.

With that thought, Annamaria turned her eyes from the desires of her heart and back to the tasks that needed to be accomplished. So close she'd been to peering over the side of her family's nest . . . only to slide back down and settle once more inside it. But it takes great courage to stand at the edge of a nest and greater courage still to fly. I'm sure at this moment you feel quite as disappointed as I do. But we must strive to remind ourselves that eventually, all birds learn to fly. It's what birds, after all, are meant to do.

Sometimes all that's needed is a bit of wind beneath those fledgling wings.

15

So you'll start when?" Julietta and Luciana had continued on, oblivious to Annamaria's plight.

"Soon. Of course, I'll have to learn better English. That's what Madame said."

"Better English . . ." Luciana didn't know any English at all, but she needed to. She had no hope of survival in this country without it.

"I told her I'd take a course at the Settlement House."

"A course?"

"A class. Where they teach you English."

"It's a . . . school?"

Julietta shrugged. She supposed it was like a school.

"Where is this place?"

"The Settlement House?" Didn't the girl know anything? "Over on Parmenter."

"And they would teach you English at this place?"

"You and everyone else."

That was something to think about. She wondered how much it would cost.

Annamaria spent the rest of the day pulling out her work and then starting over again. If she refolded the material, she thought she just might be able to hide the stain within the fold of a pleat. Julietta worked with swift hands. She wondered how many more leaves and vines she'd have to embroider. How many more flowers she would have to create before she could lay down that work forever. She imagined herself in the sleek and elegant clothes of a shop owner. Part owner. Wondered if she shouldn't start altering some of her clothes to that end now.

Just how long would Madame make her wait?

At the end of the day she gathered her things quickly and ran down the stairs without a backward glance. She needed to celebrate her good fortune by herself, on the streets of downtown Boston. She needed to align herself with destiny just as surely as she needed to visit the Settlement House.

She was at North Street before she became aware of her surroundings. Before she descended from her daydreams long enough to register a male voice.

"Buon giorno."

Angelo! She smiled as she turned.

"I've been looking for you."

"Have you?"

"I have." He linked an arm through hers, pulling her along with him.

Julietta's heart thrilled at his touch.

"You owe me something, Signorina."

"I—I do?"

"You owe me your name. I gave you mine . . . ?"

She smiled. "Julietta."

"Julietta?"

"Giordano."

"Julietta Giordano. Well. You have to stop running away from me, Julietta Giordano. So that we can get to know one another. You want to go for a walk? To the waterfront?"

Oh, but—she was supposed to be signing up for an English class. Wasn't that what Madame had said? And what if she asked Julietta what the classes were like? Or worse, asked her to say something in English!

He tugged at her elbow. "Come on."

I'd like to say that she hesitated more than a moment. I long to tell you that she refused him altogether, but alas, that would not have been true. As she stared into his eyes, she decided that English lessons could wait one day more.

They walked down to North Bennet and then turned onto Commercial Street by the wharves, Angelo saluting carters and longshoremen, until they reached the water. Amid the clop of horses' hooves, the honking of trucks, and the teamsters' cries, they stood together, gazing out at the harbor. She knew somewhere out there, beyond the wharves and ships, was the ocean. And somewhere beyond that was the old country. That land of family and tradition and la miseria. She turned her eyes upon him. "Where are you from, Angelo?"

"Roma."

Roma? It wasn't such a usual place to be from. Not in America.

"And what did you do there?"

He shrugged. "Whatever I wanted. I was a student." And so he was. He'd studied Stirner's amorality as well as Armand's free love; he was dedicated to both those causes and methodical in practicing their disciplines.

She'd suspected that he was smart. He drove a truck, didn't he? "And what were you studying?" What did people study? "Medicine?" People besides Mauro. "Law?"

"Something like that. What I was studying will cure what infects the world. And all the people in it. Nectarine?" He'd taken it from a crate when no one was looking. It wasn't an ice cream, but it was something.

He bowed as she took it from him, letting his eyes roam her face. "And what do you do?"

"I work for a gown maker. And she's going to make me her partner. She told me so herself, just this day." And telling someone somehow made it seem more official.

"Partner? In a shop?" Angelo wasn't nearly as jubilant as she was. "Why would you want to be her partner?"

Why?—men! When had they ever understood anything when it came to fashion? "It's a fancy shop. Where the finest ladies in Boston come to buy their gowns."

"Finest? By that you must mean the richest."

Wasn't it the same thing? And why did he have to speak so scornfully?

"Why would you want to become a parasite and oppressor of the poor? You don't seem like that kind of a person."

Parasite? Oppressor of the poor? "I didn't say any of that, I only said that she wants to make me her partner."

"Your shop owner doesn't actually make the gowns, does she?"

"She drapes them and fits them. Like a genius. The best in Boston."

"And then I suppose she makes everyone else put them together."

Well, of course she did. "She pays us for it." Julietta forgave him his great disdain, for how could a man be expected to know what making a gown required?

"Ah! But how much does she pay you? Not nearly what you're worth, I'd guess. She keeps some of what she makes for herself, doesn't she?"

"I suppose she should. She owns the shop."

"And yet it's you who does all the work."

Julietta had never thought about it like that. But it was true. In a way.

"She owns the shop, she's undoubtedly rich, and she becomes richer off your labor. She's a parasite. She's making all of her money from your hard work."

He made it sound as if she deserved more money. Imagine asking Madame for a raise! There were at least three girls down on the second floor who aspired to her position. Asking for more money would be the same as telling Madame to let her go! But then, he'd just come over from the old country, hadn't he? Perhaps he didn't yet understand how America worked. "Perhaps she is. But what's wrong with a pretty gown?"

Nothing. He liked seeing a pretty girl in a pretty gown just as well as any other man. He'd like Julietta's better, of course, if her neckline were lower. And the skirt even a bit higher. "I just hate to see a girl like you deceived by all that propaganda."

"And what am I supposed to do if I don't work?" She couldn't imagine such a thing.

"You could ride along in the truck with me."

All day? Much as she liked Angelo, much as she hoped her future would include him, she knew that none of her best assets would be showcased sitting beside him all day in a truck. "Maybe I could. But I'd have to ride in one first to see if I'd like it, wouldn't I?" She threw the nectarine pit into the litter-strewn water, then turned on a heel and began walking away.

"But—where are you going?"

She turned, but continued to walk, one dainty foot, one slender ankle behind the other. "Home." She smiled and gave a little wave.

"Meet me tomorrow. Here."

She nodded and then she disappeared from view around the corner.

Tomorrow! He'd asked her to meet him tomorrow. Of

course . . . she'd told Madame she'd work on her English. She almost turned around and went back to tell Angelo she couldn't see him. But . . . wouldn't he think her a child to be so unsure of what she wanted? To keep changing her mind? She was old enough to do what she wanted. Isn't that what she'd told Mama? As far as she'd seen, America was about doing what you wanted. And that's exactly what she planned to keep on doing!

16

While Julietta was talking with Angelo, Luciana was back on Beacon Hill. She'd been sent to retrieve the sample books from Mrs. Quinn. And this time, Billy wasn't going out to The Tennis and Racquet Club, he was coming back. He jogged up the steps behind her and opened the door for her. What good fortune! What great luck!

She was wearing the same gown she'd worn the day before, an ivory color, in a fabric so insubstantial it seemed to float in the air around her. It was done up with a sash that let him know that underneath all those layers she was as slender as she was lithe. He wondered anew what country she was from. Had he had the advantage of a classical education, he would have known how to speak Italian. Proper Italian. Her Italian. As it was, his mother had never let him learn it. It was the one point from which his father could never sway her.

"For what purpose?" she had always asked. "So that he can speak to those filthy, destitute immigrants? Why should he have to learn to speak to them? They ought to be learning to speak to him."

His father would always sigh and shake his head. Protest that not all Italians were like that, while his mother argued that of course they were, a peculiar sort of triumph lighting her eyes.

Billy had learned a different language instead. And he could speak it quite well, though he hadn't kept up with those studies since the war had started. German wasn't something that anyone wanted to admit to speaking. Not anymore.

While Luciana was waiting to be given the sample books, Billy slipped outside and dismissed her waiting car. Then he asked for the Packard Twin to be brought around instead. He wanted to speak to her again. Or at least try to. He knew it probably wasn't the most proper thing to do, but how many more times could he expect her to show up on his doorstep? When he was home? And in any case, he couldn't ask her permission to drive her home. She didn't understand him. He had to present it as a *fait accompli*.

She came out the door and made it down one step before she realized her motorcar had gone. She stepped back up onto the porch. Looked up the street. Put a hand up to shield her eyes from the slanting sun. Looked down the street. Her motorcar was nowhere to be seen. "Mannaggia!" She'd had to endure the strega's sharp looks and the diatribe the woman had given, and now her motorcar had gone.

There was no help for it. She'd have to walk back to Madame's. And then she'd still have to walk home. She sighed. Looked down toward her throbbing feet. She'd finally set aside enough money to buy new shoes, but she hadn't been able to afford the best quality. The leather was too stiff. They had been biting into her heels the entire day.

"Hey!"

She looked toward the sound and saw a man waving at her. The strega's son. She lifted a hand and waved back.

"I can drive you."

She smiled. Waved again. Pressed the heavy books to her chest and started down the steps. *Porca miseria.* Of all the miserable luck. She stepped out onto the sidewalk, turned east, and started the trek toward downtown.

What? She was going to— "Wait. Stop!" Billy lifted his voice so that it would follow her.

Luciana heard Billy's cries and threw a glance back over her shoulder. He'd opened the door of the car.

"I can drive you."

Was he asking her to get in? He'd been nice enough the day before, though she hadn't understood a word he'd said.

"Really. I can drive you. It's not a problem." He'd opened the door even wider, gesturing for her to get in.

No. She'd had quite enough of handsome, charming young men. She clutched the books more tightly to her chest and continued on down the sidewalk.

He watched as she turned her back and walked away from him. Rats! She didn't understand. He slammed the door shut, ran to the driver's side, and got into the car. Started the engine as she kept walking farther down the street.

He pulled up beside her. Raised his voice to be heard above the engine. "Get in. I'll drive you."

She sent a look of alarm in his direction. Began to walk faster.

"Hey—just—" He left the car idling, got out, and sprinted to the sidewalk. "Would you just—"

She dodged him and continued walking.

He skipped two steps to catch up. Tried to take the books from her.

She wrenched them free.

"Look, I just want to—"

She'd started walking again.

He grabbed her by the arm to stop her.

Luciana was frightened now. Should she shout? Should she yell? She wrested herself free, terror dictating her motions, fear flashing in her eyes.

Billy saw tremors shake her shoulders. He stopped. Held up his hands. He hadn't meant to cause such fear. "I'm not trying to hurt you."

She took one slow step backward. Then another.

"I want to help you."

She didn't know what to do. Should she knock on the door of one of those dignified houses and beg for help? But how would she make anyone understand?

"I don't—I just—" He'd completely botched it. But he was too polite to use the word he wanted to say in the presence of a woman, so he settled on satisfying sounding syllables instead. And he spoke them in German. "*Verflixt!*" Ran a hand through his hair as he turned away.

Behind him, Luciana blinked. Had he— "What is the matter with you?" Out of reflex she had responded in kind. In German.

He stopped and turned around. "What did you say?" Billy's German accent had gone a bit flat from disuse, but Luciana understood him well enough.

"I said, what's the matter with you? Accosting me like that!" His ability to speak German had cured her muteness. And it had restored her indignation and backbone too. Luciana the Immigrant had no idea how to fend off an unwanted advance. But Luciana Conti, schooled in the ballrooms of Europe, could quite handily wield every weapon in a woman's arsenal.

A smile lit his lips, giving birth to a dimple in one cheek. "You're German!" He would never have guessed it. She didn't have the fair features or light-colored hair he associated with that race of people.

"German?"

"May I offer you a ride?"

His questions were coming too fast and were too confusing. A ride? "Where?"

"Back to the shop."

"Why?"

"Because you don't have one."

She frowned. "I know it. I don't understand what happened! The motorcar was supposed to wait for me."

"I sent it away."

"You—you what? Why?"

"Because I wanted to take you myself."

"What for?"

He blinked. His intentions had never before been questioned, let alone his person scrutinized. At least not that directly. He found it rather awkward and more than a bit uncomfortable. But he fell back on his Irish charm. "How else am I to spend time with such a beautiful young woman as you?"

She wondered if all Americans were as charmlessly blunt. Now that he had explained himself, it all seemed rather innocuous. And there could be no deceit hiding within him. Not when he looked at her with such clear green eyes. She had the impression of being able to see straight through to his soul. "Then I forgive you." She nodded and continued on her way.

She?—forgave him? Billy Quinn? Unbelievable! She'd had him practically on his knees, admitting to all kinds of private thoughts and secret hopes, and now she was going to walk away? Well . . . he wasn't going to chase after her. There were some things a man just wouldn't do. "The offer's still good. For a ride back." The foreign words, uncomfortable on his tongue, paralleled his emotions.

"I don't need it." What's more, she didn't want it. She turned, determined once more to walk away.

But he couldn't just let her go. "One thing more. Before you leave, could I have the pleasure of knowing your name?"

She didn't see any harm in giving it to him. At least not the first part. "It's Luciana."

"Luciana." It fairly danced off the tip of his tongue.

The way he said her name made her remember . . . things

that she shouldn't. And so she didn't reply and she didn't stop. She kept on walking.

"Luciana."

Did he have to keep saying her name! "What?"

"You're bleeding."

"I—" Bleeding? "Where?" Her foot. It had to be. She lifted her heel up to the side so she could see it. *Verflucht!* He was right. She'd walked a hole right through one of her stockings and a gash right into her heel. And now that she'd seen it, her foot throbbed even more.

He drew the passenger door open. "May I offer you a ride? If that wouldn't be improper?"

Oh . . . *bene*. She'd accept his offer, but only because she was afraid she'd soon wear her heel to the bone. She approached the motorcar, and did what she'd always done in Roma. She climbed, not onto the front bench as Billy was hoping but past it, toward the backseat, leaving him to play chauffeur.

And he couldn't help laughing out loud. Once again, she'd outfoxed him.

It wasn't quite what he'd had in mind. But he *had* sent her car away and he *had* nearly frightened her to death, so he supposed that he deserved it. Billy Quinn playing servant to an immigrant girl? Wouldn't his mother be scandalized?

17

That Saturday, Julietta was completely regretting accepting an offer of her own. It was the night of Mauro's dance and she wished—how she wished!—she had not been so overcome by the pageantry of the war concert. If she'd had her right mind about her, she would have said no.

"No." She said it to her reflection in the mirror. And then she stuck out her tongue for good measure. But in truth, *no* did not come easily to Julietta. Not when it came to men. For there was always some task they could perform, some use they could fulfill. Even if it did not produce the result for which they were hoping.

She sighed.

There was nothing else to do. If the dance at the Sons of Avellino Hall was as close as she could get to a ball, then she might as well get on with the getting ready for it. She carefully parted her hair on one side and then spent the next hour coaxing her thick tresses into waves around her face. And then, once they had been pinned into position, she gathered up the rest of her hair and pulled it into a knot at her nape.

"How do I look?"

Josephine, passing behind Julietta, a pile of laundry in hand, paused. How did she look? Like a goddess. Like an angel. She bent to place the clothes on a stool, licked a finger, and put it to one of Julietta's curls, pressing a stray lock back into place. "*Perfetto.*"

Perfetto.

She wished it were Angelo she was looking so perfetto for, but Mauro would have to do.

"So, are you planning on eating or are you just going to stand there, admiring yourself in that mirror?"

"What's for dinner?"

"*Timpano di peperoni.* And a bit of soup."

Julietta wrinkled her nose. Peppers and garlic and anchovies? Right before a dance? "I still need to press my gown. No need to wait for me."

"No need to wait? Well, thank you very much, Your Majesty!"

Julietta rolled her eyes and then forgot completely about Josephine and her comments, about anchovies and soup, as she considered what to wear.

The dress she usually wore to the dances or the new messaline?

She reached out a hand to stroke the pink and white silk. Oh, how she'd love to wear it. She longed to wear it! But . . . no. The messaline was worthy of so much more than Mauro and a dance at the Sons of Avellino Hall.

She'd save it for something truly special.

She took a percale from its peg instead. She had convinced herself that the weave was so thin, it looked like a voile. But between you and me, her aspirations fell somewhat short of reality. In fact, it was a cheap percale that looked exactly like what it was. Although Julietta had altered the silhouette and embellished the trimmings to such an extent that if one didn't look too closely, the gown appeared quite acceptable. And rather fashionable as well.

As she stepped into it, she remembered once more the smile

that had lit Mauro's face when she had accepted his invitation. And again, she almost wished she could wear the messaline for him. But that would defeat the whole purpose of saving it for something special, wouldn't it? She turned away from the pegs so that she couldn't see it. But still the memory of Mauro's delight flickered in her mind. She'd go a bit early to the dance and take a flower off one of the tables. Push it into her hair behind an ear.

Si. That would have to do.

An hour later, Julietta was standing—still!—against the wall of the Hall. The gardenia she'd pushed behind her ear enveloped her in a sweet perfume, which completely belied the look of irritation on her face. She'd been standing there for nearly an hour. By herself.

Mauro was late.

At last she saw him enter the room, his form framed in the doorway. He pulled his hat from his head, pressing it to his chest, and stood there for a long moment, eyes searching the dance floor. Then he turned toward the people standing around the refreshment table.

Resisting an urge to wave, she tucked her hands behind her and pushed her back to the wall. Let him look. Let him wonder. Let him worry that she had gone.

It only took a moment more. Relief relaxed his features and a smile lit his face. He stepped around signora Sardo and signora Riccio. Walked around a cluster of giggling young girls and a knot of young men. Then nearly got trapped between two couples as they did the Castle Walk across the dance floor.

He halted in front of her. Made a quaint, rather gallant bow. "I'm sorry. I meant to be here before now, but signora Matullo had one of her fits."

Signora Matullo? The fish-seller's wife? Julietta came away from the wall, alarm sharpening her features. "Is she all right?"

Mauro sighed. "Who can say? At least she's sleeping now." He set his bag down with his hat atop it and flexed his shoulder blades, hoping to drive out some of the tension. He hadn't been able to stop signora Matullo's fit. He'd never been able to stop them. In spite of all the new cures and all the advances of modern science, he had nothing with which to combat a simple seizure. Oh, he could try to keep her from hurting herself and send her into sleep afterward, but he couldn't prevent them from coming and he couldn't stop them once they had grabbed hold of her limbs. It vexed a man, especially a man who was a physician as gifted, as competent, as Mauro Vitali. There he was at a Saturday night dance with Julietta Giordano and all he wanted to do was go home and pore through his books, try to find the one bit of information, the one clue that he had missed. That everyone— every doctor in America—had missed.

He closed his eyes for a moment and tried to clear his mind of the memory of signora Matullo convulsing on the floor. He opened them to find Julietta looking up at him, a gardenia glowing from her hair. Mauro put a trembling hand to the back of his neck mostly because he wanted so badly to press it to hers.

He had meant to be there early. He had meant to return home first. To wash. And change his clothes. He hadn't wanted to show up at the dance with the smell of his patient still on his hands and the reek of tenements still on his shirt. At least he'd had the foresight to eat a peppermint on the way. "I'm sorry."

Julietta reached out a hand and touched his arm. "It wasn't a problem." And indeed, it hadn't been. At least not much of one. Being able to tell the other men that she already had an escort seemed to increase her value in their eyes. And now that Mauro had taken up her hand and led her onto the dance floor, she could see the rest of the bachelors sizing him up.

For a moment, as they waited for a *mattchiche* to begin, she sized him up as well. There, among the greater community of Sheafe Street, he had ceased to be just her brother's friend. Had taken on an identity of his own: Dr. Mauro Vitali. And Dr. Vitali was more than a little bit handsome. He wore his age well. It made him seem almost . . . dapper. And really, thirty wasn't so very old, was it?

Mauro and Julietta swooped together around the dance floor in a quick and graceful two-step. Hands joined together, first pointed toward the ceiling, then toward the floor. As they swung around each other, Julietta quickly became enveloped by Mauro's scent. A hint of something . . . unpleasant. But on top of it, the smell of peppermint. Beneath it, bay rum.

And, Madonna mia, he had some rhythm, didn't he?

She'd never seen him dance before, at least not that she had noticed. But he was quick and precise in his steps. And very energetic. He twirled her about the room for three dances and by then she'd had enough. She needed a break.

"Do you think there's any *limonata*?"

"What?" He was having trouble understanding what she was saying. A flush rode her cheeks, and the effort of dancing had left her chest heaving. All he wanted to do was take her by the hand and lead her out into the alley. But, God help him, he wasn't a boy anymore. He was a grown man. And the girl standing before him was his best friend's sister. Beside which there were things that a person—a doctor, a man—just shouldn't do.

She stood on her toes, put a hand to his head, and pulled it down to speak into his ear. "Do you think there's any limonata?"

He leaned his forehead against hers for a moment, just a moment, and inhaled the cool, exotic scent of the gardenia. The tickle of her breath against his cheek sent a snaking warmth through his chest. Limonata? There had to be some. And if there wasn't, he would make it himself.

The back of Mauro's neck was damp, and the curls flopping over his collar tickled the back of Julietta's hand. She reached up and—what was she thinking? He was Mauro. Mauro Vitali. *Old* Mauro Vitali. She released him, resisting the urge to run her hand along his cheek. Took a careful step backward.

He smiled a lopsided smile. "Limonata. Right. I'll go look."

———

Just before dinner, Mama asked Annamaria to go to Zanfini's for some cherries. "Might be the last time we can find some this year."

She left the apartment so quickly that she forgot to put on her scarf. And by the time she noticed she was already down the stairs and across the street. But when she reached Zanfini's, the awnings had been taken down and the store was dark.

She knocked on the door. Waited a moment. Knocked harder still. She didn't care whether Mama got her cherries, but she wanted to see the man again. The one who had sold her the tomatoes.

As she started to rap on the door a third time, it swung open and she nearly knocked her knuckles right into that man's chest.

He almost caught that hand up in his and kissed those very knuckles. But he didn't. He swung the door wide instead. "Come in."

She nodded. Slipped past him.

"What do I get you?"

She bit her lip. It was so dim without the lights. She knew they must have cherries somewhere, but she couldn't see them.

"Tomatoes?"

She smiled as she shook her head. They still had three left over from her last visit. She made a gesture with her hand, forming her thumb and forefinger into a small circle.

She wanted something small, then. He tried to think of something small. And round. "Radishes?"

She shook her head once more.

She didn't want tomatoes and she didn't want radishes. What else could she want? And why wouldn't she just tell him? "Why don't you tell me and then I'll find it for you?"

She started to shake her head, but then stopped. And she

spoke. Why shouldn't she? What was more important: observing Mama's proprieties or getting the cherries that were needed? "Cherries."

He squinted. Leaned toward her. Had she spoken? It looked as if she had, but it was so dark and he hadn't actually heard anything. "I can't . . . I didn't hear you."

She threw a nervous glance to the door behind her. Stepped closer to him. "Cherries."

He heard her that time. And he smelled her and felt her too. Her hair brushed as lightly as the softest of feathers against his cheek. And it smelled like . . . rosemary. "Cherries! Well, they're just . . . here."

As he stretched an arm out behind her and over her head, leaning close, she held her breath. But she kept her eyes open. And she saw a tangle of hair on his chest beneath his open collar and a rash of stubble on his chin.

"Red or white?"

"What?"

He pulled two baskets from the shelf and held them out in the narrow space between them. "Red or white?"

She didn't know. Mama hadn't said. Confused, her eyes sought his.

"Rafaello?" A woman's voice floated into the store.

He grimaced as his gaze fled from Annamaria toward the curtained doorway behind them. "Just a second, Mama!"

He returned his attention to Annamaria. Held up first one basket and then the other with an accompanying lift of his brow.

She put a finger up to touch one.

He reached back behind her again, his arm brushing her as he put the other basket on the shelf. Then he scooped a good portion from the basket she'd requested out onto a piece of paper and tied it up with a string. Bowed as he offered it to her.

"Grazie." She said it in a whisper because her throat had gone dry.

"*Prego.*" He said it in a whisper that matched her own.

Their eyes held for what seemed like an eternity, and then she left. He watched her cross the street, then locked the door and went to see what it was his mama wanted.

"Rafaello. Rafaello." She repeated it like a chant as she climbed the stairs. His name was Rafaello. As she walked into the apartment, she realized she hadn't paid him. Shame colored her face. What must he think of her!

"Annamaria!" Mama had raised her voice so she could be heard above the shrieks of the baby in the neighboring apartment. She inclined her head toward the door. "Go over to Josie's and see if you can help her with the baby."

Annamaria put the cherries on the table and then gladly obeyed. Mama couldn't know that comforting a wailing baby was no work at all to Annamaria. That she would gladly set aside a hundred shirts and a thousand English lessons to take Josie's baby up in her arms.

She pushed the door open as she stuck her head into the apartment. "Josie?" She saw the baby, but she didn't see its mother. "Josie?" She pushed the door further open. Now she saw her neighbor. The girl was trying to dress her two-year-old at the same time she was trying to chase down her three-year-old. The baby lay in the middle of the floor, wailing.

"Can I help?" Annamaria crossed the floor, picked up the baby, and cuddled it to her chest. "Where are his clothes?"

"He soiled them."

"Where are his others?"

"Somewhere out there." She gestured toward the window, where Annamaria could see a line of clothes fluttering in the evening's breeze.

The baby lifted his head and shrieked in Annamaria's ear.

"There now. Of course you're mad. You've got no clothes!" Not being able to bring in the wash with the baby in her arms, she concentrated on soothing it while Josie finished with the other children. She pressed kisses to his warm, fuzzy head as she rocked from side to side.

Once the other two children went to play underneath the bed, Josie pulled in the clothes and took the baby from Annamaria, putting him on top of the table for changing.

"*Mille grazie.* Someday I'll return the favor. When you have children of your own."

A sudden, fierce pain stole Annamaria's breath and brought tears to her eyes. One of them splashed onto the baby's chest as Josie struggled with the diaper. She looked up. "Annamaria?"

Annamaria put a hand to her mouth, shaking her head.

"What did I—?"

"Nothing." She backed away from the table and fled the apartment.

18

There had to be someplace where Annamaria could go. Someplace where she could mourn. *"Children of your own."* The echo of Josie's words rang in Annamaria's ears long after she left her neighbor's apartment. Long after she had run down the stairs into the basement. That dark, dank pit where she could rail against her fate. Where she could sink down to her heels on the damp, worm-eaten floor and cry out her misery.

Why, God?

Why does it have to be this way? Why do you demand this from me? Why would you give me a desire for children, for a family, if you never meant for me to have them? It's too cruel! Is this really what you want? Is this what you want from me? You want everything? You want everything I dream of and all I have to give? That's what they say. That's what Father Antonio says. He says this is what I have to do. He and Aunt Rosina both.

But I don't want to do it. I don't want to pour out my life for my mama and my papa, my brothers and my sister. I want to give it to my own family. For myself. What's so wrong with that?

No answer came back to her through the cobweb-ridden darkness.

"What's so wrong with that!" She startled herself by saying the words aloud.

Was there anything wrong with it? When such things were commended to others? Like her sister? Why would it be honorable for Theresa and a sin for Annamaria to want the very same things? Why was she the one who had to look after everybody? Why couldn't they all—all of her brothers and sisters—join in the caring for Mama and Papa? And for each other? Surely no one would begrudge her what they themselves wanted—and expected—from life.

She dried her tears on a sleeve as she contemplated that thought.

Maybe . . . maybe this wasn't what God required at all. Maybe it was as simple as that! Perhaps all she had to do was figure out how to ask the others for help.

———

As Mauro walked Julietta home from the dance, there was something new, a growing awareness that hung suspended in the night air between them.

Julietta slid a look up at him from beneath her eyelashes. He looked almost . . . *handsome*, walking right there beside her. Didn't he? She blinked. Looked again. Si. Handsome. Definitely so. And she couldn't quite understand it. Decided that it must have something to do with the light of the moon.

For his part, Mauro could hardly believe his good fortune. Walking Julietta Giordano home. After a dance. To which he had been her escort! They reached her building. He opened the door for her.

She walked through.

He followed her up the stairs to the Giordano apartment.

How many times had he climbed those stairs? How many times had he traversed that long hall? All those times before, he had done it as family, walking through the door, knowing he would be greeted by the Giordanos as both son and brother. But this time? This night? He did it with fear and trembling, if not a bit of euphoria. He walked those steps as a stranger. One hoping to establish a new relationship. He did it as a—dare he even think it!—suitor. Filled with a surge of confidence that being with her had given him, he decided to take the third great risk he had taken in less than a month.

She put her hand to the doorknob.

He saw it turn, knew he had little time left to speak to her. In private. "I was hoping to see you again. Soon. At the *festa?*"

The festa. Saint Marciano's festa, the weekend next. With her cheeks still flushed from dancing and the memory of the mattchiche still swirling through her mind, she said yes.

Yes. Yes!

But was it the sort of yes that Mauro was hoping to hear? The sort of yes that meant Julietta would have eyes only for him?

It might have been. It was possible that she meant it to be. For *something* had happened between them at that dance. But Julietta being who she was and Mauro being someone that she had always known . . . it was difficult for her to focus clearly on a person who had always been—so obviously—there.

He might have stood a better chance at Julietta's heart if there hadn't been an Angelo. For not long after, as Julietta was walking down North Street that Monday on her way to work, an arm linked through hers as a pleasingly baritone voice said, "Buon giorno."

Buon giorno.

What was it about that phrase that sent such a thrill of delight through Julietta's soul? We can't fault the man for lack of imagination. In fact, he had plenty of imagination. It's just that he squandered it on things like treatises and speeches, which left very little imagination left to think of anything better to say to Julietta. And in any case, he hadn't ever, not once in his young life, had to think of anything different to say in order to beckon a girl to his side. What worked for Bianca and Alessandra, Mimi and Carmela, worked for Julietta as well.

Would she have cared? If she had known about the others?

It's difficult to say. She had kissed other boys herself and she understood the yearnings of a restless heart. But she also longed to be The One for someone's heart in a way that no one else ever had or ever would be. But caring and being seen to care were two different things, so Julietta simply smiled and said, "Buon giorno, Angelo," as if he walked her to work every day of the week.

He winked down at her. "Where are we going?"

"I'm going to work. Where are you going?"

"I'm going to amuse myself."

"Amuse yourself!" She wondered what exactly he had in mind to do.

"Just so. Why don't you come with me?" He tightened the loop of his arm enough to stop her. And then he threaded that arm back around her waist and turned her toward him.

"And what would we do?"

Catching up her free hand with his, he spun her beneath his arm right there on the sidewalk. "Whatever we wanted to."

She dropped a playful curtsy. "How I'd like to, Signore, but I'm afraid I'd lose my job."

He scowled. "Who needs one anyway?"

"I do." She smiled as she said it to try and assuage his frown.

"Why? To bow and scrape to someone? To serve as a pawn for the capitalists until you're old and gray? What good does that do anyone?"

Capitalists? Pawns? She didn't know what he was talking about. But since he had mentioned it, she wondered what good work *did* do anyone? Anyone but Papa to whom she always handed over her paychecks just as soon as she got them. How she wished she could do as Angelo did and just walk through the streets as though she owned them, as though the city had been made for her pleasure alone. But she couldn't. "I can't."

He dropped her hand. "I thought you were more modern than that."

She shrugged. "I guess I'm not." She walked off down the street without a wave. Without one look back. And oh, what it cost her! It wasn't a strategy she was sure of. She hadn't had to use it much before. Only with him, in fact. And so, she worried. And she would have worried even more if she had seen how his face darkened as he watched her walk away.

Once Julietta got to work, she stewed.

All morning long, while Madame was up and down the stairs, asking for Luciana to do this and that, Julietta relived her conversation with Angelo. It was the second time she had refused to accompany him. And it was the second time she had turned her back on him and walked away. She went over each word she had said and each word that he had spoken in reply.

Dozens and dozens of times.

Would she ever see him again?

Because there was no way to know and because she had never before cared so much what any man thought, she let fear and doubt worry away at her. They gnawed at her self-confidence until she could think of a hundred reasons why Angelo Moretti was lost to her forever. And because she couldn't bear to think that she had failed, she found an alternate person to blame for all her problems. It wasn't so difficult a thing to do. As she emerged from her remembered conversations and self-recrimination, there was one name that rang constant in her ears.

Luciana.

Luciana, do this. Luciana, do that.

Luciana, come take the car and go up to Beacon Hill.

Julietta was the one who deserved to take the car! She'd worked for Madame longest. Julietta was sick to death of Luciana! Hadn't everything been just fine before the girl had started working? And hadn't Julietta been the one Madame had always favored? If there was any tribulation in Julietta's world, it had to do with Luciana.

When Annamaria left early for confession that afternoon, Julietta's pent-up anxiety, her imagined inadequacies, and her jealousy exploded into a rage. "You think you can just come in here and take over the shop? Well, you can't. I'm the one who's worked here longest. I'm the one Madame's chosen to replace her."

"I don't—"

Julietta came at the girl, eyes blazing, finger pointing. "I don't care what you say. I don't care where you're from. You and your northern accent. I'd take bets you're no more than a fisherman's daughter."

"I'm not—"

"I'm the one who knows how things work here. I'm the one that Madame asks to—"

Luciana had put up her hands, hoping to deflect Julietta's wrath. At the very least to stop the blows she was quite certain were going to come. "I don't want the shop."

"It's me that Madame trusts. *Me* that she's chosen."

"I don't want your shop!"

19

Luciana's words reverberated in the sudden stillness.

Julietta looked at Luciana through the fog of her resentment and jealousy.

"I don't want the shop." At least—she hadn't. Not until then. But the more Julietta insisted she couldn't have it, the more it seemed to make sense that she should. Why shouldn't she? She couldn't spend the rest of her life sewing beads onto gowns. If that was to be her fate, she would dig her grave herself. Right now. This minute.

"But . . . you don't—why not?" The thought that someone didn't want the same thing she did was almost as offensive to Julietta as a woman wearing a gown three seasons old. Why wouldn't anyone want what she wanted?

Luciana folded her arms across her chest as she glowered at the girl. She would not be told what it was she could and couldn't do. Not by this girl. "Actually, you're right. I've changed my mind. You've convinced me. Maybe I do want the shop."

"But you can't—"

"I can. You might know how to sew, but I know how to wear

the clothes you make. And I can get on better with Madame's clients. Much better than you do."

Julietta eyes flashed. "Not if you can't speak English. Not if you keep cringing at shadows. You don't know the first thing about America."

"And you don't know the first thing about class."

They exchanged looks across a vast expanse of resentment and envy.

Julietta broke the silence, eyes spitting fire. "Fine. What do you want? More than the store?"

More than the store? Luciana had to admit that the idea of spending her life as a shopkeeper was just as distasteful as spending it sewing beads. More than the store? There was in fact one thing she wanted. One thing she needed quite badly.

"I need to learn English."

English? That was what she wanted? Then why hadn't she just said so? "Go to the Settlement House. Over on Parmenter Street. Like I told you."

"I don't . . . I—I can't."

"Why not?"

How much should she say? "I can't."

Julietta's brows crimped in annoyance.

"I really can't. There's someone looking for me. And if he finds me . . . I'm afraid of what he'll do. I saw him once. Here in the city."

"Why is he looking for you?"

"Because of something that happened in Roma."

"Is that where you're from?"

"Si."

She'd known Luciana wasn't from the south. The only mystery was just how northern she'd been. She was from Roma? Then she was among the worst of all northerners. Among the first of all those who had taxed and ignored and oppressed their countrymen into poverty. She was the cause of all the country's troubles. One more reason to despise her.

Like most of us, Julietta had no trouble holding conflicting opinions about a certain set of facts. Angelo and Luciana were both from Roma. The prejudices Julietta, as an Avellinesi, could easily dismiss for the one, she pressed like an iron against the other. And had you or I informed her of the inconsistency, she wouldn't have seen any fault in herself at all.

"My grandmother and I came here to America because we had no other choice. We had to escape him. And we can't let him find us now. We have to survive."

Survive. Julietta could understand that. That's all that any of them had wanted. At first. But Julietta was beginning to want more. She wanted more than existence, more than mere survival. She wanted triumph. That's why Madame's shop was so important. She wanted to become a part of America. She wanted to belong. To walk down any street in Boston knowing that she had a right to be there. Know that everyone else knew it too. "So what do you want me to do about it?"

"I want you to . . ." What *did* Luciana want? "I want you to show me where the school is. I can't afford to wander around looking for it. He might see me. I want you to take me there, and I want you to help me sign up."

"That's what you want." That's all she wanted? "If I help you sign up, you won't take the shop from me?"

Luciana shook her head.

"All you had to do was ask."

———

Mauro searched the crowds all day on Saturday, pushing through the packed streets in vain. Julietta was nowhere to be found. As it happened, Angelo had driven by in his truck just before Saint Marciano's procession had started. When Julietta saw him there sitting high in his cab, when she saw him reach across the seat and push the passenger door open, there was nothing for her to do but get in, to see where the ride would take her.

And what a ride it was!

Good thing she'd decided to wear the messaline. She always knew Saint Marciano was looking out for her! And she never imagined how exciting riding in a truck could be. It wasn't like the electric car at all! No. There were only the two of them and somehow, enclosed in the cab, it was very private. For several blocks she didn't know quite what to say. She snuck a look at his dashing form. Overcome with the intimacy of the moment and the speed at which things passed by her window, she lost her ability to speak. Though not for long. Soon she was smiling as if she went for rides in trucks every day of the week.

"Where are we going?"

Angelo winked at her. "Where do you want to go?"

She shrugged. It wouldn't have done to look too excited, to seem too eager. A man like Angelo wouldn't be interested in a naïve country girl. He was probably used to girls with much more sophistication. Julietta surreptitiously pushed herself back against the seat and folded her hands into her lap.

And so they proceeded, away from the city and out into the farmlands that surrounded the metropolis, lurching over potholes and honking at groups of children playing in the dusty streets, warning them to get out of the way. And once, when they came to an intersection blocked by a sturdy if stubborn cow, Angelo let Julietta press the horn herself.

After a while he turned the truck off the main road, and they jounced down a rutted, rocky lane. When the road ended at the start of a field, Angelo set the hand brake and turned off the engine.

He pushed his door open, hopped down, and reached behind the seat for something. Paused when he saw her still sitting there. "Aren't you coming?"

Julietta was surveying the field, just as she had surveyed the road that had brought them there. They were both rather . . . rough. And covered with a dense layer of dust. Being made denser still by the dust they'd stirred in their coming. It was settling down all around them—on them—she could taste it on her tongue.

Dust was one thing she hadn't thought of.

A romantic walk in a park. A picnic. But trudging through a dusty field had not been part of her plan. And anyway, she was dressed in her best. For the festa.

She put one long leg up on the bench of the truck. "I'll ruin my shoes."

He took one look up that nicely shaped, incredibly long leg, and then fixed his gaze on her eyes. "So take them off."

"Take them—take them off?"

"Take them off."

Well. She could. But why should she? And risk her gown being ruined by the dust and the dirt! She pouted, just the tiniest of pouts. "Can't we go somewhere else?"

He leaned an arm against the steering wheel. "Like where?" He thought of the picnic hidden behind the seat and his growing hunger.

"Like . . ." They couldn't very well go back to the city and risk being seen. What she'd done by leaving with him was risky enough. She didn't want to be caught in the doing of it. " . . . like . . . your place. I could meet your family." They couldn't be half as bad as her own. And if she met them and they liked her . . . wouldn't that be grand!

Angelo had raised a brow in apparent surprise. "My place?" He hopped onto the bench, slammed the door shut, and reversed the truck so quickly that Julietta's head knocked against the back window.

"Is it very far?"

"What?"

"Your place. Is it very far?"

"No." Angelo turned off the main road onto a lane that bordered more fields. Tall cornstalks rose up from one of them like spears. Hardy green bouquets of cabbages sprouted from another. He took a sharp turn onto a narrow, rutted path that outlined the perimeter of the cornfield, following until it dead-ended at a stand of trees. The engine died with a jerk.

He stepped down from the cab, inviting her to do the same.

She slid down from the seat onto gravel. This was no better. They might as well have stayed where they were.

Angelo had already started down the lane, carrying a basket in his hand.

"Wait! *Scusi.* I just . . . I can't . . ." The gravel was poking at her feet as if she weren't wearing any shoes at all.

He strode back to her, gestured for her to get back into the cab, and then he knelt on the gravel below her. "Here. I'll give you a ride." He tugged on one of her feet, seeming to indicate that she should mount his shoulders.

"I don't think . . . I really shouldn't—"

"And how else are we going to get there?"

With a scramble up onto his back and a lot of clinging to his chin, she finally settled herself onto his shoulders.

"Ready?"

"I guess I—" she shrieked as he pushed to standing. Then she began to grasp at her skirt, which had ridden up past her knees.

"Don't worry about it," he said, placing an arm over her shins and pulling them toward his chest. He felt her straighten, pushing against his neck, centering her weight across his shoulders. "I can't see anything anyway."

In fact, he could. He could see quite a bit. Shapely calves, a very fine pair of knees. But he was careful not to let on.

He was enjoying the view. And besides, she was a cute little thing. He didn't want to ruin anything before it had even gotten started.

As he strode down the lane, she felt rather liberated. She'd never ridden on anyone's shoulders. Not since the age of eight. Or nine. And then, it had been . . . had it been Mauro's shoulders she'd ridden on?

Mauro!

To Julietta's credit, she did feel bad about not being at the festa with Mauro. A little bit. A very tiny bit. But in the next moment she sent the thought away. Who wanted to think about Mauro on a day like this? With a man like this one? Mauro would never have been able to hoist her to his shoulders. Some days he seemed too weary to even carry around his old doctor's bag.

As they came to a curve in the lane, a shack came into view. A shack that Angelo seemed to be headed for. Was it . . . his house? It couldn't have been big enough for a family. Although the Giordanos somehow managed to fit themselves into their tiny apartment.

She tugged on his chin.

"Ow!"

"Shouldn't you let me down?" She didn't want his family to see her like this!

He bent his knees and released his hold on her shins to allow her to slide off his back. He nearly got choked in the process, and Julietta's gown was pulled up even higher, but neither let the other know of those indignities.

Angelo pushed the door open wide and let Julietta walk in.

It took a moment for her eyes to adjust to the lack of light. The sole window was coated with dusty grime. A table and two chairs sat in one corner. A bed in another. A crate overflowing with pink-colored papers in a third. There was hardly enough room to pass between the furniture. "And . . . where is your family?"

He reached out a hand over her head, shoved the door shut, and caught her about the waist with a hand. He bent his head and kissed her. "Family? I don't have one."

20

Julietta had been daydreaming about kissing Angelo, but she'd never imagined that his touch would fill her with fear. He didn't have a family? But then . . . that meant that she was hidden away with him, in a house that was his alone? *Oddio, sono finita!* That wasn't good. That wasn't at all what she had intended! Sneaking out into an alley with a boy was one thing, but going off somewhere alone with one was another thing entirely!

She had to get out. Now!

"What's the matter?" He'd drawn her close, against his chest.

"I think I should—"

He nuzzled her ear.

Oh. My. That felt rather . . .

"You think you should . . . ?"

"I think . . . I should." What was he doing to her neck? Whatever it was, it felt divine.

"Should what?"

"What?"

He laughed as he rubbed a hand up and down her back.

Oh! Now she remembered. She put a hand to his chest and

pushed him away. "I think I should leave." But there was a hint of regret in her eyes. He was rather good at kissing. . . .

He caught up that hand, tugging her forward until he felt his knees hit the edge of the mattress. Then, embracing her, he brought her with him as he fell onto the bed.

"Angelo!"

The springs squeaked alarmingly as she tried to roll off him. And the mattress sagged under his weight. So much so that she couldn't scramble away from him; the pitch of the mattress kept tumbling her back to his side.

He stretched out an arm and pulled her to him. Nipped at her ear. Her neck. His hand crept up her ribs.

She shoved at him. Hard. "Don't—!"

"What's wrong?" He eased away, propping himself up on an elbow to look at her.

She used the opportunity to push herself to sitting. And then to stand. Her heart was racing, and it wasn't with ardor or passion. "You can't—I don't—"

He sat up too and held up his hands as if he were innocent. "I'm sorry. This place isn't very big. I tripped. I didn't mean . . ." He shrugged. Held out one of his hands to her. "Come here."

She straightened her dress, put a hand up to her hair. Then Julietta glanced around the room before finally looking down at him.

He was sitting there so . . . forlorn.

She reached out a hand toward him.

He grasped it and immediately pulled her close. Clasped his arms about her waist and leaned his head against her chest.

She put out a hand and stroked his hair.

"I'm sorry, Julietta. I should know better."

Sì, he should!

"But you're just so . . . beautiful." He felt her relax. Heard her sigh. "I couldn't help myself."

She kissed the top of his head.

"Are we friends again?"

He was looking up at her with such hope, such regret, that she couldn't help herself from leaning down for a kiss.

That first kiss led to a second and the second one to a third. And, really, what is there to say about such things? Except that Mama Giordano would not have been happy. At all. She might have even gone at Angelo Moretti with her spoon. She knew Julietta kissed boys. Of course she did. And though it might shock you to know it, Mama didn't have anything against a little fun. But Julietta had never kissed any boy with such passion and abandon. And she'd never once before this day lost control. Always before she'd been able to stop things from going too far. With a laugh or a sigh she'd been able to end a kiss and send a boy away with a wink and a smile.

But Angelo Moretti was different.

And if he'd kept his hands to himself just a while longer, there was no telling what might have happened. But he didn't. So minutes later, Julietta sprang from his lap, straightening her dress once more. She marched to the door, more angry with herself than she was with him. She yanked it open, but stopped short of walking out. Because there was no place to go.

A cold sweat broke out behind her ears in spite of the heat of the day. She couldn't walk back to the city. Not by herself. It must have taken them an hour to get to this farm, and she had to admit to herself that she hadn't paid much attention to how they had gotten there. She couldn't stay—she wouldn't—but what was she going to do?

"Julietta. Come back. I'm sorry."

She looked at him, not knowing whether she ought to believe him. He seemed like he meant it. And his kisses! Her scalp tingled with the memory of them.

"Honest. I don't know what happened. It's like . . . you've bewitched me." He'd pushed to his feet and came to stand beside her.

Whether she believed him or not, one thing was certain. "I shouldn't have come here."

He held his hands up, palms out. "It wasn't my idea."

That's right. It hadn't been. It was her idea. The realization caused her to flush in shame.

"I'll take you home. If that's what you want."

What she wanted didn't matter much. What mattered was getting home before anyone noticed that she'd been gone.

Angelo put a hand to her back as she left the shack. He climbed into the truck on the driver's side, then leaned across to push her door open.

She climbed into the truck and soon they were bumping back down the lane. But there was an awkwardness, a tension between them that hadn't existed before. And despite the unease she felt for what had transpired between them, she couldn't bear to think that he was angry with her. Or worse: disappointed. He must think her nothing but a child. She frantically searched for something to say.

"Is your family still back in the old country, Angelo?"

He scowled. "I grew up in an orphanage."

Maybe she hadn't chosen the best of subjects.

"Not from birth. My pa left when I was three. And then Ma dropped me off when I was eight. She decided it was time to move on."

Julietta's brows rose. She'd decided it was time to move on? To where? From what? "I'm so sorry."

"So was I. They whip you there, soon as look at you."

She smiled, intent upon lifting his spirits with a tease. "I suppose you were very bad."

Angelo, thinking about that horrific place, missed her cue. "No. I tried to be good." If he had looked at her face, he would have known it was the wrong answer, but the past was painful to Angelo, and he had shared it with very few people. Each time he had, when he had taken that risk, he found it easiest to do while he was distracted. He didn't want to see the revulsion, the disgust he was sure would be revealed in their eyes. So he concentrated on driving instead, keeping his eyes on the road. "Kept thinking if I was, Ma would come and get me out. You know?"

She didn't know. She couldn't imagine her own mother, or anyone else's, abandoning any of her children. What kind of mother would do that?

He fumbled in his shirt pocket for a cigarette. Finding one, he put it between his lips and then put his hand to his trouser pocket to search for a match. "Steer for me."

"What?"

He pointed to the steering wheel. "Drive."

Drive? What did she know about driving? She grabbed hold of the steering wheel as he let go of it in order to light his match. He swore as she jerked the truck toward the right and then back to the left. After lighting his cigarette, he took control once more.

"Eventually, I ran away. I mean, who needs it, you know?" He took a draw on the cigarette. "Who needs people telling you what to do all the time? Like they're so much better than you are? Why should anyone tell me what to think or what to believe?" He paused to take a drag. "Who needs rules anyway? And why should a government tell me what to do? A religion, what to believe?"

"You aren't Catholic?"

"No."

How could someone from Rome not be a Catholic? "If you aren't Catholic, then what are you?"

"I'm nothing."

Nothing? Was that even possible? "You don't believe in God?"

He snorted. "Why should I? When I don't have any proof that He's ever believed in me."

"Then you don't . . . go to confession?" Imagine that!

"What do I have to confess? And why should I confess to

breaking someone else's rules? I'm a smart person. Can't I decide for myself what's right? And wrong?"

"But if you don't believe in God and you don't believe in . . . the government . . . then what do you believe in?"

"I believe in myself. And the capacity of man to determine his own fate. To decide for himself what he should do and where he should go."

She'd never heard of such a thing! How could anyone live without papas and mamas telling them what to do and where to go? "How do you decide? And what kind of rules do you make?"

"Rules? There are only two. I do what I want. And when I do, I make no apologies for it." He punctuated his points with a brandishing of his cigarette. He could have added that he changed the rules whenever he felt like it, but he didn't. And in any case, he didn't actually see it as a changing of the rules; he would have described it in much more philosophical terms best left to academic discussions and term papers.

No apologies? "You must not have many friends, then."

She was hoping for a laugh. What she got was a scowl. "I don't need anybody. Who really needs anybody? Sentiment hinders change. Change can only be had through revolution. And sacrifices must be made in order that revolution be achieved."

Revolution? Sacrifices? It sounded rather . . . sinister. And she couldn't keep herself from shuddering. But she didn't want to end their day with talk of sacrifices and revolutions. And she didn't like seeing him look so unhappy. So she slid closer to him. Kissed him on the cheek.

And was rewarded with a smile. And a wink.

—————

Once Angelo dropped Julietta off near Zanfini's, she ran through the North End to her street, into her building, and up four flights of stairs before skidding to a halt in front of her apartment door. She smoothed her gown, pushed the pins further into her hair. Prayed to God that no one would notice her. That no one would ask her any questions.

But Mama Giordano caught her coming through the door. "There you are! Grab the beans and bring them to the table."

Julietta froze and then moved toward the sideboard, eyes wide. That was it? That was all the attention she would be paid? The only remark that would be made? She felt her shoulders go slack with relief. Her gaze traveled the room. Everyone was there. Including Salvatore and Little Matteo.

And Mauro.

Her cheeks were lit by the scorching flames of guilt.

Mama bustled by with a serving spoon. "So where were you anyway?"

"Where was I? I was at the . . . um . . . the . . ."

Mama Giordano glanced over at Julietta, took in the dusty hem of her skirt. Her disheveled hair. The shadow that seemed to have fallen on her neck. Something . . . no, *everything* . . . about Julietta seemed somehow askew. Mama planted a fist on her hip and leveled a gaze at her daughter. "Where have you been?"

She shrugged, not willing to lie to Mama. At least not blatantly.

Mama's mind was furiously working through the list of eligible Avellinesi boys in the neighborhood, trying to come up with a pairing that made some sort of sense. But the Basso boy was after the Celentano girl and the baker's son was courting the fish-seller's daughter. So who had Julietta been with?

Everyone at the table looked on with great interest. No one more so than Mauro. Julietta hadn't been at the festa, and he knew it. He'd been down every street and alley looking for her. But where *had* she been? And who had she been with? He could see Mama's eyes getting dangerously narrow. He could tell Julietta's knees were beginning to quake. And so he did something he'd never done before in his life. He lied to Mama Giordano. "She was with me. For most of the day."

———

Julietta followed Mauro out into the hall as he left that night. She wasn't quite sure what to say, so she settled on the simplest, most expedient word. "Grazie."

He'd lied to Mama Rossi on her behalf and all she said was *grazie*?! As if he'd done her some kind of favor? He turned around to face her head-on. "Thanks for what? For lying for you? I should have let your mama find you out."

His words caused her to stop in her steps. She blinked.

He set his doctor's bag down and moved toward her. "Who were you with?"

She bit her lip. Then she shook her head. Why should he have to know?

"Don't you think you owe me that? At least?" After making him search for her all day, and worry about her all night? After he'd spent the better part of his morning shaving his face and shining his shoes and pressing his shirt?

She resented being scolded as if she were a child, and kept her eyes trained on the tops of her shoes.

In pure frustration he reached out and grabbed her by the shoulders. "Look at me!" The one fearful glance she sent him did nothing to assuage his fears. "Did he hurt you?"

That caused her gaze to fly toward his. "Ow—no! But you are."

He loosened his grip. "I apologize. But so help me, if he did—"

"He didn't. He wouldn't."

Who was he? Did Mauro know him? Because if he did, he'd put the fear of God into him. Listen to him! Put the fear of God into him? He'd wring the boy's neck with his own two hands!

She shrugged out of his grip. Stepped back. "I'm not a little girl anymore, Mauro. I can take care of myself."

"You have no idea how much I want to hope that's true."

Hope it was true? It was true! "He's not like you. He treats me like a woman."

"Like a woman? By enticing you away from your family, taking you God knows where, and marking you like a—"

"Marking me?"

He wrenched her chin to bare her neck. "Right there. Gentlemen don't do things like that!" Thugs did things like that. To whores. And girls who didn't care enough to stop them.

Che macello! She clapped a hand up to her neck to cover it. She had a mark on her neck? Was that what Angelo had been doing? How was she going to keep Mama from seeing it? And how long would it take to go away?

He was angry at her, frustrated by her, and scared for her. But more than that, he was frightened by her actions and her attitude. Terrified by the thought of her clasped in the arms of a man he did not know.

"Julietta . . ."

She raised her chin. Looked at him. "Leave me alone, Mauro. I know what I'm doing."

21

The day of the festa hadn't been any less eventful for Annamaria. She too had dressed for the occasion. On this one day in all the year, she had abandoned her head scarf in favor of a flower blossom tucked into the middle of her bun. And she tied a colorfully embroidered sash around her slim waist.

Her future suddenly seemed so broad. And bright!

Would she see Rafaello?

She hoped so! Even though he was . . . Sicilian. And Saint Marciano belonged to the Avellinesi. But that didn't mean he wouldn't be at his store, did it? And maybe she could coax Mama into buying a melon today. Just for special.

When Rafaello saw her with the flower and the sash . . . maybe . . . maybe he would smile at her again. Or take up her hand in his!

Her cheeks flamed at the thought as she jostled Theresa for the preeminent place at the window. But her victory was only temporary. They both lost out to Mama when she elbowed them aside. "Such a fine day for Saint Marciano! He must be pleased." She stuck out an arm and gave a vigorous wave to someone Annamaria couldn't see.

"Who is it?" Theresa whispered to Annamaria behind Mama's back.

"I don't know. I can't see!"

There was a scraping sound behind her. Annamaria didn't turn around to look because she thought she might be able to glimpse a view of the street. If she bent at the knees just a little, she could peer through the gap between Mama's upper arm and her body.

"Here!" Theresa shoved something into Annamaria's back.

Annamaria turned.

Theresa was holding out a chair. "Stand on this. Mama won't let me; she knows about Giovanni. But there's no one looking for you."

Oh, but sì, there was! At least she hoped there was. And she almost spoke of it right then, but prudence made her guard her tongue.

"Tell me if you see him!"

Annamaria had already put Theresa completely out of her thoughts. She had Rafaello to look for. A few moments later, as she watched high above Mama's head, she saw him come out of the store and put up the awnings.

Here I am. Look up. Right here. At me.

He did! And she almost toppled from the chair.

"Madonna mia!" Mama turned and looked up at her eldest daughter. "What are you doing up there? If you want to look, just say so. But keep Theresa away from the window. That Giovanni Sardo keeps sniffing around." Mama backed away from the window as Annamaria jumped from the chair and took her place.

"And bring me that chair, Theresa!"

For once, Theresa did some work, leaving Annamaria to revel in the luxury of having the window to herself. She placed her elbows on the windowsill and watched the street below, chin propped up in her hands.

Behind her, Theresa leaned first this way and then that, trying to see down into the street. "Move!"

"Mama said not to."

"Mama said . . . and you always do what Mama says, don't you?"

Annamaria ignored her. Because right at that moment, Rafaello came into view, carrying a crate of eggplants. He glanced across the street, up toward Annamaria, who suddenly found it difficult to breathe.

And then he winked.

Behind her, Theresa gasped. "Was that—did that boy over there wink at you?"

Annamaria pushed way from the windowsill and whirled to face her sister. "What? No."

"He did! That boy from—" She leaned out beyond Annamaria. "From Zanfini's? A Sicilian?"

"He didn't."

"I think he did! Mama!"

Annamaria grabbed Theresa by the forearm. "He didn't wink at me."

"He did."

"He didn't!"

"Then swear on the grave of Saint Marciano himself." Theresa, noting the hesitation in Annamaria's eyes, sensed victory. And a place at the window. "Mama!" She wrenched her arm from her sister's grip.

But Mama Rossi was nowhere to be found.

Annamaria, hard on Theresa's heels, followed her sister out the apartment door. They tore down the stairs, each of them trying to reach the bottom first. And then they burst out into the street, heads swiveling like marionettes, both of them looking for their mother.

Theresa gasped and clutched at Annamaria's hand. "Look! There he is. There's Giovanni!" Had you known him, you might have marveled at the excitement in her voice. But youth have a lamentable way of placing value on all the wrong sorts of things. And Theresa was no exception to that rule.

"Mama said you weren't to—"

"She also said not to talk to Sicilians."

"I never—I never talked to him." Not really. One word didn't count.

"But he winked at you?" With narrowed eyes, she probed Annamaria's gaze. But then her own gaze shifted up and over her sister's shoulder. She lifted a hand and fluttered her fingers in greeting at someone. She squeezed Annamaria's hand. "I won't say anything if you don't say anything."

"About—about what?"

"Exactly!" She gave Annamaria a swift hug and then skipped away past her and disappeared—with Giovanni—into the crowd.

The throng in front of Annamaria parted and there was Mama. Right there! But—she glanced over toward Zanfini's. *He* was there too. He had to be. And if she went back to the window, maybe she'd be able to see him. And he would be able to see her.

But what about Theresa? And Giovanni? Knowing them both, they might just get themselves into some serious trouble. But then, Theresa might land Annamaria in serious trouble too. If she told.

Indecision plagued her. Should she tell Mama? What should she do?

———

Annamaria ran up the stairs just as quickly as she'd run down them. She'd made her decision; she wanted to keep Rafaello to herself. The whole apartment was empty. She positioned herself at the window and soon after saw Rafaello come out of the store once more.

She held her breath as she watched him, willing him to look up.

He did.

He nodded—at her!—and then he proceeded to pick up an apple and polish it with his apron. And then he picked up another. And another. He polished that whole crate of apples, one after the other, all the while looking up at Annamaria.

She didn't quite know what to do.

As her cheeks grew hot, she thought that surely it must be unseemly to stare down across the street at him, but she couldn't seem to make herself do anything else. She thought, perhaps, maybe . . . she could wave at him.

And so she did.

And he saluted her with an apple, touching it to his heart before placing it back into the crate.

She felt a flush wash over her face.

But that wave—and his response—had emboldened her. She leaned forward, out over the window, and she smiled at him.

She did!

A smile so big that it was unmistakable.

And—heaven bless her!—he smiled right back.

Soon the tooting of horns, the rattle of drums, and the roar of a crowd approached. Leaning out the window farther still, she could see Saint Marciano's statue come around the corner, swaying as it was carried by a contingent of Avellinesi men.

When it paused in front of her window, she pinned a dollar on his robe. On behalf of the entire Rossi family. "Please!" She hardly dared voice her wish. But then again, she hardly dared not to. And so, she whispered her prayer as she pinned a dollar onto the statue's robe. "Please, help me, God. Please. With Rafaello Zanfini. Somehow. Some way. Please, God."

As the party of revelers carried the statue down the street, the crowds began to thin. This was her chance! She took a few coins from Mama's jar, enough to cover both the cherries and a melon. And then she went to find Mama.

She sidled up to her and waited for a pause in the conversation.

"Can I get a melon today, Mama? Since it's Saint Marciano's?"

Mama frowned.

"You know how Stefano likes them."

Her face softened. Stefano. Her precious baby boy. "Go ahead. But only one." She shook her head as she watched Annamaria cross the street. A melon. As if they were royalty.

Knowing Rafaello was in the store, waiting for her, imbued Annamaria's every thought with purpose, every movement with grace. Never before had she felt so . . . female. It came to her then that Rafaello didn't really know who she was. He must think she was just a normal girl. A girl like Theresa. She only wished she were.

She entered the store, and as her eyes adjusted to the sudden dimness, she saw Rafaello's back disappear behind a curtained doorway even as she heard someone call his name. Her heart froze. She lingered in the store, hoping he would reappear. He never did. And Mr. Zanfini grew impatient.

She pointed to the crate of melons.

"How many?"

"One." She didn't have the heart not to speak. What did it matter? It was only Mr. Zanfini. She walked back across the street, disappointment weighting her steps. She climbed the stairs up to the Rossi apartment and abandoned the melon on the sideboard.

22

That night Annamaria helped serve dinner at the Sons of Taurasi Hall. And then she helped Mama Rossi clean up afterward. Once Papa and the boys had left for more revelry, and once Mama had found her group of friends, Annamaria walked home to the tenement. Finding it empty, she pushed aside the curtains and sat at the open window, drenched in the silvery light of the summer's moon.

Zanfini's was closed now. The awnings drawn. The store dark.

If only she'd had the chance to see him! Would she have spoken to him again? Maybe . . . sì! Sì, she would have. And she would have said more than just one word.

Her gaze lifted from the store to the windows of the buildings opposite her own. And just there, across the street, one story up and one building down, sat Rafaello, his face glowing in the moonlight. They weren't supposed to speak. No self-respecting Avellinesi should speak to a Sicilian. And they could not meet, save for Annamaria's trips to the frutta e verdura, but no one could stop them from staring out the window at each other, if they chose to, of a night. And so they did. And when Rafaello burst into song, when the notes of a lilting melody drifted across the street to her window, Annamaria knew—she knew with a certainty borne of true love—that he sang those words just for her.

She couldn't understand the words; no one on her side of the street could. The song was an ancient one, sung in the Sicilian dialect. But everyone who heard them understood their meaning. You would have to, for he was singing of love. Amazing love. Fantastical love. An all-consuming love that was born when the world first began, a love that would venture to the very gates of hell—past the gates of hell!—in honor of its beloved's heart.

Children who were playing in the street below, liberated from the night's chores by the festa, soon ceased their games. Passersby stopped to listen. Even the wind ceased its teasing gusts. One old nonna cheered as Rafaello finished his song. Insisted that he sing one song more.

He did.

And then he sang another. And another one after that.

But long about midnight Mama Rossi came home, Theresa in tow, and insisted that Annamaria go to bed. "No good ever came from sitting in front of a window at this late hour. You'll catch your death. Go to bed."

"I'm going, Mama."

But before she did, she pulled the flower from her hair. Held it out over the casement and let it fall three stories to the street below. She didn't dare to look at Rafaello as she did it. She was much too timid for such obvious displays of affection.

After Annamaria had left her window, Rafaello dashed down four flights of stairs and out into the street. Rescued her flower from the sidewalk and tucked it in his pocket. Flowers and amorous glances were not for him. They did well enough for the moment, for he was in no hurry. But he knew, son of a greengrocer that he was, that things happened for a reason. That nothing flowered and fruited and ripened except when it had a purpose. So he would sing, and he would watch, and he would wait. But he had no intention of surrendering such newfound love as was his to some ancient idea of honor. Not here. Not in America. Not when he had just come to discover the very meaning of life itself.

The parade had long passed by. Night had fallen, and now even the drunks had stumbled home to their beds. At last Luciana could open her window. And leave it open for the rest of the night. She hadn't wanted to do it when boisterous groups of young men and raucous throngs of boys had still been roaming the streets. Who knew what menacing elements lurked in those crowds?

As she pushed at the window, it creaked in protest and then stubbornly jammed halfway up. Try as she might, she couldn't get it to budge. But at least she could feel the cool of the outside air. Luciana pulled the contessa's chair closer to the window, folded her arms atop the frame, and set her chin on them. She looked down into the shadowed street.

At least the contessa slept soundly in their bed. That was one thing to be thankful for. And there was so little to be thankful for these days.

What about in Roma? Had she ever once thought to be grateful for all those luxuries? All those things she had thought were necessities. Had she ever really appreciated them? What she wouldn't give for . . . a down-filled pillow. Or her carved and gilded bed. For even one pair of pumps, one gown, from her closet filled with clothes. Clothes and shoes that had been replaced in their entirety twice a year. She could have clothed the entire tenement building with her castoffs. And maybe even the building next door.

But they were alive, weren't they?

And there were some good things that had happened. Some things to be grateful for. There was . . . Madame Fortier. At least Luciana was getting paid. For something she didn't mind doing. And there was . . . Julietta.

Her lips quirked at the thought of the girl. How she'd hurried

Luciana down to the Settlement House and signed her up for a class. And she'd been persuaded to make over the ivory gown. And the others ones as well. That was another thing to be thankful for. She didn't have to wear the old yellow satin.

Had she truly once thought it was pretty?

She thought of other things too. Of the picture in the strega's house. How lovely it had been to look upon a painting again. And to stand, for just a moment, in a place of elegance and refinement. She had not known how much she had missed the estate—the house itself—in Roma.

And thinking of the estate led her again to the loss of the family's jewels. How she could use them now! And she could put them to better use than adorning her neck and wrists and fingers for parties and receptions and balls. *Magari!* What a fortune a pile of jewels like Mrs. Quinn's could fetch! And how long that small fortune could keep her and the contessa in food. And clothing. The old woman couldn't go much longer wearing her peasant's blouse and skirt. Not with autumn approaching and winter's chill to follow soon after.

What a price those gems would bring.

She sighed, pushed back the chair, and went into the bedroom. Crawling into bed, she faced the contessa's back and closed her eyes, vowing to think of other things. Things lovely and charming and gay. Things like . . . the strega's son.

When she'd been with him, she'd felt like her old self again. Such startling green eyes he had. And such a firm chin. With generous lips that seemed always to curve with good humor . . . though it often seemed his amusement came at her expense. But he did have the most noble of noses. A nose any Roman would be proud to claim. One that started from the spot between his brows and gradually curved to a decided tip at its end. An altogether agreeable son . . . born to an altogether disagreeable woman.

She wondered: Had he approached her in Roma, would he

have wanted to dance? Would he have asked to call. . . if he had known her as she was?

She turned away from the contessa and curled into a ball. As she surrendered to sleep, she prayed that God would spare her, this one night, from reliving her memories of *that* night. That this night she would be able to sleep the sleep of the innocent.

Or the dead.

But several hours later, she awoke to the percussion of an enormous thud. A dozen smaller concussions followed on its heels, rattling the window.

She knew the sound. She knew the vibrations. She knew exactly what it was.

O God! Please, save us!

She pushed from the bed, ran to the window, and peered out into the dark. Above the roof of the building across the street she could see a ghostly cloud rising to blot out the moon. A cloud that was soon lit with the flames of a fire beneath it, glowing as it hung there, suspended in the sky. Her nose wrinkled at the acrid odor. She saw people pour from the tenements into the street. Trembling, she wrestled with the window. Banged on it with her elbow. Finally managed to pull it down. Then she went back into the bedroom and shut the door. Got into bed and wrapped her arms around the still-sleeping contessa. She did not need any more information to know what the sound had been.

A bomb.

A bomb just like the one that had changed her life forever.

That night had begun like a hundred others before it. There was nothing to suggest to Luciana that anything had been about to change. There had been a dinner at the prime minister's mansion, dancing in the ballroom afterward. A ride in a motorcar back through town beneath the pale glow of a spring moon.

And there had been a man lurking in the bushes by the house.

She had blushed when she'd seen him; she knew him. He was one of the people her father had brought home. The count collected eccentrics and artists, scholars and zealots. She'd been flattered by the newcomer's attentions. Who would not have been? He was young. He was handsome. And he had existed apart from her world of society and balls. Her fascination with him, her attraction to him, had been all the greater for it.

It made her want to retch now.

But she hadn't known anything, any of it, that night, so she had looked at him as they had passed by in the motorcar. As he touched a hand to his heart.

She had been thinking of him still, of how the moon had lit the planes of his face when her father had escorted her and her grandmother to the steps of the house. But she'd paused before climbing them. She'd actually taken a step backward, thinking that she might be able to steal away, unnoticed, to spend a moment with the man. At least to steal a kiss.

But he had already begun to stroll away.

She had sent one last lingering look out into the night as she began to walk up the stairs. As she looked up toward the house, the silhouettes of her father and her grandmother had been thrown into high relief.

She had felt a sudden, scorching heat.

And then she saw.

She saw . . . she saw the flames shoot up over the top of her father's neck—his neck!—for his head was no longer there. And then his body had pitched forward into that consuming blaze. Grandmother had stood there for one long moment, outlined in flames, and then had crumpled into a heap.

Luciana remembered running up the last of the steps, taking up her grandmother's arm, and pulling her down into the drive.

And then she remembered no more. Remembered nothing more until she had awakened in the home of a family friend.

She was told that her father had been assassinated.

Assassinated!

Just like their beloved King Umberto. Just like the Russian Tsar, Alexander II. Like the French president, the American president, and two Spanish prime ministers. Elizabeth, Empress of Austria and Queen of Hungary. The king of Greece and Archduke Ferdinand of Austria. Just like them, her own dear papa had become a victim of the anarchists' rage.

They told her the resultant fire had swept through the main floor of the house. That her grandmother, though bowed by grief, was alive. That the house could be repaired, although technically it now belonged to her father's cousin, the new Count of Roma.

She had lain there in that bed for a week, trying to grapple with the life that had been left her, a girl orphaned and title-less, without inheritance or means. Trying to determine which of her sometime suitors might still be persuaded to ask for her hand. And whether her cousin might be coaxed into supplying a dowry.

But though she had lain there for the week, her cousin had never sent a motorcar to collect them. Or offered any other sign of largesse. He'd never bothered to contact them at all. She had finally recovered strength enough to go to the estate and beg a meeting with him when the letter had found her.

Written on pink paper it was addressed to Luciana. And it was brief.

> There will be bloodshed; we will not dodge; there will have to be murder; we will kill, because it is necessary; there will have to be destruction; never hope that the carabinieri and your hounds will ever succeed in ridding the country of the anarchistic germ that pulses in our veins. . . . Long live social revolution! Down with tyranny.

And to the letter he had signed his name. That was how she'd known it was him. And that was when Luciana had decided to flee.

The anarchists were everywhere. They were as numerous as fleas and as insidious as the plague. From them, there was no recourse. There was no place to hide when someone could snuff out the life of a person simply by blowing them up with a bomb. There were no policemen that could be called for protection, no guards that could make any difference when an anarchist was bent on murder.

What grievous sin had her father committed, had she harbored, that she had been targeted by such a murderer? Was it because they had been born to their positions? To wealth? Was it because they had the gall to socialize with others of the same station? Or the unforgiveable impudence to be inclined to keep the government the way it was? To retain power in the hands of the people who could manage it? To support the monarchy?

Luciana knew all about the anarchists' philosophies. She had learned them from her association with *him*. That murderer! She had almost started to believe that he was right. And, most damning of all, she had thought him mysterious and charming and handsome. But she had not known that he had intended to blow them all up.

What would have happened if she'd spurned his advances from the first? Would he have gone away? Left them alone? Perhaps not. He'd entered their circle at her father's invitation, after all. Papa had thought the man brilliant, if misguided. But if she were given just one wish, she would use it to refuse him. To rebuff that very first smile he had given her.

If only she had known!

There was only one way she had known to survive: She needed to lose herself, to hide her identity. To go somewhere he could never find her. And so she did what a million of her countrymen had already done. She and her grandmother had plunged into the great emigration. She had disguised them as peasants, and they had slipped around whatever watchmen had been posted and they had escaped, through steerage class, to America. Once onshore, she had simply immersed them in the disembarking throngs and followed along until they had arrived in the North End. And that was where she had planned on staying.

Now she didn't know what to do.

She had thought, she had hoped, that being an immigrant in Boston might be the perfect disguise. But the bombs had found her again, and she had seen him walking down her own street. There was no other place to which she could run. She would just have to be very careful. And perhaps she might even have to pray.

23

Madame Fortier, living as she was outside the North End, had forgotten that there was even such a thing as a festa for Saint Marciano. She had long ago put such country ways behind her. No respectable woman would take part in such things, pinning money onto a statue and parading it through the streets. It was all just a little too undignified.

A little bit too Italian.

She had tried, with a zeal that bordered on obsession, to erase every trace of her parentage. Being Italian had cost her . . . everything. But that morning the streets were aflutter with news of a bomb. Another one. Planted by the fiendish anarchists. Probably fiendish *Italian* anarchists.

Right there. In their very midst.

It was bad. Very bad, indeed.

Those anarchists could cost her everything she had gained. If her clients became afraid to come downtown . . . well, perhaps she would have to change her policies. Perhaps she would have to go to them. It defeated the purpose of having established herself on Temple Place, but she might not be left with any other choice.

As she sat in her dining room drinking tea, she heard the

sound of church bells giving warning of the approaching hour. She hadn't been to mass in a great number of years. Too many years to think of. Too many years now to be able to venture back inside the church. What had been done was done. Why regret it, after so many years? Except that . . . she almost . . . missed it. Almost missed the sound of the priest chanting, the smell of incense as it rose from the censer. She missed the old and familiar liturgy. Missed being surrounded by friends, by neighbors. There was a certain confidence, a sense of community gained, in knowing every person in the pews.

Indeed, she missed herself. She missed the person that she had been all those years ago. The person she had tried so hard to forget. But that was an anathema to all that she had become since then, and so she did not dare to recognize that emotion for what it truly was. She simply turned her back on all those people, all those memories, and took another sip of tea.

On Monday morning, after all her girls had filed up the back stairs and the sound of the morning's chatter had given way to the whir of sewing machines, Madame opened a wardrobe in her office to search for an old sample book. She had to rummage back into the depths of it, and in doing so she brushed up against a gown.

The gown.

And she did something she had rarely ever done. She pulled it from the closet and brought it out into the light of the room. Examined it in the same way she would have examined any of her other creations. It wasn't bad. Not for her first attempt at a wedding gown. In fact, it was rather good. Inspired, she might have once said.

Her lips twisted at the thought.

Now that it was revealed in all its splendor, she felt a bit foolish for having hidden it away for all those years. It was only a gown after all. What harm could it do anyone now? And why shouldn't it be allowed to do some good?

Why shouldn't it?

Clutching the hanger in her hand and draping the heavy material over an arm, she began the climb to the third floor workshop.

"I have a proposition."

The girls looked up at the sound of Madame's voice.

"I have, in this shop, a wedding gown that has never been worn." She held it up in front of them as she spoke, and then walked forward to lay it on the table before them.

Julietta swept her embroidery out of the way. It was gorgeous. And oh, how she wanted to touch it! It was old. She knew it at a glance. Overlaid with silk-embroidered net, the gown was a confection of lace and beaded braid that must have cost Madame a hundred hours' work. But really, with a few tucks here and there, it wouldn't look too old-fashioned. It had only the slightest suggestion of puffed sleeves, and if the lace around the throat were removed, leaving only the v of the lace collar, it could look decidedly elegant.

Madame read their faces, each one of them, and she was pleased. "I will offer it to any of you. To all of you. To whichever one of you marries first." Sì. That's what she would do. So that some good could come from all the bad. From all the disappointments and regrets.

Annamaria looked upon the gown as Luciana had looked upon Mrs. Quinn's painting. She admired the gown and appreciated the handiwork, but she did it with the detachment of a person without means. A person who is forever looking without one hope of possessing. She liked it, but she did not allow herself—not for one moment—to imagine what it would be like to wear it.

Julietta, of course, did quite the opposite. She could barely restrain herself from trying it on. In Julietta's mind, it was already hers. She could see herself in it. She could feel herself in it. If she could have possessed it through sheer force of will and wishful thinking, she would have done it right then.

Luciana was the only one who spoke. "It's lovely." Such a beautiful, ethereal thing. It was meant for the happiest of occasions, the most felicitous of celebrations. "Whose was it?" And why had it never been worn?

At once Madame realized her mistake. She had let her guard down, had cracked open the door of her heart to these women—forgetting that in doing so, she had no choice but to reveal herself. "Does it matter?" She tried to smile as she swept the gown from the table. "It's never been worn." Never been worn. The saddest of tales. A wedding gown that had never seen its own wedding.

As Madame retreated back down the stairs with the dress, Luciana's question remained suspended in the air between them. Whose was it? And why had it never been worn?

———

That night, Annamaria came home to a celebration. "What's happened, Mama?" She caught Mama Rossi's arm as the woman danced around the small room, glass held high in an ongoing toast.

"It's Theresa."

"What about her?"

"She's getting married!"

Married!? But . . . Theresa was so young. Younger than Annamaria, in any case. "To . . . ?"

"To Giovanni, of course!"

Giovanni Sardo? The one Annamaria was supposed to have kept her away from? "But she's only seventeen!"

"And I was only fifteen when I married your papa."

Fifteen. Seventeen. It made Annamaria feel old beyond her years at the age of twenty-two. As the eldest, it was true that no one would expect her to marry, but at the moment that expectation seemed patently unfair. Why should Theresa be able to marry? Why should Theresa be able to engender the good wishes of everyone in the family, while Annamaria was only given shirts with holes to be mended and dirtied plates to wash?

The thought that had been formed in the bowels of the basement began to pulse in her head. It wasn't fair. And she *would* say something about it . . . just perhaps not tonight.

As she looked around at her family's smiling faces, as she saw Theresa and Giovanni look at each other with such barefaced love, Annamaria's scarf felt as if it were choking her. She loosened the knot. Pulled it off and flung it into the corner.

Papa Rossi handed her a glass.

She took it, raised it in Theresa's direction. "*Felicitazioni.*"

Her sister smiled and then turned back toward Giovanni.

After that, no one else looked at Annamaria. No one turned to her and teased her about when it would be her turn. No one wondered when they would be raising a glass to her happiness. She took a sip from her glass. Normally, she liked the fruitiness of Papa Rossi's wine, but that evening it seemed rather bitter.

She set her glass down on the table, took up her scarf, and tied it under her chin once more.

"Where are you going?" At least Mama had noticed her leaving.

"To get some tomatoes."

"But we don't need—"

Too late. Annamaria had already gone.

———

Annamaria had meant to go to Zanfini's. She even crossed the street. Rafaello saw her coming and retied his apron strings around his waist. But when it came time to actually enter the store, she couldn't do it. She couldn't enter into that oasis of cucumbers and spinach. She couldn't bear to look on *him*. On all the joy that was forever out of reach. Oh, she might be able to convince her family to free her from her obligations, or at least to lessen them, but she knew she would never be able to convince them to let her marry a Sicilian. Even as she heard herself think the word *marriage*, her cheeks flared with the audacity of such presumption.

So she walked on past while she cursed the day of her birth.

The day that had made her the eldest daughter in the Rossi family.

If only she'd been born second. If only she were her sister. If she were Theresa, she would be planning her wedding right now. Right this minute. And she would have the privilege of wearing Madame's beautiful gown.

Rafaello watched her pass. Saw the tears that marked her cheeks.

He bolted from the store.

Mr. Zanfini frowned. Followed him to yell out the door. "Rafaello! What about the figs!"

Rafaello didn't even hear him. He jogged to catch up with Annamaria. Tapped her on the arm once he did.

She turned toward him. And then she turned away. Quick enough, she hoped, to keep him from seeing her tears.

But his hand reached out in front of her, offering a handkerchief. "*Per favore.*"

That he—of all people—should see her! Her shoulders convulsed in a despairing sob.

"Per favore. Let me help you."

Help her? He was the problem. If only . . .

"What is it?"

She turned, handkerchief pressed to an eye. There was no point in pretending. "I wish . . . I wish I wasn't me."

"But if there wasn't you, then who would I dream about?" He put a hand into the pocket of his apron and withdrew the flower that she had dropped all those days ago. Held it out to her.

"Rafaello! The figs!"

He sighed, took a step back, and yelled over his shoulder, "I'm coming!" His heart ached as he looked at her. He had no right to take her into his arms, and there was nothing more that he could say. And so he offered her the one last thing he had: He smiled. And then he turned to walk away.

But she reached out and plucked the sleeve of his shirt. When he turned, she gave the flower back to him. "It was meant for you."

He looked down into her eyes. Took the flower from her. Nodded. Placed it back into his pocket. And then he left.

He hadn't spoken more than a few words, but he left her feeling cherished.

She pressed herself against a tenement wall, handkerchief clutched to her chest as a group of children skipped past. Stepped down into the street to avoid a dog who was snuffling through garbage.

If only . . . if only she could be free.

Maybe if Papa had more money. Maybe if he could finally buy the apartment. Or even a house. If he owned a house, then maybe they wouldn't depend upon her so much. They wouldn't need the money her job provided. And maybe, if they could stop working so hard, it would make it easier for some of the others to give Mama a hand now and then. Then Annamaria would have the freedom to . . . why . . . do anything!

That's what money bought. It bought freedom. Money in quantities like that strega, Mrs. Quinn, had. To think that she could afford to attach real jewels to her gowns the way Annamaria had attached money to the statue of Saint Marciano at the festa! Imagine that. Imagine what a small fortune a pile of jewels like that would bring. Such wonderful freedom.

She could pay someone else to perform her duties.

And maybe then, if Papa and Mama could meet Rafaello, they would see that he wasn't such a Sicilian after all.

When Annamaria returned to the apartment, Mama and Theresa pounced on her.

"You have to help me with my dress!"

"You need to help Theresa with her dress."

Annamaria blinked. What dress? Hadn't she just finished mending Vittorio's shirt and undoing the hem on Stefano's trousers? There hadn't been a dress in the pile. In fact, Theresa didn't even own a dress. "What dress?"

"My wedding dress! Annamaria, you have to help me. You know I'm no good at sewing."

Her wedding . . . "I can't." I won't. You know as well as I do, that's what she really wanted to say.

"Of course you can. That's all you do all day at that fancy shop where you work."

"I do smocking, not sewing."

"I want something beautiful, something . . . well, something white, of course. You'll make it for me, won't you, Annamaria? I was thinking, if you could find some lace? And some pretty rosettes for the skirt?"

Annamaria stood there listening to Theresa babble, and it came to her that this is what her life would be like if she didn't do anything to change it. She would forever be told what everyone else wanted and how it was that she should meet those demands. And she decided right then that she couldn't stand it any longer.

"*I* was thinking that I might get married myself someday soon and that you and the boys would be able to help take care of Mama and Papa."

"Wha-at?"

"As they get older. When it comes time."

"Married?" Mama stared at her, slack-jawed.

"You?" Theresa was looking at her as if she'd suddenly sprouted horns.

Mama, having realized what Annamaria must be talking about, was all smiles. "Married once we've passed, Papa and I. Of course you'd get married then, though you can't blame me if I hope it's not too soon in coming."

"What did you mean, 'help' you?" Theresa had taken a step away from her sister.

"What I meant was that if we all work together at taking care of our family, then no one person would have to do it all alone."

Mama and Theresa glanced at each other, and then they turned to stare at her.

"*I* wouldn't have to do it all alone." There. She'd said it. And what a very great relief that had been. Of course she shouldn't have to do it all alone. Why had she been suffering so long in silence when it had been that easy to make everyone understand?

"But—you mean—you want me to help—*you?*" Theresa turned toward Mama Rossi. "She can't do that, can she? Just completely refuse to take care of you? Giovanni wouldn't marry me if he thought we'd have to take care of you. And Papa."

"Hush now." Mama patted Theresa on the arm. Then she turned toward Annamaria. "Stop your foolish talk. Don't you love your sister?"

"Of course I love her!" As much as anyone could love a self-absorbed, selfish seventeen-year-old girl.

"Do you want her to get married in that old blouse and skirt? Because that's what she'll have to do. If you don't help her."

"Of course not!"

"Do you really want people to think the Rossis aren't as good as the Sardos?"

"I didn't mean—"

"Good! We knew you'd do it."

"I can't—"

"Of course you can." Mama leaned close. "And anything you do will be much better than Theresa could do by herself." Mama winked as she nodded. She kissed Annamaria on the cheek. "You're such a good girl." She took Theresa by the hand and moved to join the others.

"I can't. And I won't. If Theresa wants a dress, then you and she will have to make it yourselves. I'm sorry, but I don't have the time." Or the inclination.

As Mama and Theresa stood there, mouths open, Annamaria stepped past them and went to join the rest of the family.

24

While Annamaria had been climbing the stairs to the Rossi apartment, Julietta was attending a meeting with Angelo. She'd been buoyed beyond relief when he had waved to her that morning near Zanfini's. Thankfully, he hadn't mentioned one word about their time in his shack. Or her neck, though it might have been nice to have been given an apology. Her toes still curled with shame.

She wasn't quite sure what to think of herself. Or of him.

He'd crossed the street when he'd seen her that morning and told her he wanted to introduce her to his friends. Not that he'd said it in quite those words. He'd urged her to attend an important meeting about the problem of the capitalists and the solution to the war.

An important meeting.

She imagined she knew what *that* would involve: sharing a stolen moment out behind the Sons of Avellino Hall. Watching while the boys played *morra* down in the alley. Even bystanding while a game of bocce ball was being played. She was amenable to any of those.

But it turned out that Angelo's meeting truly was a meeting.

And those friends of his! They were taking turns yelling at each other, eyes lit with an enthusiasm, a nearly religious zeal, that Julietta didn't understand. It wasn't money they were after. Julietta would have sympathized with that. Applauded it, even. There were such lovely, lovely things that money could buy.

But these people seemed to despise such vain pursuits.

She wished she could think of something clever to say. It wasn't in her nature to sit quietly in a room, letting everyone else have all the attention. They were speaking of capitalists, in a tone of voice that Mama Giordano usually reserved for the Settlement House ladies. And they seemed to be equally disdainful of the rich as they were of the poor—the people who did not have to work for their living and those who did. Which left Julietta feeling just a little bit confused. If they didn't want to work for a living and they didn't want to be rich, then what, exactly, did they want?

All the talk, all the shouting, the complaining, reminded her of Little Matteo when he was sulking. He didn't want this thing and he didn't want that thing; he didn't really want to be made happy at all. He just wanted to enjoy his fit of bad temper. And if he could kick somebody in the shins as he did so, all the better.

No. She really didn't understand it at all.

When they'd first come, before all the people had started in about politics, everyone had seemed very sociable. Quite friendly. There were several seamstresses from shops on Hanover Street. Another deliveryman, like Angelo. Several fellows who worked at the paving yard. Some university students. And one they called Pick. A pick and shovel man, probably. Like half the immigrants in the North End.

It was with no little regret that she marked the passing of time as the meeting went on and on. And on. She tried to concentrate on what they were all saying, talking over one another and beating the table with their fists now and then. She might not have understood exactly what it was they were hoping to accomplish, but one thing was certain the longer she listened: They hated the rich with a much greater passion than they despised the poor. And there, she could agree with them. For in her experience, the rich were those like Mrs. Quinn, who came into Madame's shop and barked orders at everyone. And a second thing was certain as well: Angelo was held in high regard by most of them for the access he had to his employer's truck. And for something he'd done back in Roma before he'd emigrated.

She looked over at him, struck once again by the beauty in the raw planes of his face. By the passion in his eyes. As he sat there, intent upon the words of the speaker, listening with such active concentration, he fairly glowed with righteous indignation. And if she heard him say words like *destruction* and *bloodshed* as he talked, she was able to convince herself that he really didn't mean them.

"Down with tyranny! Long live the revolution!"

———

"What did you think of the meeting?" There's nothing Angelo would have liked better than to have pulled Julietta into his arms, then and there. But he'd arranged to do some business with his anarchist friends, and he didn't have the time right then.

Julietta shrugged. Smiled. It wouldn't do to tell him what she really thought, and so she said nothing at all.

"I can't stand all those rich people parading about town with their fancy clothes and all their money and lists of rules. This is America. The Land of Plenty. Plenty of miseria, I'd say!"

"Not that much miseria. My papa owns our apartment. He never did in Avellino."

"Your papa ought to own a house! All of us ought to. But the government is against us. Can't you see how they're trying to oppress us? So many have so much, but even more—even worse—so many have so little. And you can see how very little those who have so much have done for the rest of us. They scoff and despise."

They? Surely he wasn't talking about actual people. She sent him a sharp glance, but she didn't see in him anything different than she always had. Anything more than his glittering dark eyes, thick curly hair, and full sensuous lips. And in any case, Julietta didn't consider herself poor, not by any means . . . though were she to come into extra money, she knew what she would do with it.

She did know something about oppression, though. And the excesses of the wealthy. "There was a rich lady, come into the shop just the other day. She came with a bag filled with jewels. All colors and sizes! And left it for Madame to sew onto her clothes. As if she wanted to be a piece of jewelry herself. Can you imagine!"

"A bag of jewels?" He slid a glance toward her. A whole bag? That was unlikely.

"A whole bag. With . . ." What had Madame called them? "Rubies and garnets and the blue ones . . ." What had Luciana called them? "Sapphires. She's a real strega, that woman!"

"They're all stregas. All the rich ones. How else could they contrive to keep all that money to themselves? But does she always do that? The shop owner, I mean. Keep her clients' jewels?" Angelo despised the rich, just as much as his friends did, but he was willing to admit that it took money to finance a revolution. And he was able to appreciate the irony of exacting that money from the very people he was fighting against.

"No. No! She was upset about it. One of the girls said Madame had tried to talk the woman out of it, but the strega wouldn't be persuaded. You know how the rich are. Anyway . . ." She linked an arm through his.

As you've probably suspected, Julietta didn't know how the rich were any more than she knew how Americans were. But she was done talking about the shop. She wanted to talk about Angelo. And the next time they might be able to see each other.

Luciana had stopped by the grocer's on her way home from work. She had finally been able to stop asking Madame for an advance on her pay. That meant she could bring home something more than just bread and cheese for dinner.

To her mind, if trouble were to find her in a store, it would be better than finding her on the street. For at least then she would have the chance to ask someone for help. So she took her time selecting a bottle of milk for the contessa and two eggs for their breakfast. She asked the grocer to measure out four ounces of a tube-shaped maccheroni. She hadn't tried cooking noodles before, but she didn't suppose they would be so very difficult to make. She'd seen the grocer weigh piles of them for customers before. She went into the frutta e verdura on her street as well and bought a zucchini and a handful of greens.

Laden with packages, she entered her building and walked up the flights of stairs. She stepped around a pile of refuse in the hallway, then paused to lean the bottle of milk against her thigh as she turned the key in the lock. Setting her packages on the sideboard, she slipped off her scarf and went to greet the contessa.

But . . . the woman wasn't in her chair.

"Contessa?"

Nothing.

"Nonna?"

She hurried into the bedroom, but the woman wasn't there either. Where had—? She knelt on the floor, looked under the bed. She ran back into the first room. But her grandmother was not there.

Had her father's murderer finally discovered where they lived?

Terror coursed through her veins.

He had to have left a note. He'd left one before. She ran her hands across the table, pushed all the food from the sideboard, searched everywhere she could think of for a note. Then she ran back into the bedroom, tore the blanket and sheets from the bed. Stripped the pillows from their cases. Upended the mattress.

But there was nothing.

25

Luciana swept her scarf back over her head, rushed down the stairs and into the street. "Have you seen my nonna?" She asked the question of everyone she met, the number of which were rapidly declining as the reach of the shadows was lengthening. People were going home for the night. Merchants were closing up their shops.

"Have you seen my grandmother?"

Answers to that question soon led her to the western end of North Bennet Street. And from there, up Salem Street, then to Charter Street. Apparently, an old woman had wandered that far. And no, she had not seemed to be in the company of anyone in particular.

The contessa had stopped, for a time, to watch a group of children jumping rope.

She had paused at a fish seller's and asked him about his eels. Tried to buy a bun from the baker, telling him to send the bill to her son, the Count of Roma. The shopkeeper had laughed as he told her that.

But once Luciana had reached the corner at Commercial Street, her grandmother might as well have vanished. No one else had reported seeing her. And, truthfully, there was nowhere else for her to have gone. In front of Luciana ran an expanse of railroad tracks, and across the tracks several trolley sheds. To her right was a slaughterhouse, the stench of which pierced her nose and roiled her stomach. Had the contessa come this far, and she undoubtedly had, Luciana ought to have seen her. There was nowhere for her to hide.

Where had her grandmother gone?

The sun had already begun to disappear behind the roofs of distant buildings. The remaining rays of light were retreating from the scene before her. A train rumbled by above her, sending a shower of soot cascading down upon her.

There were so few places to look and even those few places were quickly being consumed by shadows.

O *Signore, aiutaci a* . . . O God, help us to . . .

She paused, raised her eyes toward heaven.

Help me to . . . please. Help me to find my nonna.

It was the first time in a long time that she had prayed to God. And it was the first time she had ever prayed for something for herself. The very first time she had ever deviated from the Church's standard, scripted incantations, and she didn't know what to say. Didn't know what words to use. She only knew that among the tens of thousands of people in the North End that evening, the search for just one could not be very important and very likely not worth Signore's time. But didn't He know all? Didn't He see all? And even if He hadn't concerned himself with Luciana before, couldn't He, even now, direct her steps to the place where her grandmother had gone? Didn't He owe her at least that?

She closed her eyes, took a deep breath. Then opened them.

Luciana stepped into the street and crossed the road. Started across the railroad tracks. She still didn't know where to look, and she was more than a little bit frightened by the idea of whom she might encounter in her search, but she knew she had to find her grandmother. And she had just prayed for help.

But could she trust God?

She had to. There was no one else to help her.

She peered into the trolley sheds. Walked the fence line of a massive storage tank. Picked her way across the city's paving yard.

Stopped in at the fire station.

"Have you seen my—"

And there was the contessa, sitting at a table, firemen standing in a half circle behind her. "*Suppli! Abbacchio alla scottadito!*" She had raised a hand, gesturing as if to a servant. Nonna wanted supper. Rice croquettes and lamb chops, to be specific. Apparently, she had been asking for them for quite some time; her voice was sharp with annoyance.

"*Mi scusino . . .*" Luciana stepped over the threshold and into the room.

All eyes turned in her direction.

"Ah! Ragazza. I don't like this place. They won't serve me any food. I keep asking and asking for supper, and they won't bring me anything. Take me somewhere else." She stood with great dignity. And then she glowered at the men. "*Imbecilli!*"

Luciana extended a hand.

The contessa slapped it away. She lifted her chin, collected her skirts, and walked out the door. Luciana tipped her head toward the men, then hurried to follow her around the building and over the railroad tracks as the woman retraced the elaborate series of twists and turns that she must have taken to arrive at the station.

They stopped in front of the now-shuttered bakery. Paused in the doorway of the fish seller. Peered down a darkened alley where, two hours before, a group of girls had played at jumping rope.

Once home, the contessa sat in her chair in front of the window. "I'll have the suppli and the abbacchio alla scottadito."

What she got was some less-than-tender maccheroni, some zucchini, and a plate of greens. But she ate it all without a disparaging word, then meekly went to bed.

———

It was only later that evening, once the contessa had fallen into a deep sleep, that Luciana remembered her prayer. She had prayed, straight to Signore, by herself. And He had responded, not to some lofty-sounding petition from one of his priests, but to a plea that Luciana had uttered on her own.

Maybe He did care after all.

Grazie, Signore.

But though the contessa lay beside her, blessedly given to sleep, Luciana's problems had not been resolved. Not all of them. What about tomorrow? What if the contessa found her way outside once more? And what if she left the North End this time? What if she wandered out into the city at large? A world that would not understand an old woman's Italian mutterings? To people that would not know what to make of her words?

Luciana rolled from the bed and went to sit in the contessa's chair. She stared out the window, seeing nothing at all in that thick, hot, inky darkness.

She would have to find someone to watch her grandmother. Perhaps . . . weren't there dozens of young mothers in the building? But who among them had the time or inclination to keep an eye on her wandering nonna when they had their own children to mind?

It would be different if her grandmother, or Luciana, had some skill that could be exchanged for the favor. An extra enticement that she could offer for the trouble. But what skills did the contessa have that would lessen the responsibilities of some young mother? The contessa had never changed a diaper or cleaned a child's dirty face in her life.

Their situation would not have been so dire in Roma, with servants and diversions without number. Back there she might have devoted a servant or two to the contessa's care. Or even cared for her grandmother herself. In Roma, Luciana had nothing but time. And she had been able to give, to dispense it, as she'd pleased.

Her time now had to be used to earn money.

Why hadn't she given more serious thought to learning English back then? She used to laugh, she and her friends, at the hundreds of Englishmen and Americans who had trooped through Roma on their way to the ruins at Pompeii. They had watched them—those uncivilized, restive Americans—as they were dragged by local *terroni* all over the city. Over here: The Forum. And over there: The Coliseum. And right here, in front of you, all of the local beauties who are laughing at your uncivilized behavior. Why should she have had to learn the language of such a brash and uncouth people? That's what she had told her father, the count.

He had laughed and nodded. "Why, indeed? Our people were educating barbarians and conquering continents before their own was even discovered." Why, indeed?

Oh, the bitterness of hindsight! Oh, the irony of fate!

Maybe . . . should she go to the police? Tell them what happened in Roma? And that the man who had done it was here? She didn't know enough English yet, not enough to be able to explain all of that. But even when she did, if the American police were anything like the Carabinieri in Roma—and she had no reason to think that they wouldn't be—the voice of one lone woman would mean very little. Not if it weren't backed by power. Or money.

Once both had flowed from her hands the way the strega's jewels had poured from that pouch. But now she had neither.

She bowed her head, wishing she would never have to lift

it again. That daylight would never come, that she would never again have to shoulder the burden of their survival.

But it was no use regretting lost opportunities. No use in wishing for the past. There was only here and now. There was a job in a gown shop and a package of maccheroni on the sideboard. A bed to sleep in and a chair to sit on.

One young ragazza and one old contessa.

She returned to the bed, closed her eyes, and prayed once more.

God had listened the first time. Perhaps He would listen again.

Please, Signore. If I had money, I would know what to do with it, but I have none. I need help. If not your own, then someone else's. I don't know what to do.

26

The next day, a Tuesday, Madame signed for a box, instructed the deliveryman to place it in the back room, then gave him a tip. Once he had gone, she opened it up and peeled back layers of tissue.

Bene.

The fabric for Mrs. Quinn's gown. She would have one of the girls on the second floor cut it and then she could give the collar to Luciana for beading. She placed a hand atop the gray-colored material, stroked its lustrous length. It was perfect. Perfect for the season, perfect for the style, perfect for the strega. The woman could be nothing but pleased.

Lifting the length from the box, she took it up to the second floor, asking that the pieces be returned to her immediately upon their cutting. Several hours later, one of the girls appeared at the edge of the shop floor. Madame waited until she had finished with her client to address the girl. And even then, she didn't take the material from her. She cleared her desk of papers and ordered the pieces set down on top of it.

There was always something a little bit daunting about a stack of pieces. Something that felt a bit like trepidation . . . and excitement. Shot through with anxiety. Would they all come together the way they had been meant to? Would the gown actually fit the person it was intended for? And would the client like the result? Madame always enjoyed sitting, for just a moment, in front of the pieces and imagining herself a great, magical sorceress, breathing the gown into being. She didn't do the sewing anymore. But it was still her hands, her genius, that produced the gowns made in the shop.

As Madame sat, feeling the promise before her, the girl disappeared around the corner, feet hitting the stairs as she scurried up to the familiar environs and relative safety of the second floor. None of them liked to venture down into the shop. Though filled with fancies and stocked with all the delights that money could buy, their world was lived abovestairs. And there they preferred to remain.

Madame smoothed the top piece on the pile. Such a fine luster. And a beautiful color. One of her favorites. She left her desk to open the safe and take out the pouch of jewels. Only— *che cosa?*—what?

They were gone!

———

Alternate waves of fear and rage swept Madame, first draining her cheeks of color and then marking them with a red, blotchy stain.

She bent her head to see inside the safe. Pushed a hand into its cool depths.

Nothing. Not one bag. Not one jewel.

The witch!

Hadn't Madame maintained that she didn't want them? And hadn't Mrs. Quinn insisted all the same? Hadn't the woman always spoken of taking her business elsewhere? Well, now she could. *Buona notte al secchio.* Soon, there would be no Madame Fortier to assist her.

No Madame Fortier at all.

They had been stolen? She felt around the safe one more time before concluding that, sì, indeed they had been. And what was there to do about it? She stood there in front of the safe like a supplicant before an altar.

Please, Signore.

And what did she expect Him to do about it? When she hadn't even darkened the door of a church in the past ten years? When she hadn't ever gotten insured in the first place.

Sono una donna stupida! Stupid woman! Couldn't she have at least done that one thing?

There was a fortune in those jewels. And now she'd have to pay for them herself. Unless she found them. She'd have to find them. There was no other option. She had to recover the jewels. And in order to do that, she'd have to discover who had taken them.

Who had known of them? She'd start there. Who had known of them? The girls on the third floor.

Julietta, Annamaria, and Luciana.

She knew her girls. All of them. Knew there was no communication between the second and third floors. Luciana, in any case, didn't know any of the girls on the second floor. She hadn't come up from there. Annamaria knew them, of course, but she so rarely spoke to anyone. And with her work requiring such attention to detail, she had no time. And Julietta? That girl had enough pride about her that she wouldn't deign to speak to anyone she thought inferior.

The thief was on the third floor. The thief had to be on the third floor.

But which girl was it?

———

Eyes flashing, chest heaving from the exertion of having pounded up two flights of stairs, Madame threw the door to the third-story workshop open. All three girls jumped at the sound. And then they quailed under Madame's dark look.

Madame had rarely ever lost her temper. The first time was back in the beginning, before she'd hired anyone. She had—just once—yelled at a client. Not spoken pointedly. Not even talked distinctly. Madame had yelled. Loudly. The foolish woman had insisted on ordering a gown in dotted white voile, even though she was nearing sixty years of age, and then had the impudence to insist that she'd never ordered it at all once the gown had been made. The woman had never ventured inside the door of Madame Fortier's again. The second time was . . . well, right at that instant. And in both cases, the fear of her audience had stemmed from the same root.

It stemmed from the nature of Madame.

Back in the beginning, that foolish client had hoped against hope that Madame wouldn't act like an American. That she wouldn't shriek and scream and rage, but instead react with the remote detachment and cool reserve that the woman was certain was European. And now, the girls on the third floor were terribly frightened that Madame was going to act like an Italian. That she would shriek and scream and rage, instead of reacting with the remote detachment and cool reserve that they had long ago decided was American.

In truth, Madame was neither American nor Italian. She had not yet, and never would, obtain so lofty a goal as to be mistaken for an American, but she had tried so hard to bury her ancestry that she was certainly not then, nor would she ever again be, Italian. It was to her credit in that endeavor that the girls on the third floor could not have said from which region in the old country that she had come. Indeed, could not say for certain that she had come from anywhere at all.

"The jewels have been stolen."

Julietta's face went white as she remembered a conversation she'd had about the jewels several days before. Luciana bit her lip as she thought about how she'd dreamed of the help those jewels could buy. And Annamaria's gaze shot toward her lap as she remembered thinking how that fortune in jewels could buy freedom.

An astute observer such as you or I would have seen a stealthy look of guilt cross the face of each one of the girls. Madame, no less astute and no less observant, saw those looks as well. Saw each glance slide to the table and then to the floor. Saw hands clutch at themselves in each girl's lap.

What did it mean? What did all of those gestures signify? "You are the only three among all of my girls who knew about the presence of those jewels."

Still, no gaze rose to meet her own.

"Mrs. Quinn is to have her gown delivered on October twenty-first. The final fitting will be one week earlier. I expect to find the jewels in my safe by October seventh, in time for Luciana to work them onto the gown." She didn't. Not really. But she hoped with a fervency that would have rivaled Petrarch's for Laura. "If they are not recovered by then, all of us will be out our jobs." As she left the room, she was unable to stop herself from slamming the door.

Madonna mia. What was she going to do?

———

An uneasy silence reigned in the third-floor workroom the next day. The three girls had all had an evening to consider the theft of Mrs. Quinn's jewels and the import of what Madame had implied. It was clear that one of them had stolen the jewels.

Julietta, though she knew who had done it, was trying desperately to convince herself that she didn't.

Luciana, reliant on the shop's continued viability, badly needed for the jewels to be found. She knew what rich people did when they thought they had been cheated. They exacted revenge in very costly ways. She knew it because she used to be one of them. And so she had worked long and hard trying to figure out who had done it.

It didn't take long, that morning, for them to share what they knew. It was Annamaria who started it. She had been working on a slippery silk, smocking an intricate pattern of diamonds and double waves onto the tops of the pockets.

Pockets in a gown? you might ask. Pockets in a gown of sorts. For do not forget: Madame's was a shop that fulfilled all of her clients' needs, from the ballroom to the bedroom. And so, as often as not, Annamaria performed her handiwork on nightgowns as well as ball gowns.

"You'd think this would be just what the Germans want."

Both Julietta and Luciana looked up at her words, not quite believing that she had spoken. And not quite understanding what it was that she had meant. "What's that?" Julietta finally asked her.

"You'd think this would be just what the Germans want: for America to use up all its money on fancy gowns and fancy underthings. Can you believe that some people spend fortunes on things like this?" She lifted up the fabric and gave it a bit of a shake. "For something that only gets worn at night?" She was irritated and peckish because she had spent too much time thinking about the coming wedding of her sister and Giovanni. And too little time in Zanfini's store.

"I wouldn't say that too loudly, Annamaria."

The girl looked up at Julietta's admonition.

"Some people can't be trusted." Julietta looked not at Annamaria but at Luciana as she said it. Because if the thief wasn't the person she was hoping it wasn't—and how she hoped it wasn't!—then it had to be someone there in the room.

Luciana refused to allow her reputation to be tarnished. "I don't know, Annamaria. Greed seems to me to be part of the soul of America. Observe: Julietta just got a new hat."

She had indeed. She'd been eyeing it every day on the way

to work for over a month. It was a smart, stylish little thing. She had some money, and she didn't see why she shouldn't spend it the way she wanted to.

"How much did it cost, Julietta?" Luciana spoke to her beads as she said the words, because she couldn't bear to look upon the girl's smug, haughty face. Hadn't they just come to be friends? Of sorts? So why did she feel like Julietta's words had been thrown toward her like spears?

"Do you want one like it?"

Luciana shrugged. At other times, in other places, she might have.

"You won't be able to find it. Mine is the only one there is." Julietta had made sure of it by fixing a wide ribbon around the crown, trimming the bow with a discarded belt buckle, and then adorning the ribbon with silk flowers. She'd stayed after several nights that week in order to do it. And missed out on attending a meeting with Angelo in the process. But the result had been worth it.

"I'm just wondering where you found the money to buy it." Thief.

"I'd think you'd have enough money now to buy something of your own."

Luciana dared to look up. "You know that I don't."

"I wouldn't know the first thing about you, would I?"

"And I wouldn't sit here day after day, listening to the both of you, if it weren't absolutely necessary!" Annamaria's words echoed in the sudden and complete stillness.

27

Julietta and Luciana were both shocked into silence. Annamaria had spoken. Again! And not only that, she sounded as if she ... had she scolded them? Both of them?

"She started it!"

"She did!"

"Then you had both better finish it." She said the words with quiet vehemence.

Their glances bounced past Annamaria, toward each other, then down to their work.

"You're the lucky ones. I go home to even more work every night. Annamaria, do this. Annamaria, do that. Annamaria, go buy tomatoes from the Sicilians."

"Sicilians!" They both gasped. Buying tomatoes from Sicilians was vastly more offensive than being accused of stealing jewels.

Only Julietta dared to speak. "And do you?"

Annamaria had regretted the words as soon as she had spoken them. It was her own business, wasn't it? The only thing she had to call her own. And now she'd gone and cast it in front of both of them. But then maybe ... maybe she'd wanted to. She lifted her chin. Nodded.

"And do you ... speak to them?" Sicilians were even more of an abomination to Luciana than they were to Julietta, for Julietta had lived within sight of them for over twelve years in the North End. They had become a worrisome, if acceptable, evil. But to Luciana, Sicilians were a breed of peasants akin to the Barbary pirates of which she had only heard tales. And sordid ones at that!

Annamaria shrugged.

"What are they like?"

She shrugged again as she pulled her needle through an impressive number of pleats. "They're nice."

Julietta's eyes narrowed. It almost sounded as if Annamaria liked them. "And why do you have to buy tomatoes from them?"

"Because Maglione, the Avellinesi, sells rotten ones."

Julietta frowned, took a stitch at her own work. It was a dirty business when one couldn't trust one's own countrymen.

Luciana lifted a brow at that perplexing bit of information. A Sicilian? Selling good tomatoes? When an Avellinesi sold bad ones? Not, of course, that Avellinesis were that much better.

But Annamaria's secret had achieved what her admonition had not. Julietta and Luciana worked the rest of the day in relative silence, pondering the wonders of buying from, and actually speaking to, a Sicilian. How nice—how pleasant!—the workshop would have been had that peace reigned for even one day more.

But it could not. How could it have when both Julietta and Luciana sent withering looks across the table at each other? How could it when each suspected the worst of the other? They glowered through the morning, then began sniping at each other that afternoon. Until finally Annamaria had had enough. Again.

"Stop it! The both of you!"

They each turned from the other.

"I am sick unto death of both of you!" She might have been her own mother scolding her youngest brother. The same frustration, the same eternal weariness were evident in her tone.

"Then tell *her* to stop glaring at me."

"And tell *her* to stop insulting me." Luciana hated the way her words had come out in a whine, but Julietta seemed always to bring out the very worst in her.

"You're both at fault. Admit it. Julietta, you think Luciana stole Mrs. Quinn's jewels. And Luciana, you think Julietta stole them."

"She did!" They both said it at the same time.

"I didn't. You did." Those words, too, were spoken in unison.

It was enough to make long-suffering Annamaria want to weep. "What if *I* stole the jewels?"

Julietta hadn't considered that possibility before. "Did you?"

"No. None of us did."

She spoke the words with such absolute assurance that Julietta knew her first guess, her first thought, might just have been right. How it would grieve her heart to know it! But she couldn't admit it. Not yet. "It had to have been Luciana!"

And now Annamaria wanted to pull at her hair. But she didn't. Manifesting infinite patience, she talked to Julietta as if she were her youngest brother, Stefano. "But why would she steal them? She needs this job."

"Then it was Julietta!" Luciana had had enough of the girl's constant arrogance and scorn. If she'd been a servant in Roma, Luciana would have had her fired. Days before. Weeks even!

Annamaria turned her efforts to Luciana. "And why would she steal them? She wants to own this shop one day."

Julietta felt her spine straighten as Annamaria spoke. It was true. She did. And she was going to get those jewels back if it was the last thing she did. For how could she own part of the shop if there wasn't a shop to own?

"But if she didn't steal them and I didn't steal them . . ." The only person left, in Luciana's mind, was Annamaria.

But the girl was already shaking her head. "I didn't take them."

Luciana looked at her with all the cool disdain of the daughter of the Count of Roma. "And why wouldn't you have?"

"Why would I? I'm the eldest daughter of the Rossi family." She turned her attention from Luciana back to her work. Began a row of delicate bullion stitches. "I'm expected to spend my life looking after my family. What would I want with money or jewels?" She frowned as she leaned over her work to inspect it more closely. Using her needle to separate and count the pleats, she sighed. She'd missed one; once again, she'd have to start all over.

If Julietta didn't steal them and Luciana didn't steal them and Annamaria didn't steal them, then who did?

One of them had to be lying.

———

Two floors down, Madame had her own problems to work through. Her client, the strega, was weeping. She'd never done such a thing before. Ever. Which just served to illustrate what a manipulative and devious strega she was. Trying to make Madame feel sorry for her. For her—Mrs. Quinn! As if she had anything to weep about.

Madame could have shown her sadness. Regret. And misery? Why, Madame had miseries by the armful. By the heart-full. But Madame was nothing if not discreet. And so she drew from an immense reservoir of self-possession and spent some of it on Mrs. Quinn. Silently, she pulled a handkerchief from her sleeve and handed it to the woman.

"I don't know what to do anymore." The strega took Madame's offering, swiped at her eyes with it, then put the handkerchief to her nose and honked into it. "I've tried to be interested in what interests him. I've tried not to be interested in what interests him." She moved to give the handkerchief back before thinking the better of it. She'd have it laundered and returned—or not—as it suited her. "I've tried to help him with his rallies. I've stayed away from his rallies. I've gone to Washington when he's in session and I've stayed home. I've tried to be supportive and dutiful and . . . and good!"

Good? The strega?

"But mostly I've been resentful and bitter and hateful."

Only a strega would know such things about herself and freely admit them. "But have you tried . . ." Should Madame say it? Could it really be as simple as that? "Have you tried loving him?"

"Loving him."

Madame nodded. And then she took a step backward, behind the woman's shoulder so that she wouldn't have to see the strega's face. Loving him? Had she really suggested that?

"I married him *because* I was in love with him! Don't you understand? I was a Howell and he was nothing. Nobody! Some Irish immigrant's son from the North End, who didn't know a soup spoon from a salad fork. I made him who he is. Without me, he'd be married to some brazen Italian girl, tending a bar on Hanover Street."

Some brazen Italian girl. It was providential indeed that Mrs. Quinn couldn't see Madame's face.

"But have you never simply loved him?"

"I just told you I had!" Mrs. Quinn turned in her seat to stare at Madame. Really! She'd just poured out her heart to a shopkeeper and the woman hadn't even bothered to listen.

"I mean, have you never simply appreciated him as a man. For who he is and what he wants."

"I appreciate him every day. I've given him my money. I've given him a son. I've given him my family's contacts and a whole voting district! What more could he possibly want from me?"

"Perhaps he simply does not want you to want anything at all."

Why had Mrs. Quinn expected Madame to understand? She swept from the chair to her feet, determined to make an exit with her pride intact.

"Perhaps he does not want you to make demands on him."

Mrs. Quinn halted. Demands? And when had she ever made a demand? All she'd ever done was support him in his career. Push him, perhaps. Just a little, when necessary. And what did she require in return? "Demands? Such as . . . summer at the shore? A box at the opera? My birthday ball?" She only ever asked for those things so that people would know they were happily married. That he was her husband. And she, his wife.

Madame raised one of her slender, elegantly clad shoulders in a shrug.

"But if I don't demand those things, then I would never see him at all!"

Ah, poor Mrs. Quinn. The problem was that she had never trusted love. She had never quite believed that she might be enough, without her money, without her family, without the heir. Without her thousand petty, incessant demands. It was fear that drove her. That had caused her, month after month, year after year, to take on the person of someone else. Someone else who might, in fact, be able to deserve the love of her husband. In truth, she had tried to turn herself into her husband's first love. Or, at least, the woman she imagined that first love to be.

"What if, instead of insisting, you let him choose?"

"Choose what? To claim me or to abandon me? What kind of a choice is that? And what do you mean, have I never loved him?"

What Madame had meant to say, of course, was, *Have you never loved yourself? Have you never decided for yourself what might make you happy?* Had Madame just been able to find the words, she would have offered these: Have you never thought to be yourself? For which of us, in offering another the truest self that we have, have ever been disappointed by those who really love us? Which might have led round once more to the first question: Have you never trusted love?

Madame Fortier, for once at a loss for words, turned to the

only thing she knew. The only thing in which she was an expert. She turned to her gowns. She picked up a new spring season sample book and put it into Mrs. Quinn's hands. "Show me what you like."

"What I like?" How would Mrs. Quinn know? She had been guided for years by Madame Fortier. For years she had allowed herself to become shaped in Madame's image.

Madame gestured toward the book. "What do you like?"

Mrs. Quinn looked up at the shopkeeper, frustration etched onto her face. "How would I know? *You* tell me what looks good. You always tell me what I want."

Madonna mia! She was giving the woman a chance to choose. To throw off the fetters of Madame's rigid taste and blossom, finally, into a woman of her own making. Madame bent to turn the pages herself. "That one?"

Mrs. Quinn simply sat there.

"How about this one? It could be made up in tricotine or even in taffeta."

Mrs. Quinn, poor woman, didn't know what to do. That's what she paid the gown maker for: to clothe her in the latest fashions. And hadn't Madame Fortier been doing that all these years? Why was she asking for her opinion now? Mrs. Quinn looked down at her watch. Opened the fob. "I'm afraid I haven't any more time. You should send the book up to the house. And note your suggestions." She stood and offered Madame the book. Then she gathered her bag, put a hand to her hat, and hurried out of the shop. Before that woman could ask her any more ridiculous questions.

28

And so it was that Madame had to send Luciana up to Beacon Hill. Again. As if Madame Fortier had nothing better to do with her girls than to send them on expeditions to her clients' doorsteps. She entrusted the spring sample book into Luciana's hands. "You can return home from there."

Well, that was something, then. It was only three o'clock in the afternoon. Luciana had arranged to have a woman on her floor look in on the contessa several times a day. And leave her door open in the meantime. Luciana just had to hope that if the contessa tried to leave, the woman would see her. In exchange for the woman's services, Luciana had given her one of Madame's precious castoff gowns. With the promise of another closer to Christmas.

The woman wouldn't expect Luciana for another two and a half hours. So if Mrs. Quinn didn't make her wait, then she had at least two hours for her own. Maybe more. She could go to the Settlement House early and sit in on the English class that took place before her own.

Madame tapped the book. "But make sure—"

"That she returns the book before I leave." Luciana nodded.

Madame tried to smile but wasn't quite able to do it. They both understood how it was with the strega. And so, Luciana climbed into the back of the waiting motorcar, knowing all the while that she was bound to fail. Not twenty minutes after her arrival, she was dismissed from the Quinn mansion, absent the aforementioned book, having been told to return for it the next day.

And she couldn't have been happier!

She even smiled at the butler. And didn't mind at all when he showed her the door. In fact, it was this woman, pleased with the outcome of her errand and in a hurry to reach the Settlement House, who saw Billy Quinn lounging on the front stoop as she stepped through the door.

Her smile disintegrated into a frown. "Where is my motorcar?"

He glanced up, as if surprised to see her. "*Guten Tag.* What did you say?" he continued in German.

"Where is my motorcar!" The volume of her words had risen quite impressively for one so small of stature. A passerby cast a suspicious look at her as he walked by.

There's a word some people might apply to Billy Quinn. But I urge you not to do so. Firstly, because you oughtn't think such things of people you don't know very well. Secondly, because he was desperate to spend time with Luciana. Desperation makes people do foolish things. Thirdly, because really, it was a rather complicated relationship they were developing: an American and Italian who could only communicate in German; a Boston blueblood and a displaced noblewoman who didn't know the first thing about each other's lives. And finally, because if you had seen Luciana's eyes as she spoke, you might have noticed that beneath the anger lay something more. Something more akin to disappointment. Which means, in fact, that she expected more and greater things of him. And the whole problem with Billy was that he'd never had any expectations at all. At least not any that would call forth his best and most noble self.

He put a finger to his lips. "I wouldn't speak so loudly."

"It seems I have to. You have not yet answered my question."

"Ah—but since we're speaking in German, we might want to speak it a bit more quietly." He had dropped his voice as he spoke and picked himself up off the stoop to stand rather a bit more closely to her than she was comfortable with.

She took a step back toward the door. "Why?"

"You wouldn't want anyone to think that we're collaborators, would you?"

Her brows peaked at that suggestion. Collaborators? With the Boche? Certainly not!

"So why don't I just drive you home myself?"

No. Oh, no, no, no. Luciana shook her head. If he had dismissed her motorcar, which she had every reason to believe that he had—again!—it was for her to find her way home on her own. And she had no injuries this time to dissuade her from doing so. She'd rubbed so much olive oil onto the leather heel of her shoe that she could probably have fried an onion in it if she'd wished to. "I shall walk."

"Then I shall accompany you." He crooked his arm and offered it to her.

She ignored it, marching right past him and down the steps.

He grinned at the tilt of her pert little nose. Billy hadn't been so highly amused since . . . well . . . since the last time he had seen her. He started down the steps after her. "It's a free country you know, here in America."

Oh, sì. She agreed with that. Freer than most!

"I might just decide to take a walk myself."

She sped her pace.

He matched his to hers, easily coming apace with her in several strides. "And I might just decide to take my walk wherever it is that you're going." He winked at her.

She flushed. Winks were impertinent. When they were unsolicited. She snuck a look at him from beneath her scarf. And not so very rude when they weren't. He had such green eyes! She'd never seen their like before. And such glossy auburn hair.

They walked several blocks in uneasy silence.

"It's a glorious day."

Luciana thought about the words for a moment before responding. She could sense no trap. No reason for him to misinterpret a response, whether she agreed with him or not. So she nodded. Because it *was* glorious. A glorious September day. Summer's scorching dry heat had subsided, and even the birds seemed to know that autumn was coming. The pigeons were flying lazy circles in the air, the wind caressing her cheeks.

When she might have turned left at Beacon Street, he offered up his arm as they crossed and steered her right instead. Into the expanse of green that stretched up and away from them.

"What is this place?"

"Boston Common."

She stopped, forcing him to stop as well. Boston Common. A park? With him? It wasn't what she'd wanted to do with her extra time.

Sensing her ambivalence, he placed a hand atop the slender fingers that rested on his forearm. There was something about her . . . something that called forth from him his most gallant behavior. As well as a grin or two.

He took a cautious step forward.

She followed.

He took another. And another. And soon they were walking along those paths like a pair of lovers. As they walked along, he kept sliding glances at her from beneath his shock of auburn hair. And as she hurried to keep pace with his long strides, she kept shooting up glances at him from beneath the fold of her scarf.

Really, he didn't seem like an American at all. At least not the kind of American who had visited Roma. Those Americans had been loud and boisterous. They dined much too early and drank much too late and then cavorted in the city's fountains like children. They spent their days consulting guidebooks as if the pages were sages and speaking in their street voices beneath the dizzying vaults of the cathedrals.

He smiled with the bright enthusiasm and innocence that she remembered. But beneath those charms seemed to lie a vast well of intelligence. And she had to admit that when she closed her eyes at night, she was haunted by the memory of his tourmaline-colored eyes. And so she decided to give him the test. The test she had given every suitor that had ever called upon her at her father's estate.

"What do you think is the most beautiful thing in the world?" As soon as Luciana asked the question, she regretted it. It wasn't as if she had so many suitors here in this new country that she could afford to be discriminating. And it wasn't as if she was even looking for a suitor at all. But he made her . . . curious. She wanted to see where he might have fit into her past had he been among her circle in Roma. It was a question born of curiosity. Nothing more than that.

"In the world?" He was buying time, for something told him that her question was important. "The whole world?"

She nodded. But she did it with a tide of disappointment pooling in her stomach. He wouldn't pass. No one had ever passed. It's not that she considered herself superior, or even more intelligent, than other people. And she wasn't naïve. She'd known what was expected of a society marriage. But when she had tired of balls and wearied of dinner parties, when she had taken out her beads and gone to work, it wasn't just handsome princes of which she had dreamed. She had wished for a marriage of mutual respect. She had wanted a life that mattered. To someone other than herself.

Billy was tempted to take his handkerchief from his pocket and use it to blot the sweat that had suddenly appeared on his forehead. What is the most beautiful thing in the world? Why, it wasn't a thing, was it? And it certainly couldn't be one thing. There were many beautiful things in the world. And it was quite difficult for him to think poetically in a language that wasn't his own. "The most beautiful thing in the world? Well now, that would depend, wouldn't it?"

She looked over at him, startled from her thoughts.

"That's what they say, right? That beauty is in the eye of the beholder?"

Her spirits sagged once more. For soon he would be telling her that the most beautiful thing in the world was her. That's what all the others had said. But for the first time, here in America, she had felt hope—anticipation even—while waiting for her answer.

He knew he hadn't really given her an answer. And so it was with honesty, as well as frustration, that he tried to put into words what he had known for a very long time. "It's almost as if . . . I don't think . . . well . . ." He very nearly gave up, lacking German words to put to an idea he didn't fully understand himself, but he decided to try one last time. "It's almost . . . it's almost as if I haven't seen it yet."

"Really."

"*Ja*. I mean to say, I've almost seen it. Once or twice. As dawn broke over a mountain in the Berkshires. And one time, when I was in California, as the sun set over the ocean. I feel like if I could just—"

"See it from the other side."

"Exactly. If I could see it from the other side." He'd been taught by his father to believe in the pooka, fairies, and the mysteries of the Church. And he'd been coached by his mother to believe in the power of progress and the sanctity of mankind. But he couldn't quite help believing that there was something else. Something more waiting for him on the other side of the sunset. It was as if he'd only been granted a glimpse of something he knew had to exist in full.

Luciana began to smile. He had said the magic words. And like some princess of old being rescued from enchantment, she turned toward her handsome prince, breathless with expectancy. Hope shining in her eyes as she looked at him with great wonder.

He looked down into those eyes and, though he was feeling rather foolish, dared to ask the same question. "And what do you think is the most beautiful thing in the world?"

"That. The very same thing. Something that I know for certain exists, but something that I haven't yet been able to see."

"I can't believe—"

"And you too—"

They beamed at each other alight with the sudden knowledge, the absolute certainty, that it was Providence who had brought them together. As they walked the path, bound together in perfect agreement and intimate silence, they soon happened on the bandstand that was being set up for a rally after a Win the War for Freedom parade. Several of the musicians were tuning their instruments. Practicing phrases of the music they would play later that afternoon.

For the first time, Billy held out his hand to her, not simply for courtesy's sake or in vain flirtation, but with honor and respect. "Do you think we could . . . would you care to dance?"

Would you care to dance?

The phrase triggered a response that had lain dormant within the fiber of the daughter of the Count of Roma. She raised her chin as she offered him her hand.

He put a hand to her waist and then whirled them around a grassy dance floor.

She kept the rhythm on light feet, dancing as gracefully as she had in Vienna or Paris. Just as stylishly as she had in the arms of the Duke of Prussia or the Baron of Kubinzsky. And he guided her across that patch of ground just as ably as he'd guided Helen Putnam or Eloise Winthrop.

But what they had achieved apart on the dance floors of the

world was nothing compared to what they achieved together. And after the last musician gave up his tuning, still they danced to some melody unheard by mortal ears. They danced until Luciana could ignore the decline of the sun no longer.

"Really, I must go home."

"You can't stay? For just a few minutes more?"

She would have liked to, but no, she must not. The contessa was waiting and the ballrooms of Europe existed no more. Though how she wished she could be that girl for this man.

They walked to the edge of the park. He hailed a taxicab and then he got into it beside her. She told him to direct the driver to Cross Street. When they came within view of it, she told Billy to have her dropped there.

"This is where you live?"

"I can walk from here." It was only six blocks and a couple of alleys farther up the street.

"I'll drop you where you live." It was nothing less than any gentleman would have done. Only she was no longer a lady and she did not need—did not want—such courtesies. It would only draw attention to her. Attention that could be very dangerous. "It's fine here. I just live up there, at the corner." Six blocks up.

"Then the corner is where I'll leave you." He didn't like the looks of this part of the city. And, frankly, he couldn't remember ever having come here. For all of his mother's talk about the common man and all her professed sympathies, he had never actually met one. And he was not prepared to do so now. The girl beside him could not live in such humble circumstances. He would not believe it. Surely there was a nice, quiet street in the midst of all the filth and squalor. Surely there was a place in that warren of alleys that did not require propping up or reek of sewers.

They had reached the end of the block. "Here?"

She inclined her head, not willing to lie and not quite willing to tell the truth either. He skipped around the front of the cab and opened up her door. Offered his hand once more. "Thank you. For your time. For . . . everything."

She smiled at him. A smile that illuminated her face like the sun brightened the sky after a cloudburst. And he fell under the magical spell that it cast. "Thank *you*, Herr Quinn." She stood on the curb as he climbed back into the motorcar. Held up a hand as he leaned forward to speak to the driver.

But they didn't leave.

She waved again, hoping that the gesture would cause him to go.

He smiled at her through the window, not knowing that every second he sat in his cab on the street was causing dozens of eyes to turn in their direction.

She nodded. Turned and walked toward the nearest tenement. Paused as she stepped onto the stairs.

He waved.

She sighed. Walked up the steps and into the building. There she waited until the sound of the motorcar faded. And then she ducked out of the building, down the stairs, using the shadows to hide her as she walked home.

29

Later that evening, Luciana took the contessa to the Settlement House on Parmenter Street. Though it was only her third class, it was already quite clear that she was the teacher's prize student. Languages had never been difficult for her. And English seemed to be nothing more than a complicated blend of Italian and German. Some of the words were even quite similar!

As she had walked through the city that week, she had collected the words she'd heard. Especially the words that seemed as if they'd been spoken to her. Or about her. And that evening, after class finished, she took the contessa by the hand and went up to the front, where the teacher was gathering her books.

"Please?"

"Yes? What is it?" The woman's tone didn't have the patience it usually did during class. And her eyes were fixed on the door.

"Some . . . word."

"Yes?"

"What do they . . . mean? Please?"

"Words? What words?"

What words? Luciana had become rattled. She didn't know—

"You'll have to ask me next class." The woman took up her books and brushed by Luciana on the way to the door.

"Feel-thee. Der-tee. Sheeft-less . . ." There was one more. One more that someone had said—to her?—in a very emphatic sort of way. "Skuh-muh."

The teacher stopped mid-step. Turned around, jaw open. "What did you just say?!"

"What they mean?"

"Were you—where did you hear them?"

"People . . . say . . . ?" Was that the right word?

The teacher nodded.

"They say these word to me."

The teacher's cheeks flushed as her gaze dipped down to the floor.

"Please?"

"Filthy and dirty are the same. They mean not clean."

Sporca. Not clean.

"Shiftless means . . . idle."

Luciana shook her head.

"Lazy."

She shrugged.

"Good for nothing? . . . won't work."

"No work."

"Yes."

Sporca and *pigra*. Sì. She knew those words. Her set had used them often. To describe the peasants who had the unfortunate habit of cluttering up her fair city. "And . . . the other?"

The teacher shook her head.

"Please. I must know this."

"Scum is . . . left over from something."

Luciana didn't understand what the woman was trying to say.

"From something dirty."

Dirty. *Sporca.* Again.

"It means worthless."

"Worth less? . . . than what, please?"

"Worthless . . . as in . . . garbage. Rubbish. Trash."

But then why had—? Luciana suddenly understood. And she felt as if she had been slapped. It had been the only word spoken directly to her. Rubbish. Garbage. She'd become one of those peasants cluttering up the city. She was worth less than anything. Worth less than everything. She understood now.

"Where did you hear these?"

"People say the word to me."

"They thought you didn't understand. Or they would never have said them. . . ."

"I understand."

———

That night, at the shop, Julietta gathered her bag, put a hand to her darling new hat, and hurried out the back door of the shop. She very nearly muttered some vile things about Luciana and Annamaria as she did it. To think she'd once thought of the two of them as friends!

And she'd never needed one more than she did now. She was almost certain that Angelo had stolen the jewels. If she didn't get them back, Madame would lose the shop. And Julietta would lose her dream of partnership. But if she did get them back . . . How was she going to get them back?

And how could he have done that to her?

To think that Luciana had accused her of stealing them!

But . . . hadn't she? Hadn't she been the one to speak of them in front of Angelo?

It took her six blocks and an electric car ride to realize the full extent of the consequences of his theft. Flustered, panicked, she walked into the apartment. But then Mama provided an unwitting distraction when she asked Julietta to go down to the baker's for some bread. She ran into Mauro as she was heading back to the apartment.

Mauro!

Mauro.

She couldn't go running to him with her problems. Not like she used to. She'd told him to leave her alone. And she'd meant it. And now it looked as if he was going to do that very thing. But— "Mauro!"

He blinked. Turned as he passed by. Stopped. "Julietta."

"I—what's wrong?" There was more than indifference at work in his features. There was distress. And alarm.

He raised his bag. "Patients."

But why should that bother him? Wasn't that normal? There was no need for a doctor if there were no patients.

"The Spanish influenza. It's come."

"But—it was here last spring, wasn't it?" Hadn't the Spanish influenza taken one or two children just down the street?

"It's back." Then he turned around and started at a jog down the street. And there was something in his manner, a dire sort of urgency, that set Julietta's heart to pounding.

———

The next evening, Julietta's heart was pounding for entirely different reasons.

She'd met Angelo on her way home from work. She needed to talk to him about the jewels and talk him into returning them. But she hadn't yet figured out how to do it. Because what's the polite way to ask someone if they're a thief?

If he'd done it, it couldn't have been on purpose. He must have just . . . made a mistake. She knew he must have an explanation, and she was certain she could talk him into fixing it. If only she knew what to say. But when he pulled her into an evening shadow and began to kiss her . . . all resolution fled.

Scream, cry, yell if you have to, but it won't do any good. For when has any eighteen-year-old ever responded to reason when there was passion to be had for the taking? Julietta so badly wanted to believe that Angelo was innocent that she was willing to sacrifice her integrity for him.

Until the feel of Angelo's hand kneading her back reminded her of the yellowing bruise on her neck. She broke away from him, stepping from the shadow into the light. Shoving a pin further into her hair, she readjusted the brim of her hat, all the while sending glances up and down the street to determine if anyone had seen them. Anyone could have seen them!

Madonna mia, this wasn't what she'd meant to be doing! Why did her control always abandon her whenever she was with him? What she needed to do was talk to him. Not kiss him!

"What is it?"

"Nothing. I have to go." As she took a step from him, he reached out and spun her back to himself. Bent his head to her neck for one last kiss.

Reflexively, she pushed his head away. He had just left her when she saw Mauro hurrying up the street from the other direction. Looking straight at her. At them. Unconsciously, she put one hand to her waistband to make sure that she'd unrolled it. And the other to her neck. Putting a smile on her face, she linked an arm through Mauro's as he came abreast of her.

"Is that him?"

"Is who what?"

"That man that . . . he was kissing you." And it hurt like a twist in his gut for him to have seen it.

She said nothing.

He reined her in with a tug of his arm. "Who is he, Julietta?"

"His name is Angelo Moretti. He's new here. From Roma."

"And how long have you known him?"

Not that long, really. But she certainly wasn't about to let Mauro know! Who was he to tell her what to do? Or who to see? "Long enough."

His jaw tightened. Long enough? She'd known the man long

enough to kiss him when he'd known Julietta for all of her eighteen years?

She pulled her arm from his as they walked the rest of the way to the Giordanos' building. She wished he would ask her what was wrong, the way he had when she'd been little. He'd always known back then when something was bothering her. And he'd always said just the right thing. That's what she needed. She needed someone to know that something was wrong and she needed someone to tell her what to do about it.

But Mauro was too overwhelmed by his own pain and confusion to be able to register hers. And too overcome by the thought of the epidemic he feared was being loosed upon the city. When she moved to walk up the stairs, he didn't follow.

30

Julietta saw Mauro pause, one foot on the steps to the building. "Aren't you coming up?"

"Maybe."

Julietta raised a brow.

"Later. I've two calls left to make." And a broken heart to try to mend.

"Two calls that can't wait until after dinner?"

He shook his head and continued on his way. She went up the stairs and into the apartment, warning Mama to keep something in the pot for him. As the Giordanos ate dinner that night, Julietta marveled at her family. At how loudly they talked and how opinionated they were. How often they yelled at each other.

Just like Angelo's friends.

Only . . . his friends used such big words. Words she really didn't understand. And they didn't just laugh at each other when they were done with their yelling and go back to being brothers. They waged war with their words, as if they contained the powers of life and death. It made her question that Angelo actually called those people friends. Question that anyone would call them friends! She wondered if, like her brother Salvatore and

Mauro, Angelo would give his life—if he would give anything at all—if one of them required it. And suddenly a terrible fog of loneliness swept over her, and she wanted to hide herself forever in her family's warm embrace of fierce loyalty and fierce love. She wondered if this was what growing up was all about. And if being in love meant growing apart from all she used to know. If only we had been able to whisper into her ear, "No. It doesn't mean that at all!"

Mauro didn't appear until after the table had been cleared. But even so, Mama just smiled and put a plate before him, patting him on the head and bending to kiss him on the cheek as if he were her own child. He didn't linger long afterward. He tried, in fact, to duck out without Mama seeing.

"And where are you going?"

"Home." He didn't want to be anywhere near Julietta. And there was something out there in the city. Something new. And threatening. He'd been down to the wharves. There were sailors down there. All of them sick. Other doctors had insisted that it was the grippe. But when had the grippe ever knocked over a group of young, sturdy sailors as if they were bowling pins? It was the influenza. It had to be. And he could not sit there, in Mama Giordano's apartment, trying to pretend as if he'd never seen Julietta kissing that man, while the disease found a way to threaten the very people he had worked so hard to protect.

Mama tilted her head, squinted at him. Put a hand to his forehead. "You sick? You want some wine? You need some wine."

He tried to smile. "No. I'm not sick." But there were too many who were. And he needed to be out there. With them.

She tried to press some on him anyway. When he wouldn't take it, she pressed Julietta on him instead. "Go see him outside. Like a good girl."

Instead of protesting the way Mama was half expecting, Julietta simply slipped past Mauro, through the open door.

They were downstairs and nearly to the door before she plucked at his sleeve. "Can I ask you something, Mauro?"

Timidity? Uncertainty? In Julietta? This was something new.

"Do you think I'm smart?"

He cursed the man, that Angelo Moretti, who had put it into her mind that she was not. For who else could have done it? "I think you're brilliant." Though his sentiment was serious, he winked as he said it. He wasn't quite sure how to read her mood.

But she didn't smile in return. "I'm asking because I know you'll tell me the truth." In fact, he was the only one she knew who would tell her the truth. She had turned to the only objectively honest person that she knew. Even though she also knew that she had hurt him.

Seeing the worry and the trust in her eyes, he pushed his own worries and his own pain to the back of his mind. Set his bag at his feet and took up one of her hands. "The truth is, I do think you're brilliant. I've never seen anyone with your ability to read people. To know what they want and then how, from that, to get what you want from them."

Julietta blinked. Then frowned. Was that a criticism or a compliment?

"And I've never seen anyone with your style."

"That's nothing. I work at a gown shop, Mauro."

"But that doesn't signify that you have to know a thing about fashion. I walk through this city every day. And you're years ahead of the fashions." He was a doctor. He'd been trained to notice details. "That's not nothing. That's genius."

His own brilliance with words had assuaged her vanity just a little bit.

Seeing the glow come back into her eyes, her chin begin to rise, remembering the possessive way that man had held her around the waist, led Mauro to say something that perhaps he should have kept to himself. "And I've never met anyone like you for making me fall in love."

That luminous glow was now tempered by sadness. Why did he have to go and ruin everything? Of course, she'd suspected he had such thoughts, but as long as he hadn't spoken of them, she'd been able to pretend that she didn't know. She could flirt with him when she wanted to and discard him when she didn't, and she'd never had to answer to her conscience. But now . . . now that he had spoken the truth—he had changed everything.

She took a step closer, tipped her head, and put a hand to his cheek. Why did she feel like crying? "I'm not the girl for you, Mauro."

"I was thinking . . . hoping . . . that you might be."

She shook her head. "You need someone kind and noble. And I'm terribly selfish. You need someone calm and patient, and I'm not. You need someone . . ." Older. Didn't he? Someone much older than she. "You need someone who loves you the same way that . . ." There, her courage faltered. She didn't want to talk about love. She didn't want to talk about . . . well . . . certainly she didn't want to talk about marriage. There was a restlessness deep inside her. There were so many things she wanted to do. So many things she wanted to see. And how could she do any of them once she married? Mauro was offering his heart, and all she could see were chains.

She put a hand up to her throat, which felt as if it were throbbing. She remembered the mark on her neck and moved to cover that instead. Why was there suddenly so much that she didn't want Mauro to know? To see?

Why was there so much to be ashamed of?

She could think of nothing else to say but the simple truth. And so she stood on tiptoe and kissed his cheek. "You need some-one better than me." She turned and went back upstairs.

He stood there watching her go. Better than her? But she

was the best that he had ever found. And he wasn't settling for anything less than the best. He never had.

They'd told him he couldn't go to medical school. Because when had they ever invited an Italian into their ranks? So he'd gone back to his books and studied. Two years later they'd let him in, and he'd graduated first in his class. They'd told him no Italian would ever be allowed to set up an office on Congress Street. He'd saved up his money, and he'd gone to city hall week after week and month after month, and a year later he'd hung his sign on that very avenue.

Julietta may have refused him, but she hadn't told him she didn't love him. He was too much of a pragmatist not to have noticed that. But she hadn't said that she loved the other man either. What she had said was that she didn't think she was worthy. But she was. He had made his decision long ago, and there was nothing he'd seen since then to make him change his mind. He'd just have to wait a little bit longer until she could see it for herself. He'd never minded a wait. Not when he could see the end so clearly.

And so, when she had disappeared from sight, he picked up his bag, pushed open the door, and walked down the street. Forgetting for just a moment the specter of the influenza, he even whistled as he went.

————

Billy Quinn sat that very night in a mansion up on Beacon Hill that hemorrhaged light from its purple-tinted windows. Surrounded by eligible heiresses, he ate from a shockingly bright-colored Sèvres plate that had just recently replaced all of the staid, but embarrassingly German, Meissen tableware. Quite an extravagance for such an old Yankee family! But he hardly credited the incongruent luxuries nor the demure beauty of the girls sitting beside him. All he could think about was Luciana.

The girl on Billy's left was trying to flirt with him. She was a Cabot and actually quite pretty. At any other time he would have put his mind to flirtation, to flattering her, pushing her to see exactly how thoroughly he could make her fall in love with him. But she didn't have the cachet of a foreign accent or dark exotic looks. She didn't have the regal arrogance or the flashing eyes. She was rather dull, really.

"Do you think it's truly the grippe that has stricken all those sailors down at the pier?"

Who knew. Or cared.

"Some people think it's the influenza." She smiled, then abruptly pulled her lips together. Was there something caught between her teeth? Is that why Billy Quinn was behaving so oddly? Usually she didn't have to work so hard at conversation. "What about the war—do you think it will end soon?"

Didn't everyone hope so?

He smiled and gave her some sort of answer and then he busied himself with a dinner roll. Who was she? Where had she come from? Truly? She lived in the North End, but she couldn't be Italian, could she? She couldn't be. She was nothing like the Italians he'd seen before. She spoke German . . . although something in her diction hinted that she wasn't actually from that country. She wasn't Irish and she wasn't a Slav. He threw out every possibility until he was left with just one conclusion.

She was a goddess. Or a fairy.

Though it pleased the Irish in him and his sense of the poetic, he knew it couldn't be so. She had to have come from somewhere. And he decided that he would find out who—and what—she was.

———

Billy began his investigation the very next day, a Friday. He pulled a cap down to his eyes and stole away down Beacon Hill before it was light. He strode through a city that was largely asleep, save the deliverymen and the newspaper printing presses. Once he'd reached Luciana's street, he stood near the corner, watching delivery trucks rumble by and observing an exodus of men from the tenements, trudging off to their jobs, pails swinging from their hands. He stood in the shadows, watching the entrance to her building, waiting for her to come out.

She never appeared.

He spent all day puzzling over it and decided to try again on Monday. But it only produced the same result. Unless she had become quite suddenly ill . . . there was nothing else for him to think but that he'd remembered the building wrong.

Taking himself back up Beacon Hill, he spent the remainder of the day lounging in the shade of the back porch and playing tennis at the club. As he motored home through the streets, dodging pedestrians returning from work, he realized that Luciana would have to return to home from her job—and if he didn't know where she lived, he was quite certain that he knew where she worked! He drove past the Quinn mansion, pointed the car down the hill, and wedged it, a few minutes later, nose first into a spot between a waiting carriage and a Pierce-Arrow.

He got out and passed the time pacing back and forth in front of the shop. He waited longer than he thought he'd have to. She didn't appear until six o'clock. And even then, he nearly missed her! She'd come out a back door by way of the alley.

Leaving the car behind, Billy shadowed her all the way up to Cross Street. It wasn't very difficult. She'd pulled that detestable scarf down nearly over her eyes so that when she glanced behind her, which she did quite frequently, she never saw him. After crossing the street, he expected that at any moment she'd turn into one of the ramshackle buildings that lined the crumbled sidewalks.

But she didn't.

She walked past the first and the second buildings, past the whole block entirely, plunging them both deeper into the filth and decay of the North End.

He hid his nose in the crook of his elbow.

Deeper and deeper they went into the maze of streets and alleys that so confused every visitor to that dismal place. But finally she turned left, onto another street entirely, and began to walk up the stairs of a building he hadn't even known existed.

"So this is where you live!"

Luciana's heart stopped in her chest, and she very nearly coughed from the sudden absence of its beating. She looked down at the shadowed canyon that was the street and saw Billy Quinn standing there, one foot on the stoop beneath her.

How dare he stand there, skulking in the shadows! She wouldn't have it. Not anymore! "You followed me, Herr Quinn?"

He nodded.

"For how long?"

"From the shop."

From the shop? And she hadn't even known it? She cast a frantic glance up and down the street. Anyone could have followed her and she would never have known it.

"I waited Friday morning and yesterday morning at the place where I dropped you off. And I never saw you. I just . . . wanted to know where you lived."

"You want to know? You want to see?" She was coming dangerously close to leaving behind German altogether and berating him in Italian. The improper kind. "Come."

She whirled around, pushed open the door, and took to the steps with great strides, pounding up the stairs. Four flights of them. By the time she reached the top, he was lagging three flights behind. "Wait! Stop!"

"You wanted to see? Well, then, look!"

Her neighbors, hearing the shouts, had come to their doors. They stood there, clad in dirtied aprons, children on their hips and behind their skirts. Nothing much ever happened up on the fifth floor, and this Signorina? She hardly ever spoke, though they'd assumed she was Italian. So to hear her yelling? In some strange language? Well, that was just too good to miss!

Luciana turned her key with a violent wrench and threw the door open, disappearing within. But still she shouted, though only Billy could understand. "Here. This. This is where I live. This is where I am from!"

By then he'd jogged up to the fifth floor, leaving a trail of slack-jawed immigrant women in his wake. By then she'd realized he wasn't behind her and so she'd gone back out into the hall for him. He wanted to see? Then she'd drag him in by the ear if she had to! "You wanted to see where I live? Then come in and look!"

He'd stopped, not so certain now what he wanted. He'd thought—he'd hoped!—to see pleasure, delight even, in her eyes. Not anger. But he was here now. There was no point in turning around.

"This," Luciana said, walking to the sideboard, gesturing toward it with a sweep of her hand. "This is where I make our meals." She spun to the table. "And this is where we eat them. And there is where the c—my grandmother sits all day while I work. And in there"—she pointed to the door—"is where we sleep."

"Stop that racket, ragazza! Can't an old woman sit in peace?"

"And that is my grandmother."

"Who is it, ragazza?"

"It's a gentleman. Herr Quinn."

Upon hearing his name, Billy stepped forward, bowed, took up the contessa's hand, and kissed it.

She smiled slightly, her eyes suspiciously clear. And then she gave him a wink!

Hiding an answering smile, he straightened, looking back at Luciana. He might have laughed, but his mirth died the instant he looked into her eyes.

If she'd had the luxury of privacy, she might have sunk to the floor and wept. She would have wept for herself. For her father and her grandmother and for all that had been lost. She would have wept for her future as well. A future that could never include a man like the one who now stood before her. But you see, her breeding did not allow for such selfish displays of emotion, and certainly not in front of a man like Billy Quinn. So she stood by her bare sideboard and stared straight into his eyes, and she dared him to say what she had known all along: She was not worthy of him. Not any longer.

She was filthy, dirty, and shiftless. She was scum.

But Billy didn't know any of that. And he would never have imagined those words in conjunction with her. He only knew that she was distressed. So he violated every rule known to polite society. In both his world and in hers. He stepped around the table and took her into his arms.

Bent on maintaining control, she clenched her hands against the emotions that raged inside of her. But it was useless. She burst into tears anyway. And then she lifted her arms and clasped them about his waist.

"It's all right." He murmured the words into her hair and then pulled her closer. "Everything will be all right." As he spoke the words, he discovered that they were a promise. It was both exhilarating and terrifying to find that he cared so much for her. He pressed a kiss to her temple and then laid his cheek against her hair. "It will be all right."

She knew it wouldn't. Nothing would ever be right again. But she stayed there in his arms for a while, pretending that it was true. And the contessa continued staring out the window, the faintest of smiles upon her lips and the tiniest of twinkles in her eyes.

31

That evening, as Mama was cooking, Annamaria dropped first one and then two apples off the fire escape and watched as they tumbled into the alley below. They weren't rotten. No. They were nearly as fresh as they had been when she'd bought them at Zanfini's. But she yearned to see Rafaello again. And she couldn't think of any other way to be able to do it.

"Annamaria!"

"Mama?"

"Where are my apples?"

"What apples, Mama?"

"I thought I had four apples."

Annamaria shrugged.

"Didn't I have four apples?" She sighed. Put a wrist up to her forehead and pushed a few gray wisps of hair aside. "You'll have to go get me two more."

It was difficult to keep from smiling. Surely God would forgive her the deception. She wanted to see Rafaello. She needed to see him. She had to know that somewhere there was someone in the world who liked her for who she was and not for what she did. And she still had the money for the cherries, wrapped in a handkerchief, pinned into her pocket.

She felt like dancing as she crossed the street, but she didn't. And she felt like running into Rafaello's arms when she saw him, standing behind the counter, but she didn't do that either.

Another girl had reached him first.

He had stretched out his hand to push a tear-soaked lock of hair from her face. And then he picked her up and set her on the counter. She was sobbing as if her heart were breaking. Or at the very least, her pride.

Rafaello pulled her close against his chest. "Hush now, Eva. What's happened?"

Only eight years old, she put a grubby fist up to her face to rub away the tears, but only succeeded in smearing dirt across her cheek.

Rafaello lifted the hem of his apron and wiped the dirt away. "What happened, cara mia?"

She held out a tattered ribbon. "He ripped it out of my hair."

"He who?"

"Beppe Bertolino."

He scowled. "Beppe Bertolino is nothing but a troublemaker."

"Why does he always do that?"

Rafaello looked into her tear-soaked eyes. Sighed. Looked over the girl's shoulder at Annamaria. "Because he thinks you're the most beautiful girl in the world, but he doesn't have the words to say it."

A blush crept up Annamaria's cheeks.

"So he takes my hair ribbon?"

"Hush. Give it to me. I'll put it back in." He fumbled with it for a few moments before finally tying it in a loose, if lop-sided, bow.

Annamaria tried not to smile.

He hefted Eva beneath the arms and set her back on the floor.

"I'd steal Beppe Bertolino's ribbons if he ever wore any!"

"It's not very nice to steal from people."

"Then what am I supposed to do? To get even?"

"I'll take care of everything. I'll put his name on my list."

"What list?"

"The list of all the little boys who have stolen your hair ribbons. Then, in six or seven years, when they come around wanting to court you, I'll say, 'I'm very sorry, but you're one of those wicked little boys who stole Eva's ribbons. I'm afraid I'll have to ask you to leave.'"

"Could you maybe kick him while you say it? In the kneecaps? Because that really hurts."

He leveled a look at her.

"I wish you weren't so nice all the time." She grabbed a peach from a basket. "But I'm glad you're my brother!" She smiled at him and then skipped out the door.

He shook his head as he watched her go. And then he stepped out from behind the counter. Noticed Annamaria smiling. Smiled in return. "So. You are . . . happy?"

She blushed at the memory of the last time she had seen him. At the tears that had coursed down her face. As he stared into her eyes, she didn't know what to say. She was more than happy to be standing there. With him. She might have stayed there forever! But she was more than sad to know that he could never be hers.

She wasn't truly happy. He could see it in her eyes. But he didn't know what to do about it, so he asked the only other question he had a right to. "What do I get for you?"

What did . . . ? She blinked. Remembered. "Apples. Two."

"Two apples."

He walked back behind the counter and picked out two apples.

"I have something. For you . . ." She drew the handkerchief

from her pocket, fumbled with the pin, and held out the money to him.

"What is this?"

"For the cherries."

For a moment, he was mystified, but then his face cleared. "They are my gift to you. I don't want money."

She shook her head.

"But, sì. A gift. From me. To you."

She'd been showered with gifts ever since she'd first met him. With his glances. With his smiles. With his . . . concern. "Grazie."

"I just wish . . . I wish you were happy."

She didn't dare to meet his eyes after that, but she left Zanfini's with a smile on her face. Which was tempered as she crossed the street by the knowledge that some wishes weren't meant to come true.

———

As Billy walked into the Quinn mansion that evening, the butler told him that he was wanted by his mother. As he walked into the understatedly elegant world of her sitting room, he observed her pacing in front of the window.

That was unusual.

Mrs. Quinn took to her sitting room each day in order to undertake the enormous volume of correspondence that was her work. Unless she was out attending a rally, making visits to charities—or visiting her gown maker—she sat at her desk, writing letters, dictating notes, and holding conferences with her associates until that work was done.

A cough from the other corner of the room made him turn his head.

Father! Since when had he ever come home so early in the evening?

Mrs. Quinn gave a cry when she saw him. Hurried forward to place a letter in his hand.

He noted the return address. Raised a brow. Borrowed a letter opener from his mother's desk and slit the envelope. A single thin piece of parchment slid out into his hand.

He read it not once but three times. Each time served to dissipate the memory of his visit to Luciana's and the memory of holding her in his arms. Three times he read it, and then he held it out toward his mother. "I've been drafted."

Mrs. Quinn reached for the letter with a trembling hand, not wanting to believe him. Not willing to accept what she already knew to be true; what she had been told in a personal telephone call by the head of the draft board. She began to read it aloud.

" 'Notice of Call and To Appear for Physical Examination

To: William Patrick Quinn
Boston, Massachusetts

You are hereby notified that pursuant to the act of Congress approved May 18, 1917, you are called for military service—' "

She couldn't do it. She couldn't read any further.

Patrick Quinn came to her side and placed an arm around her shoulders.

She wanted, more than anything, to turn in toward his warmth. To accept his comfort. But she couldn't. There was too much that had to be done. "There's a physical examination first. That's what it says."

Billy nodded. "On September tenth."

"You've always been a bit knock-kneed, haven't you?"

"Mother, I hardly think that—"

"And you're terribly hard of hearing. Ever since you were a child." She glanced up toward her husband, looking for support. "Don't you remember? He always has been. He was."

"I am not!"

"Then why did you never come when I called?"

Mr. Quinn attempted to take her by the elbow, to steer her toward a chair.

She shook him off. "Stop! Just stop. There must be something we can do. You'll just tell them that—"

"Mother. I've been drafted. There's nothing to be done. I've been called upon to do my duty."

"Duty? Duty! To send you to some foreign country to die in some godforsaken place? For no good reason at all?"

"I'm not planning on dying."

"No one plans on dying!"

Billy laid a hand on her arm.

She clutched at it. Couldn't imagine what would happen if—no. She couldn't think it. She wouldn't think it. She could do anything, *would* do anything, but send her son off to war. "We'll send you to Mexico! We can do that, Patrick, can't we? I'll have the butler pack you up right now, and we'll put you on the train. Or maybe we can hire an aeroplane." The sooner out of the country, the better.

"I'm not going to Mexico."

"But you can take a . . . what do they call them? A villa! You can take a villa there. And stay for as long as you want. Until the war ends."

"Mother."

"The butler can have you packed. I'll have the cook send you with a hamper of food. And—and we can send you money, can't we do that, Patrick? There must be some way to have it wired."

"I'm going to keep the appointment for the examination on the tenth and if I pass—and there's no reason I won't—I'll be joining the army."

"Fine. Fine." He could join the army if he wouldn't be dissuaded. "Patrick." She laid a hand on her husband's arm. "You can get him a job in the War Office, can't you? Ring up the secretary and tell him you need a favor. You've done plenty of them for him. It's past time they were reciprocated."

Billy wished he could take his mother by the shoulders and shake her, but she'd already retreated to her desk. "I'll have no one in this house making me out to be a coward. I'm an American. It's my duty. And it's my right. If they ask me to fight, then I will. Don't ask me to do anything less."

"But—"

Billy stalked from the room. He couldn't stay and watch his mother cry. I'm sure you'll understand that he had too many fears of his own to be able to stay and listen to hers. What did he know about guns and wars and fighting? Some of his friends had gone down to Mexico. He always wondered what would happen if his draft number were picked. If he would join them too. Now that it had happened, he had discovered something about himself that both fascinated and appalled him.

He wanted to fight.

———

Billy spent that night awake, thinking. Planning. Dreaming. There were things that had to be done before he left. And he intended that not one of them be left undone. He started to work accomplishing them the next morning when he greeted Madame Fortier at the shop's door.

"Mr. Quinn!" She assumed that he must be there about the jewels. Somehow the strega must have found out! In her fear she released the shop key back into her bag, and had to fish for it all over again.

He grabbed her by the arm, interrupting her efforts once more. She looked up into those wide green eyes, which had always seemed so familiar.

"I need your help!"

What was—? Help? He needed *her* help?

"I need you to send Luciana up to the house again."

Then he wasn't there about the jewels? And he wanted Luci-ana? "Why?" There was suspicion in her eyes.

"I'm being drafted. And she's become . . . very dear to me." Dear? She'd become the entire world to him.

To his great surprise, tears had softened Madame's eyes. She grabbed at his arm. "Not you!"

He was moved by her emotion. And slightly embarrassed. "Yes. Me along with many others."

She swallowed the lump that had swelled in her throat. Blinked back those foolish tears. "Of course, of course. So. You want to see Luciana."

He nodded.

"And your intentions?"

"They're the most honorable of kinds."

32

Madame Fortier had once again sent Luciana to the house on the hill. And once again she had given the girl leave to go home after she'd accomplished her task. Luciana sat in the back of the motorcar as it climbed the streets, dearly wishing she could bite at her nails. But her nonna had drilled that habit out of her many years before. She sat on her hands instead.

Would she see him?

Oh, how she wanted to see him again! To take comfort in those steadfast arms. To hear him whisper her name. To have him tell her everything would be all right.

But she understood now how things were in this new country. They were just the same as they were in the old country. Only now she didn't have the wealth or the family name necessary to secure the things she desired. She was trapped on the wrong side of the social divide. And there could be nothing gained by harboring any fondness for Billy Quinn.

What could she offer him but ridicule and scorn? And the curse of an anarchist's murderous threat?

Had she been confident in her English, she might have tried to convince the chauffeur to drop the package off in her stead.

She could have remained behind, safe and hidden in the backseat. She decided instead to simply pass it off to the butler and walk right back down the steps. She wouldn't set foot in the house. He would never know she'd been there.

But Billy was waiting for her on the sidewalk. He opened her door before the driver could come and do it himself. He took the package from her hands, gave it back to the driver, and told him that Madame was expecting it.

"But she's the one who told me to bring it here!"

"Because I'm the one who told her to tell you." He took her hand, passed it through the loop of his arm. "Walk with me."

She shook her head. Turned toward the motorcar. "I shouldn't. I can't." What would be the point?

"Do you have to return to Madame Fortier's?" He knew that she didn't.

"I have to . . . no." How could she speak anything but the truth as she looked into the depths of those clear eyes?

He'd already started them off in the direction of Boston Common. She went along with his plans, simply because she hadn't the strength to protest. It had dissipated unexpectedly somewhere between her mouth and his eyes.

He walked them toward the pond and sat down on a bench, pulling her down at his side. He took up her hand and realized . . . he didn't know what to say. He may have been fluent in German, but he wasn't at all fluent in love. He was a master at flirtation, but an amateur at conviction. And now his palms had gone sweaty.

It wasn't at all what he'd planned.

"Herr Quinn?"

"Billy." He said it precisely and with not a little frustration.

"*Wie bitte?*" Pardon me?

"Billy. You know my name is Billy. Please, won't you use it?"

She nodded. She'd already been using it in her daydreams.

What a pleasure it would be to speak it aloud! Her brown eyes had gone solemn. He was so restless, so agitated, when usually he was so confident and carefree.

"Luciana . . . ?"

She nodded.

"I want—" He wanted to take care of her, to protect her. He wanted to dream about her. And most of all, he wanted to come home to her. After the war was over. "I mean—" He took up her hand as he laughed at himself. What could be more natural than professing his love to this woman, who had so quickly come to possess his heart? True, the war had precipitated their relationship, but he was as certain of her—of them—as he had ever been of anything in his life. So why was he making it all so difficult? "Will you marry me?"

She blinked.

"Will you?" Please.

Oh, improbable love! Had she still been her father's daughter. Had he not been his mother's son. Had she not been Italian; had he not been American. Had they met in any other circumstances at all, perhaps their romance would not have been doomed. But love is no great respecter of persons. And in fairy tales—the true ones—more romances end unhappily than not.

Marry? Had he said . . . marry? She pulled her hand from his and stood up. "I am not who you think I am."

He joined her. "But you are. You are Luciana Conti. And you're the woman that I love."

He sounded so . . . certain. "But—"

He took up both of her hands in his and kissed her knuckles.

"Billy." She'd imagined that saying his name would make her feel like dancing, not like crying. "Listen to me. *Bitte.*"

"I *am* listening."

"You're not."

"I can't. I can't listen." He was squeezing her hands so tightly, they began to ache. "I want to marry you. And I've been drafted."

Her heart had soared for one brief moment. Now it plummeted to the depths of her soul. He'd been drafted. Her world came to a grating, grinding, shrieking halt. The calls of the birds through the park swirled into the sound of the wind, and the laughter of the children blended with the blare of the hurdy-gurdy and then it all whirled away into a gigantic silence.

Drafted.

Why, God? Why do you have to take away everyone I love? Why do you have to take him too?

She heard nothing, perceived nothing, until he reached out and stroked her neck with a gentle hand, bending his face to hers. Placing a soft and reverent kiss on her lips.

And she was overcome.

She was overcome with the force of his emotion, with the depth of his love. And her own. For she did: She loved him despite all the reasons she'd given herself not to. Against that formidable weapon, her reason faltered. Her logic failed. And then it crumbled. And when Billy stepped away from her, she was weeping.

He drew her to his chest. "Don't worry. It will be over soon. It has to be over soon."

But that's what everyone had been saying for the past four years. And he hadn't seen what she had. He hadn't seen those poor soldiers. He hadn't toured the trenches. War was hell. It was eternal. It would never end. She shook her head.

"What is it? What have I done? Was it . . . what I said?" What he'd asked?

"You've done—nothing . . . nothing . . ." He'd done nothing but make her believe for one short instant that everything would be all right. And then he'd dashed all her hopes in the next.

"I'll be back. You'll see. Before you can even miss me."

She despaired that he would ever return at all.

"But I want to marry you. Before I go."

She shook her head once more, for she didn't trust herself to speak. There was too much still between them. Too much he didn't know. Too much left to say and too much left to overcome. "I am not who you think I am. And who I am can only be a danger to you. I could only bring unhappiness to your family."

"I know who you are. You're Italian." And his mother would just have to learn to live with it.

"I am the daughter of the Count of Roma."

She was so grave, so . . . sad, that he couldn't resist trying to lighten her mood. He knelt on one knee, took her hand in his. "Then marry me, Luciana, the daughter of the Count of Roma."

"You don't understand! I can't." She wouldn't. How could she? The anarchists were at work in the city already. And her father's murderer was among them. She knew he had to be. Their targets were the rich and the powerful. The only thing she could possibly do for Billy and his family would be to lead them to his doorstep. Her own family had been cursed, there was no denying it. But why should she bring that tainted dowry to his?

"You can."

She shook her head as tears streamed down her face.

He took a handkerchief from his pocket to try to stem them, but he would have been more successful at stopping the tide.

"Why can't you? Are you . . . already engaged?" He hadn't considered that. Hadn't even thought to wonder whether anyone else had any claim to her affections.

"No." The only other man who had come close to any such claim had forfeited all of his rights by murdering her father.

"Is it . . . your grandmother? She can come live with us. It wouldn't be a problem at all."

"I can't. I'm no good for you."

"Why not? Because you're Italian?"

Because she was Italian. Because she had nothing. Because sending him off to die of a German bullet would be easier than watching him die from an anarchist's bomb.

"I can't." She looked, one last time, into his eyes, put a hand to his cheek, and then ran away.

Luciana left Billy standing in the park, wondering where he had gone wrong, and turned, in her sorrow and heartbreak, toward the church. She didn't have anything she wanted to confess, but she wanted to talk to someone whose job it was to understand. So she stood in line behind a dozen other scarf-clad women. And when it was her turn, she stepped into the booth and shut the door.

"Bless me, Father, for I have sinned. It has been . . ." How long? How long had it been since she had bared her soul to man and to God? She hadn't done it in the week before the bomb had blown her world apart. There had been too many parties and weekends in the country. And before that had been Easter. She had been to confession at Easter. Just as she was supposed to have done. "It has been five months since my last confession."

Five months. Easter. Father Antonio sat up straighter in his chair. It must be something terribly bad to bring a soul to confession seven months before she was due again.

A doctor would have given anything for Father Antonio's cure. A doctor like Mauro would have loved to have dispensed his medicine once a year, at Easter. Would have loved for his patients to have been able to save up their sorrows and their cares, bring them all before him together, and lay them at his feet with perfect clarity. He would have loved to have given absolution instead of vague prescriptions and best guesses . . . just as Father Antonio would have given anything for parishioners who came to him on a regular basis, as needed, who let him peer into their hearts the way Mauro peered down their throats or into their ears. Disease and sin have this in common: It's much better to treat them at the first symptom than to stand witness to their last.

Father Antonio folded his hands together. Waited for the confession.

It did not come.

"Just say it, child. The burden will grow less in the confessing."

"I have nothing, Father."

"Nothing to confess?"

"Venial sins." She'd lied in a fashion by donning peasants' clothes, hadn't she? And she'd been enticed into shouting at Julietta. But her sins weren't the reason she was there. "I need help."

Help? A young woman by the sound of her. "Are you . . . with child?"

"No! No. It's nothing like that. I'm being hunted, Father."

"Hunted?"

"By an evil man."

"For what reason?"

"Because of my family. He doesn't like my father's politics."

Father sighed. He was weary to death of politics. And families. Of their grudges and their vendettas. Of people who swore they would never speak to each other again and then spoke of their feuds to anyone who would listen. "Our Lord Jesus counseled His disciples to turn the other cheek."

Turn the other cheek? She'd turned her tail and run. That wasn't the kind of advice that she was looking for. "There's a man, Father."

He tried not to sigh. There was always a man. There were

so many men. So many irascible, hot-tempered, intractable men.

"A man who says he loves me. He's asked me to marry him."

Love and marriage did not always come together in Father Antonio's long experience. "And?"

"How can I marry him, Father, when my life is in danger? How can I deliver trouble to him? And to his family? I just want to know . . . what's right. What is the right thing to do?"

"Have you told him about this danger?"

"No."

"What have you told him?"

"I've told him I can't marry him."

"Love bears all things, believes all things, hopes all things, and endures all things. And yet you've chosen to take away his opportunity to do any of those?"

"I love him too much to subject him to this. The other man means to kill me, Father. And what if this man—the man I love— is killed too?"

"You say you love him, and yet you don't trust him enough to let him decide if it's a risk he's willing to take. Perhaps . . . you don't love him."

She sat silent for a moment, contemplating his words. "I do love him."

"Perfect love casts out all fear. Let the fear go, my child. Let God grant you peace."

God. Again. "I'm not so sure I believe in God anymore, Father."

"You're here, in my confessional, aren't you?"

"God took my father. He took my money. He's taken my entire life. I have nothing left, Father, of what I used to have."

"And is what you used to have so very valuable? That you would blame God for taking it away?"

Was it? Truly? Because what had she had but a life of idle luxury in a society filled with people she only tolerated, if not downright despised? She had lost her father, it was true. But had that really been God's fault?

"Perhaps God has not stolen from you. Perhaps he has given you a gift."

A gift.

"You said you needed help. If you could put this evil man behind you, would you accept your young man's offer?"

"Sì."

"Then let him help you put that evil man behind you."

33

As Luciana was daring to dream what life might be like with Billy, Annamaria was imagining what it would be like to walk with Rafaello. In public, through the streets of the North End. Anywhere they wanted. Whenever they wanted. In her daydreams, Annamaria was free from her family, free from her responsibilities, free from expectations. She was free to love Rafaello exactly the way she longed to do.

What would that be like? To love and be loved? To take up someone's hand, not to assist them in crossing the street or return their attention to a schoolbook, but to take it up and simply hold it?

That would be . . . why, that would be paradise!

She pondered love and freedom and paradise as she walked along. As she climbed the slumping stairs of her building, as she walked the sour-smelling hall and pushed open the age-worn door—she didn't see or smell any of those things. She was walking into the oasis that was Zanfini's, smelling delectable onions. And apples. And seeing the tender greeting in Rafaello's eyes.

But she was roused from her daydreams by the tumult of her family.

"What is it?" She unfastened her scarf with fingers gone suddenly clumsy.

"A letter!" Mama was fairly bouncing with excitement. "From my sister."

Aunt Rosina?

"It's just come. In the mail!"

A letter. All the way from Taurasi? "What does it say?"

"We were waiting for you."

For Annamaria. The only one who knew how to read. She took the letter from Mama Rossi, and as the others crowded around she tore an end off the envelope and pulled out the letter.

Her Aunt Rosina. She wished she could walk into the woman's arms for just a moment. Be surrounded by her love, welcomed into her warm heart.

"What does she say?"

"She says, 'Dearest Sister, Mama and Papa are dead—' "

The family gasped and crossed themselves as one. "They're dead? How did they die?"

" '—from the grippe.' "

Mama crossed herself again as Papa patted her on the shoulder. "She'll have to come over, then. We'll tell her she has to come over. That's what we always said. Once our mama and papa had gone, she'd come over."

" 'There's not much else to tell except that I've married Cesar Fragasso. There wasn't anyone else left after everyone went to America. I'm just too old to travel.' "

Mama hissed. "Cesar Fragasso. He's a nasty one for sure! At least he always had been."

Papa cocked his head. "Didn't he have children?"

"Did he have children?! They live right down the street. The son married the Riccio daughter. And has either one of them ever said hello to you or me?" Mama gestured for the letter. "My dearest Rosina." She held it up to her lips and kissed it, then passed it around so that everyone else could do the same. At last it was returned to Annamaria so that it could be put back into its envelope.

Annamaria watched as her mother carefully slid it under the jar of olive oil, where she kept the family's most important papers.

Aunt Rosina had married Cesar Fragasso? That nasty old man? All those years of caring for Nonno and Nonna and that was her reward? Hadn't she always called Annamaria her very own girl? And hadn't she assured her, whenever Annamaria had felt sorry for her, that she would someday have a family of her own? Just a bit later, rather than sooner. After she'd done the work that God had given her to do.

As Annamaria took over the preparing of dinner, she retrieved the letter from beneath the jar. A ring of oil had already been stamped upon the envelope. Turning her back to her family, she hid it from view as she reread it.

> *Dearest Sister, Mama and Papa are dead from the grippe. There's not much else to tell except that I've married Cesar Fragasso. There wasn't anyone else left after everyone went to America. I'm just too old to travel. Your loving sister, Rosina.*

Your loving sister. The sister who had loved everyone enough to let them all sail away, leaving her stranded in Avellino, married to a man she didn't love. She didn't. Annamaria knew she didn't. How could she? He'd been a vile old man fifteen years ago, before they'd ever left. And there was nothing in her aunt's letter to make her think that he'd changed.

There wasn't anyone else left.

She put the letter back underneath the jar, but it haunted her as she cooked. Is that all the reward she had to look forward to? After Mama and Papa were gone? After Stefano had grown and married and left her all alone? Who would still be waiting for her then? Surely not Rafaello. Not after all that time.

But that was what she wanted. He was what she wanted.

And why shouldn't she have him? Why should anyone keep her from him?

Unclasping her Saint Zita medal, she set it on one of the high shelves and pushed it back toward the wall where it was hidden behind some bowls.

Toil and turmoil? No. That wasn't the life for her. Not if she had anything to say about it . . . and she was beginning to believe that she just might!

———

Madame Fortier was a lie. Two, yes, even three times over. She was not French. She was yet a mademoiselle. And she had never been a Fortier.

Fortier. Strength. Ha!

What had she done but use the sheer force of will to create a life for herself? But once that had been achieved? She had not once ventured from her gown shop outside of the city, let alone to France. She who was the most renowned interpreter of French fashions in Boston!

Madame Fortier?

Madame Farce. That's what she ought to call herself. Which made it even more important that no one ever know. No one ever suspect.

She took a collar from one of the second-floor girls and walked it up to the third floor. The third floor where Annamaria was dreaming about Rafaello, Luciana was trying very hard not to cry over Billy, and Julietta was thinking about how to get the jewels back from Angelo. She couldn't believe he'd stolen them. Well . . . yes, she could. She did. What she couldn't believe is that he'd done it when he knew how much her job meant to her. That he'd done it when she was so in love with him. With love on her mind, with love clouding the very atmosphere, it was not so surprising that when Madame came to visit them, that Julietta asked the question that she did.

"Have you ever been in love?"

Annamaria gasped. Luciana pricked her finger with the needle. This time, Julietta had pushed too far. They could see it on Madame's face.

Julietta regretted her words the moment she had spoken them. But it was far too late to recall them.

Madame Fortier blinked. She took in a deep breath, enough that it strained her bodice, looked at Julietta, and said, "No." But of course she had. What she might have said, what would have been more truthful, was *once*.

Once, she had been.

"Never?" Julietta couldn't imagine that somewhere in Madame's past there had not been some handsome fellow bent on winning her heart. In fact, looking at Madame with a speculative gaze, she became convinced of it.

"Never." Madame dropped the collar on the table and went down the stairs, a hand to the wall for support. She sat in her chair, opened up her drawer, and poured herself a shot of grappa.

There had been someone. Once. Oh!—she'd been so in love, so completely beguiled, that she had refused to listen to reason. But she was not the daughter of a tailor for nothing. Eventually, she had foreseen how the pieces would fit together and what an ill-suited couple they would have made. She wouldn't have been any good for him, and might have brought a great deal of harm to him.

She had done what she had to do. For him. On his behalf.

He had married, in any case, not so very long after she had refused him.

But what did it mean? Should she be delighted that he had found someone, or should she be offended? She still hadn't decided. Not even after twenty-one long years. And every once in a while, when the moon was full and the wind was restless, she pulled out the string of facts and worried over them like a rosary.

She had been beautiful. She still was. She had left him. And apparently he had not mourned. Not that she had expected him to. But he had married. Had he been blinded by grief? Oh, Madonna!—she hoped not. She could not have borne the guilt. Not on top of everything else. Had he just not . . . cared?

One thing was certain: She had been poor.

His wife was rich.

She had offered him beauty.

His wife had offered money.

She had spurned him.

His wife had accepted him.

So who was at fault? Was it her fault that he had married the woman, or was it his? And in the end, what did it really matter? She generally ended such musings in front of the mirror, staring at herself.

In the end, what did it really matter?

———

"Whose do you think it was?" Julietta asked the question after Madame had gone. "The wedding gown. Whose do you think it was?"

Luciana considered the question. Tried to recall the gown. She hadn't seen it for very long, but those several minutes had left several impressions. "It wasn't made recently."

But Julietta already knew that. Hadn't Madame said it was the first gown she'd made?

"And it wasn't for an older woman."

Julietta's eyes narrowed. "How would you know?"

"It was more . . . youthful. Not staid. Or matronly."

Julietta conceded. She'd thought the very same thing, though she couldn't have said why.

"Madame spent quite a bit of time on it."

Surprised to hear Annamaria's voice, Julietta turned her gaze toward her. "Why would you say that?"

"From all the seaming."

"And all those flounces and gores." Si. Julietta had to agree.

"So it was a wedding that had been planned for some time, then."

Annamaria and Julietta, having sewn gowns for a number of such weddings, knew exactly how it would have gone. The bride would have come in for an initial consultation. Madame would have sat her down in the chair behind the screen. Would have filled her lap with book after book, pointing out fabrics and flipping through pages. She would have paid special attention to the styles she thought would enhance the bride's figure . . . and paged quickly past those she thought would not. She would have talked the bride out of too much lace and too many ruffles. She would have listened to the bride's mother speak, but she would have paid more attention to the bride's face. She would have watched the girl's eyes intently, noticing when they lingered on a certain style and when they lit up at a particular fabric. And somehow, through suggestion and persuasion, she would have persuaded the bride to settle on a design that was exactly what Madame thought the bride had dreamed of.

And usually it was.

Knowing that, understanding how Madame worked, Julietta began to imagine the bride that had caused Madame to imagine the gown. She would have been . . . tall, wouldn't she have? And slender for Madame to have made a gown that defined the waist so clearly. Had there been beading on the gown? Julietta closed her eyes, trying to remember. Si. There had been. But only on the bodice where it would be seen. The bride hadn't been wealthy, then. She had wanted beads, but they had been placed where they would be most noticed. Which fit with the style of the gown. There had been no train. So either the wedding was meant to be small or the bride hadn't the money. "She was poor."

"What?" Annamaria and Luciana both looked up at Julietta's words.

"She was poor. The gown didn't have a train. It didn't have much beading on—"

"Of course it did. There were some right here." Luciana touched her own chest.

"Si. But that's the only place they were. A bride with money would have had them sewn all over. Even in places where they wouldn't have been noticed."

Luciana nodded, for it was true. In Roma she'd had closets filled with gowns that had been beaded all over. She'd never thought twice about it.

"I wonder what happened." Even Annamaria had been caught up in the mystery of it all. "Maybe she died. . . ."

They all crossed themselves as they contemplated such tragic misfortune.

"But then . . . wouldn't they have buried her in it?" Isn't that what people normally did? That's what Julietta had always seen done.

But . . . would they or wouldn't they have? She hadn't actually gotten married, that's what Madame had said. But the gown was finished. Which meant that if she'd died, it would have been quite close to her wedding day.

"Maybe *he* died." Luciana's eyes widened even as she spoke the words.

They crossed themselves again. Even more tragic! To have come within sight of the altar, only to have the marriage denied by the grave? "Then wouldn't she have wanted to keep it? As a memory of her beloved?" Poor, tragic bride.

"Maybe . . . the parents forbade it." Julietta could quite vividly imagine that happening.

"Which?" Luciana wasn't quite sure she could.

"His. She'd had the gown made, hadn't she?" Obviously hers had approved.

They considered that possibility for several minutes.

"She must have thought they'd approve. Otherwise they would have eloped, wouldn't they? If they thought there'd be a problem?" That's what Julietta would have done.

Well, that was true. Why go to the bother to plan a wedding if you weren't sure there was going to be one?

Julietta was itching to see the gown, to touch the gown. She was sure that if she could get her hands on it, she could coax its story from the threads. "Maybe . . . he left her standing at the altar." She had hit closer to the truth than any of them had that day. And very nearly uncovered Madame's secret sorrow.

They thought about that possibility too. And Julietta was the first to discard it. She could almost see the woman intended for the gown. Tall, graceful. Elegant. Slim-waisted. What man would desert a woman like that?

No man that she knew. And she knew quite a few of them. No. Somehow that didn't quite fit.

"Maybe she couldn't pay." Annamaria had always been a practical sort.

Couldn't pay?

"She was poor, wasn't she? Isn't that what you'd decided?"

Couldn't pay? For a gown that she'd ordered and Madame had made? Couldn't pay for a wedding gown? That wasn't romantic! No. That couldn't be the reason.

And so they sat that afternoon, working, thinking about Madame's wedding gown. Just as Madame herself was thinking about it down in her office.

What would those girls have thought had they known the truth? Would they have liked Madame any more? Or thought of her any less? And what of Madame? What would she have thought of their knowing? Their guessing?

She would have cursed the events that had led her to make the gown.

But why had she kept it? Why had she held on to the gown? She had let the man go, hadn't she? Long ago?

The man, perhaps.

But not the gown.

There are hopes and dreams contained in a wedding gown. And all kinds of vanity and pride. It was that knowledge that had become Madame's special gift. It was the legacy of that gown that had allowed her an unparalleled success among Boston's elite. She didn't dress her clients for events. She dressed them for their hopes. And their dreams. She dressed them as the people they wished to be, not the people they were.

If Madame had held on to the gown, then that was why. She hadn't wanted to give up the fantasy. She'd had a dream and she'd let it go. Why should she surrender the memory too?

34

That evening after work, Annamaria was sent back to Zanfini's for tomatoes. And for some onions and a few zucchini too.

Rafaello hadn't seen her coming. When he looked up from stacking nectarines to see her standing in the door, he felt—literally felt—his heart cease beating. He was struck dumb by her beauty. He gripped a nectarine with such force that his knuckles went white, bruising the fruit beyond redemption.

Annamaria walked across the floor, weaving between crates of grapes and boxes of plums.

She was—an angel! And he wanted to give her something. He wanted to offer her up a token of his heart. So he looked out on that vast display of nature's bounty. Chose the reddest, the most perfectly conical sweet red pepper he could find. And as she approached, he reached out over the box and offered it to her.

So many gifts he had given her. She hesitated.

"Si." He nodded. Offered it up to her once more. "For you."

She reached up and took it from him. Cradled it in her hand. She could still feel the warmth that his palm had left on its flesh.

"Grazie." Then she looked up at him—into his eyes—and she smiled at him.

"Please. What is your name?" Until that evening he'd simply thought of her as the most beautiful girl in the world.

She cast her gaze down as she considered his question. She knew his name. It was Rafaello. His mother and father had called it out whenever she had visited. *Rafaello, fetch me this. Rafaello, bring me that.* How was it fair that he should not know hers?

"Annamaria."

"Annamaria." The way he said it, the way he drew out the syllables and savored them made her plain name sound like the loveliest one in all the world. He bowed his head, placing a hand to his chest. "Annamaria, I am Rafaello."

She smiled back. "I know."

"You know?"

She nodded. "Your—"

His mama came through the curtained door at that moment. "Rafaello! There you—" She stopped as she saw her son and a customer share a laugh, then shook her head and returned behind the curtain to stir the pot of soup she had constantly simmering on the stove.

Annamaria had laughed! He had never heard her laugh. He put the sound of it away in the same place he stored the picture of her long, elegant fingers and the sway of her shoulders when she walked. He leaned forward, spoke in a low tone. "Could you . . . would you mind very much . . . could you say my name too?" He just wanted to hear it in her voice, wanted to know what it would sound like when she said it. He had the feeling that if she would just speak his name, that something magical, something enduring, would be called forth between them.

A flush lit the tops of her cheeks, and her gaze dropped to her toes, but she did it. "Rafaello."

Oh! He could live for months on the ecstasy that one word

had kindled in his heart. Their tongues had exchanged names; their hearts had exchanged eternities.

If Mama Rossi had known of it, she would have taken up crossing the street for the tomatoes herself.

To Rafaello, Annamaria was more beautiful than the ripest red pepper. Though we might find the comparison an odd one, to the son of a greengrocer, a red pepper was a thing of great beauty. For all the world is contained within a red pepper. The smooth and shiny skin hides the kernels of life that grow inside. When peeled, the flesh is revealed and spreads a sweet and pleasing goodness that flavors the taste of everything it touches. Sì. Annamaria was a great beauty indeed.

Though he knew he did not deserve her, though he knew that she would probably never consider a Sicilian for her hand, he determined that he had to try.

———

As Annamaria and Luciana watched Julietta leave the workshop the next evening, they couldn't know that she was not returning home. That she would not, in fact, arrive at her apartment within the hour. She was believed to be taking English lessons. By Madame. And working late at the shop. By her family. And she would do both those things. Soon. Once she had gotten Angelo to return the jewels.

And so, after leaving work, she determined to look for him in the North End, near the wharves. Once she dodged the carts and cars on Cross Street, she tugged her skirt down, pulled the scarf from her neck and tied it over her head . . . making sure to cover the last remnants of the bruise that Angelo had given her.

She was going to stay away from him today. She wasn't going to let him kiss her. She'd decided that he took too many liberties when he did.

She found him near the rickety shed, where he met his friends to argue about politics. But before she even had a chance to speak, he had taken her by the elbow and pulled her inside where a meeting appeared to be well under way.

Tyranny and oppression!

Anarchy and revolution!

As the meeting progressed, it became clear that they were no longer talking in generalities. They were planning something in particular. Something that had to do with a bomb.

Her scalp began to prickle as she glanced around the room. She'd thought these people were just overly enthusiastic—and rather rude. But never before had she realized they were crazy! She'd made a big mistake. She knew that now. Bombs and revolution? Murders and assassinations? Didn't her papa curse people like these? People who gave the rest of their countrymen a bad name?

Oh, how she wished her papa were there right now! To take her away from such madness.

She meant to wait until the meeting was over to speak to Angelo, but she decided she wanted to hear no more. She grabbed his hand and pulled him with her toward the door. She wanted nothing more than to be done with him and all of his friends.

All she had to do was get Madame's jewels back, and then she would never have to see him again. Why had she ignored that dangerous glint in his eyes? And what was it that she had found so appealing in his smile?

The air outside was just as hot as the air inside the shed, but a breeze blowing in from the harbor stirred it, offering the relief of movement and the scent of the sea.

"Why did you do that? We're in the middle of planning—I have to get back in there!"

"Those aren't good people, Angelo. You shouldn't associate with them."

He flashed a grin. "I'm not associating myself with them. They're associating with me."

"They're talking about bombs. And—and hurting people."

"Of course they're talking about hurting people. How else can we free ourselves from the government's oppression? How else will we make people listen?"

"You wouldn't really hurt someone, though." Would he?

"I'd rather not have to, of course. It's as dangerous for me as it is for them."

Not have to? As if anyone would ever ask to be hurt.

"But I have. When I had to. I killed a man once."

A chill crept up her spine, in spite of the fact that she was perspiring from the heat. He said the word as if he would have liked to have said *twice* or *three times*.

"On accident . . . ?" Please, God . . .

He shrugged. He'd done what was necessary. "He was in Parliament. He campaigned for industry and was a supporter of the king. Against the people. And quite influential. They asked me to find a way to silence him."

Silence him? What—?

"He came home one night from a party, and boom!" His eyes reflected the light of that glowing fire, the zeal of the cause, and the satisfaction of a man who had accomplished his purpose. But there was also, deep within his soul, a sliver of guilt. A tiny shred left of his conscience.

"You killed a man. . . ." Without realizing, she had pulled herself away from his side.

"But I didn't kill his family." He said it with profound regret. "They escaped."

"To where?" She asked the question in horrified fascination.

"Here. Somewhere. And when I find them, I'll do to them what I did to him." He saw that she had moved away from him. "What is it? What was it you wanted to say?"

What kind of a man would plan to kill someone? And then actually do it? It was one thing if that man had harmed him. Or one of his family. Such prices were enacted for revenge all the time. But to kill a man he didn't know? To search him out and take his life?

Angelo walked to where she stood. Filled with the enthusiasm of a zealot and drunk with the power of death, he caught her up by the waist, craving her admiration, anticipating her acclaim. "Come here. Kiss me."

———

When Angelo finally released her, Julietta ran down the street, shoes slapping against the sidewalk, trying to drive the thought of his confession from her mind.

O God . . . O God . . . She didn't have the nerve to finish her prayer. She didn't know what to ask. She didn't know what she wanted. She only knew that—

She pitched herself against a wall and vomited onto the sidewalk.

Afraid to refuse him, afraid to contradict him, she'd allowed him to kiss her. But she'd imagined herself far away in a crowded fifth-floor tenement. Safely hidden inside.

She vomited again.

O God, how can I ever—how can you ever—?

She felt so . . . so vile. So dirty. She rubbed her lips against the sleeve of her blouse. Pulled a handkerchief from her pocket and scrubbed at them. Narrowly avoided retching again by taking in long, deep breaths through her nose.

When she arrived at her building, she didn't have to enter the apartment to know that they had already started eating. She could hear the clinking of utensils and smell the scents of garlic and oregano through the door.

"Julietta, you're late!" Mama Giordano never missed anything, even though she could be found perennially at the stove, back turned toward the door.

"Papa wouldn't wait for you," Little Matteo whispered as she passed by.

She had the good sense to recognize that Papa Giordano could usually be talked out of a foul mood. Especially when he was eating. Anger tended to sour a stomach, and what was the point of that? Not wanting to talk about where she'd been or what she'd done, about the horror of—no. She would not think about it. Not right now. She squeezed behind the chairs lining the table and approached her father. Kissed him on top of the head, right where age had pressed its thumbprint into his hair. "I'm sorry, Papa! Madame asked us all to work late. There's a big dance coming up next month. It seems no one wants to wear a gown they already own." True. All of it. Most of it.

He reached up to pat her cheek at the same time that he pointed a fork in Little Matteo's direction. "That's fine, cara mia. Go eat your dinner. And tell that young *giovane* that he whispers much louder than he thinks he does."

Julietta brought her plate to the stove, enduring a glare from Mama as she did so. She smiled as she waited for her plate to be filled, or tried to. And then she made a show of breathing in the aroma as it wafted up from the plate. "The best in the North End, Mama!"

Mama Giordano gave a halfhearted shake of her head as Julietta sat at the table. And then a puzzled frown. There was something about that girl . . . something . . . not right. There was something about the way she had smiled. Something that would bear pondering. The eyes had been too bright while the smile had been too sharp. Si. She would have to do some pondering.

35

Luciana, too, had had a change of heart. And now she was ready to talk. But would Billy listen to her? Would he even agree to see her? She knew, of course, where he lived. But she also knew that she couldn't just march up to that formidable mansion and knock on the door. Request to speak with him. She might have lurked on the sidewalk by the gate, but feared that sooner or later she would be shooed away. And she did not want the attention.

She could have sent him a letter. If he spoke German as fluently as he did, then certainly he could read it as well. But a letter would have taken a day or two to reach him. And a letter like that—written in German—might also have drawn the censors' attention.

But she needed to speak with him, and soon. He'd been drafted. That's what he'd said. If she didn't see him soon, she might not be able to see him at all!

In her frustration and discouragement she drew on her scarf and told the contessa they were going out.

"Going where?"

"To the Duke of Prussia's."

"Whatever for?"

"For a turn in his garden."

"You'll hand me my shawl, then."

Her shawl? Luciana handed her a moth-eaten scarf, and the contessa arranged it over her shoulders as if it were cashmere.

They walked the thirteen blocks from North Bennet Street to Boston Common. There was nowhere else she knew to go, and her thoughts had been on Billy's proposal all day. Why shouldn't she have gone to the one place they had always been together?

And why shouldn't he?

"Guten tag, Contessa."

The contessa looked from the swans, swimming in the public garden, up into Billy Quinn's handsome face. "Guten tag, Herr Quinn. Have you come to the duke's garden too?"

"And why else would I be here?" He looked not at the contessa but at Luciana as he spoke.

She smiled at him.

He took it as an invitation to speak. Lowered his voice so the passersby wouldn't hear him speaking German. "If I offended you in any way at all—"

She stepped closer, as close as she dared. "Nein."

"If I presumed anything that I shouldn't have . . ."

She laid a hand on his cheek. "*Nein.*"

"Then . . . ?"

"*Kommen.*" She took his hand. "Listen. I have a story to tell you."

He let her lead him to a bench, and then he listened with the intensity of one whose destiny hung in the balance as she began to speak.

"I was born Luciana Conti to the Count of Roma and his wife."

She looked at him as she spoke, discerned no doubt, no suspicion in his eyes.

"The counts of Roma are related, by blood or by marriage, to most of the noble houses in Europe. And Russia."

He nodded.

"I grew up in Vienna and Paris. I knew that my father had a seat in Parliament, but I never really understood what it was that he did. While he was agitating for war and becoming known as a supporter of the king, I was dancing and flirting in some of the finest ballrooms on the continent."

He could imagine it. He could imagine all of it.

"And then he began receiving letters. From no one in particular. They were signed 'The Anarchist Fighters.' And they warned him he would suffer great harm unless he stopped pushing the king's warmongering policies."

"And what did he do?"

She shrugged. "He scoffed. He was the Count of Roma. Why should he pay attention to threats made by cowards too frightened to sign their own names to a letter?"

"How long did these threats go on?"

"I have no idea when they started. But they ended on the twelfth of April. That's the day he was killed by a bomb."

He took her hand into his own. "I'm very sorry."

She accepted his sympathies, but she had no time, not right then, for the words or for the sentiment. "I know who the bomber was. I saw him. I knew him." Her gaze dropped from his. "I once thought I loved him. My grandmother and I escaped. We fled to the estate of a friend. But even there the letters found us."

"The same ones?"

"The very same."

"And they . . . ?"

"Threatened us with death. And so, under cover of night, Grandmother and I escaped. We boarded a ship in Napoli and sailed here. To Boston."

"You left everything behind?"

She nodded. "It was no longer ours. The estate had passed

to a male cousin. The next in line. But he didn't even bother to come see us. To try to help us."

"But certainly if you'd stayed, he could have—"

"What? Kept that murderer from finding us? Truly? Is that what you think?"

"Why didn't you inform the police?"

"What are the police? They're lazy. Corrupt! And if that monster was able to kill my father, then why wouldn't he be able to kill me? He's an anarchist and they're everywhere, even here."

"Ja."

"Even here." She whispered the words, certain that if she said them too loudly, she would summon their specters. *His* specter. "So now you know why I said that I could not marry you. It is not a question of love. It's a question of life."

Billy had followed Luciana's story, even understood the reasoning of everything she had said up until those last three sentences. "Nein. I don't. I don't understand at all."

"I can't bring such misery and misfortune to your doorstep. I won't place your life in danger. Don't you know what would happen if we married?" She knew how society weddings worked. "It would be printed in newspapers around the world. It would lead that anarchist right to your house."

"Why are you so sure that would happen?" Billy's voice had risen in frustration.

A man walking by looked over sharply.

Luciana leaned closer toward Billy as she continued to speak in German. "I've seen him. Here." Her whisper was tinged with fear.

"Who?"

"The person who killed my father."

"Then come with me and we'll have him arrested."

He made it sound so easy. If only it was.

He had pushed to his feet and was holding out his other hand.

"I can't." She'd seen him, it was true. But she didn't know where he lived. Didn't know if he had taken another name. Didn't know if she could even trust the police with her story. She only knew one thing. She placed her hand in his. "Please. I am only trying to save you. I love you."

Billy only really heard that last part. "You—you do?" He'd hoped. He'd prayed. But he hadn't been at all sure. For the first time in his life, he was going where no one had led before.

Luciana nodded. She couldn't speak for the tears that flowed down her cheeks.

He took her into his arms. "Then I would rather risk a thousand bombs than have to live without you."

Luciana clasped him about the waist. When he tipped her chin up, she accepted his kiss and offered her own in return.

"So . . . that really is your grandmother?"

"Ja." Luciana smiled through her tears. "And she truly is a contessa."

"A contessa." Wouldn't his mother love that! "Which one was that again?"

She laughed. She could not help herself. It could not matter one whit which contessa she was or what title she held. None of it mattered here in America. "The Contessa of Roma."

"Then perhaps we should ask the Contessa of Roma what she thinks of my proposal."

Before she could stop him, Billy had knelt before the old woman and asked for Luciana's hand in marriage.

The contessa listened to his proposal, made in German, and then turned a keen eye on Luciana. Spoke to her in Italian. "Do you hear what he asked me, ragazza?"

"Sì."

"He seems nice enough, and I suppose that he's as good as you can hope for. You should accept his offer while you can. It is doubtful anyone will ever ask again."

Billy didn't understand what the contessa was saying, but

he could interpret the melancholy and the sadness in Luciana's eyes. She was gazing into the future. Into a life spent beading in Madame's workshop. Hurrying home after work to her grandmother. Running from shadows and jumping at strange noises in the dark. And if she married him? Wouldn't she still be running from shadows? And jumping at strange noises in the dark? Si. It was doubtful that anyone would ever ask again. And if they did, she knew what she would tell them. She turned back to him. "I can only place your life in danger. How can I expect you to marry me?"

"I love you. And you love me. How can you expect that I would not?"

As Luciana and Billy were speaking of their future, Annamaria was grappling with her present. With the expectation of the services she was pledged to provide the Rossi family. For the rest of her life.

Mama had heard her come in. Hardly allowed her to take off her scarf before putting her to work. "Go help Stefano with his studies."

Annamaria shoved her scarf into a drawer, smoothed her hair, then sat down next to her youngest brother. "Where are you?"

He flipped through the book, stopped at a page near the middle.

Annamaria sat for several minutes, trying to work out what it was that he was supposed to be learning. "It looks like you're to choose the right word to complete the sentences."

He shrugged. "I know."

"So what's the problem?"

"I don't want to do it. Will you do it for me?"

"If I do it for you, then how will you learn to do it yourself?"

Mama clucked as she listened to their conversation. "Do it for him, Annamaria. He's too young to quit school and too old to still keep going. Do his homework for him so he can go out and find his friends."

And after that? Would she be told to do the rest of his school-work as well?

Stefano was already sliding away from the table, but Anna-maria reached out and grabbed him by the ear. "If you want your work done, then do it yourself. I've work of my own to do."

He blinked, not quite understanding what she meant. Work of her own? But her work was to finish everyone else's.

She left him at the table as she rose to help Mama Rossi.

"Why aren't you doing it for him?"

"Who's going to help him speak English when I'm not there? When he's twenty-three or thirty-three and I'm not there to help him?"

Mama looked at her for one long moment and then shrugged. Handed her the broom. "If you're not going to do that, then you can sweep the floor."

So that's what she did.

Wondering at Annamaria's sudden stubbornness and not wanting to push such a normally agreeable daughter, Mama went down to the fish seller herself for the night's dinner. And she came back with more than she had bargained for.

———

Annamaria jumped as the door slammed shut.

Mama stalked right up to her and shook a finger in her face. "Signora Tubello and signora Rimaldi told me that you talk to those Sicilians."

The blood drained from Annamaria's face, and her heart began to beat so loudly that she could hardly hear herself speak. "I—I did. I do."

"I thought we told you not to speak to those people!"

She wound her hands up in her skirt. "You also told me to go buy tomatoes from them."

"Buying from them is one thing. Speaking to them is another!"

"How can I buy anything without speaking to them?"

"You were told not to speak to them!"

And Mama Rossi didn't speak to her at all until it was time for dinner. Annamaria spent that intervening hour pulling in laundry, mending a shirt, and generally staying out of Mama's way, hoping she'd forget about the transgression.

But Mama was not so forgiving as that. As soon as the Rossis had crossed themselves in a blessing and the fish had been served, she wasted no time in telling Papa what she had heard.

He sucked in his breath. Turned a sorrowful eye upon his eldest daughter. "You spoke to a Sicilian?"

Annamaria didn't dare speak. But she nodded.

He turned an accusing eye on Mama. "I told you no wife of mine was going to cross the street."

"And I didn't! Annamaria did." Mama would not be accused of something as terrible as that!

"I only did it because you told me to."

Mama waved a fork in her direction. "And look! Now she's talking back and speaking to Sicilians!"

"Did he speak to you first, cara mia?"

Annamaria, responding to her father's gentle voice, looked up into his eyes. Nodded.

He shrugged at Mama. "There. See? He spoke to her first."

"Of course he spoke to her first. He's a Sicilian!"

"But I wanted to, Papa. I wanted to speak to him." It wouldn't have been right to be dishonest about the whole thing.

Mama Rossi crossed herself. "It's bad business mixing with those people. We can't have Annamaria speaking to Sicilians. What will people think of us?"

Of course it was a bad business. He didn't see anything to disagree with there. "So what are you saying?"

"I'm saying she shouldn't speak to them."

"Are you saying you don't want their tomatoes?" Because isn't that what had started the whole thing in the first place?

"I'm saying . . . I'm saying we all do what you say, Papa."

Papa's right brow lifted. He chewed on his mustache for a while as he considered what to do. Annamaria shouldn't be speaking to Sicilians. That was a fact. But he couldn't go back to eating rotten tomatoes. That was also a fact.

But Mama wasn't done. "They told me that Annamaria was smiling."

Smiling! "Were you smiling, Annamaria?"

She glanced up from her plate. Looked around the table. "Si." She fixed her eyes back on her plate.

"Why were you smiling?"

"Because."

They waited for whatever was to come next, but after Annamaria picked up her fork and began to eat, it quickly became apparent that she didn't plan to say anything else at all.

But Papa couldn't let this strange behavior go unquestioned. "Because why?"

Annamaria finished chewing. Set her fork down. "Because I wanted to."

"You wanted to." Mama couldn't credit it. "Have they bewitched you?"

Yes! "No."

Papa couldn't believe it either. "You *wanted* to smile. But why?"

"Because they're nice people."

Nice people? That provoked no little consternation among the Rossi clan. Nice people? What did Sicilians have to do with being nice? And if they were being nice, then what was in it for them?

"You're going to have to go over there, Papa, and tell them to stop being nice to Annamaria."

He glanced over at Annamaria as he listened to Mama's tirade. How had things come to this? And why had he ever left Avellino if the consequence of his leaving was to expose his daughter to Sicilians?

36

Luciana had gone to the fish seller's after Billy had escorted them home to the North End. Starry-eyed and enveloped in dreams of eternal love, she hadn't dared to think past the wedding, which Billy had assured her would take place soon. And she kept her thoughts from the other—from the draft. Why mar such glorious thoughts as weddings when he might not even pass the physical?

She very nearly walked right into a man who was striding up the sidewalk, dancing out of his way just in time. She blinked and vowed to keep her mind fixed to the task at hand. She hadn't attempted fish before, but how difficult could it be? As she walked along, she stepped across a newspaper that was being blown, end over end, down the sidewalk. Its headline was tall and boldfaced. It was, perhaps, information she might have wanted to know. But as it was, she was in a hurry. And even if it had blown beneath her, right side up, she still might not have been able to discern its meaning.

And so the pronouncement of an epidemic of the Spanish influenza blew past and continued on down the street. In truth, not so very many people in Boston that day paid any more attention to it than Luciana did. Only enough to note that there were some soldiers sick at Fort Devens—poor boys—just west of the city. The place was filled with soldiers returned from the trenches and those readying to go. If a Hun's bullet didn't get them, then the influenza just might. It didn't quite seem fair.

At the fish seller's she bought a fat, fresh cod. There was much to celebrate after all! The fish seller wrapped it up in newspaper and tied it with a string. Luciana, package pressed to her chest, nodded her thanks and pushed out into the quickly darkening night.

And it was then that she saw him.

———

There was joy at work in Billy's heart, an elation that flowed through his veins. Luciana, daughter of the Count of Roma, had consented to be his wife.

She had said yes. Yes! The war might be raging in Europe, the grippe might be sweeping the city, but in his heart, the world was a bright and happy place.

He entered the Quinn mansion through the front door and came upon his mother in the hallway. She had just finished changing the menu for her birthday dinner. Again.

He took up her hand and waltzed her across the floor. " 'The bells are ringing for me and my gal; The birds are singing for me and my gal; Everybody's been knowing, to a wedding they're going . . . the parson's waiting for me and my gal—' "

"What on earth—?"

"I've met the girl of my dreams, and I'm going to marry her." He dipped his mother as he said it and then swiftly brought her upright.

"Marry—what did you—? Did you say marry?" Mrs. Quinn was not opposed to marriage in general. In fact, she was quite in favor of it. To the Putnam girl or the Cabot daughter in particular. It was expected that Billy would make his choice between them. She just hadn't imagined it would happen so soon . . . although he had been drafted. And that changed everything. A surprise wedding wouldn't be so terribly unconventional under such circumstances.

"And which one is it?"

"Her name is Luciana."

"Luciana? Why, the name sounds Italian."

"It is. She's from Rome. *Roma*. That's how she says it."

"She's Italian?"

He nodded.

"You want to marry an Italian?!"

We'll forgive him for not reading his mother's face more closely, for most men aren't adept at such things. But we'll cringe for him all the same. Poor lad! He didn't understand her objection. He didn't want to marry an Italian. He hadn't set out to, in any case. He wanted to marry Luciana, and she turned out to be Italian, and that's just how it happened to be.

"No son of mine is going to marry some rude, filthy Italian peasant."

He dropped her hand. "She's not rude or filthy. Or even a peasant, for that matter. She's the daughter of—"

"Is she pregnant? Is that why you think you have to marry her?"

He felt the blood drain from his face. "What?"

"Did you get her pregnant?"

His mother had done many things over the years to embarrass him, but this was the first time that he realized just how often she had embarrassed herself as well. "I'm not going to answer that."

"You did, didn't you? We'll talk to your father about this. He'll know just what to do." She left him standing in the hall, sat down behind the desk in her sitting room, and went back to her work.

But she didn't work for long. Before she had even completed one letter, there came an insistent knocking on the front door.

She sighed. Put down her pen. Expected that the knocking would stop once the doorman answered it.

It did.

But then the shouting started.

Mrs. Quinn rose and stalked into the hall. "What is the meaning of this!"

The doorman was trying to shut the door on whoever it was that was yelling. Some woman, from the sounds of it.

"I can't understand a word that's being said!"

"Bee-lee!"

The doorman was trying to bat the woman's arm away as he leaned against the door.

"Bee-lee!"

"Remove her from the premises. At once." Mrs. Quinn went back into her sitting room and closed the door. Stopped her ears to the noise and got on with her work.

The doorman had almost succeeded in shutting the door when Billy, alerted by the clamor, came down the stairs. "What is it?"

"Nothing, sir."

"Bee-lee!"

Was that—? Billy pushed the doorman out of the way and opened wide the door, causing Luciana to fall into his arms. "What is it?!"

"I saw him."

There was no need to ask to whom she was referring. Her pallor and fear-filled eyes told him what he needed to know. He pulled her close, trying to stanch her trembling. "Where?"

"On the street. On my street."

"Is your grandmother all right?"

"I don't—I'm not sure. I just ran."

"Did he see you?"

"I don't know. I don't—" She lapsed into Italian.

If only he knew what she was saying! He motioned for the doorman to shut the door and then took Luciana into the kitchen.

Had one of the servants bring her some tea, asked another to get a shawl from his mother's wardrobe. Luciana's hands felt like ice, and night was fast descending.

As he placed the shawl over her shoulders, she was still muttering in Italian, rocking back and forth, though some of the panic had gone out of her eyes.

"Luciana." He placed his hand over hers.

She stopped speaking. Looked up at him.

"It's not safe for you to go back to your building." He spoke slowly and in German.

"Nein."

"We're going to drive back to get your grandmother, and then I'm going to take you to The Lenox."

"What is this . . . Lenox?"

"A hotel." The finest one in the city.

"What if he sees us?"

"You'll stay in the car. I'll go up and get your grandmother."

"I'm afraid."

He stood and pulled her into his arms. "And so am I. But if he's here in the city, that means the police can catch him."

———

It didn't take long to reach the North End. And Billy didn't have to say much to convince the contessa to come with him. He simply extended his hand.

She took it.

He looked for some clothes to take with him, but he only found a few gowns, and those didn't seem worth taking. He'd get them what they needed in the morning. But his plan hit a snag when he tried to register Luciana and her grandmother for a room.

The clerk coughed. "I don't believe there are any rooms available."

"I don't want a room. I want a suite."

"Our suites aren't available either."

"You've no suites at all?"

"Our suites aren't available to people like *them*." He indicated Luciana and her grandmother with a nod and a sour expression.

"People like them. You mean the Contessa of Rome and her granddaughter?"

"They could be the Holy Father himself for all I care. We don't take Italians."

"You can send the bill to Congressman Quinn at the United Bank Building."

"This is highly irregular, sir. I know the congressman wouldn't take up with Italians. I voted for him myself."

"And I know the congressman as well. I'm his son."

———

Billy and Mrs. Quinn were waiting, the both of them, in Mr. Quinn's study when he finally came home that night. He didn't like the looks of the faces which greeted him. Not the rage in his wife's eyes, nor the stubborn resolve in his son's. So he pretended they were angry constituents that he had an obligation to appease.

He sat down behind his desk and folded his hands in front of him. It was his signature gesture, and it made him look both patient and wise. It also kept him from reaching out to strangle people's necks. He tried charm first. And his brogue. He smiled. "It's not every night a man comes home to the warm embrace of his closest kin."

Mrs. Quinn had been fixed upon the thought of the debasement of her family's reputation for the entire day. And she was not about to be persuaded from her position. She knew battles were often won by those who fired their weapons first. "You've let your son get drafted and now he wants to marry some Italian girl!"

He looked from his wife to his son. But the boy didn't look away. He squared his shoulders and met his father's gaze straight on. Patrick cleared his throat. "You've already spoken to your mother about this, then."

"I have."

"And you want to get married."

"I do."

If he'd given his heart away, then Patrick Quinn had to trust that it was to someone who loved him in return. "If Billy loves this girl, then he should marry her."

Mrs. Quinn blinked. Raised her brow. Bellowed, "He's only marrying her because she's pregnant! He thinks he has to. Tell him he doesn't have to."

Billy rounded on his mother. "I will *not* have you speak about Luciana like that! She's not some scheming, desperate—" he couldn't bring himself to say the word he knew his mother was thinking—"girl."

"No. You're right. She's not. She's a scheming, desperate Italian."

"Do you love her, son? Truly?"

"I do." There was no hesitation in his reply.

He looked back at his wife. "Then I see no reason why he shouldn't marry her."

No reason? No reason! What about appearances? What about the family name? What about position and politics? Everything they'd accomplished together as Mr. and Mrs. Patrick Quinn had always been about position and politics. It's why he'd married her, wasn't it? And it's why they'd sent their son to Harvard. It made no sense. There was a legacy to be had here. A dynasty to be made. And Patrick was going to let them throw it all away for some Italian?

For an Italian!

And then, with a searing flash of insight, she knew. She understood. And suddenly it all made sense. "It's because of *her*, isn't it?" Her voice wasn't filled with any of the rage or injustice or humiliation that she felt. It was devoid of all emotion. It was completely and utterly flat.

Billy might have been mystified, but there was no need for Mr. Quinn to ask to whom his wife was referring.

"You're allowing this because of her. This isn't about Billy and it isn't about me. You don't care what they'll say. You don't even care about your career. You don't care about any of us at all."

There was a searching exchange of looks between them, and then Mr. Quinn sighed and ran a hand through his graying hair. "You can go to bed, son."

Bed? At ten o'clock? Like some schoolboy? But Billy rose, shot a puzzled look at them both, and then left without comment. There was much for him to do. There were forms to be filled out for the wedding and the priest to contact. A physical to prepare for. His entire life was rapidly changing, and yet it couldn't change quickly enough for his taste.

Mrs. Quinn waited to speak until the door had closed. "You're letting him marry his Italian because you couldn't marry yours."

He pressed his hands flat against the desktop. "I don't—I don't know. Perhaps I am."

"You would throw her in my face?"

"Her name was Rosa."

"You would do that? To me?"

He looked away from his memories and into his wife's eyes. "I've never been unfaithful to you."

He hadn't.

"Have I ever embarrassed you? By flirtations with other women?"

More than politics required? "No."

"Have I ever been anything but cordial?"

"No." But neither had he been affectionate or adoring. She felt like a schoolgirl being called before a principal, caught for passing notes. "I love you." Passionately. Desperately. And without any hope of redemption.

Ah, now this was familiar territory. Here, he knew just what to do. He smiled. Winked. "And I'll take it all the way to the voting booths."

That's how he had always responded to her statements of love. And that's what she'd always done. She'd allowed him to take her family's name, all her earnest hopes—and her love—all the way to the voting booths.

She used to be thrilled, jubilant even, at the thought of being Mrs. Patrick Quinn. At the idea of opening to him the corridors of power, of ushering him into the arena of politics. She used to think of herself as the chief advisor behind the man. Used to dream of all the good that they could accomplish together. But that was when she thought that he had chosen her. Before she knew about the Italian girl. About . . . *Rosa*. Back before she realized what had really happened. Before she understood that she had chosen him.

"It's always been about her, hasn't it?"

He sighed. Shrugged. "I don't think, honestly, that—"

"No. Don't. You told me. Before we were married, you told me. And I married you anyway. That's my fault. But she left you, Patrick. And I took you. So when does it start to be about me?"

37

Patrick Quinn made his way to the stairs and pulled himself up with a hand on the rail. Halfway up, he stopped. Sat down on the step. Loosened his tie. Ran a hand across his lined, though still handsome, face.

Rosa De Luca.

He hadn't thought of her for years. He hadn't let himself. Every time he'd felt the specter of her presence, every time he'd sensed her skirting his thoughts, he'd thrown up the barricades of faith and family and career, and refused to let her in.

And now Billy was doing the same thing he had. Following the same path. And why shouldn't he?

Patrick Quinn knew what love was. He'd been young once, hadn't he? He'd been ready to risk it all, risk everything for love. It still galled him that he hadn't been allowed to. Hadn't that been his decision to make? Hadn't he deserved at least that chance?

It had taken him a while to figure out why she'd done it. And when he had, it had hurt him even more. Hurt him more than it had to stand up in front of the church with the priest, waiting ten minutes. Twenty. A full hour.

It hurt him even more because she'd been right. She'd been

right! What had anybody ever said but, *"I told you so. Italians can't be trusted. You're better off without her."*

How would they know? How would they ever know what it had cost him to continue on without her? How would they know just how many dreams he had never been able to realize because she hadn't been there by his side. To love him. To believe in him.

She may have been right, but that didn't make her decision any less wrong. They could have found a way. There had to have been another way.

He sighed, then pulled himself to his feet and continued on up the stairs. If Billy wanted to marry his Italian girl, then that's what he ought to do.

———

The next day Annamaria went to confession. She cleaned up early, pulled on her scarf, and hurried from the shop toward Saint Leonard's Church. Her heart had grown heavy with the sins of the week. With the guilt of an unsanctioned romance.

She walked into the church, dipped her fingers into the holy water, and crossed herself. Waited her turn in line. Once inside the booth, she didn't waste any time in speaking. "Bless me, Father, for I have sinned. It has been a week since my last confession." Actually . . . a bit more than a week. She'd meant to have gone on Tuesday, but with Theresa married and gone from the apartment, leaving all the work in Annamaria's hands . . . here it was Friday already.

On his side of the booth, Father Antonio recognized the voice. It was Annamaria Rossi. He felt an unseemly blossoming of pride for the girl. So pious and devout. Just the way a good Catholic girl should be. A quick confession of venial sins, a short prayer, and she would be done with her confession and gone from the booth. He put up a hand to smother a yawn.

"I have . . ." What? Spoken sharply to the girls at the shop?

Shoved two apples out the window? Regretted her mother's stubbornness? Spoken to a Sicilian? Sì. And smiled and laughed with him too. But what wrong had she really done? What sin had she truly committed? And didn't a person have to commit a sin in order to confess it?

Father waited.

"I have . . ."

That was odd. She sounded so hesitant. It was very strange. "You have . . . ?"

"I have . . . nothing to confess." She fairly laughed the words. Smiled them in any case. She was in love with Rafaello Zanfini. Her mother would call her a whore and her father might call her a traitor, but she had nothing—absolutely nothing—to confess.

"But—"

"Thank you, Father."

He slid the screen open, looked through to the other side, but the girl had already gone.

———

The next Monday, Annamaria and Julietta left the shop at the same time after work. They walked toward the North End together, though not by design. They had been pressed toward each other as they pushed their way through a crowd of thousands, who lined the streets waiting for a Liberty Loan parade to start. A symphony of coughs and sniffs accompanied their progress. The man pushing through the crowd in front of Annamaria couldn't seem to stop sniffling. Eventually, he parted from them at Congress Street, but not without first sneezing on her.

Julietta handed her a handkerchief.

Annamaria used it to dab the spittle off her face. Then she pocketed the square, planning to return it after it had been washed. Only she forgot that she put it in her pocket, and she missed the gathering of clothes for washing that Mama did that night.

She shrugged when she realized and put it on the sideboard so she would remember the next time. Only Mama found it first. "Where did you get this, Annamaria?" She was holding up Julietta's handkerchief.

"From a girl, Mama. At work."

Mama nodded and set it to one side. She would make sure it was included in the next wash. But it being white and reminding her of one of her own, she grabbed the handkerchief and used it to wipe off the lip of a cup that tumbled to the floor. And then to blot up the spill. Since she had the cup in her hand, she decided to fill it up again. She poured some more wine into it and then put it to her lips. Savored the taste of it as it went down her throat. "Bene. Va bene!" Papa should be getting his grapes from the country delivered soon. And then they'd have a feast. A big party, when he made his wine. And an even bigger one when he uncorked his supply in the spring.

She took another sip.

Mama could feel the warmth enlivening her blood and flowing to her bones. They were old, her bones. *Alla bell'e meglio.* Who knew how long they would last? She just wished they'd stop complaining so much. Creaks every morning getting out of bed, and aches every night sliding back in. Not like her girls. They were energetic. And sprightly. Though Annamaria had seemed a bit . . . moody . . . following Theresa's betrothal. Mama Rossi could understand. It was hard to be the oldest. But her Annamaria was a good girl, with a good heart . . . when those Sicilians weren't talking to her. And maybe someday when the youngest boys had married, she could spare her eldest daughter. Annamaria was meant for family. Anyone could see that. *Se Dio vuole.* Maybe someday. Just as soon as she could spare her. And then she'd find her Annamaria a nice Avellinesi boy to marry.

Stefano wandered by. Such a boy he was, wearing his breakfast still at the corners of his lips. Mama licked her finger and reached out to scrub at his face. Then she dabbed the rest away with the handkerchief, passing it across his lips once or twice for good measure. He licked up the trace of wine that it left on his mouth.

Later that evening, when her oldest son, Vittorio, came home from his work, he picked the handkerchief up to catch a sneeze. He'd been doing that lately. And coughing too. He pressed its folds beneath his nostrils to catch one last drip.

By next afternoon, Mama Rossi was sniffling too. And Theresa was sneezing.

"Watch what you're about!" Vittorio wiped the traces of Theresa's sneeze from his cheek with a swipe of the hand, from his ear toward his mouth. Then he reached across the table, picked up the bread that was left from lunch, broke it in half, and offered some to Stefano. They finished it together as Mama Rossi watched them, pride of family on her face.

She'd finished her cleaning. And some of the cooking. She took another sip of wine as she looked over at her sideboard. Maccheroni, onions, salame, garlic. And . . . no tomatoes.

"Annamaria? I need some tomatoes."

The girl jumped up from the bed where she was hemming a pair of trousers, grabbed her basket and her shawl. Mama watched her daughter leave, wondering that she had been blessed with such a magnificent family. And then she crossed herself just in case. Just in case fate was tempted to take away all of the blessings that it had granted her.

Several minutes later, once the onions had been cut and the salame sliced, Mama Rossi went down to the street, carrying a chair with her. She had several moments to spare, and she'd decided she'd rather spend them on the street with the scent of the sea perfuming the air than looking out the window onto the scene below.

The other women greeted her by making room for her chair.

Signora Tubello reached out and jabbed at Mama with an elbow. "Your Annamaria's a sly one."

"Annamaria?" Didn't the woman mean Theresa? That girl had been sneaking about with Giovanni for weeks before they'd become engaged.

"Sì. The one who crosses the street."

"I know she crosses the street. I asked her to cross the street. That Maglione was selling me rotten tomatoes." She dabbed at her dripping nose with her sleeve. Muffled a sneeze in her palm. "Do you know what he gave me for tomatoes?"

They knew. They all knew. They'd heard the story a dozen times. Or more. But they were all friends and their work was done for the moment and they had nothing better to do than to sit on the sidewalk and watch the world pass by. "What did he give you?"

"He gave me wormy ones and yellow ones. He gave me squashed ones too. With extra onions on top of them. Just to . . ." Mama Rossi had started on her story and was halfway into it before she realized that Annamaria hadn't yet returned. Her words tapered off.

"Just to hide the rotten tomatoes, sì?"

"Sì, sì. It's just . . ."

"You didn't tell about when you got them home yet. How they weren't even fit for *conserva di pomodori*."

"Or how Signor made that face when he tasted his parmigiana di melanzane."

"That sour one. Like this." Signora Tubello pulled a face, and the other women laughed at her. Everyone liked Papa Rossi. And they would have liked him even more if Mama Rossi would have talked a little less.

"Where's my Annamaria?"

"She crossed the street."

"Sì. I know it. I sent her."

Signora Rimaldi shrugged. "She always stays for a while. To talk to the Zanfini boy. Like I already told you."

Mama Rossi blinked. "To what?"

"She talks to him."

Talked to him? *Her* Annamaria? Still? She thought they'd been clear about that, she and Papa. Annamaria wasn't to speak to them anymore. Mama Rossi left her chair and started off across the street.

38

Indeed, Annamaria was talking to the Zanfini boy. She'd been doing that lately, ever since she'd told him her name. And smiling at him. And once in a while, to Rafaello's great delight, she laughed as well. Her laugh had the sound of bells in it.

That very afternoon, Mama Zanfini had asked Annamaria to give her pot of soup a stir. A very great honor. Mama didn't let just anyone fool with her soups. She sold them to the customers. For some extra money on the side.

When Annamaria had done the honors, she stepped out from the curtain and went to join Rafaello, who was standing behind the counter.

He'd been watching her. "You look like a plum."

You or I might have laughed at the sheer absurdity of the comparison, but Rafaello wasn't thinking about shape. He was thinking about Annamaria's sweet, earthy scent. About the sheen in her dark eyes. And the pleasing firmness of her dusky skin. It was clearly a compliment, and Annamaria took it the way it was intended. She blushed.

"The loveliest of plums." He picked one up and held it to her cheek.

She put a hand up to touch his.

And that's when Mama Rossi burst into the frutta e verdura with all the righteousness of a saint. She smacked Rafaello's hand away. The plum tumbled from his grasp, bruised itself on the floor, and rolled away behind the counter. "We told you not to speak to these people!" She grabbed Annamaria by the elbow and spun her from the boy. At least, that's what she intended to do.

But Annamaria would not be moved. She had blanched at Mama's appearance, but she made no move away from him. "Mama, this is Rafaello Zanfini."

"He could be the angel Gabriel himself, for all that I care!"

"It's Rafaello, who sells me your tomatoes." What she really wanted to say was, *It's Rafaello, whom I love.*

"I forbid you to speak to him!" She turned her wrath on Rafaello. "And I forbid you to speak to her!"

She grabbed hold of Annamaria's sleeve and turned toward the door, but her daughter would not have it. She disengaged herself and, after sending Rafaello a look of apology, walked from the store under her own power. Unfortunately, what her mother did next was not under Annamaria's control.

Mama Rossi turned on her daughter in the middle of the street. "Consorting with Sicilians!" She broke for a cough. "For shame. You of all my daughters! You disgrace me! You must despise me!"

Of course, Annamaria did no such thing. At least she hadn't until her mother had made their private words so very public. "Let's go home, Mama." It was getting dangerous standing there in the middle of the street with carts rattling by.

"I'll do no such thing! I'll have no traitor under my roof! Consorting with Sicilians! What do you have to say for yourself?"

"I love him."

"What do you—what?"

"I love him." She was sure, certain beyond any doubt, beyond all reason, that she loved Rafaello Zanfini.

And that confession, that declaration of love, is what finally moved Mama Rossi off the street and into the tenement building.

"There will be no talk of love. Not with a Sicilian!" She would have liked to have slammed the entrance door behind her, but it had an annoying way of catching against the threshold.

Annamaria said nothing, not one word during the time it took to climb three flights of stairs. Which took longer than usual, for Mama kept having to stop to catch her breath. But at the top of the stairs, she whirled around and began yelling once more. "I order you not to speak to him!"

Annamaria said nothing—still—as Mama fumbled with the key and door.

Vittorio, hearing them from the other side of the door, opened it for them as Mama kept up her tirade. "I forbid you to cross the street. Never, never again. I promise you!" She shoved Vittorio aside and slammed the door shut behind them for extra emphasis.

"I would as soon stop breathing."

Mama Rossi stepped forward, yanked Annamaria around with a hand on her forearm, and slapped her across the face. "That I should live to see my daughter shame me! May my name be lost in your home!"

Annamaria gasped. Mama had just disowned her.

"You have—you have—" Mama clutched at her chest, her lips turning blue.

"Mama?"

She gasped—a long, wheezing gasp that ended in a cough. "Don't . . . don't—" She crumpled into a heap on the floor.

Annamaria, cheek still tingling from her mother's palm, dove to the floor and picked up Mama Rossi's hand; it was cool. She put her hand to Mama's forehead; it was burning hot.

Over the next three hours, each one of the Rossis collapsed, felled by the Spanish influenza. First Mama, then Stefano. Vittorio and Vito, Theresa and Papa. Annamaria tried to get them all into their beds, but the boys were bigger than she could handle, and they didn't have energy enough to help her. She finally ripped the sheets and the pillows from the mattresses and placed them on the floor. By pushing the kitchen table back against the far wall and rolling them to the sheets, she succeeded in making each of them a bed on the floor.

After that, her thoughts had turned to food and water. But she was so very tired. They were sleeping now, all of them. But she didn't like the blue blotches that rode high on Mama's cheeks; they looked unnatural.

She decided that she'd sit down for just a minute. A minute wouldn't hurt anybody. And then she would try to get them to take some water. But as she sat down, she missed the chair entirely and dropped straight to the floor.

———

The next day, Annamaria didn't show up for work.

By that time, the city knew they were facing an onslaught of the Spanish influenza. And Julietta, warned by her conversations with Mauro, knew that the sickness was something bad. Something terrible. Something to fear. While Luciana and Madame were hoping that Annamaria would return to work the next day, Julietta was hoping—praying, in fact—that she was still alive.

Midday, Madame came up the stairs to offer them their customary bottle of wine.

"She still hasn't come?" Madame knew that she hadn't, but she couldn't help hoping that she had gone up the back stairs unnoticed.

Luciana shook her head.

Madame scowled at the table where Annamaria had left her work so neatly folded. She didn't know what to do. The newspapers were warning people against congregating in groups. They were counseling the use of gauze masks and whiskey rinses, the inhalation of turpentine fumes. There had even been a ban placed on sneezing. She wasn't sure she ought to leave the relative safety of the shop in order to find her missing employee. And even if she did, she wouldn't have known where to look. "Do either of you know where Annamaria lives?"

Neither of them did.

"I guess we'll just have to wait."

———

By dawn's meager light on the third day, all seven of the Rossis were stretched out on the hard, worn floor. The influenza had pounced on them, just as it would pounce on tens of thousands of other Bostonians. They had gone from coughing and sneezing to gasping for breath in the space of three hours. From sitting at the table to slumping to the floor.

A knock sounded at the Rossi door that morning. Most of the family was awake by then. Too weak to respond, they turned their eyes toward the sound. Somewhere, beneath the fog of their illness, they knew that they needed help. And somewhere, beneath that heavy malaise, they knew that they ought to answer.

But it seemed such a very great effort.

Much too great an effort. It was easier not to move. And so, soon after their ears had registered the knock and their eyes had focused on the door, they found the sound fading and their vision blurring as they surrendered once more to the illness.

All of them but Annamaria.

Annamaria was the one who rolled over onto her side. And Annamaria was the one who, despite a debilitating headache and a chest that felt like it had been weighted with rocks, crawled to the door. She clutched at the doorknob. Pulled on it with all her feeble might to stand. Leaning against the doorframe, panting and spent, she unlatched it and drew it open.

Rafaello's eyes widened as he saw her, as he caught her. All the color had gone from her face. Her eyes were nearly hidden by the great dark circles that ringed them. He looked past her, saw the rest of the Rossis lying on the floor. He carried her to one of the chairs at the table. The table that hadn't seen breakfast or lunch or dinner in over three days. "I hadn't seen you. I didn't know . . . if I had only known!" He hadn't seen her yet that week, and she always came into the store on Tuesday. Always. He'd woken that morning knowing that something was wrong. And hearing reports of the plague that was stalking the North End, he'd known he needed to find her. To see her. To help her, if help was what she needed. He prayed that he wasn't too late.

Madonna mia! She could hardly hold her head up. He carried her to the bed in the corner, pulled a blanket over her trembling form. "I'll be back, *amore mio*, don't you worry. I'll come back."

True to his word, he returned not half an hour later, hefting a pot of some of Mama Zanfini's *stracciatella*, with a loaf of bread tucked beneath his arm. Though the Rossis were quite literally starving, they had no strength, no will, to do anything but watch as he set the pot on the cold stove. They could only stare as he scrubbed out a bowl. Only gaze as he ladled some of the soup into it.

Rafaello knelt by Stefano first. Put a hand beneath the boy's head to raise it. He wanted to cross himself at the sight of his blue lips and raspy breathing, but he decided that physical ministrations should come before spiritual. He worked his way around the room, spooning soup, wiping brows, and straightening blankets. Each one of them would remember, in the coming years, the infinite gentleness of Rafaello Zanfini as he moved around that room.

And finally, he reached Mama Rossi.

She recognized him. She turned her head.

Across the room, from her vantage point on the bed, Annamaria saw the gesture. "Mama. Don't."

Rafaello tried again. Again, Mama refused his aid.

Annamaria stretched out an arm, wishing she could turn her mother's head. "Let him."

"I am only trying to help you, Signora."

She tried to shake her head, but it took too much effort. "Why? Help?"

Why help? He thought that she was questioning his sanity. He thought she was wondering why he would expose himself to the deadly plague of the influenza. His answer was swift. And very simple. He slipped a hand beneath Mama Rossi's head. "Our blessed Savior once said, 'If you've done it to the least of these, you have done it unto me.' "

But Mama Rossi wasn't inquiring about his theology; she was disparaging his ancestry. "Don't want . . . the least . . . not to me . . ." She turned her head away.

Rafaello followed her mouth with his spoon.

From somewhere deep inside her scandalized Avellinesi soul, she summoned the strength to knock it to the floor.

39

Annamaria was not the only one who had failed to report to work at Madame's shop. Half the girls on the second floor had been absent for the greater part of the week. In the North End, it was easy to tell that something was wrong. The wharves were much less busy than usual; there were fewer ships in port and there were far fewer teamsters and longshoremen than there should have been on weekday afternoons. Julietta's little brother, Matteo, hadn't gotten up for breakfast that morning. An ominous sign in any ten-year-old. And Salvatore had gone to work with a cough. She herself was beginning to feel a hitch in her chest whenever she breathed, although she'd been able, so far, to keep from coughing.

They'd tried to find Mauro, but the good doctor was nowhere to be found, though he was rumored to be everywhere. Everyone in the North End had seen him, but no one could find him. Julietta had already torn out her work three times from lack of concentration. She had already been tense with worry, and thoughts of Little Matteo only added to her great burden.

Luciana had worries of her own. Much as she tried not to think of it, the date of Billy's physical was approaching. They'd

SIRI MITCHELL

come to seem so much like a family—she, the contessa, and Billy. He treated her grandmother with such kindness. He took her to museums and out to tea. Over to Boston Common for walks in the public garden. He'd set them up at The Lenox and bought them entirely new wardrobes. She'd even caught the contessa trying to teach him Italian. But it was all just a fantasy.

He hadn't formally introduced them to his family.

He'd be shipping out soon.

And her father's murderer was still out there, somewhere, in the city.

He couldn't understand why she insisted on keeping her job at Madame's. The reasons were several. There was no one else who could do what she did. Madame needed her. But Luciana also needed Madame. She was afraid to hope. She was afraid to trust in Billy's bright dream for their future. She needed to know that she could take care of herself.

Before Julietta and Luciana could leave the shop for the night, Madame paid them a visit. "I don't want you to come to work next week."

They both looked at her, alarm in their eyes. If they didn't work, they wouldn't be paid.

"Don't worry, you can make up the work some other week, after this plague has passed. I doubt very much whether the Putnams will be holding their party or the Winthrops their dinner when so many people are unlikely to attend. There's no great hurry anymore for these gowns. And you may be risking more by coming to work than if you stayed at home."

They couldn't argue with her. They had both become experts at dodging those who looked ill. And they had both become adept at ignoring the alarming numbers of carts that were wheeling bodies through the city, and the stacks of corpses that were piling up outside doctors' offices.

"Only—before you go." Madame pushed a piece of paper

toward each of them and followed it with a pencil. "Write your address for me. Just in case . . ."

———

Julietta used the time off to her advantage. She didn't tell Mama or Papa about Madame's decision. Mama was busy enough with Little Matteo, and Papa would only start worrying about the money. Her cough hadn't seemed to worsen any, so she rose as she always did on Monday morning and left the apartment as if she were going to work. Only when she spied Angelo's truck in the neighborhood, she went right up to him and tugged on his sleeve.

The courage it had taken!

She was quaking in her shoes and everything within her screamed at her to run away from him. But she couldn't. He'd taken Madame's jewels—she was more certain of it now than ever—and Julietta had to get them back. Her honor, and Madame's business, depended upon it.

Angelo turned around and smiled. Winked at her. "Look what's fallen from the clouds!" He opened the truck door for her, but she shook her head.

"I need the jewels back, Angelo."

The smile disappeared from his face as he slammed the door shut. To his credit, he didn't dismiss her accusation. "What if I need them more?"

"You don't understand. They weren't even Madame's. She was keeping them for a client. If they aren't returned, she'll be ruined!"

He shrugged and leaned a shoulder against the cab of the truck. "What's that to me?"

"They aren't yours. You stole them!"

"You should thank me. I've freed you from the bonds of oppression."

She attacked him. Lashed out at him with a fist. "I don't want to be freed! I want my job! I like it!"

He blocked her fist with his arm and considered her for a moment. He'd had more trouble trying to sell the jewels than he thought he would. So in spite of their promise, they hadn't given him much return on his trouble. But she still had something he wanted. "How much are they worth to you?"

"What—what do you mean?"

"How much are you willing to pay for them?"

"I don't have much money—"

"I'm not talking about money. You give me what I want, and I'll give you what you want. How's that for a trade?" He put a finger to her cheek and drew it down past her neck.

———

By midweek the Rossis were recovering, for the most part. Everyone but Mama. She had used the last of her strength to refuse Rafaello's help. There was no known cure for the Spanish influenza, but those who kept warm and those who stayed nourished greatly increased their chances of recovery. Sadly, Mama Rossi would do neither. Not when it was a Sicilian who was offering the aid.

Annamaria watched from her bed, watched as Rafaello spent his days cleaning for them, as he fed them, and as he cared for them. She watched as her mother took her last breath . . . watched as her soul slipped away.

It was Rafaello who waited as she dressed Mama in her wedding dress, and Rafaello who carried her body out to the street and arranged for someone to collect it. Then later, it was Rafaello who found out where she had been buried.

She may have looked as if she were fifty. She may have acted as if she were sixty, but Mama Rossi had been just forty years old when she'd died.

———

Madame's shop was deserted. The impossible had happened. It was the last week in September and the most preeminent gown maker in Boston had no appointments and she kept none. She had no girls and she needed none. There was no work to be done. The Spanish influenza had halted the city's business just as surely as if the world had come to an end.

But she rose every day and went to the shop in the morning just the same. She didn't want to be alone in her house with her thoughts. She didn't want to worry about *him*. At least at the shop, her fears could be pushed aside by the hundreds of things that needed her attention.

But still she worried. She hoped he was still . . . fine. Still . . . Alive.

Still alive is what she hoped he was, but she didn't want to—wouldn't—think it in those words.

She was so proud of him. As proud as if she were standing next to him. Prouder still, perhaps. For she knew that he would have accomplished nothing had she in fact been standing there. It had been so plain to everybody. She only wondered that she had not realized it before. And wondered still more that he had realized it not at all.

He was an Irishman. She was an Italian.

Italian.

It wasn't the word that condemned her, for she hardly thought of herself in that way. Not anymore. No, it wasn't the word; it was the tone. It was the tone in which these Americans spoke it. A tone that had been passed down from generation to generation. From mother to son. From father to child. *Italian*. With a half-dozen qualifiers strung along in front of it in order to debase that epithet even further.

What would he have become if she'd married him? Just what did he think he would have done? It was her quick thinking, her sacrifice, that had saved him. But did he ever think of her, in the dark hours of the night? Did he ever wonder?

He must know. He must know by now. He must be grateful. He must thank God every day that she had done what she had. If he thought of her at all, it must be as a man who looks back on an illness that nearly took his life.

He must be grateful.

That was the thought upon which she had built her life: He must be grateful. Madame assured herself, as she always did, that she had done what she had out of love.

One of the many tasks she performed that morning, just as she did every morning, was the opening of her safe. She peered into the interior as had become her habit. Pushed a hand inside just to see, just to make sure, that the bag of jewels had not been magically returned during the night. She spread her fingers wide as she reached toward the back.

But they closed around air. There was nothing there.

She didn't know what she would do.

There had been so many jewels in that bag. And not only seed pearls. There were piles of sapphires and stacks of garnets. The strega, it seemed, had wanted to wear her entire fortune on her chest. Ridiculous woman.

Ridiculous.

The word was Madame's greatest insult. And it was reserved chiefly for that witch, Mrs. Quinn.

Strega.

There were so many other words Madame would have liked to have called her. So many other things she had thought up through the years. But strega was the only one that really, truly applied, and so the strega, Mrs. Quinn remained. And now the strega's jewels were gone. If Madame thought too long about that obligation, worried too much about how she would ever repay their worth, her stomach tied itself into knots, her breathing grew shallow. She had almost fainted one morning. And so this morning she stopped her thoughts from running ahead to the seventh of October. She threw up a barrier. To there she would think and no further.

After the world had righted itself and the influenza was gone, there was Mrs. Winthrop to be received and Mrs. Kennedy to be fitted. A second fitting. There was Mrs. Putnam to be measured and the order for Mrs. Cabot to be placed. There were a dozen things that needed to be done before this day was over and a hundred to be done before the seventh of October. And at some point in between then and now, she desperately hoped that the jewels would be returned.

She had to hope. She hadn't the money to be wrong.

But she puzzled over their disappearance. It had to be one of her girls who had taken them. She wouldn't stoop to calling them stolen.

Julietta.

Annamaria.

Luciana.

Which of them had it been? And why?

Julietta had been wearing new clothes recently. Madame recognized that they had been remade with bits and pieces from the workshop. From leftover trims and braids. Madame wasn't concerned about that. She applauded such resourcefulness and creativity. But Julietta had a new hat . . . a very pretty, very stylish new hat. Still, Madame considered herself a good judge of character and she would have told anyone, had she ever been asked, that Julietta, though vain, was reliable. That's why she was hoping to train her as an assistant.

So she wouldn't have said that it was Julietta.

Luciana?

The girl was new. And that lent a certain trace of suspicion to her character. But she came from a good family. Madame would have sworn to it. She was poor, but then, so were many of her girls on the second floor. That didn't mean they lacked in honesty. In fact, Madame insisted upon it.

No. She wouldn't have said that the thief was Luciana.

Annamaria?

That was something to think about. She wouldn't have even considered the possibility a month—even two weeks—ago, but there was something different about the girl. A certain attitude. A new kind of knowledge in her eyes. And she had the look of a girl who kept a secret. She was hiding something. That was certain. Madame had to hope that it was the jewels. She had run out of other options.

Annamaria.

She wouldn't have thought it. But she would just have to pray that it was true.

40

As Madame was keeping busy at the shop, Julietta was getting ready to go out. She was getting ready to meet Angelo. She bent at the knees so she could see her reflection in the little mirror Mama Giordano had hung by the door.

Mama came to stand behind her. "Have you seen Mauro lately?" Mama was waiting for her daughter to turn around. Her youngest, dearest, most beloved daughter who insisted on wearing that hat! Madonna mia! In Avellino, only the wealthiest or the loosest of women wore hats . . . though sometimes they were one and the same. Scarves had been good enough for the rest of them. They still were! She didn't know why Julietta insisted on wearing the hated thing. Although she'd been insisting on so many things recently. She'd insisted on coming home late. She insisted on disappearing at community events. She seemed to be . . . seemed to be . . . leaving. If that were possible.

"Mauro? No. Why?" She didn't want to see him for another hundred years. Couldn't bear to think of seeing him, knowing she would never again be able to look him in the eyes again. Not after she finished paying the price that Angelo had demanded for the jewels.

"He said he hadn't seen you either. Not even when he went by the shop last week. He said it wasn't even open."

Julietta closed her eyes. She was so tired of lying. So tired of pretending. So tired of feeling so dirty. She opened her eyes, took one last look at herself. Told her reflection to act like that girl in the mirror. The one that looked so confident, so American with her darling hat and her newly altered blouse. All she really wanted to do was to throw herself into Mama's arms and confess everything. Confess that she had run around with a stranger; confess that the stranger had turned into a murderer; and confess that the murderer wanted to turn her into his whore.

But how could she?

If she confessed to having told Angelo about the jewels, wouldn't that implicate her in the crime? And if she confessed to having walked out with him, wouldn't that make her exactly what she would shortly become?

Though she wanted to confess to Mama, what she really longed to do was run to Mauro. He had always protected her, always listened to her in the past. And he might have done it again if she hadn't thrown Angelo in his face.

She'd dug a hole for herself that there was no way out of, and there was no longer anyone she could ask for help. Her only option, her only chance to right all those wrongs, was to do exactly what Angelo wanted. Her virtue wasn't worth so very much, after all. Not after she'd lied, and cheated, and allowed him to steal from Madame's safe.

"Mauro said the shop was closed."

Julietta answered her mother without turning around. What was one more lie? "Madame did close the shop. For a few days. For most of the girls."

"He said he knocked on the door. He asked after you."

"Sometimes Madame sends me out on deliveries." Or she might have, had Julietta proven herself more able for the job than Luciana. How she wished she could speak to Mama without having to lie. How she wished she could just be Julietta again. She had no illusions; she knew her faults just as she knew her weaknesses. She was vain and not particularly devout, just as she was not fickle or cowardly. In most instances. But as she stood there, trying to keep from looking Mama in the eye, she wished for the time when she was truly a part of the family. A family that she didn't have to hide from or flee. The family that they had been before there was Angelo.

She'd thought he'd offered excitement and flirtation and fun. But what she'd gotten was lies and deceit and the death of everything of value. He'd destroyed everything that was good in her life.

Mama cocked her head and looked at this daughter whose eyes seemed to have such trouble meeting hers of late. "Is there anything you want to tell me, cara mia?"

Those bewitching eyes, startled, swerved to meet her mother's in the mirror for just a moment.

Help me! Pray for me! Rescue me!

But Julietta didn't deserve anyone's help, just as she didn't deserve any prayers. She'd wanted to experience life on her own two feet, uncommitted and free. Well, she'd gotten what she wanted, hadn't she? And now she would have to pay for it.

"Anything at all? We are both women, cara mia. Both Avellinesi."

There was a moment when Julietta might have told her mother everything, might have admitted to seeing Angelo, might have admitted to going to those meetings . . . even told her mother that he was a murderer and a thief. But her mother was exactly what she had said. She was Avellinesi and she would never have understood. So Julietta turned around, giving her mother a swift hug and a kiss on the cheek before she opened the door and walked out.

Julietta met Angelo in front of Zanfini's, the way they had arranged. Angelo assumed she lived somewhere near there, although the truth was she lived some three blocks up and three blocks over. She was glad now for her deception. She didn't want anyone to see them together. Not ever. She sat beside him, meek and silent, while he completed his deliveries. And then as he pulled the truck to a stop by the wharves.

She let him kiss her. Let him embrace her, not moving, trying not to react until she felt a breeze pass across her chest. She pushed him away and discovered that her blouse had come undone.

A flush lit her cheeks as she fumbled with the buttons. She'd have to sew the holes up smaller when she got home. As she was trying to regain her modesty, Luciana's lavaliere fell from her open collar, sparking a gleam when it swung into an errant ray of sun.

Angelo caught it up in his hand. "Where did you get this?"

She answered by grabbing the necklace from him and dropping it back beneath her blouse.

"Where did you get it?" He grabbed her by the forearm.

"I—I was given it. As a gift."

To her mind, it was. It was worth far more than the few hours she had put into altering Madame's gowns for Luciana.

"A gift."

"Si." She spoke with her eyes downcast.

"Because the last time I saw that crest, I was in Roma."

Roma? But—that's where Luciana had come from. How did . . . ? "It was given me by a friend."

He was staring at her chest, at the place where the lavaliere dangled beneath her blouse. "I've changed my mind."

She looked up at him, startled.

"If you introduce me to your friend, then I'll give you the jewels back."

"If I—" Did that mean . . . ? She was freed? And all she had to do was introduce him to Luciana? She tried to stem her rising elation. It didn't make any sense. Her eyes had been opened and she knew now that he had been trying to seduce her for weeks. So why should he discard her now? When he could so easily take what he wanted? And why did he want to be introduced to Luciana so badly? She slid to the far side of her seat and opened the door, wanting to slip away before he pressed her further. "I'll see." He was going to have to leave it at that. Because he was never going to meet her. Not as long as Julietta had any say in the matter. Something didn't seem right.

———

Julietta couldn't leave quickly enough after work the next Monday. She wanted to be home. Back at the tenement. The shop was too quiet, with none of Madame's clients visiting. And outside, on the streets, it was so eerie. There'd been no mass on Sunday; church had been canceled throughout the city. No bells had rung, no people had promenaded in the streets in the afternoon. And today there had been no cars. Motorists had been ordered to keep them garaged. It was strange. And frightening. As if the world had come to an end. And now, Angelo wanted to meet Luciana. That thought was frightening too. Because niggling away at the back of Julietta's mind were several remembered conversations, which all pointed to one horrifying conclusion.

It was with great shock, then, that she observed him as she pushed open the door to the alley. "Angelo!" Fearful of being seen with him, and yet wanting to take him far away from the shop—far away from Luciana—her eyes swept the alley. She discovered there was someone else, another man, lounging in the shadows.

That man was Billy. He was waiting for Luciana so that he could take her to city hall to sign the papers necessary for their wedding. He'd borrowed one of his mother's servants to stay with the contessa.

Angelo smiled at Julietta. It was a lazy smile that didn't quite spread from one side of his mouth to the other. "Did I surprise you?"

"Sì. Of course you surprised me."

He wrapped an arm around her waist and gave her a kiss that nearly made her retch. She broke from his embrace. "Why are you here?"

"To meet your friend."

She wasn't about to let that happen! She linked an arm through his and began to hurry him away.

But the door squeaked open at just that moment, and Angelo turned back toward it.

Julietta knew who it had to be.

Angelo had gone completely still. His eyes were the only thing in motion, and they burned with an unearthly glow that made the hairs on Julietta's arms stand on end.

For her part, Luciana, who had just come through the door, had also come to a halt. And her face had gone deathly pale. It was just as she'd known. Just as she'd feared. Her father's murderer had found her, just as he'd promised. But the fear, having washed over her in a horrific wave, rolled past and left a quickly rising anger in its place. Her face burned red. "Assassino!" Her voice was hoarse, her tone low. But then she said it again with all the outrage her slim frame could muster.

Billy had pushed away from the wall. He moved past Julietta and Angelo on his way to Luciana's side.

But Luciana paid no attention to him; indeed, didn't even seem to see him. In fact, she marched right past him, up to Angelo, and slapped him across the face.

Julietta gasped as her mouth fell open.

Angelo just stood there, a livid outline of Luciana's hand making an imprint across his cheek.

But Luciana wasn't yet done. She spit at his feet. Twice. She might have done it a third time, but Billy grabbed at her arm and Julietta pushed herself between Angelo and Luciana.

Julietta put a hand up to his chest. "What do you think you're—"

Angelo shoved her to the ground with a force that knocked the breath from her. Then he took a step forward toward Luciana. "I've finally found you." The sneer on his face changed into a leer.

Billy stepped between them. "Luciana?"

Behind them all, Julietta was trying to get up, but her arm had been bent back at a strange angle and it hurt with a pain so sharp that it made her draw back the breath she had just let go.

Luciana sidestepped Billy and launched herself at Angelo, tearing into his face with her nails. "You killed my father!"

Julietta could only sit and stare as Luciana attacked. It was true, then. Everything Angelo had told her was true. Each and every despicable thing.

Billy had grabbed hold of Luciana's waist and was trying to pull her away from Angelo. "Luciana—*bitte!*"

"It's him. He's the man who killed my father!" The man who flirted with her and lied to her. The man who had betrayed her love and trust; who had played her for a fool. "He's the one!" At that admission, all of her indignation and fury deserted her. She promptly burst into tears and collapsed in his arms.

Billy eyed Angelo, who was edging away. The assassin tripped over Julietta in his haste, then righted himself and continued on. As he neared the end of the alley, he sent one last triumphant smirk over his shoulder.

It was that which sent Billy into action. Leaving Luciana on the back stoop, he ran in Angelo's direction. All those afternoons at The Tennis and Racquet Club stood him in good stead. Angelo heard Billy coming, but by the time he turned around to look for him, it was too late. The only thing he saw was Billy's fist as it smashed into his nose. He started to raise a hand to ward off subsequent blows, but Billy's other fist boxed him in the ear. Angelo had already blacked out by the time his head hit the ground.

Billy turned his back on the man. His hands had gone stiff. He flexed them once, twice. Then he reached down and extended a hand to Julietta, helping the girl to her feet. By that time, Luciana had come down off the steps and flown into his arms. *"Danke."* It was the least of what she wanted to say to him, but the only sentiment that she was able to put into words.

"We need the police. To come and take him away." He opened the door of the shop and ushered Luciana through it, then turned to look for the other girl.

Julietta had walked over to where Angelo lay on the ground. "I can't believe I ever kissed you . . . I can't believe I ever thought I loved you . . . I can't—" A sob tore at her throat. She kicked him in the stomach. And again for good measure. Oh, but the effort made her arm ache. "You filthy, miserable . . . *malfattore!*"

Once inside, Billy alerted Madame to the goings-on in the alley. She telephoned for the police. But by the time Billy had met them at the entrance to the shop and led them through to the alley, Angelo had gone.

The policemen looked up and down the alley, but found no sign of him. They came back to where Billy was standing. "An assassin? One of those anarchists?"

"Yes, sir."

"Says who? You?"

Billy looked over at Luciana, who had hung back by the door. She nodded hesitantly.

"Says Miss Luciana Conti, daughter of the Count of Rome."

———

Madame helped Julietta tie up her arm in a scarf. It still hurt—it hurt excruciatingly—but at least it wasn't bumping against her side at every step. She left the shop by the front door as the policemen went out the back.

She pondered her fate as she walked home.

Mama would have to be told what had happened. Mauro would have to be called to look at her arm. She would have to spill the whole shameful story. And it was a shame. All of it. A deep, abiding, humiliating shame. And that was the worst of it. The deep, deep shame. A shame that kept Julietta's gaze on her feet all the way home.

She hadn't known he was like that, had she? At first? She had once thought Angelo bold and visionary, but she had discovered him to be so much less. She was shamed now that she would have to admit to a relationship with him. Shamed even more that it was Mauro who would have to be told.

———

Julietta might have told Mama everything that evening, but the astounded woman began clucking over her daughter's arm just as soon as she saw it, and didn't stop exclaiming over it until Mauro had been called. And once he had come, she stood right over his shoulder as he examined Julietta's arm, as he pronounced that it needed to be set in plaster. He had his own ideas—culled from the way she refused to meet his eyes and the fading finger-shaped bruises on her forearms—about how she had happened to break her arm, but he decided to keep his suspicions to himself. Which left Julietta feeling even more shamed as she went to work the next morning.

Madame was able to rig a sort of vise to hold Julietta's work as she went about her embroidery, but it was slow going and awkwardly done, and by the time the day was over, Julietta was wishing for nothing so much as her bed. But she had amends to make first.

"I owe you something, Luciana."

Luciana looked up from her work in surprise. Julietta hadn't spoken for the entire day. Luciana eyed the girl with suspicion. "I don't know what you mean."

"I want you to have your necklace back. I don't deserve it. I've brought you nothing but trouble."

"You earned it. You altered the gowns for me."

"But it's not mine. It's yours. It belongs to you. Angelo recognized . . . I mean, I didn't know he was like that. Not really . . . not until . . ." She said it like a plea.

Luciana's eyes softened. "Neither did I. He deceived me back in Roma. The same way he did you."

"But I didn't know! Not at first."

"Neither did I." Luciana still couldn't believe she hadn't known. Hadn't realized.

"I feel so . . ."

"Stupid? Foolish?"

"Si." And angry, too. "Please . . . take it back."

It was a pendant made in the design of the Conti family crest, and of all the pieces she'd had to let go, it was the one she had regretted the most. Luciana nodded.

"You'll have to unfasten it yourself." She lifted her useless arm as she bent her head, baring her neck.

Luciana undid the fastener, pulled the chain free, and then put it around her own neck. The gems twinkled as the lavaliere fell back into place beneath her blouse.

41

"Look what I found!" Stefano had called out to Annamaria from across the room.

She turned from the stove toward him, glad to hear a note of excitement in his voice. There had been so little to delight over, so little joy in the apartment since Mama had died.

He was swinging a familiar silver medal as he waited for dinner, the chain whirring as it spun an arc through the air. "I found it on the floor underneath the shelf."

She held out her hand.

"It's mine! I found it."

"Give it, *bambino mio*. You don't want a medal of Saint Zita." No one did. No one with any hopes or dreams.

"It's mine."

Vittorio was watching from his place at the table. "What? You want to turn into an old maid like Annamaria? Give it back to her. That's who it belongs to."

"An old maid?" Stefano pulled a face. Threw it at her. "I don't want it anymore. You can have it."

She threw up a hand and caught it before it could hit her in the face. Saint Zita. Patron saint of single women and servant girls. Saint Zita had beckoned her back, called her home. How could she think of doing anything now but caring for her poor motherless family? She bowed her head to fate and slid the chain back over her neck.

Stefano suddenly and unaccountably ran over to her and threw his arms around her waist. "You won't leave us, will you, Annamaria?"

All eyes at the table turned in her direction.

Leave them? Now? Now that Mama had died? How could she? How could anyone? A small voice inside her insisted that this wasn't what she wanted.

"Now you have to stay with us, don't you? You can't leave. Not ever! Not like Mama did."

Tears glistened at the corners of her brother Vittorio's eyes. Papa had bowed his head and put a trembling hand up to cover his face.

Closing her eyes, she bent to kiss him on the head. "Now I have to stay with you."

"Promise! Promise you won't leave."

"I won't leave."

She fell asleep that night clutching the medal, praying that God would give her the strength to stay. And the grace not to regret it.

———

Before he began his rounds on Saturday, Mauro stopped in at the Giordanos to take another look at Julietta's arm. He pronounced her well enough to do nearly anything. "But nothing too strenuous, Mama." He didn't bother to give the instruction to Julietta, because he knew she would ignore it.

But Julietta didn't have plans to do anything strenuous. There was only one place she wanted to go and she went there that very afternoon, sliding into the confession booth at St. Leonard's a little after three o'clock.

Julietta crossed herself. "Bless me, Father, for I have sinned. My last confession was six months ago."

The priest waited for the voice to continue, but it said nothing. "My child?"

"I need . . . help, Father."

"You can't remember your sins?"

Julietta nearly smiled. "No. I can remember them." She remembered all of them. "It's just that . . . there are so many." How had she come to collect so many of them? And why was it that she had waited so long to confess them?

"God has been waiting for you, my daughter."

Have you, God? Truly?

"To offer you peace and forgiveness. Mercy and wholeness."

You would do that, God? For me? Even after . . . everything?

"The Holy Scriptures tell us that all have sinned and that in Christ alone we have redemption and the forgiveness of sins. He can forgive you. He will forgive you. If only you will confess."

Forgiveness. That's what she wanted. She wanted to start all over again. She wanted to feel clean.

"It's always best to start with your mortal sins. Confess the worst one first."

Mortal sins. All of them had been mortal sins. They were all grave sins, and all had been committed with Julietta's full knowledge and full consent. "Then I confess to . . . lust." That one was the worst. That was the one that had led her to Angelo and then kept on drawing her back. "I confess to hatred, wrath, strife, sedition, envy . . . reveling." She listened to the words as she spoke them. She meant every one. "I confess to anger." She'd been angry, hadn't she, that her family hadn't been more American? She'd been angry that they kept living as if they were still in the old country, and angry that they couldn't be made to see any sense. That they wouldn't change. And the anger had led to shame. Or had it been the other way around? "I confess to neglect of my Sunday obligations, to lying, and to sins against love. I've been very ungrateful, Father. I've despised my family for their . . . love." Because that's all they'd ever done, wasn't it? All they'd ever done was love her. All they'd ever done was wanted the best for her. "And I confess to pride."

"How many times have you committed these sins?"

Times without number. "Too many times to count."

Father Antonio was rarely surprised by the sins his parishioners committed, but he had never ceased to be saddened. "You committed yourself to the path of rebellion, my child."

She nodded, though she could not speak for sorrow.

"Do you wish to turn from this path?"

"I want to, Father. I'm sorry for these and all the sins of my past life." She hadn't before realized just how far away from her family, how far away from love, her sins had carried her. She'd undertaken some of them as a lark. She'd made a game of trying to keep her family from knowledge of Angelo. She hadn't realized how dangerous that game had become.

"You must go from here and confess these sins to your parents."

Her heart quailed within her. But as she bowed her head, as she listened to the words of the priest, she realized that he was right. She'd already confessed her sins to God. Now she needed to confess them to the people she had hurt. And when, at last, she was invited to, she sincerely spoke those timeless words of contrition. "O God, I am heartily sorry for having offended you and I detest all my sins, because I dread the loss of heaven and the pains of hell. But most of all because I have offended you, my God, who is all good and deserving of all my love. I firmly resolve with the help of your grace to confess my sins, to do penance and to amend my life. Amen."

The priest sighed, both in sorrow over the transgressions of this beloved daughter of God and in happiness that she had come to accept a measure of His grace. "May our Lord Jesus Christ absolve you; and by His authority I absolve you from every bond of excommunication and interdict, so far as my power allows and your needs require." He crossed himself. "Thereupon, I absolve you of your sins in the name of the Father, and of the Son, and of the Holy Ghost. Amen. Now, may the Passion of Our Lord Jesus Christ, the merits of the Blessed Virgin Mary and of all the saints obtain for you that whatever good you do or whatever evil you bear might merit for you the remission of your sins, the increase of grace, and the reward of everlasting life. Give thanks to the Lord for He is good."

Julietta had received the ministrations with eager gratitude, and now she was forgiven. Renewed.

Give thanks to the Lord for He is good. For His mercy endures forever. And it extends to such as me.

———

Madame Fortier had gone to her shop on Monday morning, trepidation spotting her palms with sweat. Today was the day. The day she would either discover the jewels to have been returned . . . or the day she would have to fire one of her third-floor girls. Only one outcome was acceptable. The other would leave her reputation in tatters, her business in ruins.

It was a day when she wished—how she wished!—to be her father's daughter once more. To find him in his tailor's shop, mouth filled with pins. To walk into his warm embrace. To sit on Papa's lap, sheltered by his arms, and tell him all that was wrong. But she was no longer a girl; she was a woman grown. And she was no longer her father's daughter. She was Madame Fortier.

She busied herself first with settling some bills, then with writing up some orders. She did a hundred things that morning which kept her from opening the safe in her office. She heard the steps of her girls going up to the second-floor workshop. And three sets of steps going up farther still. *Grazie a Dio*, Annamaria had finally returned!

It was time.

Madame considered fortifying herself with a drink from the bottle she kept in her drawer. Then decided she'd better not. The theft had nothing to do with the strega. It was her own fault that she'd hired a thief, if a thief there proved to be . . . though she'd always been so certain of her judgment. In any case, if she had to fire one of her girls, she wanted to have all her wits about her. But she sat there behind her desk for several minutes more, staring at her fear until she became annoyed by the stubbornness with which it had dogged her. And it was then that she finally summoned the anger necessary to continue.

But it was at that moment—that very same moment—someone pushed into the shop. And shoved the door shut with such energy that the building itself shuddered.

Madame dropped her hand from the lock and left her office to see who it was.

The strega.

Her eyes widened. All her hopes plummeted from the secret shelf in her heart where she had put them, hoping, praying that the jewels would be returned. There was no doubt. Mrs. Quinn knew. By some dark magic she must have discovered the theft of the jewels. She had discovered the theft and now she was going to demand payment.

"Where is she?"

Madame Fortier came out from behind the counter onto the shop floor. She tried to make sense of Mrs. Quinn's words, but there were only so many ways to rearrange those three short words and none of those combinations made any sort of sense. "Where is . . . who?"

"Her!"

"Which *her*?"

"The girl who stole Billy."

Stole was a word that fit Madame's expectations, but . . . "Billy?"

"The girl who's seduced my son. That Italian girl!" Mrs. Quinn's face flushed bright red, and her eyes flashed dangerous glints of steel.

Madame took a step back toward her office. "I assure you, I have no idea of what you speak."

"And I assure you that one of your girls has trapped Billy into marriage." It had taken her a while—three weeks, in fact—to find out who it was that Billy was so bent upon marrying. And even now she didn't know who the girl was.

But Madame did. And she liked Luciana. She wasn't about to throw her to the strega. "Which girl?"

"The Italian one!"

"I have several Italian girls working for me. To which one do you refer?"

"I don't know. They all look the same to me!"

Madame Fortier's right brow had risen dangerously high. She'd had enough! Enough of being tied to the orders and whims of a woman whose only goal seemed to be to make life complicated. "*I* am Italian. Perhaps you are speaking of me."

Mrs. Quinn took a step backward, away from Madame's wrath. "Of course you're not Italian. You're . . . you're . . . French!"

"As French as an Italian can be."

"I don't understand. I don't—"

"Out." Madame pointed toward the door with one majestically outflung finger.

"I don't think—I mean—"

"Get out of my shop."

"If I leave, I may never come back."

"Bene. May it be a promise between us." Madame opened the door herself and then pushed the strega through it with an unyielding hand.

42

She passed her office wondering if . . . but no. The jewels could wait until later. Until after she had determined what exactly the strega had to do with Luciana. She had turned the corner toward the back stairs when she realized something. She had dealt with the strega—ordered her out of the store even!—and she hadn't needed a drink to do it. She felt absolutely fine. She felt as fine as she'd felt in over twenty years.

She almost stopped right there with her foot on the first stair and laughed. From the sheer exhilaration of it all. From the look of outrage on the strega's face. If she lost everything she'd ever owned tomorrow, if Mrs. Quinn found out about the jewels, she'd still have done—still have said—the very same things.

Go ahead, cheer if you wish to. I did the same myself.

Madame walked past the second floor and on to the third. She stood in the doorway, surveying her girls. Which of them had lied to her? Though she'd been ready to ask each one, ready to put the theft of the jewels to rest, she put that matter aside. Concentrated on the question at hand.

"Is there something one of you wishes to tell me?" A flush simultaneously lit each girl's cheeks, though none of them said a thing. Curious. "Something that pertains, perhaps, to one of my customers?"

Now, only Luciana's eyes refused to meet her own.

"Something that concerns that customer *very* greatly?"

Luciana remained silent, yet she truly wanted to speak. The only thing she lacked was words. What words could she use to speak to Madame of treachery and betrayal? Of family lost and found? Of strangers' kind help and astonishing propositions?

"I must know what's going on!"

Luciana bowed her head. Of course, Madame should know what was going on. It concerned a customer of hers. In a way. "Billy Quinn has asked me to marry him."

Julietta's eyes widened. Madonna mia! Billy Quinn? The strega's son? Her gaze shot toward Madame, but the woman didn't seem at all surprised. "Billy Quinn. He asked you to marry him."

"And I told him no. At first. I told him that I couldn't. Because . . . well . . ."

"Because it would be better for him, for his family, if you didn't."

"Si." Yes. That was it exactly.

Madame looked back, alarmed that the girl would be so willing, so ready, to commit the same mistake that she had so many years ago. "But you *must* marry him."

"Si. And I—"

Madame turned and rushed from the room, leaving her astonished third-floor girls with only one directive. "Don't do anything—don't say anything. I'll be back. Just wait until my return."

———

Madame let herself out of the shop, and instead of turning toward her home, she set out across Temple Place and then down the street, oblivious to both man and woman, carriage and car.

She marched to Washington Street and then past it to the United Bank Building. There, she climbed the front steps, pushed through the door, got into the elevator, and told the attendant to press the button for the fifteenth floor. The top. That's how far she was going. All the way to the top.

When the elevator stuttered to a stop at the fifteenth floor, she stepped out of the cage and walked down the hall in search of the president's office. As she found the office and entered it, a man glanced up at her from behind a desk. He stood.

"Mr. Quinn, please."

"The congressman? I'm afraid—" He abandoned his customary excuse at the look she was giving him beneath her imposing hat.

"You may tell him that Miss De Luca is here to see him."

"Miss De Luca. That's fine, but really, he can't be—"

"And I'll see him now."

"I . . ." He surrendered to the iron resolve he saw in her eyes. "One moment, please." He returned a minute later, surprised that his boss had agreed so readily to see a woman who had never, not once in the ten years he had worked for Mr. Quinn, come to see him before. If she had, he would have known it. He would have remembered. Like all those involved in the machinery of high finance and national politics, contacts were his currency and memory was his chief asset. "If you'll follow me."

If? She had no choice. Not really. If she did, she would still be in her shop, the haven she had built for herself after that morning in the church so many years ago. She would still be standing there on the shop floor, the shrieks of Mrs. Quinn still echoing in her ears. But she had been forced to come. So that Luciana would not make the same mistake that she had, trading love for reason. Practicality for passion.

Patrick Quinn glanced up from his desk when she entered his office. "Rosa."

Oh, why did he have to say her name? And why did he have

to say it with such gentleness and . . . love? She wanted to say his name too, just once. To give it voice, to recall the life she might have had, the person she used to be. But she was the one who had let it all go. She was the one who had given up her rights to say it. And so, she simply carried on with the business at hand. "I've come about your son."

"Billy?"

"He's fallen in love with one of my girls. At the shop. I'm a . . . a gown maker. Have been for quite some time."

He didn't say anything.

"I want them to be able to marry. She's a good girl. From a good family, as she's a northern Italian." At least, that's what Madame supposed. "She's . . . she's perfect. For him. They deserve to be together."

"In the same way that you and I did not?"

Is that what he thought? That it had been about what they deserved? "What I did—everything I did—I did for you."

He folded his hands and placed them on the desk. But he was gripping them so hard that his knuckles had gone white.

"Please. Give them a chance."

"You're asking the wrong person. I was always willing to give you a chance."

"I'm sorry. I'm so sorry I left you. I've always been sorry I left."

"I didn't care who you were or where you came from. Didn't you know that? To me, you were always just . . . my Rosa."

And now she was Rosa to no one. No one but this man remembered the daughter of Cosimo the Tailor. Rosa was gone. Madame had abandoned her, punished her. Killed her. She had exorcised the memory of that girl by trying to become the image of the woman that Patrick Quinn ought to have married. The woman she had stepped out of the way for him to marry. But her plan had gone wrong. He hadn't married that woman at all. Si, he had returned to the altar—just as she had intended—but he had come away with the strega, Mrs. Quinn. "But you married anyway. You found someone else."

He shrugged. "I did. She wanted me. And I wanted no one. But we shared the same dreams. The same goals. And I thought that at least I could make one person happy."

But she wasn't. Mrs. Quinn wasn't happy at all.

"Didn't you trust me? To love you?"

"I did. I wanted to." She choked on her tears. "I didn't trust myself. Why did you ever want me? What could I ever do for you?"

"You thought . . . that it was about what you could do for me?"

Or couldn't. She didn't dare to look him in the eye.

"It was about sharing our lives. Building a dream. Starting a family. Together. It was about life being so much richer, so much fuller, just because I knew you would be by my side."

Oh, if only she had known! If only she had known that he had thought beyond her and beyond him. If she had known that he had thought chiefly of *them*—together—then she might have believed. Love had been there for the taking, and she'd pushed it aside. "Then why didn't you come after me?"

A cough in the doorway made them both turn in that direction.

Mrs. Quinn.

Madame wasn't surprised. She was a strega, after all.

Mr. Quinn's past and present were together in the same room. Two different lives; two different women. Neither of which had ever trusted him with their love. "Adeline. This is Miss Rosa De Luca."

"Miss—Oh! *Rosa*. But—" Mrs. Quinn was momentarily stunned by the realization of who, exactly, Madame Fortier was. She stretched out a trembling finger and pointed it at the woman. "She's the one. She's the one, isn't she?" Mrs. Quinn searched her husband's face, but his eyes revealed nothing. "And it's one of her girls. It's one of *her* girls, Patrick, who's stolen Billy."

"No heart can be stolen unless it wants to be."

"The girl's an Italian! A filthy, wretched Italian."

"Whom Billy loves."

"If you would just have told him to go to Mexico, this never would have happened! He's only getting married because he got drafted. And she's probably pregnant. He's only trying to be a gentleman. Why should he have to ruin his life? Write the girl a check. Make her go away."

Madame had gone white at the insult to Luciana's character. And her own.

"And what's *she* doing here?"

"The Italians that I've met have only ever been decent and hardworking. I will be honored to welcome Billy's bride into our family. And so will you. Miss De Luca came here to inform me of the wedding. Which will take place . . . ?" He turned his attention from his wife to Madame.

"Tomorrow at eleven o'clock." At least, Madame hoped that it would. "At Saint Leonard's Church."

"Wedding? But that's what I'm here to tell you. There will be no wedding. There can't be. I won't allow there to be one."

"There can be no true marriage when two people don't love each other, but in this case I don't think there's any cause for concern. This is Billy's decision to make, and he should be allowed to make it."

"But I—you—"

"We'll both be present at the church at eleven tomorrow. Thank you so much, Miss De Luca, for coming."

"Then we've lost him!"

"That's absurd. It is only by refusing to believe in them that we lose the people we love." He looked at Madame as he said it.

———

Madame hurried back to the shop, heart alight with wonder and the unexpected, magnificent gift of Patrick's grace. She wanted to do nothing but revel in the meeting, commit every line that she had noticed on his face to her memory. But she couldn't. There was work to do. So very many things that had to be done.

Once she arrived at the shop, she headed straight for her closet and pulled the wedding gown from it. She took it up to the third floor and draped it across the table. "There will be a wedding. Tomorrow at eleven o'clock. And you will have a gown."

Luciana smiled up at her. The wedding had never been in doubt. She had been filling out the various forms with Billy, supplying the information he needed, talking through their plans, laying the foundation on which they would build a life together. Madame had simply misunderstood.

Julietta, looking at that confection of lace and beading, could only think that she had never deserved to wear it anyway.

Annamaria was the one who whisked it from the table. "If you're going to wear it, then it will need a final pressing."

Julietta was re-threading her needle even as Annamaria was speaking. "And a final fitting."

Madame backed out the door, leaving the girls to their work.

43

Later, after they had readied the gown for Luciana and improvised a veil, encouraging Luciana to leave early—and sleep well!—Julietta accepted Annamaria's help in cleaning up her space. And together they went out into the evening's chill and October's early twilight. They parted ways on Salem Street, and it was there that Julietta saw him. She would have recognized the truck even if she hadn't recognized his voice.

"*Buona sera*." He was beckoning to her from the cab. She could see one of his friends from the meetings sitting beside him.

She didn't move from the curb.

"Come on. Get in." He looked up the street and then down. "We've a mission to undertake. Tonight."

He must be truly crazy. To think that she would ever want to go anywhere with him again.

"Get in!"

He really thought she would? "No, Angelo."

Sighing, he pushed open the door, got out, and came over to the curb to speak to her. "The other night—"

"You're a murderer and a thief. You asked me to betray one

of my friends." For each step he took toward her, she took one back.

"Did she tell you her father voted for the war? For death. And that he supported the king and all his mismanaged policies?"

"Does it matter?"

"Does it matter?! How will we ever have the chance for real change when people like that still live? When people like that are still in control?"

"You, and all those people at the meetings, can vote."

"Vote? You want me to vote? *That's* what you want me to do?"

"You. Me someday, maybe. That's what they say."

"Vote? You can't be serious."

"This isn't just your country, Angelo, it's everyone's. You scoff at the king telling people how to do things, but how are you any different? He does it with rules and decrees, but you take away everyone's choice with a bomb. That's not freedom. That's you deciding for everyone else. Why not take your cause to the people you say that you support? Let them decide."

"Because they don't understand us. They've never understood us. They don't understand the reasons we do what we do."

She stopped then. "And what do you do, Angelo?"

"What do you mean, what do I do?"

"What do you really do?"

"Whatever I want."

"You destroy things. You've destroyed everything you've ever touched."

He shrugged. Shoved his hands into his pockets. He didn't destroy things. He struck blows for the cause. He made people listen. What was wrong with that? What was wrong with doing what he wanted, when he wanted to do it?

"You don't even stay anywhere long enough to claim your actions."

"That's not really—"

"That's what you do. That's what you all do. But what about the future? What about family? What about people?" What about love. That's what she really wanted to say. What about love?

"There is no future. It's an illusion. An illusion held out to you by the capitalists. Meant to—"

"Leave those people, Angelo. Let them go. Let them make their own choices. Come home with me." The man standing in front of her was contemptible and vile, but she knew that he was also searching for something. That he was . . . lost. And because of that, she took a chance. And a terrible risk. She reached out her hand toward him. "Come home with me."

Home. There had never been such a place in Angelo's life. Not that he could remember. *With me.* He could hardly contemplate the thought. Him? Who would want him? Isn't that what life had taught him? No one wanted him. Not for anything good or for any length of time. He was a man who had never gotten over being a boy, and so he worked up a sneer and tossed it at her. "Who needs you anyway?" He was only saying what had been said to him a thousand times over the years.

She flinched as if she had been struck.

The anarchists needed him. They needed his truck. They needed his plans. And his courage. This girl, standing there looking at him with such sadness in her eyes—why did she care what he did? Why did she insist on clinging to her bourgeois values? For hating him for his natural impulses? She'd wanted him just as much as he had wanted her. He knew she had. But it was over now. So why didn't she just leave? She was bound to anyway.

"Come home with me." She was almost certain that if she could just get him home . . .

He laughed at her. "What? Like some stray dog?" He turned his back on her, got into the truck, and drove away with his friend.

Mauro had been coming down the street when he saw Julietta stop along the curb. Walking closer, he realized to whom she was speaking. He'd been tempted to turn away, tempted not to even dine with the Giordanos that night, but indecision delayed him, and by the time he had decided to go, Julietta had already turned toward him and seen him.

Julietta blinked, eyes wide. But not wide enough to hide the tears that had collected in their corners. "Buona sera, Mauro."

She seemed to have shrunk inside that sleek coat of hers. He nodded.

"Are you coming for dinner, then?"

"I was . . . I don't know . . . anymore."

She looked at him, noticing that his face lacked a certain intensity it usually had. A certain interest it used to display whenever he had looked at her.

If truth be told, he was looking at her right then the way he looked at his patients. The way he looked when he was trying to decide how best to go about the treatment of a stubborn, if chronic, illness. It was, in fact, the very question he was asking himself. What was the best way to rid his heart of the ailment otherwise known as Julietta Giordano?

"Do you know, I saw that man today."

He blinked. "Pardon me?"

"I saw Angelo Moretti."

"You did." Of course she had. Hadn't he just seen him drive away in his truck? "And what did you say to him?"

"I asked him to come home with me."

"And what did he say?"

She shrugged. Thought about attempting a laugh, but she realized she probably wouldn't be able to summon one. So Julietta decided on telling the truth instead. She tugged on his arm until he looked right down into her eyes. "I made a mistake, Mauro. A big one. A mistake I don't ever know if I'll be able to fix. He wasn't the person I thought he was. The person I hoped he'd be. He wasn't . . . he didn't . . . he wasn't you."

He gathered her into his arms as she began to cry. He wasn't quite sure what to do, but he knew for certain where she ought to be. "Let's go home."

———

Julietta arrived at the Giordano apartment just in time for dinner, with Mauro on her arm. Mama Giordano's heart soared as she saw the two of them walk in together. "You bring Mauro, Julietta?"

She glanced at the man beside her. "No, Ma. Mauro brought me."

"Oh." What was the matter with the two of them? Back in Avellino, when a girl met the man she was meant to marry, then she got on with the doing of it. Why couldn't the girl see that she was meant for him? Like bread and cheese. Onions and garlic. But it was like making custard, she supposed. If you stirred too quickly, you made all sorts of bubbles. And if you took it off the stove too soon, it didn't set at all. She shook her head as she ladled out some minestrone.

"Tell me about this influenza, Mauro. How many people died this week?"

All he wanted was to get Julietta alone so that he could talk to her. So he could make sure he understood what it was that he thought she had said. But he could see that there would be no privacy that night. So he scooped up a spoonful of the soup. Blew on it. Tipped it into his mouth. Mama Giordano might have thought he had nowhere else to eat, but people asked Dr. Vitali to dine with them all the time. And all the time he replied, "Thank you, but no," for he was expected at home for dinner. The Giordanos' was as much of a home to him as his own once had been. But his parents had moved out of the North End to Roxbury five years ago. And the Giordano brothers were his closest friends. He went to visit his parents on Sundays, but during the week, when all he wanted was some time away from his work and a good bowl of soup, the Giordanos' was where he came to eat. So when Mama Giordano asked him about his doctoring, he responded as he would have to his own mother.

"In the neighborhood? One or two hundred. And in the city? Eight hundred? Or nine?" He couldn't be sure. No one was sure. "It's better than last week."

All those poor souls. Mama Giordano crossed herself. "You've been working hard."

He hadn't been working hard enough. Hadn't worked long enough. Hadn't worked smart enough to be able to save even a third of his influenza patients. It had come, this sickness, with such swiftness and ferocity that he couldn't even say that it was influenza at all.

"You need sleep, son." Papa Giordano saluted him with his spoon from the end of the table. "That's what you need."

"I'll sleep when people stop getting sick."

"Stay here tonight and you won't be called out."

He took a few more spoonfuls of soup. "I would if I could— but I can't. What would my patients think? A doctor who's not home to take calls?"

"They'd think you were out on a call."

His smile was wry when it came. "Be that as it may, I really should go home." They hadn't been, none of them, to his house since he'd moved out of the North End. If they had, they might have been embarrassed at the accommodations they had just offered him. Unlike the Giordanos, he slept on an actual bed, in a room by himself. When he woke in the morning, hot water ran through his faucets. When he stepped out of his house onto the street, it was filled not with refuse but with young mothers wheeling their babies up and down the streets. And when he walked to the curb, it was to get into his own car.

Oh yes! He had one, though none of Julietta's family knew it. He used it for making calls in the city proper and for visiting his parents, but he'd never driven it into the North End. He was too fond of the place, of its people, to want their opinion of him to change in any way.

And so the Giordanos continued to press their hospitality upon him, and though he wouldn't have minded sharing the floor with Salvatore and Dominic, and though he would have liked to have spent more time with Julietta, he pushed from the table to his feet around eight o'clock, bid Mama good-night with a kiss on the cheek, and walked out the door.

But before he'd made it halfway down the hall, he heard the shuffle of footsteps behind him. Heard Julietta calling out his name.

"Grazie, Mauro Vitali. For bringing me home."

He waved off her words. "It was nothing."

"For understanding, then."

Ah, now that was something he couldn't reply to because he didn't understand. Not at all. He didn't understand what a girl like her saw in a boy like Angelo Moretti. He didn't understand why she would allow herself to be so ill-used. And he didn't understand why anyone wouldn't have come home with her when she asked. "I'm leaving, Julietta." He said the words without intending to, but once he had, they felt right.

She bowed her head. Of course he was. What reason had she given him to stay?

"They're sending all the doctors they can spare out to St. Louis and San Francisco. Seattle, even. Everywhere that's been hit hard by the influenza." He had meant to tell all of the Giordanos, but maybe his leaving now, at this time, meant something different than he'd thought it had. Maybe it was all for the best.

"I'll miss you." She stood on her toes and pressed a kiss to his cheek, hugged him fiercely, and then she turned and ran back to the apartment.

I'll miss you.

What did it mean? What did she mean?

He wasn't you. I'll miss you.

He stood there for a long moment, then sighed and walked toward the stairs. What did a girl like her see in Angelo Moretti? He worried over the question all the way home. Realized, finally, that something completely irrational and unpredictable, something outside the boundaries of science and medicine, controlled the heart.

Not for the first time in recent weeks, he thought about giving in to despair. About conceding defeat. He'd first thought about giving up during the onslaught of the influenza, when he realized that his diagnoses were nothing more than death sentences. When he was shoved out of the way at the hospitals in favor of the orderlies and nurses. He'd been tempted to take up his doctor's bag and go home. And then that evening he had been tempted again as he stood on the sidewalk, watching Julietta with Angelo Moretti, knowing that he had nothing to offer, nothing to say that would change her mind. Knowing that he could only stand and wait.

Well, he'd stood and he'd waited, and the scourge of influenza seemed as if it might be retreating. He'd stood and he'd waited and Julietta had bid that man good-bye. But he didn't know. He really didn't know how much longer he could stand and wait for her to see him. To love him.

Sickness and madness.

There was so much sickness and madness in the world. Didn't a man have to fight for what he wanted? Didn't a man have to do something about it?

He was too tired to get ready for bed, so he simply took off his collar and tossed it onto a dresser. Unbuttoned his shirt, shrugged off his suspenders, and fell into bed. And he slept there all night, motionless. Dreamless. Alone in a bed built for two.

44

Once Julietta had slipped back into the apartment, Mama Giordano drew her away from the family, went to the bed, and pulled a package from beneath the mattress.

"There was a boy come here for you."

"A boy?"

"He brought this." She held the package out as if she did not want to. And indeed she didn't. Her daughter accepting gifts from some unknown boy? And worse, him insisting that they were hers? What kind of girl would give a man something of value? For him to keep for her?

She'd always thought her Julietta good and kind. If she scolded her once in a while for her vanity or her selfishness, it was because she could see there was such goodness inside her wanting to come out. The girl was still young; that was the problem. She was still a girl. But this boy, now? She hadn't liked the boy. Hadn't liked the way he looked around the place as if he might want to belong there.

Julietta took the package from her mother. She walked over to the bed, sat on the mattress, and undid the string and the wrapper. Held up the pouch that was revealed. Loosened the ribbon and let the contents spill out. Even in that dim apartment, the jewels sparkled. They lay there like blinking stars, all of them. All of Mrs. Quinn's jewels, along with a note.

I shouldn't have asked for payment.
Angelo

Mama gasped at the sight of the gems. Then she crossed herself. "Julietta, what have you done!"

But Julietta was shaking her head as she trembled, tears coursing down her cheeks. "Nothing, Mama. I've done nothing." Which wasn't exactly true. And hadn't the priest told her that she needed to confess her sins—all of them—to her parents? "But . . . no. I mean—I have done something. Some things." She sniffed a long, loud sniff. Wiped her tears on her sleeve. "Listen, Mama. I have some things to tell you."

Later, after Julietta had told Mama Giordano about Angelo, after she had tried to explain about the anarchists, and the jewels, and . . . everything. After all of Mama's questions had been asked and answered, Julietta had one question of her own. "Do you hate me, Mama?"

"Hate you? Because some boy came along and turned your head?"

Julietta didn't nod, didn't do anything. Didn't want to acknowledge that she'd been silly and foolish and . . . wrong. But Mama remained silent, and Julietta had no choice but to look up at her.

"How can I hate you, cara mia, when you come to me and you tell me everything?"

"Because I made the wrong choices."

"And then you decided those choices were wrong and made the right ones." Mama paused and frowned. "After you made some more wrong ones."

"That's—that's all you're going to say?"

Mama pursed her lips, narrowed her eyes as she thought about that. "No. No, that's *not* all I'm going to say. I'm going to tell you that I've been worried to death this whole time that there was something wrong with you that you weren't telling me. I'm going to tell you that you're a foolish, stubborn girl who can be much smarter than you have been, and I'm going to tell you that Mauro loves you. So why don't you love him back?"

"I do, Mama. I think I might have always loved him. I must have. I just didn't realize what I . . . I mean, I mistook the one thing for the other."

"You confused lust for love."

Julietta flushed and then nodded.

"It's not the mattress that makes the marriage, cara mia, it's the man."

"I know." She said it in a voice so low that Mama wondered if she'd even heard it. "But I don't deserve him anymore."

All of Mama Giordano's indignation evaporated. That response wasn't one she'd expected from her Julietta. Her carefree girl had been wounded and chastened. And now all the spirit had gone out of her. She sat there looking so forlorn and pitiful and . . . young. So Mama simply kissed her on the forehead and patted her cheek. "Who has ever deserved anything they've been given? Love is not about deserving, cara mia. It's about giving. And accepting. And sharing. The most worthy heart is also the most courageous. *Coraggio!* Don't give up. Not just yet." She'd leave Julietta to Mauro. He would fix her; he would know just what to do.

———

That evening, Luciana decided that it was time to be honest with her grandmother. With the marriage, everything would change. She knew the woman probably wouldn't understand, but Luciana wanted to give her the chance to. It was selfish, perhaps, but she wanted her nonna to be at the wedding. Not the contessa.

Luciana helped the old woman from her chair and then guided her into the bedroom of their suite. She seated her on the bed and then knelt in front of her. "There are some things I need to tell you."

The contessa frowned.

"I saw him, Nonna. I saw the man who killed Papa."

The contessa blinked.

"A week ago it was. Here, in Boston. He came here looking for us."

The woman began to tremble.

"I told people what he'd done. I told Herr Quinn and then he told the carabinieri. They're honest here. And they're looking for him, Nonna. They're going to find him. And when they do, they'll put him in prison. For a very long time."

"The one who killed . . . my son . . . ?"

"Si."

"My son is dead, isn't he?" Tears had begun streaming down her cheeks.

Luciana nodded, tears of her own blooming in her eyes. "Papa is dead."

"My son is dead."

Luciana threw her arms around her nonna's waist and buried her head in the woman's lap, finding the solace she had sought for so long.

A bomb exploded that night, in front of a city councilman's house. But it was harmless. Its placement had been odd—underneath a bush on the front lawn—and such that it did more damage to an ornamental cypress tree than to the house itself. It was only the next morning, while the explosion was being investigated, that a human hand was found. Then a foot and a shred of an orange-colored shirt. And an observant journalist noticed a produce delivery truck that seemed to have been abandoned on the street. Once the police had pieced all the facts together, they came to a startling conclusion: It seemed the bomber had blown himself up as he was attempting to position the bomb.

The detectives wrote up a report. They sent it up to head-quarters and then they sent an extra copy to Congressman Quinn as well.

———

At eleven o'clock the next day, Luciana stood in the narthex of Saint Leonard's Church. Her gown, cunningly altered by Julietta, was stunning and the veil only added to her ethereal glow. Her nonna had already been helped into a pew in front. Luciana stood alone.

And that's where Billy found her. "I have something for you."

Something more? On this day? Something more than himself?

He placed a telegram into her hands.

She slit the envelope. Slid the message out. Read it, lips moving. How he wished he knew Italian! "It's from my cousin."

"Ja. I know. I sent him a telegram. Last week."

"Last week?" But . . . that was . . . she'd only told him about what had happened in Roma a few weeks before. "How did you know? How did you know how to find him?"

He winked at her and caught up her hand. Pressed a kiss to her knuckles. "I have friends in helpful places." Granted, a few of those friends had been his father's, down in Washington, but they had been helpful indeed. "So what does he say?"

"He says . . ." She looked from the telegram up into his eyes. "I've been wrong. About everything. It's not that he didn't want to help us, Nonna and me, he didn't know what had happened." How could he have? He'd been at the front, commanding his troops. "He's working with the carabinieri. He says . . . I'm to come home. And he's wiring money for the trip."

Billy was smiling. He'd hoped it would say something like that.

"But I can't go! Not now. I'll have to tell him."

"We'll go together. After."

After. After the wedding. After the war. Together.

"And another present." He took the telegram from her and replaced it with a different piece of paper.

"What is it?" She'd been getting better at English, but she knew she couldn't decipher the page's miniscule, cramped writing.

"It's a police report. It seems that Angelo Moretti has blown himself up."

She held the paper to her face with trembling hands. Kissed it through her veil. The perfect wedding present.

A man walked up and touched Billy on the elbow. "You should probably . . . " He inclined his head toward the altar.

"Luciana, this is my father."

"Patrick Quinn." He held out his hand.

She looked up into eyes that were just like Billy's and placed her hand into his.

He grasped it and then covered it with his own. "I'm delighted to welcome you to my family."

Tears flooded her eyes as she realized just how mixed up everything had been. She was marrying Billy, and she had just now met his father. Maybe things were happening too fast. Maybe they should wait. Maybe . . . but no. What was it the priest had said? Maybe what God had done was give her a great gift. She'd come to this country helpless and friendless. She had been given both friends and a family.

"May I have the pleasure of walking you down the aisle?" Patrick crooked his arm so that she wouldn't have to guess at his intent.

She slipped her arm through his. "Si. Grazie."

That walk seemed to last an eternity, but at last they reached the front of the church. Billy took her hand in his as they faced each other.

The priest had been warned that the couple spoke different languages, so as he read Luciana's vows, he recited them in Italian.

"*Io*, Luciana Conti, *prendo te*, William Howell Quinn—"

She interrupted him. "Please. I say." She looked up into Billy's eyes. "Me, Luciana Conti, take you, Billy Quinn, as my husband and promise to be faith to you always."

He couldn't have been prouder or more pleased to hear her speak those words.

Once she had said her vows, the priest turned to Billy. "I, William Howell Quinn, take you, Luciana—"

Billy held up a hand to stop him. "Please. Allow me. *Io*, William Howell Quinn, *prendo te*, Luciana Conti, *come mia sposa e prometto di esserti fedele sempre . . .*"

Luciana burst into tears as she heard those precious words spoken in her own language. Billy finished his vows, one arm around her shoulder, supporting her as he searched in his pocket for a handkerchief.

———

It was a small, intimate ceremony. The contessa, Madame, Julietta, and Annamaria sat on one side of the central aisle and Mr. and Mrs. Quinn on the other. Once the ceremony was finished, it was time for introductions. Billy did the honors. With Luciana on one arm and the contessa on the other, they walked over to where his parents were standing.

"Mother, this is Luciana."

Mrs. Quinn speared her with her glance. "Yes. We've met."

"And this is her grandmother."

The old woman extended her hand toward Mrs. Quinn as if she were granting a very great favor.

Mrs. Quinn didn't know what to do with it.

"Who is this woman that she will not kiss my hand?" Only Luciana and Billy knew what it was that she had said, for she had spoken the words in German.

"But—the woman's a Hun!" Mrs. Quinn blanched white and reached out to grip the back of the pew for support.

Billy stepped closer to Luciana's grandmother. "She holds the title of the Contessa of Roma."

"She what?"

"Mia nonna." Luciana tried to explain as best as she could.

"A countess." Mrs. Quinn scoffed at the very notion. But then she noticed the woman's ring. The ring that displayed a coat of arms, decorated with glittering diamonds and rubies. Realizing her mistake, she reached out and took up the woman's hand, planting a hasty kiss upon it. "Why did no one tell me . . . ?"

"I tried, Mother. And you insisted that Italians were rude and filthy. 'Peasants,' you called them."

Mrs. Quinn raised her chin against the accusation, though she did not deny it.

The contessa resisted the urge to wipe off the kiss as she turned away from the young people. She was old. She was tired.

Mrs. Quinn stepped closer to her son so that she could speak into his ear. "You ought to have told me."

Billy took a step back, placing an arm around his wife. "And you ought to have let me speak."

"Well. We'll have to write up an announcement for the newspapers."

"For a marriage you were determined wouldn't take place?"

"It may be, perhaps, that I was wrong."

———

Annamaria and Julietta thought the gown had looked perfect, Luciana angelic. Mrs. Quinn had scowled through the ceremony—was scowling still—but she'd been born a strega and would probably never change. They saw their friend's grandmother had been left standing alone, looking rather forlorn. So they each took up one of her hands and led her to a pew where she could sit.

"Grazie." Such nice friends her granddaughter had. Such a nice wedding it had been. "Did you know, back when I was a newly married contessa, that I danced with King Umberto at his coronation?"

Julietta looked over at Annamaria and winked. Julietta squeezed the woman's hand and said, "No, Nonna. Why don't you tell us about that time?"

They stayed with the old woman until Billy and Luciana came to collect her. Luciana slipped a piece of paper into Julietta's hand. She glanced down and was able to decipher the words *Police* and *Report* before Luciana threw her arms around Julietta's shoulders in an embrace.

Patrick turned, for just a moment, as he left the church. Caught Madame's eye. Nodded.

She returned the gesture.

There was nothing more to be said. They had loved once. They had lost each other. But they had also prevented the repetition of their doomed history in the next generation.

45

Annamaria walked home from the wedding, a thought stirring in her mind. It had to do with the Quinns' son and Luciana. With the way they looked at each other, even as the strega had scowled. At the way they loved each other. As she crossed the street, her foot scuffed against the cobblestones, causing her to stumble. As she threw her arms out for balance, the Saint Zita medal swung free from her blouse. It swung up toward her chin, glinting in the light. After she had regained her step, she reached for the medal and drew it away from her chest. She looked down at the worn design.

Perhaps God had willed that Saint Zita's life be given over to service, but had God willed that for her? Truly? If it had been all right to hope for more while Mama was still alive, then why wouldn't it still be all right to hope for more now that she was dead?

She crossed herself as she remembered her mama. Fiercely loving, fiercely loyal, fiercely . . . wrong. In the end, her mama had been wrong.

What did Annamaria owe the dead? Was there anything to be

gained by sacrificing herself—her hopes and dreams—on Mama's dusty altar of tradition?

She wrenched the medal from her neck, wincing as she felt the clasp give, and dropped it into the gutter. Winking, it rested for a moment atop a pile of rotting garbage, and then it disappeared as it sank into the morass.

She worked that afternoon in the Rossi apartment, thinking of burdens lifted and dreams renewed, and how exactly to go about the doing of what it was she was about to do. Simply. Honestly. Wasn't that the only way that it could be done?

"Papa?"

He looked up from the table. He'd been sitting a lot at the table since he'd recovered from the influenza. Sitting at the table, doing nothing, staring at something only he could see.

"Papa, I want to go get some turnips."

He nodded.

"And when I do it, I'm going to speak to the Zanfinis."

The Zanfinis? Who were the Zanfinis? He looked up at her, a blank look in his eyes.

"To the people who own the store."

"The Sicilians?"

Annamaria nodded.

What was it about those Sicilians? Papa Rossi was trying to remember exactly what it was about them that had caused such great problems. "And why wouldn't you?"

"Mama . . ." Annamaria crossed herself as she spoke the word. "She had forbidden me to. Told me she wished her name to be lost in my home." She stood before her father, head bowed, waiting for his judgment.

"Your mama said that?"

She nodded again.

"Before she . . . well, now. Let me think."

Annamaria's heart sank to her toes. For when had Papa Rossi asked to be given time to think when he had not, after great deliberation, repeated Mama's words exactly? And why should anything be different now that she had gone?

"Your mama said, 'May my name be lost in your home'?"

"Sì." There was no point in trying to deny what had taken place between them. Better for it all to be spoken, all the words to be said now.

"She didn't want you speaking to those Sicilians."

"No, Papa."

"But she didn't know them, did she?"

"No, Papa."

He thought on that for a minute. His beloved wife hadn't really known them. She hadn't ever met that nice boy. And she hadn't realized what kind of people they were. They were Sicilians, that was certain. But it seemed there were Sicilians . . . and then there were Sicilians. "I'm sure she didn't mean those words, Annamaria. She was dying, you know."

Annamaria looked up into her father's eyes, not certain that she understood. "But she did know, Papa. She refused their help. Rafaello came to help us, and she refused to even look at him."

Papa smiled, a faint smile that hardly turned his lips. "She was always a stubborn one, wasn't she? Once she got a thought stuck in her head . . ." He shrugged.

"So . . . can I go, Papa?"

"Sì, sì." He waved his hand toward the door.

She could go!

"And when you see them, Annamaria, don't forget to thank them."

And so Annamaria Rossi crossed the street once more. She crossed without worrying who was watching, without hiding her intentions. She crossed it smiling.

When she opened the door and walked in, Rafaello's face glowed like the sunrise. "Annamaria." He drew out the syllables of her name and savored them as he spoke each one. Che bella. She was even more beautiful than he had remembered.

"Rafaello."

An exchange of names. A meeting of souls. Two hearts united once more.

He came around from behind the crates of onions to take her hands in his. Bent down to press his lips against hers. They were warm enough to banish the chills of a thousand influenzas. Gentle enough to assuage her grieving spirit. And strong enough to unite them together. For good.

He turned around, placing an arm around her shoulders, sheltering her in his embrace. "Mama! Papa!"

His parents hurried to the shop floor.

"You know Annamaria."

Of course they knew Annamaria! Hadn't they been praying for her and her family?

He looked down at her.

She put an arm around his waist and nodded up at him.

"She is going to be my wife."

———

When Julietta came to work the next day, instead of trudging up the back stairs, she went to Madame's office and knocked on the door.

"Enter."

Julietta walked up to Madame's desk, reached into her lunch bag, and pulled out a bundle. She placed it atop a stack of papers.

Madame laid a hand atop it. "What is this?"

"The jewels."

The jewels! Madame's brow rose. In the rush of Luciana's wedding, she'd forgotten about them entirely. You had probably forgotten about them as well. But Julietta hadn't. She'd spent all day and half the night thinking of what needed to be said. And still her knees were shaking.

Madame turned her attention from her astonishing lapse in memory back to Julietta. "Perhaps we should talk."

Julietta remembered the last time that she had been invited to talk to Madame. It had been three short months before. Julietta had been offered Madame's trust. And in return she had promised to learn English. But, in the interim, she hadn't proved that trust, neither had she bothered to polish her language skills.

Madame drew the package toward herself and unwrapped it. "Tell me how you came by these."

"I didn't . . . It wasn't—" Julietta took a deep breath and decided to try again. "There was a boy." There was pain in the words she spoke; it was the pain of self-knowledge and bitter regret. "There was a boy I . . . knew. Used to know. I told him, once, about the jewels. I wasn't thinking about what I was saying. If I had been . . . well . . . I wouldn't have said it. But he came here and stole them." She waited in silence for the punishment, the diatribe that she was certain would come.

Madame, looking at the girl, recognized the regret in her expression. "Grazie."

Grazie? Julietta lifted her gaze, not quite daring to believe that this was the only thing Madame would say. "They are all there." At least she hoped they were.

"I am certain that they are." Madame pushed the bundle to the side, if not entirely out of the conversation. And then she stood. Julietta was being dismissed.

The girl contained her sigh with the realization that she didn't deserve Madame's trust. But she would. If she worked hard enough, if she showed herself worthy of that high regard, then maybe someday she would.

———

A week later, Mrs. Quinn turned her attention from her work to the noise in the hall. It was truly and terribly annoying! That girl. Walking around the house conversing with servants, coming and going with Billy and her grandmother. Down to the Settlement House, over to The Tennis and Racquet Club, up to the United Bank Building. She had no sense of dignity. No propriety. Laughing and chattering. When they were all just waiting for Billy to be shipped out to the war! It was grating, that's what it was. It was as if she didn't understand that everything was being taken away.

And her accent was indecipherable!

But Mrs. Quinn wasn't planning on saying anything. Nothing at all. Because she knew that her son and her husband expected it of her. And she wasn't going to oblige them.

The butler came in with an envelope.

She was tempted to simply throw it on top of her stack of correspondence. To open it later. But the truth was she had lost her train of thought. She was trying to decide what to do about Madame Fortier. An entire season's worth of gowns were still on order and all of her jewels were still at the shop. She sighed and put a hand to her throbbing temple. She fingered the envelope. Why not open it? What kind of work was she going to get done anyway? *The draft has been postponed. Due to the influenza—* She blinked. Stood up. "The draft has been postponed! Billy! You don't have to go!"

———

The epidemic of influenza retreated and then faded away by the end of October.

The armistice was signed. Madame gave all her girls the day off. The city went wild with frenzied flag-waving and parade after parade marched up and down the streets. In his fifteenth-floor office at the United Bank Building, Patrick Quinn began dictating telegrams to send to his contacts in Europe. Up on Beacon Hill at the Quinn mansion, the strega was busy in her sitting room drafting letters, while upstairs in a second-floor bedroom, Billy and Luciana had a private celebration of their own.

Mauro was tending to influenza victims in San Francisco, and though he heard church bells ringing, he wasn't told until the next day what the celebration had been about.

The next week, Annamaria got married. In Madame's gown. And Rafaello, beaming at her as she walked down the aisle of St. Leonard's Church, knew she was the most beautiful woman the world had ever known. She found a way to keep her promise to Stefano. She didn't go away, she didn't leave; she simply kept crossing the street from the other direction. And soon no one in the neighborhood seemed to recall that there had ever been two sides to North Street.

As winter edged toward spring, Madame began to make plans for a trip to Paris. She seemed almost . . . *cheerful* about the whole thing. Annamaria and Julietta didn't know what to make of it. And adding to the odd state of affairs was the fact that Madame was wearing a new gown. And not just any gown. It was a decidedly vivid shade of green. It was emerald.

"She's never worn green before." Julietta was sure she hadn't. Didn't she always wear dark blue or brown?

Annamaria wasn't quite sure what she thought of it, but she felt she might be rather inclined to like it. It made Madame seem less dour. And more Italian.

When it was time for lunch one day in February, along with the customary bottle of wine, Madame offered them a stick of salame. And not just any salame.

"It's a Felino. From Genoa."

Julietta shook her head. And Annamaria, seeing her do that, did the same.

"You don't like salame? Neither of you?"

She did. They both did. They looked at each other. Julietta shrugged. "Won't it stink?"

"What if it does? We can open the window, can't we?"

363

Annamaria had to slide her hand beneath her thigh to keep from crossing herself.

"You won't be upset?"

"Why should I be? I'm Italian, aren't I?"

Was she? Truly? For so long she had tried not to be. But her encounter with Mr. Quinn had changed her. It had redeemed her. He had given her life back. He had given her self back. She had believed that love had died? It hadn't. It had endured. And while she'd banished herself from it, even while she'd sat in a cage of her own making, it had reached out to her. It had rescued her. Patrick Quinn had believed in her. Patrick Quinn believed in her still.

She poured three glasses of wine and sat down in Luciana's old chair to eat with them.

"You both know that I plan to go to Paris this year. Once the fashion shows resume."

They nodded.

"I will need both of you in order to ensure that the business of the shop continues smoothly in my absence."

Both? Julietta looked up at that declaration. Both of them?

"Annamaria, I will need you up here, overseeing the third-floor workshop. I have several girls from the second floor that I want to bring up."

Oversee? Annamaria didn't know if she could do that. She was only a smocker after all. But if Madame thought she could . . . then . . . perhaps.

"Julietta, I will need you downstairs."

On the second floor? Her hopes fell, tripping over themselves on the way to the bottom of her stomach. She *was* being punished for the jewels, then. But she took hold of her tarnished ambitions, promising herself that she would indeed fulfill them. If she had to spend time back on the second floor, then she'd make sure she surpassed Madame's expectations as she did so.

"I will need you to help me with my clients."

Her . . . clients?

"There is nobody else I can trust with them while I am gone. You have the style and charm. When you want to."

"I will want to. I promise you, I will want to."

"And you must learn to speak better English."

"I will. I'll start today. This evening. I'll go by the Settlement House on my way home."

"Bene." She surveyed the two girls, saw the change that her announcement had wrought. Already Annamaria sat straighter, held her chin higher. Already Julietta had cast off that air of indifference and insouciance. Madame could tell that it would not be long before assurance and sophistication would take their place. Sì. She had chosen wisely. It would work out well. "There's no way to know when Paris will resume the making of her collections, but we'll need to be ready when she does. Understood?"

Both Annamaria and Julietta nodded, dedicated in their resolve to do—to be—what Madame needed.

46

On an unseasonably springlike day in late February, Luciana had the chauffeur drive her to Madame's shop. She decided she couldn't wait any longer. Though she'd had Julietta up several times since the wedding, she had yet to see Annamaria. And she had news to share! So once Mrs. Quinn disappeared into her sitting room that morning, Luciana crept down the back stairs to find the chauffeur.

She no longer looked like a peasant. She was wearing clothes now that befitted her new station in life. Gowns from her favorite houses, Pacquin and Chanel, purchased at the most venerable of establishments. Other than Madame's. Mrs. Quinn had insisted upon it. But once she and Billy's new home in Brookline was completed, once she'd moved out of his mother's house, she intended on patronizing Madame Fortier herself. On her own.

She was feeling out her new life slowly. Carefully. Trying not to lose herself in the great euphoria and enthusiasm that was America. Trying not to let Mrs. Quinn push her into doing anything she didn't want to do. Next year, perhaps, she would undertake a trip to Italy. With Billy and her nonna. They would meet her cousin, and she would show Billy the family estate. She would introduce him to Roma and then they would decide—together—what they wanted their life to be.

It was this woman, this bride of Billy Quinn, this daughter of the Count of Roma, who descended from the motorcar with the aid of a chauffeur. As she entered the shop, Madame appeared from the back in much the same way that she had the first day Luciana had walked into the store.

"Bella Luciana." Madame opened her arms to the girl and Luciana walked into them.

Madame kissed her on both cheeks.

"I have come with a special request."

"Then I shall try to fulfill it." Madame led her to the chair behind the screen.

"I expect that I'll require a whole new wardrobe by summer. I have reason to believe that I'll be needing some gowns that don't fit quite so tightly."

Madame smiled then. One of the first smiles Luciana had ever seen cross her lips. And it was lovely. "I am so happy for you."

"Grazie."

Madame brought out her sample books, and they spent some time examining the pages, talking about colors and new styles and about the number of gowns that would be needed. Then Luciana stood, collected her things, and walked toward the back stairs. Then she stopped and turned for a moment. "Thank you. For everything."

———

Madame Fortier sat in the back pew of a West End church that Sunday morning. And as she sat there, as the words of the mass were intoned, she looked at the structure that surrounded her. It was so stylish and elegant, so coldly formal. She hadn't been in years—but it had been exactly what she'd wanted when she'd left the North End. A church with dignity and pride. A church absent any mawkish emotions and ingratiating displays of devotion. A church where people came on Sunday and then left to go about their business for the rest of the week.

It had none of the earthiness, none of the shabbiness, none of the ridiculous displays of fervor that were rife at St. Leonard's. But there was no joy at church that morning, or any other Sunday morning, she suspected. No spirit. No patron saints; no festas. There were plenty of jewels on display and a multitude of stylish hats. There were men looking down at their pocket watches, and children swinging their legs back and forth, wriggling in their seats, ready to make a break for the aisle just as soon as the priest had said the concluding rite.

She slid to the edge of the pew, slipped around the edge into the aisle, and pushed through the door. If she hurried, she thought she just might be able to make the eleven o'clock mass at Saint Leonard's.

———

Three months later, Julietta had just grabbed hold of the shade on the door of Madame's shop when Mauro Vitali's face appeared in the window. Her heart leapt at the sight, although she frowned at him. As she drew the shade down, he kept pace with the descent, giving her full view of his smiling face in the process.

She smiled too as she snapped it closed. They'd exchanged letters since he'd gone, and she'd heard he had returned to the city, but she hadn't yet been able to manage arriving home in time for dinner. Not with Madame gone to Paris and all the work that had to be accomplished at the shop. But if truth be told, she hadn't really tried.

She was afraid.

She was afraid that when she finally got the chance to look into Mauro's eyes, she would find not love, but friendship waiting for her. And she wasn't quite sure if she could bear it. So she waited a moment longer and then she pulled on the shade sharply, letting it snap open suddenly.

But Mauro was—gone.

She pressed her forehead to the glass for a moment, looking up and then down the street. He was. He was truly gone. Perhaps . . . well, he was a doctor, wasn't he? Maybe there'd been a sort of emergency. But disappointment weighted her steps. She walked to the counter, pulled the key from the drawer, set her hat upon her head, and then secured the shop for the night. Turning away from the door, she started out onto the sidewalk and ran right into Mauro's sturdy chest.

She put a hand up to steady herself, then moved to pull it away. But she thought the better of it. "There you are!" Her tone, infused with all the questions and all the longings she had lived with for many months, was not quite as light as she had meant to make it.

"Here I am."

"I—" She disengaged herself from him and looked up into his eyes. Those very dark, very solemn, very *dear* eyes. And she discovered in them something that thrilled her to the very core of her being. He seemed . . . had he missed her just as much as she had missed him?

"I came by to check on your arm."

"My . . . arm?"

"But I see I'm too late."

"Too late?" Just the idea, the mere suggestion of it, prompted her to thread that arm through his in such a way that he would have to try very hard indeed to free himself of it.

"You've already closed up." He nodded toward the shop door.

"And who says you have to examine me in the shop?" It was one of those magnificent late-spring evenings when the air was still warm, the birds were still singing, and colorful patches of flowers brightened the long shadows that the sun had begun to cast. She started off down the sidewalk and pulled him right along with her.

He glanced down at her. "Do you have somewhere else in mind?"

"I do."

They walked on a few steps in silence.

"Are you going to tell me where it is?"

"Maybe. It's a small, intimate kind of place. Very famous in the district."

"Is it new? Since I've been away?"

She looked over at him. Lifted her chin. "You might remember. It's called Mama Giordano's."

"Mama Giordano's."

"Quite exclusive. You have to know someone in order to get a table there."

"Do you, now?"

"Sì."

"I'd like to think I know some people."

"Well, you can't just walk in there like you're family."

"I can't?"

"No. That will do you no good at all. Mama's likely to just treat you like one of her boys."

"And that would be bad?"

"Extremely so."

"Then what do you suggest? To get the best sort of service?"

"Why don't you tell her you're my beau?"

He looked down at her to see if she meant the words she had said, and he read nothing there but apprehension. And hope. Hope! Exactly where he had looked for it, longed for it, waited to see it for so many years. As he put his hand over the one she had curled around his arm, he looked down into her eyes. "Why don't I do that."

They walked on for several more blocks, trading glances with each other, trying to stop the smiles that had begun to curve their lips. And then Julietta had a thought that made her pause mid-step. "You're not the kind of man that would make a girl stop working once she's married, are you?"

Mauro, tugged backward by her sudden stop, turned around and laid a finger on her lips, though what he dearly wanted to do was kiss them. "What does that—why would I make you—? Stop thinking so far ahead, *tesorino mio*. Let me get used to courting you first. Then we'll see what happens next."

See what happens next? That was just another way to say *wait*. And Julietta was tired of waiting. She'd waited nearly her whole life to discover what had been right in front of her the whole time. And now that she'd seen it—seen him—she didn't want to waste any more time. What was wrong with him that he didn't feel the same way? She could picture life with Mauro so plainly. And she couldn't wait—*wouldn't wait*—to get there.

She ignored his finger and reached up to fling her arms around his neck. "I love you, Mauro Vitali. Don't ever leave me again!"

He had no choice but to drop his doctor's bag and embrace her. And once she began to kiss him, there was no other option left but to kiss her right back.

After a few moments, he tried to speak. "I—"

"*Zitto!* Don't talk."

People were beginning to stare. But what did he care? He closed his eyes, determined to ignore them. To ignore everyone. Everyone but the girl who was finally caught within his embrace.

They moved on several moments later, walking up the street and then taking the electric car to the North End. It was so crowded that Julietta was able to refuse a seat without too much trouble. She didn't want to be parted from Mauro for even an instant.

She'd wanted excitement? She'd found it in the arms of a man. A man who wasn't just a boy in disguise, but a real man with true convictions and honest passions. Her heart had thrilled at the longing in his kiss, and she blushed at the depths of the desire she now read in his eyes.

Five short blocks and they were home. Four flights of stairs and they were at the apartment.

Mama turned from the stove at the sound of the door.

"You brought Julietta, Mauro!"

"No, Mama, *I* brought *him*."

She blinked. Stopped stirring. Turned. "You brought—? You mean—?!"

Julietta was smiling so broadly that all she could do was nod.

Mama wanted so badly to weep with happiness, but that wouldn't have done. So she gave Little Matteo a pinch on the cheek instead.

"Ow! What was that for?"

"Get up. Congratulate your sister. She's getting married!"

And then, because she couldn't contain her emotions any longer, Mama gathered them both into the wide expanse of her embrace. Looking up at Mauro, she frowned. Just a little bit. "It took you long enough! What were you waiting for?"

Julietta stood on her tiptoes and kissed him right on the lips. "He was waiting for me."

A NOTE TO THE READER

The Great Italian Emigration to America began in 1880 and ended in 1921. It is estimated that 4.2 million people left Italy to settle in the United States. Four *million* people. It was a migration unheard of in modern history, many times larger than the sweep of the Mongol hordes across Asia or the Huns through Western Europe. Entire Italian towns were emptied. The reasons for the migration were many: drought, earthquakes, volcanic eruptions. Tidal waves and famine. The systemic oppression of southern Italians at the hands of their own government. The immigrants referred to their native land as *La Miseria*. Misery. And who could blame them?

Though the vast majority of Italians came in peace, with no thought but to settle and begin their lives anew, Americans, alarmed at their vast numbers and horrified at their odd customs, reacted with xenophobia and fear. The only other race more frequently lynched during the time period were African-Americans.

On the gradient of acceptable classes, there were white Anglo-Saxon Protestants, white Anglo-Saxon Catholics (among which northern Italians were included), southern Italians, and African-

Americans. The label *Italian*, however, confused the newcomers. Italy had only taken its modern form and come under united rule in 1860. The immigrants still considered themselves Avellinos, Abruzzis, and Sicilians. Neapolitans, Genovese, and Calabrese. When the immigrants came to America's shores, it was only natural that they settled in right beside those they had lived with in their homeland. Those who married in America most often married someone from their same native region or town. While it was frowned upon to marry outside of one's ethnic region, it was oftentimes more acceptable to marry any nationality of Catholic (Irish included) than to marry a Sicilian.

Along with the peaceful immigrants, however, came a different sort of breed, with a different kind of goal. They called themselves anarchists. Long before the Twin Towers in New York City were ever built, early twentieth-century anarchists had determined that their most powerful weapon was the bomb, their most expendable asset, themselves. Like modern suicide bombers, a surprising number of anarchists blew themselves up—inadvertently or on purpose—in the process of dispatching their brand of violence. Anarchists terrified America in the early decades of the last century, mailing package bombs, distributing pamphlets with dire warnings, and lacing food with poison. In Europe, they especially targeted nobility. The Italian King Umberto; the Russian Tsar, Alexander II; a French president and an American president; two Spanish prime ministers; Elizabeth, Empress of Austria and Queen of Hungary; the King of Greece; and Archduke Ferdinand of Austria were all victims of assassinations committed by anarchists. Many other people of nobility had attempts made upon their lives during the epoch as well. But the anarchists' worst and most long-lasting punishment was inflicted upon their own countrymen. *Italian* swiftly became synonymous with *anarchist*. The vast majority of honest, peaceful immigrants soon became viewed as radical zealots. And none of their indignant protests could convince the average American otherwise.

Americans grappled strenuously with their own justice system and immigration laws before deciding to entrap and deport known anarchists living within their borders. But with the accumulation of threats and explosions, with the destruction caused by the Wall Street Bombing and the collapse of the North End's Molasses Tank (at first erroneously attributed to the work of anarchists), Americans had had enough. In 1921, Congress voted to set permanent quotas on immigration from certain undesirable countries. It was a historic law in America. For the first time, quotas were applied to immigrants, allowing the United States to clearly favor some nationalities over others. On the foundation provided by this law, the barriers to Jewish immigration during World War II were erected. The quotas were enforced so strenuously during those years that some of them even went unmet. It fell to other countries to do the work that America ought to have done.

With the bill's passing, the Great Italian Emigration came to an end.

But in the midst of the crucible of undeserved oppression and rabid xenophobia, a strange thing happened to the immigrants. The experiences they lived through, the prejudices they endured, did something that Italy had never quite found a way to do: It turned a disparate collection of provincials into a united group. Though they came to America's shores as Avellinos, Abruzzis, and Sicilians, when confronted with the harsh realities of the New World, the immigrants finally found a way to stand together. They called themselves, for the first time ever, Italians.

1918 was also the year of the Spanish influenza. It did not originate in Spain and it may not have been influenza, but it was a pandemic the likes of which had never been witnessed before. It first appeared in the spring of 1918. Hitching a ride on the troop transports that circulated between America and Europe, it resurfaced in the fall, seeming to appear everywhere at once. After its third wave in the spring of 1919, it retreated from whence it had come, never to be seen again. Scientists have still not been able to identify its particular strain.

The Spanish influenza killed an estimated twenty to fifty million people worldwide in its frenzied paroxysms of death. It ambushed its victims, often felling them in the course of hours. Its method was pneumonic; it shredded the fabric of the lungs. Its victims quite literally drowned to death. The Spanish influenza *infected* an incredible five hundred million people. And it hit those living in close, cramped conditions like the North End especially hard. When it didn't kill people, it left them so drained of energy that some families died simply because they had no access to food and water, and none of them had the strength or consciousness to go get any.

The Spanish influenza killed ten times as many Americans as World War I.

It is astounding to me, based on numbers alone, that the Great Italian Emigration and the Spanish influenza have largely been forgotten. But if history repeats itself and human nature rarely ever changes, it might be worth the effort to examine our current physical and sociological ills through the lens of the past. History is a wise teacher . . . if only we will listen to her speak.

ACKNOWLEDGMENTS

The concept of this book owes much to Beth Jusino, who helped me to grow the seed of an idea. I owe a debt of gratitude to Maureen Lang, who cheered me on during the endless weeks it seemed to take to write this, and to my agent, Natasha Kern, who challenged me to improve upon my first draft. The omniscient point of view in which the book was written can only be blamed on my editors, Dave and Sarah Long, who strenuously urged that I use it and then trusted me to get it right. To Linda Derrick and Trudy Mitchell, my encouraging first readers. To my Facebook fan page subscribers who chose Little Matteo's name. *Merci mille fois* to Dr. Paul Aoki of the University of Washington's Language Learning Center for responding so quickly to my desperate plea for help; and to Christophe Jamot and Jennifer Keene who forwarded the message. *Mille grazie* to Sabrina Tatta of the University of Washington's Italian Studies who graciously corrected my terrible Italian. Any mistakes still remaining are mine, not hers. And, finally and forever, to my husband, Tony Mitchell. Everything I write is because of you.

Discussion Questions

1. Most people in modern cultures have immigrant roots in one way or another. Where did your family come from?

2. Have you ever felt like a stranger in a strange land? What was most disorienting about the experience?

3. Do you see any similarities between American society in 1918 and modern society today?

4. This story revolves around Julietta, Annamaria, and Luciana. Which character did you most like? Why?

5. What flaws did you notice in the novel's main characters? How were these flaws overcome?

6. As the story began, what did each character want? Were those goals achieved?

7. Julietta flirted with the ideas of anarchy. What appealed to her about this philosophy? Do you see any elements of these beliefs at work in our culture today?

8. Annamaria's dreams were opposed by the expectations of her parents. Did she handle this conflict in the right way? When is it acceptable to disobey your parents?

9. Luciana found herself in a dire situation and yet she would not ask for help. Why not? What would you have done had you been in her place? If she had gone to the authorities, what do you think might have happened?

10. Each main character in this story learned the same lesson in the end. What was it?

11. Which man embodies your ideal hero: Rafaello, Mauro, or Billy?

12. Define the "American Dream." How did each woman articulate this dream? Did she achieve it? What is your American Dream? Has it changed over the years?